A Nineteenth Century Irish Sex Scandal

MURDER
—AT—
SHANDY HALL
The Coachford Poisoning Case

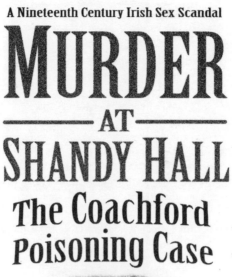

MICHAEL SHERIDAN

POOLBEG

Published 2010
by Poolbeg Books Ltd
123 Grange Hill, Baldoyle
Dublin 13, Ireland
E-mail: poolbeg@poolbeg.com
www.poolbeg.com

A catalogue record for this book is available from the British Library.

ISBN 978-1-84223-439-6

Typeset by Patricia Hope in Sabon 11 / 15.5
Printed by CPI, Mackays, UK

www.poolbeg.com

A Note About the Author

Michael Sheridan is the bestselling true crime author of *Death in December*, an investigation into the murder of French film producer Sophie Toscan Du Plantier, *Frozen Blood: Serial Killers in Ireland; A Letter to Veronica; Tears Of Blood* and *Bloody Evidence*. He is co-author and ghostwriter of *Don't Ever Tell: Kathy's Story*, an account of Kathy O'Beirne's traumatic childhood, which spent 22 weeks in the UK top ten and was a *Sunday Times* bestseller.

Michael previously worked for the *Irish Press* and the *Sunday Independent* as a freelance journalist.

Acknowledgements

For all the loneliness associated with the writing process, the result could not be obtained without a sometimes unwitting team whose support is vital for achieving the result and includes family, friends and professionals. I owe a great debt to all of these.

To the team at Poolbeg, whose faith in the project was unstinting: Kieran, Paula, Dave and the other staff. And to Brian Langan who recognised the potential of this story.

To Anthony Greene from Coachford who was unfailingly generous in sharing his knowledge of the case, which he studied closely two decades ago. I will be eternally grateful to him.

To Hilary McDonagh of Irish Ancestry Genealogy Research Services for helping to solve many of the riddles that remained a mystery after shorter accounts of the case appeared many generations ago. She was both brilliant and unflappable in delving into matters which have not come to light until now.

I am indebted to the staff of The National Library of Ireland and The National Archives, two wonderful institutions of which we should rightly be proud. And to Robert Mills, Librarian of The Royal College of Physicians who unearthed the invaluable address by Dr Pearson to the Royal Academy of Medicine in Ireland. Also to Catriona Mulcahy, University Archivist, University College Cork, for the wonderful photograph of Dr Pearson.

Thanks to Marty and Sarah for their constant enthusiasm, which also was shown by my agent and sister Christine, and to Debbie, Niall and John and the staff of Higgins who watered the dry horse when he needed inspiration. To my mother Patsy, who has never given up on me even when she had more than one reason to. The same applies to Anne and Dave, my siblings.

Last but not least I cannot praise enough my editor Gaye Shortland for her amazing intellectual rigour, commitment and creativity and whose professional stamp is all over this book. Without her involvement, well, I cannot even imagine what might have come to pass. We had plenty of debate, but not one row. She is truly a gift that every author should have.

To Ger, Cian and Fionn
And the memory of Mary Laura Cross
Who still lies alone and palely loitering in
Magourney Graveyard.

Contents

Introduction

*"For-thi [therefore] men sais into this tyde [time],
is no man that murthir may hide."*

Circa 1325 – *Cursor Mundi*

"Murdre wol out that se we day by day."

Circa 1390 – Chaucer: *The Nun's Priest's Tale*

"Truth will come to light; murder cannot be hid long."

1596 – Shakespeare: *The Merchant of Venice*

*"Death will close the ears and eyes against the sight and sounds
of earth; but even the tomb secures no secrecy.
The dead themselves declare their dreadful secrets,
open-mouthed to the winds."*

1864 – J Sheridan Le Fanu – *Wylder's Hand*

American author, William L Beck, writing in 1867 noted: "Murders are the same [as other epidemics]; when one occurs, others follow in quick succession, until the blood turns cold at reading the details of the tragedies."

And, referring to a small town murder: "Taken, all in all . . . the whole thing, from beginning to end is an unfathomable mystery."

Right now, in the era that we live in, those observations seem so bitingly familiar. There is nothing ever new under the sun and the fact of murder echoes in our ears, in our hearts and in our minds. And yet it is an enduring mystery – one that drove the greatest writers over the generations, like Dickens, Dostoevsky, Wilkie Collins, Conan Doyle, Camus, Capote and Mailer to even greater heights of expression to get to its essence. And thousands of others in both fact and fiction.

There are no doubt "murders of their time" but always so prescient in nature that they defy the passage of time. At their core, they possess a fascination with the simple proposition: why does one human being want to take the life of another, with all the consequences looming, in the very minute and second of that act, like the rope in the 19th century and our own versions of the same in the 21st?

This murder is of 19th century vintage, but when doing the initial research I was visited – with no particularly strong analogy, save one of the killing of a wife, the presence of a triangle and huge media attention – by the manslaughter of Celine Cawley. And the very same question: why not just walk away, given the basic difficulties that arose from the circumstances? Lies and cover-up were eventually exposed in both cases but the enduring mystery remains nonetheless. The thing that comes into one's mind, repeatedly, is the why, why, why, when there was another way out? But in the absence of a confession, that remains the question which despite the best efforts of the investigators and the court process will remain without an answer. Only the killer knows the whole story as the victim has been denied a voice.

However, in the murder at Shandy Hall, the victim spoke from the grave in a most extraordinary manner. There are, however, particular features in this case which spring very much from its times.

In the 19th century it was thought that crimes committed in life would affect the eternal progress of the soul. The punishment was not simple retribution, but a path the criminal could walk to a destination of divine forgiveness and redemption. The ultimate punishment was ever present in the capital offence and the judge urged the condemned to approach his or her Maker with a sorrowful mind and a penitent heart. This was necessary if they were to pass muster when they stood before a higher tribunal, unmatched by anything on earth.

Meanwhile, the earthly tribunal for an offence of murder was considered the greatest show in any city or town and tickets were issued for admission, as to a theatre; for the more salacious or notorious cases queues formed. The sensation was enflamed and promoted by the newspapers before, during and after the famous, minute-by-minute accounts of the trials.

The plots, the themes, the twists and turns of these courthouse dramas defied the best imagination, proving again and again the old adage that the truth is more often than not stranger than fiction. The piece of legal theatre was rendered immeasurably more compelling by the fact that one of the main players, the prisoner at the bar, would live or die by the unscripted final act: the decision of the jury. And of course the ever present shadow of the hangman.

But as much as there was evil in the air of one particular house in Dripsey in the summer of 1887, not many miles away in Cork there were two advocates of good: District Inspector Henry Tyacke and Doctor Charles Yelverton Pearson, who would ensure that the darker side of the human condition would be rightly and justly challenged.

Having embarked on a road down the past and admittedly not having read the book in advance, I would have to acknowledge that Kate Summerscale's *The Suspicions of Mr Whicher* later gave me great inspiration and encouragement to go on.

Chapter 1

The Backdrop

"Thou shalt not covet; thou shalt not cast an eye of desire; out of the heart proceed murders; – these dreadful realities shape themselves from so filmy a medium as thought."

J Sheridan Le Fanu, *Wylder's Hand*

Over a century ago, the pioneering English historian of law FW Maitland observed: "If some fairy gave me the power of seeing a scene of one and the same kind in every age of history of every race, the kind of scene I would choose would be a trial for murder, because I think it would give me so many hints as to a multitude of matters of the first importance."

For many decades Maitland's remark was ignored as historical scholarship passed over murder trials as "far too atypical and sensationalistic" as to merit serious study, leaving them to amateur devotees of courtroom drama and detection mysteries.

The Victorian era is so foreign to the era we live in, the century's strict rules for sexual behaviour and the salacious popular press a striking contradiction. You could not talk about sex or indulge in it safely but there was no problem reading about it, particularly through the great conduit: the criminal trial.

1

These trials, as Maitland observed, revealed a lot about other matters and were viewed as social dramas, soap operas, which as might be expected created great public interest and debate – and often long after the trial ended. And, even peripherally, the narrative of the cases involved the fundamental values and conflicts of society as a whole.

In the second part of the 19th century, murder along with treason was the remaining capital offence, and therefore involved trials with the highest stake – life – and adversarial argument at its most intense. To say nothing of the gory detail of the crimes and an intimate view of the lives that surrounded the events, revealed in what the newspapers described as the "minute to minute" accounts published in their pages.

As far back as 1792 Friedrich Schiller, one time the favourite writer of Dostoevsky, appraised the phenomenon in an introduction to a German edition of criminal cases published that year: "We catch sight here of people in the most complicated situations, which keep us in total suspense and whose denouements provide pleasant employment for the reader's ability to predict the outcome. The secret play of passion unfolds before our eyes, and many a ray of truth is cast over the hidden paths of intrigue. The springs of conduct, which in everyday life are concealed from the eye of the observer, stand out more clearly in motives where life, freedom and property are at stake and therefore the criminal judge in a position to have deeper insights into the human heart."

The invention of the steam press in the early 1800s, allied to the removal of heavy taxes on newspapers, resulted in a huge growth in the number of all sorts of publications, including daily papers and journals of all descriptions, to suit all tastes. These fanned the flames of public interest in domestic murders.

The case of Madeleine Hamilton Smith in 1857 is a classic example. This was the case of a wealthy young Scottish woman who was accused of killing her less prosperous lover to protect her reputation and her engagement to a more appropriate suitor.

Criminal perpetrators who came from the middle class or the gentry attracted a enthusiastic audience to the court, who had to queue for a ticket of admittance as if the venue was a theatre. When it came to drama and entertainment value, nothing could compare to the capital trial where the black cap of the judge, the scaffold and the noose provided the hair-tingling backdrop. The Victorian courts, let it be said, had far less accommodation for the audience than Drury Lane. That audience was from the privileged classes and court reports were invariably prefaced by a list of the notable members of society present as well as "a gaggle of females".

A reporter at the Smith trial commented on the last phenomenon: "A dozen females, or perhaps we should designate them ladies, were in court, and some of them evinced such a determination to sit out the proceedings that they brought their work with them and commenced stitching as soon as they sat down." (In neighbouring France over half a century earlier they would have taken their place beside the guillotine.) Perhaps later, if the verdict took a certain course, they would join the rabble at the place of public execution, but hardly when they could simply read about that event in the most blood-thirsty detail in their daily newspaper.

The 19th century trial had features which we would consider peculiar. The prosecution was comprised of victim, if available, and witnesses giving their sworn statements to the court. The defendant had no right to give sworn evidence, but made a statement at the end of the case. Although this seems harsh nowadays, the old tenet that a man was "innocent until proven guilty" was strictly upheld, and, as a result, the court often came down on the side of the defendant, unless a strong case was put forward.

The ladies would not keep their stitching up for long in the case of the very pretty twenty-two-year-old Madeleine, who on the morning of Tuesday the 30th of June appeared before the High Court of Justiciary, Edinburgh, charged with the murder of her young lover. The prisoner at the bar was a vision out of the ordinary, dressed in a white straw bonnet, black silk mantle, grey cloak, brown silk gown and lavender gloves; she carried a silver-mounted smelling-bottle in her hand. She was the first child of an upper-middle-class family in Glasgow. Her father James Smith was a wealthy architect and his wife Janet one of the twelve children of famous architect David Hamilton. They lived at 7, Blythswood Square, Glasgow.

So the scene was set for the trial of Madeleine Smith who was accused of the murder of her former lover, a Frenchman, Pierre Emile L'Angelier. He was a lowly packing clerk and she the daughter of a famous Scottish architect who had forbidden the relationship. The young couple were apparently passionately in love, as evidenced by a series of letters from her found in his lodgings after his death. However, she had broken off the relationship after she was engaged to be married to William Minnoch, a friend of the family.

Madeleine, who had burned Emile's letters on his instruction, for fear of discovery in her home, wrote two letters to him after the break-up begging him not to expose their past love and sexual encounters, as it would bring great shame on her and would result in her being thrown out of the family home.

The Frenchman was devastated by her decision to marry another and tried to salvage the liaison by reminding her of the letters in which she poured out her feelings for him in passionate and explicit detail. This posed a threat to her future as the lover was not willing to go away broken-hearted but clung on, and she saw her promised status begin to crumble. She was now a very desperate young woman with her past haunting her at every turn.

She went to a local chemist and purchased arsenic and when L'Angelier called to her house, she passed him out a cup of cocoa through the bars of her basement-bedroom window, or so he told a friend. She asked him to return her letters but instead he threatened to use them to expose her. She made more purchases at the chemist and there were other frantic meetings between the two, during which she again fed him arsenic. At least this was the case the prosecution presented.

However, there was evidence that L'Angelier was an "arsenic-eater", a dangerous Victorian habit thought to improve the complexion and virility. He had also talked of committing suicide over affairs of the heart.

Whatever the truth of their dealings, just after 2 a.m. on March the 23rd, 1857, L'Angelier stumbled through the streets to his lodging house, crippled by pain. His landlady helped him to bed and at 5 a.m. called a doctor who prescribed laudanum laced with water and a poultice. The doctor returned at 7 a.m. and again at 11 a.m. when he was told by the landlady that L'Angelier was sleeping peacefully. But when the doctor examined him he turned to her and said: "The man is dead."

There was a great scandal surrounding the trial, caused as much by the sexual relations of the accused and the fact that she had broken another Victorian taboo – consorting with a lower class of person – as the murder charge itself. The evidence was of course largely circumstantial and complicated by the fact that over the three weeks before L'Angelier's death there were no witnesses to the meetings between him and Madeleine.

Although unlikely, because of the passions involved and the rejection who could say that the unfortunate Frenchman did not commit suicide as a result of his disappointment?

After a six-day trial, the jury came to a verdict of that particular Scottish complexion: Not Proven. This did not mean they thought she was innocent but that the prosecution had not done enough to prove her guilt. Madeleine Smith was discharged.

It could justifiably be said that some crimes are of their time and that case was such. There was perhaps a greater sense of private and public outrage at the details of the sexual aspect of the case and the fact that a young girl who should have been a virgin until her marriage night had taken such an active and, it could be said, leading role in the sexual liaison. All the worse considering her social status. That was not the way that things were meant to work in Victorian times.

The moral climate of Great Britain throughout Victoria's reign was markedly different to that of the previous Georgian period. The respective monarchs set the tone. The image of Victoria's uncle, George IV, was that of a pleasure-seeking playboy while Victoria was deemed to be the very essence of propriety.

For the term "Victorian" Chambers dictionary gives the definition: "strict but somewhat conventional in morals, with connotations of prudery, solemnity and sometimes hypocrisy."

Victorian etiquette considered it improper to say "leg" in company – instead, the euphemism "limb" was used – and this notion of prudery is generally considered to spring from the character of Victoria herself. The queen apparently did not enjoy sexual relations and informed her daughter that a bride was like "a lamb being led to the slaughter". However, while she claimed not to enjoy her husband's baser passions, she did co-operate to the degree that he fathered nine children on her; she loved him to excess and mourned his death from typhoid for many years.

A recent exhibition *Victoria & Albert: Art and Love* demonstrates that Victoria had "a passion for nudity" and, among many other nude paintings and sculptures, gave a present of *Florinda* by Franz Xaver Winterhalter to Albert in 1852. It hung opposite the couple's writing desks. It shows a group of fleshly all-but-nude maidens being spied on by Roderick, King of the Spanish Visigoths. Victoria described it in her journal as "a most lovely picture containing a group of beautiful women, half life-size". Considering the scene depicted is the preface to the rape of Florinda by Roderick, as the legend goes, it seems that our preconception of Victoria is indeed being challenged. Which calls to mind the fact that Albert sported a "Dressing Ring", a penis-piercing now called a 'Prince Albert' in his honour – an uncomfortable thought.

But it seems such complexities were part and parcel of the Victorian psyche. Historians now regard the era as a time of many contradictions. Social movements concerned with morals co-existed with a class system that permitted harsh living conditions for the majority. The apparent contradiction between the wide-spread cultivation of the outward appearance of dignity and restraint and the prevalence of social phenomena that included prostitution and child labour were two sides of the same coin. Various social reforms and high principles arose from attempts to improve conditions.

In the same way throughout the era, movements for justice and freedom and other strong morals opposed greed, exploitation and cynicism. The writings of Dickens, in particular, observed the harsh conditions of the time. The stress on individualism became even more expressed in the establishment and rise of the middle classes. The Victorian period began with the aristocratic elite in total control of society and politics. The elite was made up of 300 families established as the traditional ruling class. The upper class valued history, heritage, lineage and continuity of the family line. They believed they were born to rule, a type of divine right, and wanted to preserve this way of life. They took a paternalistic view of society: *noblesse oblige*. Then came the rise of the middle class and the elite were obliged to open up their ranks. The idea of the self-made man became a dominant value for the middle class. If a man could work hard enough, he could aspire to wealth and ownership of land.

However, if the new individualism granted man his freedom from the class system, woman was still in bondage, whatever class she belonged to.

Not until the 1857 Matrimonial Causes Act was divorce made accessible; no sooner had the court opened its doors than it was presented with 253 petitions in England. This was a time when a husband could beat his wife within an inch of her life, and sometimes kill her but either be acquitted or get a ludicrously small sentence, especially when drink was involved.

While the misery of lower-class marriages was aggravated by poverty and drink, upper-class marriages were pressurised because of the property at stake and the social power accorded to the husband.

But the experience of Mary Eleanor Bowes, the great-great-great-grandmother of the Queen, makes the fallout of other aristocratic unions look like tea-party stuff. In 1875, Bowes applied to the London Consistory Court for a divorce from her second husband, a fortune-hunting conman named Andrew Robinson on grounds of: "adultery, beating, scratching, insulting, provoking, tormenting, mortifying, degrading, tyrannising, cajoling, deceiving, lying, starving, forcing, compelling and wringing of the heart." She understated the case, omitting her husband's blackmail and the time he abducted her and dragged her through the wilds of Scotland.

Violence in the home, in particular, was coming to seem more commonplace. Charles Dickens who did so much for the image of the home as the heart of English life, complained in 1851 that: "The fact of a woman being the lawful wife of man, appears to impress certain preposterous juries with some notion of a kind of right in the man to maltreat her brutally, even when this causes death."

The prevailing belief and practice of Victorian marriage was absolute control by the husband and absolute submission by the wife. The dominant ideology sought to relegate women to the domestic sphere and keep them submissive. All women shared a special status as females, and all women suffered particular disadvantages with regard to law, marriage, money, business and employment, regardless of social class. They had no social class on their own account but that which was derived from fathers and husbands.

Eliza Lynn Linton in *Ourselves* in the 1860s wrote: "No true-hearted woman that ever lived who loved her husband, desired anything but submission; it is the very life of a woman's love – her pride, her glory, her evidence of self-respect."

The woman who embodied the Victorian feminine ideal was the wife and mother selflessly devoted to her children and submissive to her husband. Queen Victoria remarked on women's rights when Lady Amberley expressed views on the emancipation of women in 1870: "I am most anxious to enlist everyone who can speak or write to join in checking this wicked folly of 'women's rights' with all its attendant horrors, on which her poor feeble sex is bent, forgetting every sense of womanly feeling and propriety. Lady Amberley ought to get a good whipping." Women, the royal message was, should be restricted to domestic work and child rearing.

In 1887 Eleanor Marx and Edward Aveling wrote: "Women are the creatures of an organised tyranny of men, as the workers are the creatures of an organised tyranny of idlers."

Most women were, of course, dependent on men for their very survival. For those who were forced to work by circumstances, women's work meant low pay and status. Most lived in poverty. For the lucky ones, there was the chance of being employed as a servant in the houses of the elite and, from the turn of the century, the employment of at least one female servant had become an important qualification for any family which wished to be considered middle class.

* * *

Ireland was part of the British Empire and espoused amongst the ruling class and the gentry the very same values, morality, laws and government of the Mother Country, which was after all only fifty miles of sea away. There were streets of the capital Dublin and rural areas and vast estates and small villages that were no different from their counterparts across the water.

There were rural spots steeped in hundreds of years of history and tradition and the lands and big houses and estates handed down through generations of the same family, their fortunes tied to the Crown, their names a by-word in the localities and many tied to the military profession of their forebears.

The aristocracy and the gentry sent their male children to boarding school in England and later universities or military academies, and the girls were educated at home by governesses. Their homes and estates were manned by servants and tenant farmers and the tradesmen and shopkeepers of the villages depended on them for much-needed income, as well as what little local industry existed, which in the extreme south of the country was not a lot.

It is this southern part of the country that concerns us and specifically a very small part of the largest and most fertile county, Cork, where in living memory a domestic tragedy of such horror had not been recorded nor one which received worldwide press coverage.

However, just three years before there had come to light an event in another small County Cork community that also aroused horror and that also commanded the use of international cablegrams.

Chapter 2

The Castletownroche Murders

Samuel Lewis, publisher of the 1837 *A Topographical Dictionary of Ireland*, described the sylvan setting of the village and surroundings of Castletownroche, County Cork:

"The town is pleasantly situated on the declivity of a steep hill rising from the west bank of the river Awbeg, over which is a neat bridge of five arches and on the high road from Fermoy to Doneraile; and with the castle and the church has a highly picturesque appearance, on the approach from the east bank of the river . . .The surrounding country-side is beautifully picturesque; and the river Awbeg . . . is celebrated for the richness and variety of its scenery."

As Lewis noted, the soil was fertile, the wheat raised of the best quality and the gentry had introduced the Scottish system of husbandry with success.

Until the rigours of the Famine years (1845-1852), there had been little to disturb the peace of the town or surrounding countryside since the siege of the castle during the Parliamentary wars in 1649.

In this setting, in 1884, there unravelled a story of an atrocious triple murder carried out in extraordinary circumstances, involving an impending marriage, a dowry and division of family assets, and a classic example of the very long reach of the arm of the law.

In the year 1877 William Sheehan, about thirty years old, lived on a farm situated four miles from Castletownroche with his mother, brother and sister. His elder brother John managed a pub belonging to his mother and lived in neighbouring Rockmills. William wished to marry Mary Ann Browne, the sister of a neighbour and friend David Browne. However, his family and mother in particular were opposed to this union on the basis that the prospective wife's family was not well off and she would bring with her only a modest dowry. The matter caused friction and division in the Sheehan family, and was a problem that seemed incapable of resolution. Then, at the end of October, William told neighbours that his mother Catherine (Kate), brother Tom and sister Hannah had left – for Fermoy first, to visit an ailing friend, and then for America. After they had left, he told Catherine Duane, wife of a farm labourer whose cottage was on Sheehans' farm: "There will be plenty of room for the girl now!" About ten days later they married.

Sheehan was renting sixty acres of land at £2 an acre but six years later, in July 1883, he had fallen into arrears and was evicted for non-payment of the rent. He then, with his wife and two young children, emigrated to New Zealand.

That might well have been the end of the story but in 1884 John Broderick, the occupier of a neighbouring farm, employed a man named William Fitzgerald to clean out a dried-up well on his farm which had long been used as a dump for rubbish. On descending, Fitzgerald made a horrific discovery at seventy-two feet below: the skeletons of two women and a man. Various scraps of clothing were also recovered, and boots which were easily identified as those of the three Sheehans: the "laced boots" of the mother, the "elastic boots" of the daughter and the "strong boots" of the son.

In his eventual confession Sheehan described how he had killed his brother with a blow of an adze [a cutting tool], lured his sister into the barn and cut her throat with a razor, then went to the house and dispatched his mother in the same way.

He invited Mary Ann and her younger sister to the house that evening and they sang and danced and played the concertina well into the night. After these festivities, he loaded the three bodies on a cart and took them to the well on the neighbouring farm where he disposed of them. He claimed he did this alone.

To return to what was testified in court, on the Sunday after his family disappeared he invited James Browne, the father of Mary Ann, to a goose dinner (cooked by Catherine Duane) and arranged to marry Mary on 9th November.

Sheehan continued to explain the absence of his mother, brother and sister by telling friends and neighbours that they had decided to stay in America, after first intending to make only a temporary visit.

As a final grotesque wrapping-up of the affair, he gave various items of the clothing and footwear of his murdered family as gifts to his employees and new in-laws, almost as bribes to ensure their support of his version of events.

After the identification of the bodies, information gathered by police for the inquest led to a warrant being issued for Sheehan's arrest and contact was made with the New Zealand authorities who tracked his whereabouts and assigned an undercover police-man to keep him under surveillance while members of the local police force set sail for New Zealand.

The surveillance was on a 24-hour basis, highly sophisticated for the time, and the man in charge, Superintendent Thomson, received a written report every morning detailing Sheehan's routine and movements. The team had also secured a provisional arrest warrant from the Resident Magistrate.

When the necessary documents from the authorities in Ireland were in place, a squad of police arrested Sheehan in Waikomiti, Auckland, and he was brought to the district court. Despite the objection of his lawyer he was remanded in custody while the warrants for his arraignment and return to Cork were put in place. Back in Castletownroche, Mary Ann Sheehan's brother David Browne was arrested and charged with being an accomplice in the crime.

* * *

Auckland *Star*
22nd December 1884

The Castletownroche Murders

Full Particulars of the Tragedy

Great excitement was caused throughout the city and suburbs last evening by the announcement in our yesterday's impression of the arrest at Waikomiti of William Sheehan on the charge of murdering his mother, brother and sister at Castletownroche, County Cork, in 1877. Paragraphs have recently appeared amongst the items of our Home News stating that William Sheehan was supposed to have committed the murders in question, and that he was known to have left England for New Zealand; but the probability of his having settled in our community does not appear to have settled in the minds of many of our readers.

Hence it is not surprising that news of his arrest in our midst should have created such a sensation. He has been in Auckland for some time and appears to have made quite a number of acquaintances during that period.

His Arrival in Auckland

Sheehan arrived here by the *Doric* with his wife and children about eighteen months ago, and so far as is known proceeded immediately afterwards to Mr William's station at Pakaraka, Bay of Islands. Information was recently received by the police authorities in Auckland that he was supposed to be in the colony and a description of his personal appearance came to hand in due course.

The case was placed in the hands of Detective Walker, who has shrewdly and cleverly performed the task allotted to him. There was no difficulty in discovering that a William Sheehan had come to Auckland by the *Doric* at the time indicated, but whether he was the man who was required was a different question.

The description of his personal appearance did not exactly tally with accounts given by those who had seen him, but there were some points of resemblance between the two descriptions. It was, however, considered unlikely that two families of Sheehans would be coming out to the colony at the same time, and little doubt existed in the mind of the detective that the Sheehan in Pakaraka was the man who was required.

The Return to Town

While the police were prosecuting their inquiries, information reached them that Sheehan was about to come to town. Detective Walker faithfully met the steamers on arrival and his persistence was at length rewarded. Some weeks ago he met a man coming off one of those steamers, who he knew at once to be Sheehan. From that time until the arrest, Detective Walker has kept the prisoner under strict surveillance. Sheehan went to live for a week or thereabouts at Mrs Gleeson's hotel, representing himself to be in the want of work. Mrs Gleeson obtained work for him. Odd jobs such as painting carts and filling coal were given to him to do by Mr Craig, coal merchant, and he discharged his duties satisfactorily and faithfully. Sheehan took a small house in John Street where he lived with his wife and family for a time. Rather more than a week ago he completed the purchase of a five-roomed house and twenty-acre farm at Waikomiti from Mr Berger. The stock on the farm included three cows, two horses, a cart and a hundred fowl. The price paid was £310. The family went to live out there but Mrs Sheehan did not like the place because of her loneliness. She persuaded her husband to come back to town and try and get work there, and on Sunday last he brought his family back to town with him.

The Arrest

The plans of the police were now fully matured, and fearing that the suspected murderer had got wind of their intentions and was about to take a speedy departure, preparations were at once made for his arrest. Instructions to this effect were received by telegram from Colonel Reader on Sunday night. A warrant was made out yesterday and signed by Mr GH Seth Smith, Resident Magistrate.

It stated: "That William Sheehan did feloniously murder and kill Kate Sheehan, Hannah Sheehan and Thomas Sheehan at Castletownroche on the 27th October 1877." Mr Thomson proceeded to Waikomiti in a cab yesterday afternoon to direct the arrest. He was accompanied by Detectives Walker and Twohey. The party met Sheehan driving a horse and cart. He was on his way to town to sell the horse and cart. Mr Thomson stopped him and read the warrant, when Sheehan said: "I did not murder them." On the charge being first made to him, Sheehan seemed confused and disconcerted, but he soon recovered his self-possession. He reverted to the subject repeatedly during the drive into town. He admitted that he was William Sheehan of Castletownroche. He said that his mother, brother and his sister had gone away to America and he had never heard from them since. He knew the well at Broderick farm in which the bodies were found, and indicated its position from the residence which had been occupied by the Sheehans. He ridiculed the idea that he should have murdered his mother and said that he was on the best of terms with her.

Singularly enough, he said he had not read any of the newspaper paragraphs, recently published, in which he was stated to be suspected of having committed the crime.

Sheehan's Family

Mrs [Mary] Sheehan was married to William Sheehan in Castletownroche about a month after the disappearance of the relatives whom he is now charged with murdering, and they lived on the farm for about five years afterwards. They rented the farm of about sixty acres but in consequence of their landlady pressing for rent, they concluded to emigrate to New Zealand, and arrived in Auckland by the *Doric* about eighteen months ago. They were paying £2 an acre rent for 60 acres of land [in Ireland], and the family consisted of the husband, wife and two children. Mrs Sheehan is a woman of about thirty years age, of robust habit, and although of course greatly upset by this sudden turn of affairs, resolutely refuses to answer any questions. On their arrival in the colony, Mr and Mrs

Sheehan [already] had two children, who are now about six and four years, respectively, and since their arrival in Auckland, another child, a boy who is now about two months, was born.

The Prisoner in Court – His Appearance

A large concourse of eager sightseers gathered around the precincts of the courthouse at 10 o'clock this morning in the hope of catching a glimpse of the prisoner as he crossed over from the police station. Their patience was rewarded in due course. He was escorted by several guardians of the peace, and the crowd made no demonstration. They surged into the court, however, in order to witness the further proceedings.

His Worship, the Mayor and Mr F Maguire occupied the Bench, the central table was hemmed in by lawyers, reporters and police representatives, while afar off an artist sat ready with a pencil and sketch-book to limn the features of the accused. After a few time-worn "drunks" had been disposed of, William Sheehan's name was called, and a moment later, amid a hum of conversation, a little pert-looking man made his appearance in the dock.

He was clad in a loose, unbuttoned and heavy brown tweed coat, beneath which was displayed the front of a dark vest, and above the vest a limp, unstarched cotton shirt. In fine, the dress was that of an ordinary labouring man. There is little or nothing about the visage to arrest attention. It certainly has not a villainous appearance, but there is just the suggestion of a furtive look about the eyes. As already implied, the prisoner is rather undersized, but his frame is athletic. His hands and features are small. The face is oval, the broadest portion being the forehead which is both ample and high while the chin is correspondingly small. From the centre of the forehead, the hair which is black has disappeared, and indeed with the exception of a sparse bridge of hair across the top of the head, that portion might be described as bald. There is plentiful fringe at the sides and back, however. Mild brown eyes, a rather small nose, somewhat tip-tilted, and black side-whiskers, with shaven upper lip and chin, complete the picture. It may be added that the man's complexion is slightly sunburnt, and that his demeanour was quiet and thoroughly self-possessed.

Having answered to the name William Sheehan, he was briefly charged with having on or about the 27th October 1877, feloniously killed and murdered Catherine Sheehan, Thomas Sheehan and Hannah Sheehan, his mother, brother and sister.

His solicitor Mr Napier had previously whispered an instruction to him, and he therefore remained silent.

Superintendent Thompson's Statement

Mr W Napier then said: "May it please Your Worships, I appear to watch the proceedings on behalf of the accused."

Superintendent Thomson said: "In this case, Your Worships, I may state that the present proceedings have been taken under the 16th Section of the 2nd part of The Fugitive Offenders Act of 1881, which was passed by the Imperial Government in 1881, and brought into force in this colony by Proclamation of His Excellency the Governor on 31st of October last.

The circumstances concerned with the arrest of the prisoner are briefly these. On 2nd November last I received intimation from the head of the Department in Wellington that a cablegram had come to hand from Earl Derby, requesting the police of the colony to keep under supervision one William Sheehan, who it was supposed had come to New Zealand with his family, as he was suspected of murder.

In consequence of this intimation, I took steps to ascertain his whereabouts and place him under supervision. From further information I received, I believed him to be in The Bay of Islands District, and I accordingly despatched thither Constable Herbert from the Thames, as he was unknown in the north. He proceeded there in the disguise of a gumdigger with swag, billy and gum spear and after being there a day or two he ascertained the prisoner's whereabouts.

He was found to be working for Hon Henry Williams of

Pakaraka. Herbert obtained work on a road contract close by in order that he should have the prisoner under close supervision. It appeared that he was under engagement for a period of 12 months, and at the expiration of the term, which was then near at hand, he came down to Auckland.

He had previously intimated his intention of going to Sydney, and therefore increased vigilance was rendered necessary here. As soon as his arrival had been made known, he was placed under a strict supervision, which was maintained, quite unknown to himself, night and day. I had a written report supplied to me every morning giving information of his movements from the time he made his appearance in the morning until he blew out his candle at night.

About a fortnight ago he entered into negotiation with a man named Burgess for the purchase of a small farm in the Waitakerei Ranges. A bargain was struck, and he took possession a week later. All I could do meantime was maintain the supervision over him as I had no instructions to [arrest] unless he were leaving the colony. As a means of preventing this, Detective Walker some time ago laid information before the Resident Magistrate, and obtained a provisional warrant to arrest under the section already mentioned, and enabling us to hold the prisoner until the arrival of an endorsed warrant, and duly authenticated documents, to authorise his conveyance to the county within which the alleged crime was committed.

On Sunday last I was directed to effect the arrest as soon as possible. Accordingly, I proceeded yesterday to Waikomiti with Detectives Walker and Twohey, and Detective Walker, by virtue of the professional warrant, arrested the prisoner. Without going into the details of the murder, which I suppose are familiar to most persons, I may say that the circumstances of the alleged murder are briefly these:

On the 27th October 1877, the prisoner's mother Kate Sheehan, his brother Thomas Sheehan and his sister Hannah Sheehan suddenly disappeared from their farm. From what the prisoner stated at the time, it was generally understood that the prisoner's relations had gone to America, and nothing more was thought of the matter until in the early part of September last, when the remains of three human beings – two women and a man – were found in a well on the adjoining farm about half a mile from the house formerly occupied by the prisoner's missing relatives.

The police since then have been investigating the matter, and eventually such evidence was obtained as to justify them issuing a warrant for the prisoner's arrest on a charge of murdering three persons. In connection with this, I understand that a detective officer armed with the warrant is now on his way hither, and if he has not yet arrived in the colony, he is expected daily.

Under the provisions of this act I have now to apply for a remand for the usual term of eight days, pending the arrival of the warrant issued by the Imperial authorities. In further justification of my application, I may state that the prisoner, after being duly cautioned admitted that he was William Sheehan, that he had lived at Castletownroche, County Cork, and that his mother, brother and sister had gone to America.

It seemed to be a relief to him to talk after the surprise of the arrest was over, and the statement he then made was as follows: "I came from Fermoy, my mother Kate, my brother Tom and my sister Hannah left on a car about that time for Fermoy. The farm was six miles from Fermoy, four miles from Castletownroche, and twelve miles from Lismore. They bade me good-day when they were leaving. They said they were going to Fermoy. They had spoken before about going to America, but I did not know they were going then. I never saw or heard of them after that. I did not kill them. We always lived on good terms. We had 60 acres of land rented from Miss Oliphant at £2 an acre. She was a hard landlady. If she had been married, maybe I would be there yet. We had a servant girl called Mary Reilly. She was out for the cows when they left in the car. I don't know who was the driver. It was a Derby car. Duane was at the house at the time. It was between 11 o'clock and 12 o'clock in the morning. They had told me they were going to America, to stay about a fortnight and come back again. Broderick's farm was the second farm from ours. I know the well on it. It was about 40 or 50 feet deep. It was a mile and a half from our house to the well. My brothers John, James and Edward are still in Ireland. The farm has never had a tenant since I left. I had a letter from home about six months ago. If Duane knew anything, he could not keep it so long as this. He would let it out in five minutes. I was married to Mary Ann Browne, in November, seven years ago. My mother was never against marrying her."

Superintendent Thomson concluded: "That is about all that is necessary for me to state on the present occasion, and if Your Worships think it necessary to put Detective Walker in the box to prove the arrest, it can be done.

I understand that Mr Napier, who appears for the prisoner, does not object to the remand."

Mr Napier, while offering no objection to the application made by Superintendent Thomson, pointed out to the Bench that this information had simply been laid by Detective Walker upon hearsay evidence. However, he did not intend to raise any objection on this ground. The prisoner was anxious to clear himself from the charge; he had not changed his name, and he had made no effort to conceal his identity.

The circumstances, therefore, went to show that he was an innocent man. Pending the arrival of the warrant, however, he had to apply for the prisoner's liberation on bail. Mr Napier went on to urge that the liberty of any man, however horrible, was sacred and that it should not be lightly interfered with.

Superintendent Thomson strenuously opposed the application, pointing out, as he did so, that it was neither strange nor exceptional. It would be both strange and exceptional, however, if the man were liberated. Their Worships then adjourned the hearing and remanded the prisoner till the 31st to appear before the Resident Magistrate.

* * *

Sheehan was brought up before the RM on numerous occasions after that and remanded for seven days on each occasion. It was then arranged that the original depositions taken in Ireland and the warrant issued to arrest him should be produced.

On the 18th of March Sheehan was brought before the Police Court. Evidence was given by Sergeant William Dunny of the RIC who had arrived from Cork and also by Detective Walker on the details of the arrest.

The depositions were read, made under oath by John Sheehan, Mary Reilly, William Fitzgerald, Dr Denis Quinlan (who had examined the remains of the bodies), James Browne, Catherine Duane, Michael Spillane (brother-in-law of Sheehan), Elizabeth Magnir (widow of Michael Magnir, the ailing man the Sheehans supposedly intended to visit in Fermoy), Thomas Roche servant boy to Sheehan, and John Duane.

Together the testimony built up a fairly clear and convincing picture of what had happened on the fateful day.

The star witness for the prosecution, however, was John Duane's son David who was serving a five-year prison term in Mountjoy for burglary. The charge was stealing £200 from a public house and lavishly and openly spending it. He deposed that on the night after the Sheehans had supposedly left, he had been drawn to their house by the music of a concertina. He had stood listening at the wicket gate leading to their garden until the music ceased and the lights went out in the house. He then saw William Sheehan, David Browne and a third man emerge. Duane went on to describe in telling detail how the men had rigged up a horse and cart, brought the bodies from the stable and loaded them on the cart. He said he then followed the men and cart and witnessed them throw the bodies into the well on Broderick's farm.

The Irish police believed his testimony carried weight because he had been heard to make remarks about William Sheehan's guilt before the bodies were ever discovered. Also, as he had been convicted and incarcerated on the 26th July, about five weeks before the bodies were discovered he had no way of knowing anything about the details of the case.

Sheehan was committed to Mount Eden Gaol to await his return to Ireland on the charge of murder and was sent home in April on the RMS. *Ruapehu* in the custody of Sergeant Dunny and Detective Walker.

On Sheehan's return to Ireland, he and Browne (in complete contrast to Sheehan in every way, "a large, flabby, fair man . . . who seemed sunk in hopeless anguish" according to the *Cork Examiner*) were charged but the proceedings were postponed due to the indisposition of the prosecuting counsel: the new Tory Solicitor John Monroe who had defended Parnell in the State trial of 1880 had been selected to prosecute but, visiting the well where the bodies were discovered, Monroe was overcome with horror and had a seizure.

Then, when the court met on 27th July, the trial was postponed to the Winter Assizes "due to the scandalous conduct of the Cork papers in publishing an unsworn statement concerning the prisoners and thereby prejudicing them in the eyes of the community from which the jury would have to be drawn". The statement was one purporting to come from John Duane and amounted to a confession of being an accessory to the murders.

In December 1885 Sheehan and Browne were separately arraigned before Judge O'Brien at the Cork Winter Assizes. They both pleaded "not guilty".

Sheehan's trial was first up and after five hours of deliberation the jury failed to agree. On the following morning a second trial commenced.

Auckland *Star* (from the *Star's* London Correspondent) 11th February 1886

The second trial of William Sheehan terminated – as you of course heard by cable – in his conviction. The jury were in consultation for over an hour, and it was feared that there might be a repetition of the previous failure. But all doubt was at an end when at twenty minutes past three they had agreed, and handed in a verdict of guilty.

The prisoner, in reply to the usual question, if he had anything to say why sentence of death should not be pronounced, stood up in the dock and made a long and partially incoherent statement.

He protested his own innocence and that of Browne. He declared what Duane had said was quite wrong. Browne never even entered his house. Would they be such fools, he asked, as to let a man like Duane see them commit a crime of this nature? There was no obstacle to his getting the farm, because his mother was at all times satisfied to give him the farm. He contradicted his brother, in this respect, because he said his mother had been living at Rockmills, and was but a short time living in the farm with him. There was no mystery about the matter, and he had asked his brother to write to Ennistymon and other places about his mother, sister and brother. James Browne was wrong too, in his statement, and his [the prisoner's] own wife could prove the amount of fortune he received, and that it was paid over. Why, James Browne had offered £260 odd as his daughter's portion, and his [the prisoner's] brother was witness of it. His mother asked £300 for it, and the brother divided the money. His mother was satisfied, and so was James Browne, and she was to give up everything on the farm but her things. As to the boots that were given away to Duane, they were his own boots. The dress was one left by his mother, and was it not a creditable thing to give it to a poor woman? With regard to the boxes, it was true he had the boxes, but it was arranged between him and his mother that he was to take charge of them until she would want them. This was a wrong charge, he repeated, and he was surprised the jury were so narrow-minded as to act on the statement of a young convict.

The prisoner then complained of his treatment in Auckland by Sergeant Dunny, the Irish policeman who went to arrest him there, and referring to his arrest, said he was taken by six men in Auckland, who arrested him on the very day he was going to settle about a property he had purchased there.

He complained bitterly about Sergeant Dunny. "Sergeant Dunny," he said, "that is the man who has the whole thing done. I had to report that man's conduct coming from Auckland into Wellington. I had to go there to the kind-hearted President of New Zealand and the Governor of the gaol to tell them of this man's conduct. He is a shame to Ireland. He is nothing but a downright brute. I have met many of my countrymen and I never met a bigger brute in charge of any person. That gentleman (the Governor) took me from the gaol and gave me in possession to the doctor on board the boat, and he said I should be treated properly, as I left the colonies, for I did not come to New Zealand a poor man. I took up a position in New Zealand. I had a property purchased in New Zealand. Two days before I was arrested in coming to Auckland to arrange my property, six men came up to me in a by-part of the road and rammed up against me like that." (The prisoner clapped the palms of his hands loudly.) "And when they read out the statement I said I was not guilty of the like. Walker gave a very wrong statement of what I said. The man that came here with Dunny, that man gave his statement, and he told me several times that Dunny offered him money to come here and tell what he had heard on board. He gave his deposition as McFarlane but on board he was called William Fitzgerald. Is that a proper thing to do, swear a man's life away? I think I have no more to say, my Lord."

The prisoner showed remarkable self-possession and awaited his sentence with extraordinary composure.

Mr Justice O'Brien then addressed the prisoner:

"William Sheehan, after a trial in which every effort that could be made by ability on your behalf, you have been found guilty by the jury of the terrible crime of taking the life of your own mother, your own brother and your own sister; and I owe it to the jury, and to the justice of the community, to declare my entire and absolute concurrence in that verdict.

Without a violation of the duty imposed on them by the law, it was simply impossible for a jury of the City Of Cork, consisting of men of high position, integrity and intelligence to have arrived at any other conclusion. If young Duane had never been examined, I would have myself concluded that the evidence against you demonstrated your guilt beyond all possibility of doubt.

If the remains of your murdered mother and sister and brother had never been found, I would have concluded from your conduct and language that you were author of this crime. I have but as the minister of the law to announce to you your doom. It is not even the law condemns you. I have no power to dispense mercy, and I cannot hold out to you any hope of mercy.

I would be disposed to give you the mercy of my silence about your crime, and to say not one word that would aggravate your painful and terrible position. But I owe it to the position I hold, to say that you, William Sheehan, have been brought from the ends of the world by the arm of avenging justice to stand trial in this county, and to meet a charge depending upon evidence long supposed to be buried in obscurity as profound as the grave, but which has risen out of the depths of the earth and the night of time to bear witness against you.

You are an awful example of a man being led by temptation or by passion – the passion of greed or other passion – to commit such an awful crime as that which you have committed against your own mother and brother and sister, in taking away their lives, when they suspected no harm, sending them before their God with all their sins upon them by your cruel, wicked and treacherous deed.

Your shattered roof-tree in your native home, your own approaching doom, and the death of your mother, and your brother, and your sister are the end of your great crime. Your own end now approaches; time for you, William Sheehan, is all but over, and you now have to prepare for eternity; and during the short interval of time you will be given to make your peace with God, I exhort you to turn from the vain appeal to human mercy, that cannot be awarded to you, to that throne of mercy before which we all must appear, and by which it is promised even that deep scarlet of your awful crime may be made whiter than snow."

Mr Justice O'Brien assumed the black cap.

"The sentence of the court is, and I do adjudge and order that you, William Sheehan, be taken from the bar of this court to the prison in which you were last confined, and that on the 20th of January which will be in the year 1886, you be taken to the common place of execution within the walls of that prison and that you be hanged by the neck until you are dead and may Almighty God, in his mercy, have mercy on your soul."

"Browne is innocent," said the prisoner and then he turned around, a faint smile on his lips and was led away to the cell below.

Te Aroha News, New Zealand,
27th February 1886

The trial of David Browne for complicity in the Castletownroche Murders took place on New Year's Day and, much to the surprise of local prophets, resulted in an acquittal.

For the defence it was contended that no motive was proved, and that the story told by David Duane was inconsistent and improbable. Counsel asked the jury not to convict the prisoner upon the testimony of a man who had foresworn himself on several occasions.

At the instance of Sergeant O'Brien, William Webb, a warder of Cork Prison was examined to prove that the date of David Duane's committal for burglary was the 25th July, 1884. He was transmitted to Mountjoy Prison on the 7th August 1884. The purport of this evidence was to show that he could have had no communication with any person outside the gaol and he could not have known what was going on after the remains had been found.

Sir J O'Brien for the Crown said that neither Mrs Sheehan nor Margaret Browne were examined for the defence in order to throw light upon the statement that they were at Sheehan's house that night playing the concertina. His Lordship, in charging the jury, said he could not avoid alluding to the comment made by Counsel for the Crown upon the absence of any evidence given by Mrs Sheehan or Margaret Browne. It was certain that they were present when the empty house of Catherine Sheehan was made a scene of festivity which now appeared revolting and ghastly in the face of the details with which they were acquainted. The case depended, as they had been told, upon the opinion they formed of the two Duane witnesses, and upon the credit they attached to them.

The jury returned at quarter after two with a verdict of not guilty.

The Crown entered a *nolle prosequi* in the other charges against Browne and he was discharged.

* * *

Tim Healy, the famous Irish barrister, recalls this anecdote in his *Legal Memories* about the peculiar nature of the proceedings:

"Browne was there and [Counsel] Dick Adams appeared for him. My brother [Maurice Healy, for Browne's defence] at Petty Sessions had cross-examined the Crown witnesses, and thus enabled Counsel from written depositions to contrast inconsistencies between the evidence then given and finally tendered. When the case for the Crown closed the Crier Ford (a crony of the judge) came with a meaningful air to warn Adams: 'Call no witnesses'. Believing the hint came from his master, Adams acted on it and no witnesses for the defence were examined. The judge's charge, however, pressed powerfully against Browne, and he commented on the failure to call witnesses. Adams was panic-stricken, and when the jury retired he turned on Ford: 'Why did you tell us to call no witnesses?' The Crier trolled out: "Because I hate alibis and perjury." Adams threw up his hands and told him to let the judge know that the prisoner's Counsel wanted to see him. Regarding themselves misled, they begged O'Brien to modify his charge. He refused but Browne was acquitted. His [Browne's] gratitude to his lawyers was such that he would not pay them a copper for his defence, though it cost my brother hundreds of pounds."

William Sheehan was duly executed on the 20th of January, 1886, in Cork Gaol by the official hangman, James Berry, who travelled from England for the duty and about whom we hear much more later in this story.

The extraordinary aspect of the Castletownroche murders was that no suspicion was aroused about the disappearance of the victims in the interval which elapsed before the discovery of the bodies in the well and provided a stark contrast to a case which just two years later would arise in an entirely different strata of the social caste in County Cork and not a far distance from the scene of those awful killings.

Chapter 3

A Place Fit for the Gentry

*"The thing most necessary to be devised is to increase the
English order, habit and manner, and to expel and put away
the Irish rule, habit and manner."*

ENGLISH STATE PAPER NO. 64. 1533.

In 1599 Colonel Cross and John Gillman came to Ireland in the
Earl of Essex's army and they were part of that year's disastrous
campaign, the implications of which for the young earl, once
favourite of the Virgin Queen Elizabeth I, would lead to his
execution. He had the largest ever army sent to Ireland, but was
involved in what could only be described as a number of
skirmishes, failed to subjugate the Irish clans, made a truce with the
powerful O'Neills and returned to England before his time and
without permission.

Colonel Cross settled in Carrigrohane, not far from the city of
Cork, and John Gillman settled in nearby Curraheen; their families
would become staple parts of that part of the Barony of Muskerry,
County Cork, for generations to come.

The lands of Muskerry which, under the Gaelic laws of Tanistry, had been in common possession of the local clan, came to be held in severalty by their occupiers about the beginning of the 17th century. The chieftain was reduced to the role of landlord and his clansmen tenants. Among the independent McCarthy families that became founded in this manner was that of McCarthy of Aglish whose manor stood in the meadow on the south bank of the Lee, opposite to the townland of Fergus which adjoins Cronody.

The founder of the family was Teige, third son of Cormac, 16th Lord Of Muskerry, and the representative of the family around 1636 was Charles or Cormac McDermod McTeige MacCarthy who in that year sold for £600 the townland of Cronodymore and the impropriate tithes of Aglish to one Richard Hawes who was described as an English settler. Hawes bought other lands, among them Mourne Abbey, from another McCarthy and also took on lease for 300 years from the 2nd of May, 1636, several other lands near Aglish from the aforesaid Cormac.

These were all open contract transactions, having nothing to do with forfeitures, and illustrate how many English families became settled in County Cork soon after 1600. Taking of a lease or taking a "dairy of cows" from a native gentleman were ordinary and usual dealings. Before that Hawes had acquired lands near Bandon. He had been early in the locality, being recorded as obtaining a fee farm grant dated the 1st April 1613 from Henry Becher of the townland of Gurteen-Connocher Oge on the north side of the River Bandon and three miles from the town.

Hawes was to pay £10 Irish per annum forever and was to provide "three footmen with shot and pike" to serve Henry Becher and to be employed in the king's service. On the other hand Becher covenanted that "Richard Hawes should have the benefit of letters patent made to the said Henry Becher, for the liberty of transporting commodities of the said lands, and also freedom from taxes, as fully as said Becher had power under letters patent."

By purchases and leases in these ways, Hawes became owner of many townlands. He had a favourite residence in Cronodymore, though his will was signed at an address in Bandon Bridge. He married Elinor Elwell, the widow of one of the family who were among the first Bandon settlers. The widow had a daughter Mary Elwell from her first marriage. Hawes had no children of his own and by his will dated 19th July 1654, after leaving to his wife a life interest in all his lands in the barony of Kinalmeaky, and a small legacy to a Robert Colthurst, his tenant on the lands of Coolatubrid, parish of Carrigrohane, he bequeathed the residue to his stepdaughter Mary.

That was with the proviso that she was not to marry too early and only with the consent of her mother and the overseers of his will; but if "the said Mary Elwell be headstrong before 18 years of age and marry without the foresaid consent, the lands would be left to others and to the poor of Bandon". Mary married, with full consent, Philip Cross, second son of Epenetus Cross of Carrigrohane Castle, Cross's Green in Cork and other lands. Philip was the brother of Capt Epenetus Cross, High Sheriff of Cork, who was attainted at the time of James II.

Philip, according to reports, was a dashing handsome officer of the local army forces at the time and met Mary on one of his many salmon fishing expeditions up the Lee. They inherited Hawes' lands but lived in a residence near Blarney. Mary died in 1684 and Philip on 26th March 1685 executed a settlement of all the estate held "by right of his late wife Mary Elwell-Cross on his eldest son Hawes, lately married (1683) to the daughter of Thomas Mills of Ballybeg". Hawes Cross like his uncles was attainted in the troubled times of James II and at some stage had to flee Cork.

In 1837 Samuel Lewis's *Topographical Dictionary* described the parish of Magourney which included the villages of Coachford and Dripsey thus:

"A parish, partly in the barony of the Barretts, but chiefly that of East Muskerry, County of Cork, and province of Munster, on the road from Cork to Killarney, containing with the parish of Kilcoleman; and the post-town of Coachford, 2,397 inhabitants. The parish is bounded on the south by the River Lee, over which is a stone bridge at Nadrid; and intersected by the River Dripsey, a mountain stream which falls into the former at the Dripsey paper mills in the adjoining Mattehy and over which is also a bridge of stone on the new road to Macroom.

The land, with the exception of about 150 acres of bog and waste, is of good quality and in a state of excellent cultivation; the system of agriculture has been greatly improved under the auspices of the resident gentry; and more especially of Messrs Colthurst, Good and P Cross, who have been extensively successful in raising green crops. Stone of good quality is quarried for building and for mending the roads, which throughout the district are kept in excellent repair.

The principal seats are Dripsey House, the residence of JH Colthurst Esq.; Myshell of Dr Barter whose demesne of 200 acres, formerly an unprofitable waste, has, since 1826 been reclaimed and brought into a state of high cultivation; Nadrid of H O'Callaghan Esq.; Classis, of H Minhear Esq.; Carhue of J Rye Coppinger, Esq.; Beechmount, of Dr Godfrey; Abbeville, of Mc Mahon Esq.; Broomhill of H Cross Esq.; Shandy Hall of P Cross Esq.; Lee Mount of T Golloch Esq.; Riverview of Mrs Welstead; Oldtown of S Crooke Esq.; the glebe house of the Rev H Johnson and Green Lodge of R Coppinger Esq.

At Coachford, a sub-post-office to Cork and Macroom has been established; petty sessions are held monthly at Dripsey, and fairs at Nadrid on January Ist and October 10th. The living is a rectory and vicarage in the diocese of Cloyne, united perpetually to the vicarage of Kilcoleman, and in the patronage of the Bishop; the tithes including those of Kilcoleman, which has merged into this parish, amount to £684. The glebe house, toward which the erection of which the late Board of First Fruits contributed a gift of £100 and a loan of £1,350 in 1812, is a handsome residence; the glebe comprises 73 acres. The church, a handsome structure, was enlarged in 1818, for which the same board granted a loan of £200 and the ecclesiastical commission have recently granted £224 for repair.

In the RC divisions, the parish forms part of the union of Aghabollogue; the chapel, a neat and spacious edifice, is situated at Coachford, where there is a national school. A small parochial school is aided by the rector; and there is also a private school.

In Dripsey demesne are the ruins of the Church of Kilcoleman, and the ancient castle of Carrignamuck which belonged to the McCarthys and was built in the 15th century by the founder of Blarney castle; it is situated on a rock on the bank of the Dripsey, and is surrounded with trees, forming an interesting feature in the picturesque scenery of the parish."

As far back as 1771 a list of members of the Muskerry Constitutional Society included Philip Crosse of Shandy Hall, Epenetus Crosse of Dripsey and Mr Hawes Crosse of Dripsey, confirming that the descendants of Colonel Cross of the army of Essex had settled and wielded considerable influence among the gentry of the area. In the burials at Magourney were recorded on the 7th July 1772, Mr Hawes Cross son of Epenetus Cross Esq., and on the 20th May, Eleanor Cross the daughter of the late Hawes Cross of Broomhill, who died at Shandy Hall and was buried at Carrigrohane.

* * *

Fifty years on nothing much had been changed in the succession of the gentry in the area. Shandy Hall was now the home of Dr Philip Henry Eustace Cross, a retired British army surgeon, the eldest son of six children of Philip Cross born in 1801 who had married Elisabeth Margaret Johnson in 1822 in Magourney. Philip Henry Eustace was born on 18th August 1823 and baptised in the local Church of Ireland in Magourney on 19th April 1824; Elisabeth Philippa Henrietta was baptised on 5th December 1825; Abraham Benjamin on 19th July 1827; Charles Epenetus on 23rd March 1830; Henrietta Maria on 10th July 1832; and Edward on 1st December 1839.

Their father was known as Philly Céad Cathach (Philly of a Hundred Battles) because of his constant recourse to the law. He was the tithe proctor for Agahinah and was known as being in collaboration with other gentry as an at best semi-legal money-lender. During the Famine he was a paid relief officer and there is a record of him looking for an increase in his pay.

Stories about Cross Senior were a Munster Bar tradition. Once he sent a pack of hounds to Liverpool for an English hunt, but scarcely had the ship arrived than the hounds dashed ashore and scattered through Lancashire. Cross took a legal action for damages against the steamer company which was heard in the Court of Passage Liverpool.

He swore the hounds were worth £10–£12 a couple. The opposing Counsel asked him to confirm it which Cross Senior did.

"Yes, I swear it," replied Cross.

"Thank you, sir, you may step down," advised the Counsel.

"Are you done with me?" enquired the litigant.

"Oh, yes."

"Ya!" roared Cross. "That's not the way they'd cross-examine me on the Munster circuit!"

Apparently his eldest son was a bit of a wild card until he was sent to the Royal College of Surgeons to study medicine, which he did successfully and joined the British Army as a surgeon, a role in which he would be involved in arenas of war in which acts of great heroism would be experienced alongside great suffering. It might have been a long way from the peace of Dripsey, County Cork, but that was the journey which the young doctor took.

The Army Surgeon

As Recruit No. 4992, appointed as an Assistant Staff Surgeon on 22nd December 1848, Dr Cross's first posting was in the British Army in Turkey where he served for six years. On the 3rd of April 1849 he was appointed Assistant Surgeon in the West India Regiment. In 1854 he was posted for service in the Crimean War made famous by the "Charge of The Light Brigade", the work of Florence Nightingale and the live reporting to the *London Times* by William Howard Russell who followed no official agenda and pulled no punches in his dispatches which were highly critical of the British Army.

At the age of thirty-one, Dr Cross was involved in the siege of Sevastopol, the major action of the Crimean War which lasted from September 1854 for a long year of attrition and where he experienced the trench warfare that was to be the tactical precursor of the First

World War. There he encountered constant horrendous sights of deprivation and death from both battle and disease. Thousands of British and French soldiers perished from the battle action, but the vast majority died from disease, cholera, dysentery, fever and typhoid fever.

From army surgeons' accounts of the war, he also was witness to hundreds of deaths from lack of proper training and hygiene in the hopelessly inadequate field and base hospitals. As one medical witness noted: "The official medical services in the Crimean War were not only inadequate in extent, but also enmeshed in bureaucratic inefficiency and inertia with appalling human consequences."

The military surgeon's role on the battlefield – if the soldier lived long enough to reach a base hospital – was to perform heroic lifesaving procedures and speed was vital as any prolonged surgical procedure could lead to blood loss, terrible pain and death. The only outcome generally was amputation as complex surgery on internal organs was impossible. The patients had to be held down by a number of assistants while the surgeon amputated a limb or performed other basic procedures as quickly as possible. Many died of shock or the pain caused by the operation and if they survived that there was the likelihood of death by infection picked up by unclean hands and instruments. If the soldier lost a lot of blood there was no way of replacing it. The only effective method of stopping blood loss was to use ligatures to the blood vessels, a skill introduced by a French military surgeon some centuries before and still practised.

Anaesthesia was also a problem. In 1847 a Scottish obstetrician introduced the use of chloroform which was highly effective in alleviating pain in childbirth. But the practice was slow to be adopted because other doctors were not convinced and believed that pain was a natural condition of labour and should not brook interference. It was not until it was administered to Queen Victoria during labour that it was widely accepted.

Chloroform was used in the Crimean War but, for a variety of reasons, including resistance by the medical authorities and problems of supply, sparingly.

The great Russian writer Leo Tolstoy served as a second lieutenant in an artillery regiment, in the same theatre of war as Dr Cross and wrote of his undoubtedly similar experience in *Tales From Sevastopol*:

"You will witness these horrible heart-rending scenes: you will see war without the brilliant and accurate alignment of troops; without the drum roll; without standards flying in the wind; without the galloping generals – you will see it as it is in blood, suffering and death."

In the trenches the occupants were listening to the noise of cannonballs splitting the air, the rumbling of the cannon, striking terror into all, and the crack of the rifles of the sharpshooters. Constant noise, constant fear and constant death. Sun followed by rain, by snow, followed by unimaginable misery on both sides of the divide.

Tolstoy recorded another scene: "Now, if your nerves are strong enough, pass through the door on your left, into the room where wounds are dressed and operations are performed. There you will see surgeons with their arms bespattered with blood up to the elbows, their faces pale and stern, engaged at something at a cot upon which a wounded man is lying under the influence of chloroform. His eyes are wide open and he is muttering as if in a delirium, sometimes uttering words of endearment.

The surgeons are engaged in the revolting but beneficent task of amputating a limb. You see the sharp curved knife pierce the white healthy flesh; you hear the man suddenly come to with a frightful, bloodcurdling scream and a volley of oaths and you see the feldsher throw the amputated limb into a corner . . ."

On the other side of the battle coin where Cross served, Somerset Calthorpe, aide-de-camp to Lord Raglan described surgeons at work in a regimental hospital: "Here might be seen the surgeons hard at work in their terrible but merciful duty, their arms covered in blood, the floors strewn with limbs just amputated, and slippery with gore. The enormous amount of wounded quite overwhelmed the increasing efforts of the medical officers."

By later testimonials, Dr Cross, one of over a hundred Irishmen who served as British army surgeons in the war, was brave and unflinching in the exercise of his duties and recognised by promotion in the midst of the conflict on 15th May 1855 to Staff Surgeon of the 2nd Class. While the French allies suffered far greater casualties, the British lost 2,755 killed in action. There were 2,019 deaths from wounds and over 16,000 perished from disease.

Edward Mason Wrench was only twenty when he was posted to the war by the Army Medical Service and was put in charge of the British Military Hospital in Balaclava, a former Russian military building, where the wounded from the battle of Inkerman were being treated. There he was witness to the same horrors which so appalled Florence Nightingale at Scutari.

He wrote: "I had charge of twenty to thirty patients, wounded from Inkerman, mixed with cases of cholera, dysentery and fever. There were no bedsteads or proper bedding. The patients lay in their clothes on the floor which, from rain blown in through the open windows and the traffic to and from the open-air latrines, was as muddy as a country road."

Whether on or off the battlefield the doctors were confronted with appalling suffering, if not from wounds then from the unstoppable spread of disease.

All their problems were exacerbated by the fact that the army doctor before 1854 received little special instruction in the medical or surgical problems encountered in active service and there was an almost total neglect of the principles of hygiene and preventative medicine. On top of all that, as if these obstacles were not bad enough, they were burdened by unbending ignorant bureaucracy which made their jobs harder and led to more suffering for the soldiers.

As the *Lancet Malta* correspondent observed: "Let us have an overwhelming army of doctors to combat disease. Let us have a staff, full and strong, of young, active and experienced men. Do not let our soldiers be killed by an antiquated imbecility. Do not hand them over to the mercies of ignorant etiquette and effete seniority." Edward Mason Wrench was transferred and was involved, as Cross was, in the prolonged siege and the trench warfare south-east of the Russian naval base of Sevastopol.

Lawrence Knox, a nineteen-year-old lieutenant from Sussex, of Irish parents, served in the 63rd regiment in the same arena and in the trenches, along with the other horrors, witnessed courts martial and floggings. In addition to all this, the soldiers were persecuted by swarms of flies in the intense heat of the summer.

Knox wrote in his diary: "All about the walls of Sebastopol, the war rages; Cossacks and Cavalry joust. British and French riflemen embedded in the trenches try to pick off Russians on the walls protecting the city. Russian batteries in two redoubts, the Redan and the Malakoff, shower attackers with cannonballs. Casualties on all sides are appalling." Knox later became a journalist and founder and first editor of the *Irish Times* in Dublin.

On the 25th of August, 1855, the Allies started the sixth bombardment of Russian defences of Sevastopol and two days later thirteen divisions and one brigade of 60,000 men began the assault on the city. The British assault failed but the French under a general of Irish lineage, de Mac-Mahon, seized the Malakoff redoubt. By the morning of the 9th of September the Russian forces abandoned the southern side of the city and the city was captured. The fall of Sevastopol led to the Russian capitulation in the following spring and the end of the war.

Dr Cross's first war experience therefore exposed him and his colleagues to desperate conditions and made him witness to abominable privation suffered by the soldiers, the vast majority of whom died from disease. He served according to his military record at least until the armistice in February 1856, but possibly was stationed longer with a holding section of the army.

He would be not waiting too long before being sent to another, and in some ways more traumatic war zone.

On 10th May 1857 Indian soldiers, both Muslim and Hindu, who were stationed in the central town of Meerut revolted and killed their British officers and then with an increasing number of mutineers marched south to Delhi and took possession of the city, slaughtering every Christian man, woman and child within it. A British force arrived in pursuit and occupied the old cantonments outside the city, known as the Ridge. But the army preparing for the siege numbered only 5,000 men while the rebels holding the city had over 30,000 soldiers, daily increasing in number.

The British, unused to fighting in spring and summer, apart from being depleted by lack of armaments, were affected by heat stroke and cholera. Reinforcements were needed and were met by John Lawrence who organised a siege train of guns and ammunition. In the interim, to deal with the mutiny which was breaking out in other areas, British army regiments were mobilised and set sail from home and others which were still based in the Crimea began to move overland to India.

Among the 110 army surgeons from the Crimean conflict who were ordered to India, to add much-needed experience to those already on the ground, was Dr Philip Henry Eustace Cross. They would, if such a thing was possible, face even greater horrors than those that were still fresh in their minds.

The mutiny spread and rebels attacked two other cities, Lucknow and Cawnpore, 250 miles south-east of Delhi. Cawnpore, 42 miles from Lucknow, was a large station with many European and Eurasian families, but with a very small defending force which after heavy losses accepted terms of surrender. On June 27th the remnants of the garrison walked out. On July 15th news came that a British force was approaching. The rebels executed the remaining prisoners and the women and children were butchered in a building where they were being held and their bodies dumped in a nearby well.

When Havelock's relief force arrived they were faced with this awful slaughter and their reaction became set in stone – revenge at any cost and by any means. Captured rebels were to be executed by hanging and by being placed in front of cannon and blown to pieces – and they were.

Havelock moved on then to effect the relief of Lucknow which he did on 25th September but then could not break out of the city again.

Beforehand, the Lucknow defenders had been heroic in defence during the months of continual attack and bombardment, while suffering losses both from military action and disease. In the heat of battle there was little opportunity for reflection but the hospital scenes could not be avoided, as one survivor, LE Ruutz-Rees, wrote: "The hospital presented one of the most heartrending sights imaginable as it was quite new and unexpected . . . People grew callous from a continued sight of pain, in the same way as they become accustomed to danger. Men covered in blood, some with mangled limbs, their muscles contracted with agony, their faces pale, their bodies almost cold, some with the death rattles in their throats . . . The surgeons and apothecaries were to be seen, busy enough, cutting, probing the wounds, amputating and bandaging. All the horrors of war were at once laid bare."

In the interim, earlier in the month, the siege of Delhi had been completed and accompanied by the policy of massacre revenge.

Edward Vibart, a nineteen-year-old officer, recorded his experience after the fall of Delhi: "It was literally murder I have seen, many bloody and awful sights lately but such a one as I witnessed yesterday I pray I never see again. The women were all spared but their screams on seeing their husbands and sons butchered were most painful. Heaven knows, I feel no pity, but when some old grey bearded man is brought out and shot before your very eyes, hard must be a man's heart, I think, who can look on with indifference."

The retribution by the British Army was considered justifiable back at home, in a Britain shocked by the barrage of press reports about the atrocities carried out by the "mutineers" on Europeans and Christians which raised hysteria to a high pitch and grasped the imagination of the nation like no other event in the 19th century. It could be also accepted that anyone who served in the brief war and came home to tell the tale would be considered a hero. On 9th November, Sir Colin Campbell advanced on Lucknow, with 5,000 men, a mix of native and English regiments, and after a number of engagements, one which left 2,000 of the enemy dead, proceeded to not just relieve Lucknow but lead away the survivors successfully under the nose of the opposing force of 50,000. In one or two at least of these major conflicts of the Indian war, as part of the elite medical corps numbering in total 300, Dr Cross was exposed to the worst examples of man's inhumanity to man as well as the climatic savagery of the effects of heat and disease and in particular cholera.

As in the Crimean war he was part of a corps who performed their duty bravely and admirably, some of whose greatest practitioners lost their lives in the attempt to save others, amongst those Superintending Surgeon John Boon Hayes, Surgeon William Robert Boyes, Surgeon Nathaniel Collyer, Surgeon Arthur Wellesley Robert Newnham – all at Cawnpore, 27th June 1857.

There was no indication that the staff surgeon from Shandy Hall was any different from his medical colleagues in their admirable pursuit of saving as opposed to taking life. But no doubt, as the Lucknow defender had observed, he became understandably immune to the sight of slaughter and to feelings of danger.

He then went on to serve in the brief but equally tough, in its own way, British campaign in China in 1860.

These army surgeons would have personified the advice a well-known medical professor used to give to his generations of students: "Gentlemen, you must serve your profession bravely as soldiers do. Perils may be yours, but do not let craven fear o'ertake you. The calm consciousness of dangerous duty nobly done is what brings peace at the last."

Thus Philip Henry Eustace Cross, who in the course of a six-year period as an army surgeon had participated in the toughest theatres of war, beyond most soldier's fearful experience, miraculously emerged physically unscathed and deserving that peace to last for the rest of his life. It was his due and it seemed that fate would deliver him no less when he returned to his base in England.

The Wife

On the 17th August 1869, Dr Philip Henry Eustace Cross married Mary Laura Marriott in St James's Church Piccadilly in London, apparently without much approval and perhaps outright opposition from her family. They did not marry in her local parish from her home, Abbots Hall, with the fanfare and celebration the nuptials of a woman of her status would normally occasion. Instead, they married in haste, by licence, in London, as he was due to rejoin his regiment which was then stationed in Canada. This smacks of Cross's impetuosity – but perhaps also of her father's rejection of him as a son-in-law. At any rate, there was no marriage settlement.

He was forty-six years of age to her twenty-nine. On her part, no doubt this adventurer – this six-foot medical hero of Sevastopol and Lucknow, with the confident Irish swagger and energy he had inherited from his father – was immensely attractive. She was also twenty-nine years of age and dangerously close to being left on the shelf. Cross must have seemed a true knight in shining armour. He swept her off her feet and carried her off to a new life over seas.

And by any reckoning this was a very advantageous marriage for Dr Cross who hailed from what could at best be described as a country gentleman's residence. Mary Laura, who had been brought up in Abbots Hall near Shalford in Essex, had come from a far superior background and a house steeped in history.

Abbots Hall took its name from the ancient manor which belonged to the monastic Abbey of St Osyth. It continued with the monks until the 28th July 1539, when it was surrendered to the Crown as part of the dissolution of the monasteries. Henry VIII leased it for £6 per annum to Sir Roger Wentworth. He did not hold it too long as the king on the 10th of April 1540, granted "Ye maner de Abottes and all the messauges and lands in Shalford, appertaining to the said monastery" to his secretary Thomas Cromwell (1485–1540), the chief architect of the dissolution of the monasteries and appropriation of their income for the king.

Cromwell, who hailed from a poor background, had risen to the rank of Henry VIII's chief minister in 1853 but like many of those who take on the reins of power, he made enemies as he tried to modernise government at the expense of the privileges of the aristocracy and the clergy. Although in the king's inner circle, many of his colleagues were willing him misfortune. His downfall came with his part in the arrangement of the king's marriage to Anne of

Cleves which was a disaster acknowledged by both parties, and caused Henry a lot of heartache which turned to anger. It was the opportunity that Cromwell's enemies were waiting for and he was cast in the role of scapegoat. Despite being made first Earl of Essex on April 18th 1540, he was arrested the following month.

He was stripped of all his rank and brought to the Tower of London to await the King's pleasure and the annulment of the marriage to Anne of Cleves. On the night of 27th July his enemies both noble and ecclesiastical, attended a big banquet in honour of his demise. The following day he was executed; the same day that Henry married Catherine Howard. Cromwell's head was boiled and set on a spike on London Bridge.

By an ironic twist of historical fate, over a half a century later another Earl of Essex, Robert Devereux, favourite of Henry's daughter Elizabeth I, fell into disfavour after his disastrous military campaign in Ireland in 1599. In his army Colonel Cross, the direct ancestor of Dr Cross, was a prominent member. After an aborted rebellion against Elizabeth in 1601, the Earl of Essex was tried and condemned to death, the word of the Lord Steward echoing in his ears as they had in those of the previous earl: "You must go back to the place from whence you came, there to remain during Her Majesty's pleasure; from thence to be drawn on a hurdle through the streets of London, and so to the place of execution, where you shall be hanged, bowelled and quartered, your head and quarters to be disposed of at Her Majesty's pleasure; so God have mercy on your soul."

It took three blows of the executioner's axe to kill Devereux whose head, eyes open and expression unchanged according to witnesses, was then raised by the dispatcher for all to see as he cried: "God Save The Queen!" The earl was thirty-three years, three months and fifteen days and it is recorded that the Queen, who died two years later, mourned his passing and was as consumed by it as Henry VIII had been by his Earl of Essex's state murder.

His epitaph had a strange and resounding echo that would be heard in another part of the kingdom where his colonel had settled, almost three centuries later: "Endowed with talents and qualities that place him far above the majority of men, his unrestrained and ungoverned passions ruined himself and many of his friends." All Thomas Cromwell's estates reverted to the King, who made Abbots Hall part of the jointure (maintenance) of Anne of Cleves (1515–1557), his former queen, who ironically had been recommended by Thomas Cromwell. After her death, Abbots Hall again reverted to the Crown.

On the 8th June 1588, Elizabeth I granted the manor to Richard Braithwaite and Roger Bromley who quickly within a month sold it to Thomas Tyrell of Fulton in Cambridgeshire and his son of the same name. It passed by marriage from this family to Michael Dalton whose descendants sold it to James Gray, a lawyer from the Middle Temple in London. It was then sold on to one family and another until in 1790 it was purchased by J and R Marriott, antecedents of Mary Laura Marriott and then it stayed within that family for generations.

In 1848 White's *Directory of Essex* noted:
"Shalford, a scattered village, in the vale of the river Pant or Blackwater, from four to Five miles North North West of Braintree, has in its parish 832 souls, and 2,407 acres of land, finely undulated, and having a varied but generally fertile soil, in some parts gravelly, upon a white and yellow sand, which is beneficially applied to the wet heavy lands. For a long period most of the parish was held of the honour of Clare, and was divided into five manors, several of which were afterwards united. Richard Marriott, Esq., owns a great part of the soil, and is lord of the principal manors, and has a handsome seat here, called Abbots Hall."

Mary Laura Marriott was the daughter of the above-mentioned Richard Marriott and Sophia Lucy Stephenson and was born on 12th November 1840 at home in Abbots Hall. She was the seventh of at least nine children. She had three brothers, Hermine, Humphrey and John, and five sisters, Ellen, Olivia, Emmeline, Sophia and Augusta. In the May prior to her birth, three of her siblings died. Hermine died on the 11th of May, aged three years; Olivia died aged just one on the 18th of May, and John died aged five years on the 31st of May.

Despite their great wealth, living in a big house and a vast estate, the Marriotts, who had married in 1829, could not escape the slings and arrows of outrageous fortune and no doubt the birth of Mary Laura in November of a terrible year must have brought the parents much joy and just a little consolation against the awful backdrop of burying three of their children in the same year. It could be said, without much speculation, that Mary Laura Marriott was brought up as a much-cherished and loved child, evidence to god-fearing people that there was always the possibility of hope in the face of tragedy. There was life after death. It was also reasonable to expect that the girl child was cherished and cosseted, and perhaps in the long term not necessarily to her advantage.

But there was further misfortune for the family to bear when Sophia Marriott died in 1864 at the age of fifty-eight, the grief and memory of which Mary Laura would mark by calling her fourth-born child after her mother.

The grief would not end there, for six years later, one year after her marriage to Philip Cross, her father Richard died. Mary Laura inherited something over £5,000 on his death, equal to over £357,000 nowadays. Whether this money was paid in full at that point and whether, if so, it was in the control of Mary Laura or her husband is not clear. Humphrey, Marriott's eldest surviving son and heir, also gave her £50 a year, the equivalent of £3,570 today, and this may well have been an arrangement set up with his father before his death. In an age where women had no property rights, out of concern for their daughters fathers often worked "pin money" into a legal prenuptial agreement or specified property or money which a wife was to possess for her sole and separate use, not subject to the control of her husband, to provide her with an income separate from his. Squire Marriott may have entrusted Humphrey with this duty.

The sum of £5000 was a considerable amount of money, huge compared to the average earnings of local Essex factory and agricultural workers which amounted to less than thirty shillings a week. Whether or not he had control over Mary Laura's money, and with his brash personality and her meek one it would seem likely he had, Dr Cross with his own country residence and 500 acres of good land should have been well pleased.

While Richard Marriott's antipathy to his son-in-law was noted and much later put on record, there was no explanation offered; but it would prove to be beyond dispute. For some reason he objected to the marriage and clearly did not trust Dr Cross. There is little doubt that, given the tragedy of losing three children just before Mary Laura was born, her father would have been very protective of her. She, on the other hand, at twenty-nine years of age would have been considered an old maid – which may have told its own story as far as the relationship with her father was concerned. There may have been an element of over-protection, perhaps underlined by the fact that she was not and would never be described as a very attractive woman.

Richard Marriott was a man of both wealth and accomplishment whose intelligent and efficient running of the large estate would ensure that it would remain in his family, not just for longer than any other incumbent but for generations to come. It might be idle to speculate that he was a good judge of character but something in his experience of Dr Cross put Richard Marriott off him as a prospective husband of his daughter. Thus far in the scheme of things there did not seem to be anything that justified that attitude.

After the marriage, Cross and his new wife went to Canada where the 53rd regiment to which he was attached was stationed. The couple's first three children, Elizabeth, Henrietta and Robert, were born in Canada. The family returned to London in 1875 where their fourth child Sophia Mary was born on the 29th of August and baptised in St John's Church in Notting Hill. In the same year Dr Cross, last attached to the Army Medical Department, retired on half pay from the rank of Surgeon Major to which he had been promoted three years previously.

That year Dr Cross, his wife and their four children returned to

Shandy Hall, Dripsey, where two years later on the 16th of November 1877, their last child Henry Eustace Cross was born. Dr Cross was by then fifty-four years of age and Mary Laura was thirty-seven.

Dr Cross and his wife settled into the life of the country gentry in the quiet and peaceful area of Dripsey with their family of three daughters and two sons. Two of the girls were thought not to be "of strong mind" and were subject to epileptic attacks.

Also resident in the house was Dr Cross's sister Henrietta, almost ten years his junior – for whatever reason, the classic spinster aunt. She had been travelling before settling there.

Dr Cross was not of a lazy disposition and ran the homestead as a farm and had, as his status demanded, four servants in the house – one of them Jane Leahy, who had been with his father before him – and a number of others employed about the modest estate. As time passed, in the Victorian tradition the boys were sent to boarding school in England and the girls would eventually be given the service of a governess. In the meantime such a domestic life must have had its lack of attraction for a man, probably inheriting some of his father's abrasive character, whose earlier life was full of such intense drama and action.

Tim Healy, the nationalist barrister and MP, recalls in his *Legal Memories*:

"I was counsel against Dr Cross of Shandy Hall, defendant in an action by Phil Connell, a farmer who had objected to Cross hunting over his land. Cross with a blow of a whip struck off Connell's ear and rode on. The wounded man recovered £200 damages . . . Dr Cross was notable in County Cork as the son of a father who used to drive a tandem composed of a horse and bullock to every Assizes, Quarter Sessions and Petty Sessions as a litigant."

Dr Cross later fell foul of the local hunt and was boycotted and banned from hunting with the Hussars in Ballincollig.

Clearly he was experiencing the lack of the stimulation of his early years, as terrible as they had been, as if his survival of them had brought a frustration in their wake. He was an older man looking back on his greater days and more than likely feeling that they would never return. And the winds of inevitable political change that were about to sweep across the land would never have the involvement, one way or another, of a man of his breeding and military background. The memories of the battlegrounds in which he had been a participant had faded. Perhaps he felt he was past it all, despite the fact that he was over six feet tall, of strong and endurable physique, and in his own mind ready for anything.

His wife, Mary Laura, it seemed, was of somewhat delicate health and suffered from a sensitive stomach, sometimes having to leave the kitchen where the normal smells of cooking would affect her. She was of a nervous disposition, which might have had something to do with her husband, given his nature and the local conflicts that he engaged in, that were entirely foreign to her and her breeding.

Or her nervousness might have been aggravated by an underlying condition which had all the symptoms of the epilepsy her daughters suffered from.

Her servants were witness to fits during which Mary Laura would literally fall to the ground and then usually recover some minutes afterwards. She suffered palpitations of the heart during which she would clutch her chest, a feeling of nausea, hallucinations of smell and taste, giddiness, and also brief feelings of extreme fear, anxiety and depression. Though these symptoms may have had other causes, they are common premonitory sensations signalling the onset of an epileptic seizure.

There has been, throughout history, a stigma attached to epilepsy. For centuries it was considered a curse of the gods. In the early 19th century, people who suffered from it were confined to asylums, and seizures were falsely thought to be contagious. Early studies in that era added to the stigma. George Man Burrows from 1815 studied the condition and said: "If an early death does not supervene, the malady induces demency, idiotism or incurable insanity. Of all the modifications of mental derangement, there are none so terrible as that complicated by epilepsy."

He was somewhat more accurate in his assessment of the symptoms, which in time would lead to better understanding of the condition: "The epileptic attack may be preceded by a furious paroxysm or merely by elevated ideas, by great depression of spirits or mental imbecility, forgetfulness, etc. Or the reverse may obtain and the fit and the sequel of the fit may exhibit these morbid conditions."

Dostoyevsky, who himself suffered from the condition, gave vivid accounts of seizures in his novel *The Idiot* published in 1868: "Next moment something appeared to burst open before him, a wonderful inner light illuminated his soul. This lasted perhaps half a second, yet he distinctly remembered hearing the beginning of a wail, the strange, dreadful wail, which burst from his lips of its own accord, and which no effort of will on his part could suppress. Next moment, he was absolutely unconscious, black darkness blotted out everything. He had fallen into an epileptic fit."

Later in the century, by the mid-1800s, the three English neurologists, Russell Reynolds, John Hughlings Jackson and Sir William Richard Gowers, added a much greater knowledge of the condition without, however, removing the stigma. However, the definition of the condition was made more exact, divided mainly between what was described as grand mal, petit mal and hysteroid, classified by Gowers in 1881. In grand mal the patient suffers a convulsion in which muscles stiffen on both sides of the body, followed by muscle jerking. Consciousness is lost from the outset and the patient falls straight to the ground. There is champing of the teeth, a cry at the outset, blue colouration of the lips and facial skin, and the bladder or bowel may be emptied. In the lesser petit mal, there is no falling to the ground, consciousness is not lost and the experience may even be momentary. A hysteroid attack, as the name suggests, is triggered by emotional stress.

It would seem from the servants' experience that Mary Laura suffered from the more extreme form. At the time the medication used was potassium bromide which combined the effect of a sedative and anti-convulsant. This came in the form of a white crystalline powder, freely soluble in water and had a bitter taste. It strikes one therefore as a perfect vehicle to facilitate the administration of arsenic or strychnine. Curiously, also, as we will later learn, some treatments for epilepsy actually contained minute amounts of both arsenic and strychnine. However, while being an effective medication for epilepsy, potassium bromide had quite considerable side effects. These included, in high concentration, nausea, sometimes vomiting, loss of appetite, weakness, general malaise, rashes of the skin and the face, depression which the condition was already contributing to, as well as mood swings and occasional hysteria.

There is one thing certain: at this time and indeed for many years after, anything which concerned a malady related to mental illness would have been kept a family secret, an unwanted skeleton in the cupboard, to be joined by any others that might rise in the course of events at Shandy Hall.

Mary Laura's illness could not have been eased by the burden of looking after two girls who had their own health problems, the worry about her other children in boarding school, entirely natural to any mother, and the gruff and aggressive nature of her husband who it seemed did not have such concerns on his list of priorities. Under such circumstances it is not likely that the couple had an active – or indeed any – sex life.

Their social life included mainly visits to friends and neighbours and in particular the Caulfield family a couple of miles down the road in Classas. Captain John Caulfield was also a retired British Army officer whose family were descended from the Viscount Charlemont of Donamon Castle in County Roscommon. At one stage in the mid 19th century the family owned estates in a number of counties, totalling over 10,000 acres.

Captain John was born on 10th October 1830 in Benown House, County Westmeath. Four of his brothers also served in the British Army. Captain William Caulfield served in the same theatre of war as Dr Cross and was killed in action while with the 44th Foot regiment in the siege of Sevastopol on the 18th June 1854. Captain St George Caulfield was based in India for 19 years and his brothers Robert and Henry also served in India.

John married a distant cousin in 1870 in London – Theresa Eliza Stafford Caulfield who was born on the 15th of March 1850 in Bhagalpore, Bengal, India. In Classas in 1886 the couple, John, forty-seven, and Theresa, thirty-seven, had five children: Gwendoline, twelve, who had been born in Southampton; Walter, eleven; Edith, six; Geraldine, 4; and Gordon just one year of age, all born in Classas.

Clearly, Dr Cross had more than common ground with his neighbour and there were many visits, talks and card games and a period during which Mary Laura became very friendly with Theresa, being of similar age and with the same size family. By all accounts this was a good and fruitful relationship on both sides until what appeared to be a quite innocent occurrence in the summer of 1886. One that surely, on the surface, should not have sparked off a series of events that would have an unforeseen and awful impact on both families and, indeed, on the immediate community.

Mrs Caulfield, obviously under pressure from rearing a young and active family, engaged the service of a governess to help out both with the daily routine and the education of the girls in particular which was the accepted convention of the time.

On the 22nd of June, Effie Skinner a young and beautiful woman of impeccable background and credentials arrived in the house to take up that position and was apparently, at twenty years of age, full of energy and enthusiasm. She immediately impressed her employers by her handling of the children and devotion to her duty.

The Governess

It is worth now contemplating the background of this young woman – to understand where she came from, and if possible where this would lead her. Effie, as she was and would continue to be called, was born as Evelyn Forbes Skinner on the 30th of July, 1865, in the parish of St Andrew's in Scotland to Robert Skinner, a clergyman of the Scottish Episcopalian Church, and his wife Annie Henrietta Skinner (née Sangster).

According to her birth record, her parents were married on the 3rd of July 1856, in St Andrew's Church. Her middle name of

Forbes was inherited from her great-grandmother Janis Forbes. Her father Robert Skinner was one of five children born to Robert Skinner, an engineer, and Anne Black. He was born on the 8th of August, 1827. According to Tron Kirk, Edinburgh, parish records her grandfather John Robert Skinner was born on the 19th of December 1786, to James Skinner, Esq, writer, and Janis Forbes.

In 1871 the Skinner family was living in Lea Marsden in Warwickshire, where Evelyn's father was a vicar of the local parish. The census return confirms that Evelyn was one of at least five children: the siblings included Harry, Florence, Annie and Constance. Evelyn went on to attend school at Winchcombe in Gloucestershire in the Cotswolds.

This, for the moment, just provides a partial picture of Evelyn or Effie Skinner's lineage.

Her father Robert was connected to a very famous family in Anglican Church history in Scotland, a family whose bravery, constancy and character in the face of poverty, danger and oppression was indisputable. A legacy of which Effie was undoubtedly aware but might not have been a subscriber to. Such is the attitude of most succeeding generations, then and now.

Her most famous ancestor was Rev John Skinner, Dean Of Aberdeen, a great Scottish Episcopalian churchman, poet and songwriter of note, a friend of and hugely admired by Robbie Burns. Not only a writer of poetry in English but also in Latin, he was a scholar imbued by Christian zeal, described by his contemporary, Bishop Grieg, as: "the brightest ornament of the Scottish Episcopal Church during the latter half of the 18th century – one who would have been a bright ornament of any church in any century."

John Skinner was born in 1721 at Balfour in the parish of Birse, Aberdeenshire, about thirty miles from Aberdeen. His father John, a parish schoolmaster, married the widow of the Laird of Balfour, Mrs Donal Farquharson (née Gillanders), who died two years later, with John the only child. His father was appointed Master in Echt, 12 miles from Aberdeen where he continued to teach for fifty years. He re-married there a few years later and had numerous children only one of which, the youngest son James who became a writer of some standing in Edinburgh, survived into old age. It was from this branch of the family that Effie sprang. John, the only son of the first marriage, taught and then joined the Episcopal Church and married a clergyman's daughter, Grissell Hunter, on the island of Shetland. They had six children: three sons, James, John and Marianus, and three daughters, Margaret, Grace and Elisabeth.

The family lived in Longside in a small thatched cottage which was the Rev Skinner's tiny home for life. He was a victim of the religious persecution in the mid-eighteenth century and in May 1753 was cast into prison in Aberdeen for six months where his second son John, later to become bishop of the city, insisted at eight years of age in joining his father and was allowed to do so by the authorities.

The Rev Skinner was a man who suffered such iniquity with fortitude and a strong heart. It was said of him: "He was not a man to rest content with any mere alleviations of an evil or any merely negative advantages of any sort. He strove manfully to extract from passing evil some positive and lasting good to himself or his people."

He always lived on the cusp of poverty and in 1758, like many clergy, to supplement their tiny stipend took on a farm. But, as in many cases and in his, things went from bad to worse which he expressed in verse thus:

> *"Thus farm and house demands come on together,*
> *Both must be answered, I can answer neither;*
> *I put them off till Lammas, Lammas comes,*
> *Our vestry meets, and I get in my sums;*
> *The half year's stipend makes a pretty show,*
> *But twenty ways poor fifteen pounds must go*
> *Scarce one night does it in my coffers stay,*
> *Like Jonah's gourd that withers in a day,*
> *First come, first served with me is still the way."*

Two of his sons, James and Marianus, were of restless disposition. The first took to the sea and ended up in Philadelphia, where suffering from the troubles of the rebellion he was dead before 1789. Marianus took off abroad and was not seen or heard of again. The second son, John, went to university in Oxford and later went on to a great Church career, as did his son William. Between them they held the Bishopric of Aberdeen for three quarters of a century: 1782–1857.

Rev John Skinner's lasting artistic legacy was the song "Tullochgorum" which was not only favourably compared to "Auld Lang Syne" but also excited the praise of the author of the latter. Bishop Skinner bumped into Burns one time and spent an hour in his company. The great Scottish poet was fulsome in his praise for his father, calling him the "author of the best Scotch song Scotland ever saw". During an exchange of letters with Burns, John the elder mentioned his brother James, a writer in Edinburgh – technically speaking, his half-brother – and great-grandfather of Effie Skinner.

Effie's grandfather John Robert Skinner was born on the 19th of December, 1786 to James Skinner, writer, and Janis Forbes. As part of the Anglican Communion, Effie's father Robert was destined to serve both home and abroad.

In Berne, Switzerland, in 1845 the authorities gave permission for English services to be held in the chapel at Burgerspital. A group of innkeepers undertook to pay the cost of bringing over a chaplain from England. There were plans to build a church based on plans by English architect George Edmund Street but as not enough money was raised a local grant was revoked.

In 1859 the Colonial and Continental Church Society undertook to support an English chaplain in Berne and in 1861 George William Mackenzie took up the position. Many years later, in 1881, Robert Skinner was appointed to Berne and stayed there with his family until 1886. He had studied at Hatfield Hall in Durham, been made a deacon in 1853, was ordained a year later, and had served in Wickham, Durham, Aberdeen, Lea Marston, Dacre and Shrewton. The Berne posting was recognised as one of the most underpaid chaplaincies in Europe with pay of between £130 and £150 a year, without a house for a married man. This was considered totally inadequate.

There was no church and services were held in an Old Catholic Church of St Peter and Paul with a very small congregation.

A report in an Anglican Church magazine summed up the scenario in which the Rev Skinner worked:

"Our little congregation was lost in the stately church which, in spite of a well heated stove, was icy cold. The pulpit, too, was so far removed from the congregation that some of us had great difficulty in understanding the whole of the sermon. The chief fault lay with us being so few in number, even in summer when the season was at its height, and everyone knows how chilling is the sight of a place of worship, all but empty."

In 1887 the correspondent noted with great joy that the congregation had moved to the hall of the Leber School that Christmas and had an increased number of attendees, numbering forty, which apparently was further reason for rejoicing. This gives a somewhat depressing picture of what the Rev Robert Skinner had been experiencing.

By then, happily perhaps for him and his family, he had moved to Cologne.

But the improvement was slight. Up to two decades previously William Haseldine Pepys was instrumental in bringing Church of England services to the city. (Pepys was an English scientist and researcher who was director of the Imperial Continental Gas Association, which was introducing gas illumination to cities and towns across Europe.) However, after the British Consulate was moved from Cologne to Dusseldorf, the small government support for the chaplain was discontinued. Then Henry Ferdinand Hartmann, who had been ordained in the US, arrived back in the city and, using some of his own financial means, brought together a community and obtained the use of a building called the Temple Lodge. However, the maintenance costs became too high and Mr Friederich, proprietor of the Hotel Du Nord, offered premises for the community's use. The hall had been originally designed as a billiard room. He renovated the premises and had stained-glass windows installed. Dedication of the building took place in 1883. Two years later a British company took over the hotel and the lease to the chaplaincy continued.

In 1886, when Rev Robert Skinner took over the chaplaincy

from Dr Hartmann, the congregation numbered one hundred which must have seemed a great improvement compared to his previous posting. It was that fateful year that his daughter Evelyn took up her position with the Caulfield family.

On 12th May of the same year a letter from the Rev Skinner was published in the Edinburgh *Evening Courant* in reference to his and Effie's famous antecedent John Skinner of Longside:

Having observed in your impression of yesterday an extract from Erasrers Magazine regarding the origin of Skinner's song, "The Ewie Wi' The Crookit Horn", and describing it as the metaphor of a whisky still, I beg to state that it is an entire mistake. The author was my grandfather's brother, and I have often heard my late father say he had seen "The Ewie" himself at Lineshart in the author's lifetime. I have myself seen a picture of it in the possession of the late Bishop William Skinner, who was the grandson of the author, and whom I have often heard repudiate the story. The words of the song are to be taken in their natural sense.

I am, etc,
Robert Skinner.

Young Effie Skinner came from a family of great character but one of straitened circumstances and not familiar with luxury or privilege of any kind or indeed expectant of anything that might equate to worldliness. Her lineage was of those who lived and died by their forceful religious belief and personal integrity. Her education qualified her to teach and mind the children of the privileged and introduced her to a lifestyle that was not just beyond her experience but also her imagination.

Her engagement by the Caulfields introduced her to this world of wealth in a community that seemed to be rarefied in every sense and divorced from the vicissitudes of life that her family had been exposed to – where the shillings, every last one of them, were of no consequence, where the past, present and future coalesced in a manner that was to her entirely foreign. She fitted in well, worked hard, the children took to her. Surely her future had promise.

Two miles up the road at Shandy Hall, Mary Laura Cross was in a depressed state of mind and her spirits were very low. Her late father's feelings about her husband had proved to be prescient. She was troubled, isolated and lonely despite her good relations with neighbours. Inside the door of her own house, she experienced little but stress and unhappiness. In a word she felt trapped.

She longed for the comfort of her relations in England and in July 1886 she returned to Abbots Hall for an extended stay which provided temporary relief from the claustrophobia of her life in Dripsey.

In her absence Dr Cross was a frequent visitor to the house at Classas, whiling away many evenings playing cards with his friends the Caulfields – with their young governess making up a fourth player at the table.

The evidence is that he fell passionately in love with the attractive young woman.

Perhaps this was as a result of the redundant relationship with Mary Laura and the boredom of country life, which could not satisfy a man who had seen such extremities of experience – which most of his age and status would have been more than happy to consign to the dim territory of distant memory.

A man of tough and vigorous constitution, he was nonetheless not immune to the invasive insecurities of age, which given the life expectancy of the time, were considerable. The thought that there was not much left to him to look forward to, beyond the constant and dominating encroachment of memory eating away at every precious moment left to him, must have been painful – moments which could be taken away by any sudden visitation by disease or infirmity. He suffered a delayed mid-life crisis, in which he envisioned all his perceived achievements diminished by the passage of time. For all he had done in his life, it might have seemed that happiness had eluded his grasp, a happiness he had not sought earlier but which he now craved. Such thoughts are the common hauntings of age. As are the jealous thoughts of and desire for the elixir of youth. And what better way to satisfy that desire but engagement with the young of the opposite sex?

Perhaps in this way he could somehow brush away the cloying cobwebs of time, transform the regrets of the past into the hopes of the future, banish the dark clouds that had descended over Shandy Hall and allow the sunshine to lift the spiritual depression that had ground his existence down. That would allow him to truly live as opposed to exist and deny for some time the yawning space in the vaults of the family burial ground in Carrigrohane. There might yet be something to show for all the efforts and all the negative aspects of his days, then and now; so passion would force blood coursing through his body and give him life as he knew it could be, once and for all.

It had been a long time since the Surgeon Major had experienced danger of any hue and the mental stimulation and sharpness that accompanies the cut and thrust of battle, as adrenalin readies the human body for fight or flight. The strong attraction to a very young woman was for a man in his position and familial status highly dangerous, a further incentive to the ageing doctor.

And a powerful antidote to what a man of his past and eccentric character would have found as the insufferable boredom of the life of a country gentleman. Perhaps as intolerable as the life of genteel poverty that faced the ambitious governess who had become the object of his affections. And added to the personal mix, the coalescing circumstances that facilitated behaviour that otherwise would have never been imaginable, not to mind possible.

The soldier who becomes stuck on what could happen the next second or minute might as well face the certainty of that consequence – something which would have been anathema to Dr Cross, the proud bearer of a military tradition that stretched back centuries. Like Tolstoy in Sevastopol, he went about his ghastly business, ignoring the bigger picture. Neither man would have hesitated for a second to move from one trench or battlement to another. Fearless they might be described as, but it is as much to do with banishing the thoughts that produce fear. And that means not dwelling for one minute on the consequences of any of their actions at the time. The Russian author was fascinated at times by the ability of the soldiers, under the threat of death at any second, to go about their business as if nothing out of the ordinary was happening. They could not have avoided insanity or cowardice otherwise. It is doubtful if any human being can ever properly survive such constant bombardment on their mental and physical resources and exposure to unrelenting horror. They more than likely carry the legacy of their experience intact throughout the rest of their lives.

Some such things in Cross's psyche drove him down a path that most men in his position, and sense or sensibility, or indeed instinct of self-preservation, would have avoided like the plague. But perhaps that is what surviving the risks of war does to a man. Or was it a matter of being simply overcome by the seductive fantasies of lust? Or was it love?

For a number of reasons the svelte, pencil-thin waist, the lush dark hair and the exquisitely defined features proved a powerful aphrodisiac to the doctor. Understandable maybe, as any man of his age in any age would find such a creature delightful to look at and think about but then with a sigh place their fancy where it belonged, in the realm of fantasy. Not the master of Shandy Hall. And in a society in which privilege and wealth were great prizes for any young woman of vulnerable status, he could take his chance with a certain degree of confidence.

He fixed on her across a not-so-crowded room, through a cloud of the Turkish cigarettes he had become accustomed to in his years of service, and something of his attention must have been reciprocated, however fleetingly at first, even if he had adopted the persona of the gruff and arrogant country gentleman awash with experience of far-off foreign lands.

And there must have been some communication and more than likely a job offer which Effie would have naturally taken some time to consider as she had been employed for such a short period at the Caulfields. The result, however, was that at the start of October 1886, Effie gave notice to Theresa Caulfield that she was leaving the following January.

Her employer responded by firing her with a month's notice, indicating quite clearly that she suspected something was afoot. That must have been confirmed when Effie Skinner went straight into the employment of Philip Henry Eustace Cross at Shandy Hall. It was nevertheless a strange reaction on Theresa Caulfield's part, the purpose of which could only have been to set the governess adrift without a job, so that she might be forced to leave the district and thus frustrate the interest on Dr Cross's part.

It had the opposite effect by catapulting Effie Skinner permanently into the Cross household, straight into the arena of temptation so to speak.

In time, Theresa would regret her ill-considered decision most bitterly. It was an action of such unforeseen but great consequence that it would haunt her and Captain Caulfield for the rest of their lives.

Some two decades later a well-known chronicler of crime, Charles Kingston, in a very short account gave a rather fanciful, inaccurate, but not entirely uninteresting view of the events of that time, leavened with some speculation that had a ring of the truth. He posited that Dr Cross was a man with a modest army pension, impaired digestion, overbearing manner, who had a dislike for female society while at the same time giving the impression that he was a devoted family man. He occasionally hunted and fished but his tall, military figure was conspicuous because of its aloofness. Had it not been for Mrs Cross's popularity, there would have been few visitors to Shandy Hall. The writer then proposed a scenario with entirely fictitious dialogue on the matter of the entry of the young governess into the household.

This scenario was in most aspects the opposite of the truth, not least in the idealised portrait of a pretty winning young girl which bears little resemblance to the striking, intelligent and forceful young woman we know her to be.

Kingston presents it that Dr Cross, in the presence of the young governess, "fell for her dainty figure and graceful movements, her musical laugh and never-failing cheerfulness which appealed to a man of gloomy and taciturn nature". Philip Cross then worshipped in silence, until he could contain himself no more, and startled the young governess by kissing her, uninvited, in the hall: "Unable to resist the temptation of the lovely face raised to his, the merry grey eyes dancing with a wonderful light, he impulsively pressed his lips to hers." According to this account, Effie then ran up the stairs, and nothing was subsequently said about the incident. He later apologised to the governess and pleaded for forgiveness but she had no intention of putting up with any more of such familiarities – which rings true because the governess had too much to lose: reputation and employment. But clearly the elder gentleman's attention, in either looks or body language, could not be contained and Kingston probably rightly assumed that Mrs Cross noticed and first focused her justifiable jealousy and resentment on the governess. And, classically, secondly on the errant husband. While Miss Skinner is out on a walk with the girls, the challenged mistress of the house confronts the husband and tells him that the task falls to him to tell the girl that she has to go. He baulks, according to another imagined account, but gives in because of the overwhelming necessity of maintaining Victorian respectability.

But Dr Cross delivers the awful news, according to Kingston, in an entirely lewd, lying and at the same time seductive manner. He says this is all because of his wife's unreasonableness but he will continue to act as her protector. Effie, he promises, will not be at any loss as a result of this awful consequence, in which he has played no part. She is a mere victim of his wife's ludicrous and jealous behaviour. Perhaps a fanciful view, but containing elements of truth which would be borne out by facts in the future.

How quickly Dr Cross's attentions were reciprocated is not clear but they must have been, as subsequent events would indicate. The question arises then why would a young, beautiful woman like Effie Skinner get romantically involved with a man old enough to her grandfather? Quite apart from the fact that it was not the first time such a liaison was formed in the history of male-female relationships, she may have felt an attraction to a powerful male figure, possibly more vigorous than his age might suggest, his status carrying extra power and somehow fulfilling an innate personal need. A need that could be established with some personal information, but perhaps more so in the context of the social circumstances of the time and in particular her and others of her working status: the status of the governess and her limited expectations in terms of marriage and future position.

According to Olwen Hufton in *The Prospect Before Her* (1995), the daughters of parsons were particularly likely to remain spinsters: "Anglican clergymen's families . . . were large, and it would appear to have been normal to have married no more than a couple of daughters per generation (usually to other clergymen), leaving the rest to serve as housekeepers, governesses, ladies' companions, or simply to stay at home to tend aged parents." Hufton is referring to the Georgian period but by Effie Skinner's time nothing had changed and, in fact, clergymen's daughters were often educated specifically to equip them to become governesses.

This is not to say that desire for social advancement and security was Effie Skinner's primary motivation, but it does provide a clue to her involvement. It was obvious that the risks of such a liaison were enormous and that she may have baulked at her master's initial advances. But she eventually walked down the dangerous path, the destination she clearly had no way of knowing. But one of which she had no doubt been given an expectation – the ultimate one for a young woman in her position: marriage to her master, to a man far beyond her social standing and by all means her saviour. Otherwise where would she be going? On the other hand, it could be assumed, given her genealogy, that she was not without some moral conscience. Unlike Edward Rochester of Thornfield Hall, the wife of her employer was not a lunatic locked in the attic; she was alive and running the household. And Effie, like Jane Eyre, whatever her feelings about Dr Cross, would never have been content to remain his mistress.

Up to this time she had led a peripatetic existence as one of the family of a travelling clergyman, going from one impoverished posting to another, with no permanent home and little or no prospect of ever having one. Effie would never have had to be taught self-denial; it was an inescapable condition of her life and one which she might justifiably have wished to escape. She was educated, energetic, bright and intelligent and must have viewed her status of governess as a stepping-stone.

She did not fit the stereotype of the governess as a severe "Plain Jane" type of woman; she was young and beautiful and therefore presented a threat to the peace of mind of the master and indeed the lady of the house. And she lived in a society which considered an unmarried woman as a social failure, alternately treated with pity and contempt, a social pariah at a time when the very raison d'être of the female was defined by the male. Little wonder that, for Victorian women, the issue of marriage was a huge one and a source of great anxiety.

In Charlotte Brontë's *Jane Eyre*, Mr Brocklehurst, proprietor of Lowood School, describes the goal of his institution: "My plan in bringing up these girls is not to accustom them to habits of luxury and indulgence, but to render them hardy, patient and self-denying." Experience which Effie Skinner had no need of being taught.

Neither family member nor servant, the governess held a peculiar and ill-defined role in Victorian society which found middle-class female employment anxiety-producing.

In a review of *Jane Eyre* in December 1848, the *Quarterly Review* discussed the curious status of the governess for its upper-class readers:

"There may be, and are, exceptions to this rule, but the real definition of the governess, in the English sense, is a being who is equal in birth, manners and education but inferior in worldly wealth. Take a lady, in every sense of the word, born and bred, and let her father pass through the *Gazette* [i.e. be declared bankrupt], and she wants nothing more to suit our highest *beau ideal* of a guide and instructress to our children. We need the imprudencies, extravagancies, mistakes or crimes of a certain number of fathers, to sow that seed from which we reap the harvest of governesses. There is no other class of labourers for hire who are this systematically supplied by the misfortunes of our fellow creatures. There is no other class which so cruelly requires its members to be, in birth, mind and manners, above their station, in order to fit them for their station."

Employed in England since the reign of the Tudors, governesses initially only associated with aristocratic houses, but by the turn of the 19th century economic progress brought the middle classes into the bracket of affording one, and indeed having a governess was regarded as a status symbol. Together with employing nurses to care for younger children, the Victorian mother was thus freed of the primary obligation of looking after her offspring – while the children either suffered at the governesses' and nannies' ineptness or were filled with fondness for women who were closer to them than their own mothers.

This resulted, for the governess, in a difficult relationship with the mother of the house who handed over the moral and intellectual responsibility for the upbringing of her children to a paid employee.

The governess had to learn to love children, something which should have come naturally to the mother, and yet could be subject to insolent and malicious behaviour by the children. There were a lot of instances in contemporary accounts, letters, journals and fiction describing public humiliation and degradation by employers.

Fictional accounts based on fact and experience by Harriet Martineau, Charlotte and Anne Brontë showed governesses suffering miserably as a result of repeated humiliations, sexual repression and intense loneliness. The governess was not equal to the employer, not considered a servant and not able to socialise with either group. Charlotte Brontë's miserable and unhappy years as a governess did come in useful in her writing but left her understandably bitter. Her father was of course a clergyman of pathetically limited means.

Trapped in such a social vortex the governess was fair game for both the children and the servants and ultimately the employers. Too low for the family, too high for the servants, she had even less opportunity than the downstairs staff to attain the ultimate safety for women in Victorian society – marriage – and in a market where there was a surplus of women. The figure of the spinster was all too common in Victorian society.

If she was possessed of good looks, she could not do anything to enhance her appearance for fear on the one hand of exciting the attention of the master of the household or, on the other, the jealousy of the mistress. And she had neither the means nor the time to establish friendships, particularly male, outside the household. Since one of the main functions was to teach manners and the conventions of society, the governess had to be the epitome of propriety and maintain whatever self-pride and dignity she could possess in such a position.

Whether in romantic fiction or fact, there was an undercurrent of ambivalence in relation to the governess and the master of the household, as if she secretly desired to take herself out of her lowly status by snaring the master through some sort of flirtation.

The character of the governess became popular in fiction of the time and later, precisely because of her underdog status and vulnerability. And her character could be meek or submissive or independent and rebellious. In *The Governess* (1839) the main character Clara Mordaunt comes from a wealthy family until her father's suicide as a result of bankruptcy consigns her to the role of orphan. But her life as a governess in various families leads to marriage to an aristocratic master and she is not just saved but returned to her former prosperity. The huge gap between the governess and master in wealth, caste and custom provided a powerful fictional frisson. But the reality was also encompassed in Mrs Fairfax's advice to Jane Eyre: "Try and keep Mr Rochester at a distance. Distrust yourself as well as him. Gentlemen in his station are not accustomed to marrying their governesses."

Mary Atkinson Maurice, in *Governess Life; Its Trials, Duties and Encouragements*, published in 1849, put it thus:

"In some instances again, the love of admiration has led the governess to try and make herself necessary to the comfort of the father of the family in which she resided, and by delicate and unnoticed flattery gradually to gain her point, to the disparagement of the mother and the destruction of mutual happiness. When the latter was homely, or occupied with domestic cares, opportunity was found to bring forward attractive accomplishments or by sedulous attentions to supply her lack of them; or the sons were in some instances objects of notice and flirtation, or when occasion offered, visitors at the house."

The attraction by the master of the house for a young governess was not exclusive to Victorian England in fiction and fact, as evidenced in Dostoevsky's *Crime and Punishment* and a scene that has quite extraordinary echoes of the unfolding events in Shandy Hall. Writing to the central character Raskolnikov, his mother explains how his sister Dounia took up a position as governess to alleviate her brother's financial problems, with quite traumatic consequences. The master apparently concealed his feelings by being rude and arrogant in her company, an attitude that Kingston attributed to Dr Cross as an initial wooing tactic, designed to hide the truth of his intentions from others. And quite a clever one, it has to be said. Despite the kind and generous behaviour of the master's wife, Dounia was subject of his unwanted attentions "especially when Mr Svidrigailov, relapsing into his old regimental habits, was under the influence of Bacchus . . . But at last he lost all control and had the face to make Dounia an open and shameful proposal, promising her all sorts of inducements and offering, besides, to throw up everything and take her to another estate of his, or even abroad."

Dounia could not leave at once because of her financial situation or the risk of arousing her mistress's suspicion and being the cause of a rupture in the family and scandal. The scoundrel was pushing his attentions on the young governess in the garden one day when his wife Marfa came on the scene and wrongly blamed it all on Dounia, screaming and refusing to listen her, even striking her, while the cowardly husband held his tongue. Dounia was fired. Her reputation was however later cleared when the master held up his hands and told his wife that the governess was innocent; and, as the mother related in her letter, "The evidence of the servants, too, cleared Dounia's reputation; they had seen and knew a great deal more than Mr Svidrigailov had himself supposed – as indeed is always the case with servants."

There the parallel with the Cross situation ended. The outcome in Shandy would prove to be different and even more Dostoevskian.

Whether marriage was involved in Effie's mind at that juncture is possibly doubtful but for whatever reason she became involved with the master of the house, perhaps to the extent of accepting his advances, which would have further inflamed his passion and in a natural progression turned him against his wife, because such is the inevitable chemistry of such liaisons. If there had been indifference in the Crosses' relationship prior to this, it now would have changed to dislike, if not something more as an inevitable obstacle to Dr Cross's passion and happiness.

What was inevitable was that Mary Laura Cross did become aware of the situation between the governess and her husband and confronted him about it, a very stressful thing for an already delicate woman who would have been put into an extreme state of anxiety by the fact of such a thing happening under her own roof and the possible consequences for her status as a wife and loving mother.

Whatever courage Dr Philip Cross had shown in his exemplary military career now deserted him. He did not stand by the young governess and obviously promised his wife that nothing of the sort would happen again and he would remain faithful in future to his marriage vows. The result was that Mrs Cross asked Effie Skinner to leave her employment in January 1887, although she had the decency to give her the train fare to Dublin and expenses to cover a hotel for an overnight stay. And it may be that Mary Laura was even more generous: Effie was going to visit relatives in Scotland and afterwards to Carlow where she was to take up a new position as a governess. It would appear, therefore, from the rapidity with which the new position was arranged, that Mary Laura was generous enough to provide the erring governess with a reference and may even have secured the position for her through contacts. This suggests that she blamed her husband, not the governess, for whatever indiscretions she had observed. She wanted her out of the way of her husband but did not want to ruin the young girl's life and livelihood. Unless, of course, it was Philip Cross himself who pulled strings and secured Effie her new position.

In any case, in and around this time there was a marked change in Cross's attitude to his wife, marked by cursing and threatening behaviour, as if he was blaming her for the agreed departure of the young governess. If it had been agreed that he would not contact Miss Skinner, that did not turn out to be the case.

Some weeks later Cross went to Dublin on business and stayed at the Hibernian Hotel for three days, an unusual occurrence for him, and perhaps too much of a coincidence to be explained by whatever excuse he had offered Mary Laura. She may have thought little of it, but there was one member of the household who later claimed to know exactly the purpose of the absence.

Death in Dripsey

At the end of the same month of January, Dr Cross happened by chance to meet a neighbour, Mrs Madras, in Cork and when she enquired about his wife's wellbeing he said that she was so poorly he would not be surprised if she was dead when he got home. A response that somewhat puzzled Mrs Madras, as she was not aware that her friend was in such poor health.

During the following months there ensued a correspondence with the former governess, which the doctor concealed by sending his letters to the local post office by his employed messenger and on occasions collecting the replies in person from the post office.

Around that time Mrs Cross was affected by a number of fainting fits, possibly as a result of her underlying condition but intensified by an entirely new stress in her marital situation.

At the end of March, Dr Cross went away for a couple of days, to the Punchestown Races. And he again went away for a time around the 20th of April.

On the 29th March an old school friend of Mrs Cross, Miss Mervynia Jane Dunnington Jefferson, came to visit for a prolonged stay.

Mervynia was a daughter of Joseph Dunnington Jefferson, Rector of Thorganby, Yorkshire, and Justice of the Peace for the East Riding, who had died in 1880. Her father had also been "a landed proprietor" and left his family very well provided for, enabling his widow and Mervynia (unlike the run of clergymen's daughters) to live comfortably on "independent means". She never married as she was an "Associate" of an Anglican religious order called The Sisters of the Church, which was formed in 1870 by Emily Ayckbown. The order's professed aim was "to combat social evils and to raise the status and increase the opportunities of women". The women they had in mind included themselves, as religious life freed women from the Victorian compulsion to marry and allowed them an autonomy they could achieve in no other way. They were, therefore, feminist in outlook. They focused their efforts on practical works of mercy: setting up clothing depots, Bun Schools (Sunday Schools where they fed waifs and strays on milk and buns), free day schools, night shelters, mobile carts distributing food at the docks, and orphanages. They especially valued leisured Associates (almost invariably ladies) who lived in their own homes by a simple religious rule of life and had both the means and the time to devote themselves to such projects. Such was Miss Mervynia Jane Dunnington Jefferson who was attached to their Orphanage of Mercy in Kilburn.

We can speculate that that Miss Jefferson, at forty-six years of age, must have been a formidable woman. She met her match, however, in Dr Philip Henry Eustace Cross, as we shall see.

The visitor knew that her friend had been despondent for some time but her spirits seemed to have been raised somewhat. The weather was cold but dry, as it had been the previous two months, and ideal for walking and going out. But there was not going to be much opportunity.

During the early days of Miss Jefferson's visit Mary Laura had a number of fainting fits and complained of the actions of her heart. Mervynia gave her sal volatile {smelling salts) on a few occasions. For some reason she later professed not to have interpreted those fainting episodes as epilepsy, though from the servants' later descriptions it seemed to be. Presumably she was sensitive to the fact that it was an unmentionable affliction for a person of good family and background.

On the 10th of May, Mary Laura became ill, suffering from vomiting and diarrhoea, and was confined to bed for a week. On the 18th she was well enough to walk halfway to Coachford with Mervynia but was ill again two days later. On the 22nd she was well enough to get up and go to the garden but soon was ill again. On the 24th an uncle by marriage of her husband, a retired Doctor

Godfrey, visited her, diagnosed a bilious attack and recommended medication. Over the following few days she was visited by a number of neighbours and friends who noted that she was very ill and weak.

Mervynia Jefferson had a conversation with Dr Cross and it was decided that she would return to England on the 2nd of June. It is not clear why she chose to leave her good friend at this critical juncture, nor did she later offer any excuse or explanation.

Dr Cross, with a few of the servants, was attending to his wife's needs. He was sleeping in the same room as her in a bed across from her. Mary Laura complained to Mervynia that her husband did not hear her when she made requests for help or sustenance.

The months of March, April and May had been consistently cold and dry, the normal showers and rainfall of the first two notably absent. Then at the beginning of June came a great and dramatic change. The temperature rocketed into a heat wave that would last until 10th July, making the summer the hottest on record and it would remain so for another century. For thirty-four days the sun shone over County Cork like a fireball in the cloudless blue sky. Not a drop of rain fell. For Ireland, then and now, this must be considered a phenomenon.

It was the time of the year when the days were the longest and the sun at its maximum altitude. The sun played on the pastures, on the corn; the young turnips and the grass would soon begin to turn to yellow and dusky brown and the turnips would shrivel and scorch in the boiling earth. Cork was affected more than any county in the country or any other part of Britain. The farmers saw a disastrous harvest looming, but August would bring the rains and the pastures and root crops were mercifully saved. Meanwhile, Mary Laura was suffering from constant retching, purging and a thirst, witnessed on the 1st of June by the servant Mary Buckley about five o'clock in the evening. Mervynia Jefferson saw her about ten that night.

Later, after going to sleep, Mary Buckley heard a number of screams coming from Mrs Cross's room but went back to sleep.

The following morning, between six and seven, Dr Cross woke

the servants and announced that their mistress had died at one o'clock in the morning.

Mervynia Jefferson left Shandy Hall for London at nine o'clock, an inexplicable reaction to the situation on which no light was ever thrown.

Mary Laura's death was registered by her husband as typhoid fever with the local medical officer Dr Crowley. She was buried in Magourney cemetery in Coachford early on the morning of Saturday 2nd of June. The quickness of the burial the husband explained by the infective nature of her illness and the fact that Sunday was the Papists' "pet day" for burials.

On the Thursday of the following week Dr Cross travelled to England, ostensibly to visit his children who were in boarding school. On the 14th he visited Miss Jefferson at her mother's home in Piccadilly and explained to her the cause of his wife's death.

He returned to Shandy Hall on the 21st and the next day visited the Caulfields.

Three days later he went away and on the 26th of June came back with the new mistress of Shandy Hall, the former Miss Skinner.

The communities of Coachford and Dripsey needless to say were stunned by this development and rumour and counter-rumour were transformed into something far more concrete. The body of Mary Laura Cross was not yet ready to be left in peace, far from it.

The Policeman

Around the beginning of July, a member of the community contacted the office of the RIC District Inspector Henry Tyacke in Ballincollig (a village six miles west of Cork City) to tell of the suspicion of recent events in relation to Shandy Hall.

The Irish police force, as evidenced by its involvement in the Castletownroche murders and brutally efficient dealings with Fenian uprisings, was considered so equal to tasks put before it that it was held out as the model for policing in all other parts of the British Empire. It was supervised by a corps of men who were specially recruited and trained to be its officers. The competitive examinations for the officer class covered a broad range of subjects, including a number of disciplines of law, and was sufficiently rigorous for nominees to hire special tutors to prepare for the exams. Men could progress through the non-commissioned ranks to become Sub-Inspector, which after 1882 changed to District Inspector.

While the officer positions were mainly held by Protestants, the rank and file were representative of the general population and later Catholics would rise through the ranks.

The discipline was considered tough and the wages not great; the officer salaries were supplemented by allowances for lodging, servants, special duty and travel. Unlike other police forces there was a military ethos with the use of carbines, barracks and military drill which distinguished it from the Dublin Metropolitan Force and forces in Britain.

The cadets were well-educated men in their early twenties. A significant number were university graduates, former government clerks and ex-military officers. They came from the lower social end of the gentry: professionals, magistrates and clergymen. Successful cadets were trained at the depot of the Phoenix Park in Dublin with a strong emphasis on the bureaucratic end of the business, including accountancy and report writing. The targets were set on the high side, the aim being that they should become officers as accomplished as the best in the world. The force performed a range of civil and local government duties as well as the normal policing, integrating the constables with the local communities. Strict measures were taken, however, to maintain an arms-length relationship between police and the public. A recruit was not allowed to serve in his home county or that of his wife or relations. In the early days strong links were established with the local gentry and the magistracy but, as the century progressed, such ties were also given distance.

When Sir Edward Jenkinson succeeded Sir Henry Brackenbury as head of the Irish police force in 1882, there were six police divisions outside the separate Dublin organisation, with each under the charge of a Special Resident Magistrate, later redesignated Divisional Magistrates and seven years later given the title of Divisional Commissioner.

But, like any police force the world over, it would ultimately depend on the ability of the individual investigator to get the job done. DI Henry Tyacke was definitely of that class.

He was born in 1859 in the village of Constantine in Cornwall, the seventh of twelve children of John Tyacke, born in Constantine 1819, and Eliza, born in London in 1825. His father was a gentleman farmer with 300 acres, employing nine men and boys and his uncle was Henry Philip Tyacke who commanded the 106th regiment, retiring as Honorary Major General.

The baptismal records of the village outline the remarkable progress and expansion, it has to be said, of the Tyacke family: 1) Eliza Sophia, 24th June 1846; 2) Mary Georgina, 25th January 1848; 3) John Wingrove, 7th June 1849; 4) Ellen Rosalind, 29th August 1853; 5) Patience Emily, 24th April 1855; 6) Katherine Laura, 26th April 1857; 7) Henry Donate, 3rd February 1859; 8) Edward De Garoche, 13th January 1861; 9) Arthur Romanus, 25th July 1862; 10) Linda Charlotte, 19th June 1864; 11) Percy Philips, 12th April 1866; 12) Francis Herbert, 10th November 1867.

Constantine, a village standing on a branch of the Helford river, five miles south-west of Falmouth, at the time had agriculture, mining for copper and iron, and quarrying for granite as its main economic activities.

The man from Cornwall, either because of or in spite of his background, embarked on a career entirely different from his community. Most of his acquaintances would have ended up in the dark shafts of a mine; at the age of 21 he chose another path that would of necessity also lead down into darkness, this time not in search of metal but the deeper recesses of the human mind. Obviously he must have been equal to the task as at the relatively young age of 29 he had attained the status of District Inspector.

Thus when he got wind of the seemingly suspicious events at Shandy Hall, as punctilious as his methods had and would prove to be, he opened a file and gave it a number and a note. The reference number he wrote down was 11492; the note: *Cross, Mrs, suspicious death of, proposed steps.*

Those steps must be recreated from subsequent events, for ultimately, for one reason or another, the file so faithfully kept by the inspector would go missing. But the outline and reference numbers of the file still survive, to confound the best efforts of those who chose to remove and destroy its contents.

DI Tyacke would have taken a deep breath before proceeding along the line of any planned investigation. The purpose in the first instance would be to persuade the coroner that there was reasonable suspicion to hold an inquest. Unless he could establish that suspicion he would be going nowhere with the case which, after all, at this point was nothing more than a result of rumour. A rumour that was directed against a member of the local gentry of a lineage going back generations in the locality and, what's more, regarding a retired Surgeon Major of the British Army with an apparently superb service record.

The bare facts alone were not very promising. On the other hand, his informant was very familiar with the facts and a close friend of the deceased woman. It was said that the object of the rumour, Dr Cross, was absent from the house on a number of occasions after the departure of his young governess, one an extended period after which his wife became ill, died a number of weeks later and was buried quickly on the 4th of June without much ceremony. Dr Cross and the former governess returned to Shandy Hall on the 26th of June as man and wife.

A very strange course of action. Why, if there was anything sinister afoot, would Cross draw attention to himself in such an obvious way? There could be any number of reasons why people would take a bad view of Dr Cross's timing. But, as the detective well knew, human behaviour did not always fit the perception of what it should be. Since there had been no violence involved, the only criminal method by which the death could have been commissioned was by poison, suggested strongly by the fact that Dr Cross was his wife's medical attendant during her illness, with the exception of a visit by a retired doctor and relative, Dr Godfrey. The proper and ethical thing to do was to have the local dispensary doctor to attend to his wife. There was no reason not to follow this normal procedure. Dr Cross had been retired for at least 12 years. DI Tyacke might have let this pass, but barely so in normal circumstances. These, it appeared, were anything but commonplace.

The fact that prompted him to action most at this preliminary stage was one he had confirmed by a visit to the dispensary medical officer Dr Timothy Crowley. Cross had signed the death certificate himself, giving the cause as typhoid fever and delivered it to Dr Crowley for registration. There had been no epidemic of the disease in the locality; in fact the dispensary officer could hardly remember when last there had been an outbreak.

He also conducted a lengthy interview with Mrs Caulfield, whose evidence would be crucial to the coroner's enquiry, since she had first received news of Dr Cross's marriage to the young governess – an interview during which a letter from Miss Skinner's mother in relation to the marriage was produced. It is not difficult to deduce that it was most likely Theresa Caulfield, one of Mrs Cross's best friends, who contacted DI Tyacke in the first instance and set the series of events in motion.

Tyacke instructed Acting Sgt Gorman to interview and take depositions from Dr Godfrey and a servant in Shandy Hall, Mary Buckley. Having read through those depositions, Tyacke decided there were enough questions left unanswered to proceed. A path he would have to take with both caution and speed.

He gave notice of his intention of proceeding by furnishing the coroner with preliminary reasons for an inquiry by Dr Charles Yelverton Pearson, the appointed Crown medical analyst and a professor in Queen's College Cork (the present-day University College Cork). He also, because there was no precedent in his career, went to visit the professor to take advice on the further investigation, if deemed necessary, of such a crime.

The doctor, naturally, reminded the inspector that while he was acting as a medical expert on behalf of the Crown, he was not an advocate, but could make general remarks that might provide some help on the matter of crime by poisoning and its particular difficulties. He warned that it would not be an easy crime to solve because of the secretiveness under which the perpetrator could operate within a household, especially with no direct witness to link him or her to the administration of the poison. And while each poison has its own characteristic symptoms, they could vary radically depending on the method in which they were given and the form they took – in, for example, a solution and dissolved as opposed to a solid state.

For a case to be made, and even more importantly succeed, it would be necessary to discover traces of the poison in the body of the deceased and prove that these were capable of destroying life. However, in the case of arsenic, the most popular choice of poisoners, it had traditionally been discovered by analysts in the organs of those who had died from its effects even after long periods of burial. The poison is absorbed into the bloodstream and when not found in the stomach can be detected in soft organs, like the liver. However, if the doses are small and the person has survived the effects for a certain period, it can be expelled from the body through purging, vomiting and through the urine and even the skin in perspiration. In such a case, which on the basic facts might fit this one, it would not be likely that the poison would be detected in the soft organs.

In these circumstances, given that the bar for conviction had been raised much higher since mid-century when analysis was less sophisticated, it would be most unlikely that the prosecution would succeed. If chronic or slow poisoning was properly orchestrated, it was entirely possible that the perpetrator could get away with murder. The deceased might have survived long enough for the whole of the poison to be expelled from the body. Dr Pearson recalled a case history in which a man had died eight days after a very small dose of arsenic. His body had been exhumed after two years, and no trace of arsenic could be detected. Apparently he had vomited all through the period before he expired. It was highly difficult to establish with accuracy the period required to eliminate the poison from the human system. But this, the doctor would have added, was the worst-case scenario. But best to know that before proceeding.

Now, while this was all the specific area or responsibility of the medical man, it was also vital to corroborate any of his findings by evidence of the symptoms that occurred during the life of the victim before death intervened. The gathering of this evidence was the remit of the District Inspector. In the words of pioneer toxicologist Alfred Swaine Taylor, "symptoms might be suspended for a while, or slightly modified in their progress, but sooner or later, the poison would affect the healthy, and the diseased, the old and the young with a uniformity in its effects not to be easily mistaken."

Pearson went on to explain: what makes white arsenic or arsenious acid such an ideal weapon is that it is cheap to purchase, easily dissolved in liquid and then concealed in food, and has no taste discernible to those who consume it. And it is deadly in small doses: between one and a half and two grains can constitute a fatal dose. [Grain: the smallest British weight, average weight of a seed of corn. A teaspoon can hold 150 grains.]

In cases of acute poisoning, with larger doses taken, death can occur within a short period of time, hours as opposed to days; with chronic poisoning, in which small doses are given over a longer period of time, death is slower. The usual progress of symptoms is that the individual first experiences faintness, depression, nausea and sickness, with an intense burning pain in the stomach. This pain becomes more severe and is followed by vomiting. There follows diarrhoea and more vomiting, which is made worse by any substance taken into the stomach. Discharges in some instances are of a yellowish colour. There is sometimes, but not always, an intense thirst and cramps in the calves of the legs. Close to death, sometimes coma, convulsions and spasms are experienced.

With chronic poisoning by a slow method of administration, if the person recovers from the first effects, there is also a suffusion of the eyes, intolerance to bright light and irritation of the skin. This method often masks some of the usual characteristics and could be confused with certain diseases such as gastroenteritis. While they would be in a much better state of knowledge after a post mortem, Dr Pearson went on, there were matters of investigation into events in a household where poisoning was suspected to have taken place, which DI Tyacke might well take note of.

He would need to enquire into the symptoms, the time and nature of their occurrence, the order of their occurrence and most importantly if they occurred after food, drink or medicine. He should establish whether there was any remission or intermission in their progress, and if they became more aggravated before death. It was important to establish whether the victim was healthy or suffering from any other ailments in advance of the last illness. He would need to question everyone who had any hand, act or part in providing relief and refreshment to the victim and prepared food or drink or dispensed medicine during the symptoms and especially at the end. It would be necessary to find the time of death as precisely as possible and question anyone who was present before, during or immediately after the death.

If permission was granted for a full enquiry, he should make a thorough search of the rooms in which medicine, food and drink were stored. And he would need to pay close attention to the room in which the victim expired and take possession of any vessels used to dispense anything to the victim and any that had been used for purging and vomiting. He should interview anyone who prepared the body for burial or even saw it.

The rest of the investigation, Dr Pearson judged, should follow usual procedures. Their next communication would await the coroner's decision. DI Tyacke was much relieved and comforted by the result of the meeting. He had a much clearer picture of the task ahead and how to tackle it if necessary.

He was also cognisant of the fact that Dr Cross would have had the opportunity to dispose of or destroy vital evidence. But he also knew that might pose a risk for Cross down the road and it was a risk that DI Tyacke guessed he would not take.

If the coroner was amenable, permission for the exhumation of the body of Mary Laura Cross would have to be obtained to coincide with the hearing.

Another step he would have to take as a matter of his own investigation as opposed to the coroner's enquiry, was confirmation of Dr Cross's marriage. He had been informed that this took place in St James's Church in Piccadilly on the 17th of June, so he set about obtaining a copy of the marriage record through contact with

London police authorities. He also set about assembling a list of members of the Cross household, including servants and workers, and then neighbours and friends. If Dr Pearson found grounds for a full investigation, Tyacke would have to move very quickly.

Apart from the inquest, there was another obstacle to be reckoned with: a Magisterial Inquiry with a Grand Jury, which would decide on evidence presented whether this case would proceed to trial. This enquiry would follow almost immediately and therefore the inspector would have to provide very good and solid grounds for a full and complete investigation.

The Grand Jury Inquiry was instituted as far back as 1166, before the introduction of the trial jury. It was later used as a safeguard against unjustified prosecutions and to determine if there was enough evidence for a trial. In Ireland in the 19th century the grand jury operated as a local government authority at county level as well as a judicial functionary for serious criminal cases.

While everything on the unfolding landscape of his preparations would hinge on the results of the post mortem, DI Tyacke put everything within his limited powers in place.

On the 17th of July he had a letter delivered to the coroner's office outlining his case for an inquest and by return received confirmation that it would take place in Coachford four days later. Permission was granted for the exhumation of the body of Mrs Cross in the presence of a member of his investigating team, Dr Pearson and the dispensary doctor Timothy Crowley. The post mortem was to take place in Coachford Courthouse on the same morning as the inquest, which would be conducted next door in the local hotel.

DI Tyacke opened another file, serial number 17688 with the title, *Cross, Mrs, exhumation, body of.*

The inspector had no idea at this point where this case would go. All would depend on the results of Dr Pearson's post mortem, which he had indicated would take the best part of a week of chemical tests after the preliminary examination. This essentially meant that the inquest would be opened but then adjourned until the results of the chemical analysis were delivered.

It could not have escaped the inspector's thoughts that this was a most unusual case, nothing like he had ever encountered in his career or might encounter in the future, with very complex features of which he had previously no experience, little of which his training had prepared him for. It resembled something more from a book than police practice. And one in which he would be relying on the work of a forensic scientist not only to kick-start the normal collection of evidence but also provide the very core of a case.

He would have been made aware from his conversation with the Crown analyst of the particular difficulties of proving a crime which is usually hidden from view. What set such cases apart from other crimes of violence was the potential difficulty in discovering that a crime had occurred at all.

It might have intimidated a man of less solid character, given the arena it would be played out in, but Henry Tyacke was built of similar human durability, as time would prove, as his colleague in this unfolding drama, Charles Pearson, whose training and background was as far removed from policing as could be imagined.

The coalition of detective/forensic skills would in that same year get a fictional affirmation in the work of one of the greatest crime writers of all time and in factual terms in generations to come. In 1887 Sherlock Holmes made his first appearance in *A Study in Scarlet*. It is generally now forgotten that his creator, Sir Arthur Conan Doyle, was a physician.

But neither Tyacke nor Pearson had any real idea of the benefits of that coalition and were relying on reason, scientific fact and instinct in the situation that was presented to them. And time, they both realised, was of the essence.

Chapter 4

The First Inquest and the Post Mortem

The inquest commenced on the morning of Thursday, 21st July 1887. The *Cork Examiner* was in attendance.

The *Cork Examiner* (now the *Irish Examiner*) was a broadsheet primarily circulated in the Munster region surrounding its base in Cork city, though available throughout the country. It was founded by John Francis Maguire in 1841 in support of the Catholic Emancipation and tenants' rights campaigns of the great Daniel O'Connell. Maguire, like O'Connell, was a barrister and also an MP who supported an independent parliament for Ireland. Therefore the *Cork Examiner* from its birth was an advocate of constitutional nationalism, priding itself on its independent spirit. In 1842, a 15-year-old boy from Kerry, Thomas Crosbie, began to work for the paper. He later became its editor and, on Maguire's death in 1872, became owner as well. It has remained in his family ever since.

On that day in July 1887, its reporters were poised to do justice to this rare local sensation, when at half past nine MJ Horgan, solicitor and coroner, opened the inquest at Coachford into the circumstances under which Mrs Mary Laura Cross, wife of Philip HE Cross of Shandy Hall, Dripsey, came to her death. The coroner was a well-known nationalist who had been the election agent for Charles Stewart Parnell, had been who was best man at his wedding.

Cork Examiner
22nd July 1887

Considerable anxiety and uneasiness prevails among the people of the [Coachford] district in regard to the attendant and subsequent circumstances, which in their opinion surrounded the lady's death with a suspicion that it was accelerated by some sort of foul play. Poisoning was suggested as the cause of death and, for the purpose of ascertaining if the suggestion was justified, the lady was exhumed by Dr Crowley and Professor Pearson of Cork. The latter person has taken charge of the internal organs for the purpose of analysis, the result of which will be laid before the coroner's jury, this day week.

Mr Cross drove into the village with his sister and two servants, one of whom was examined.

The inquiry was held at Burke's Hotel. The jury was fairly mixed, as will be seen by the names.

Mr Thomas Rice, S.C.P. attended on behalf of the Crown and DI Tyacke represented the constabulary. Mr Cross was not represented by a solicitor. Before the jury were sworn, Mr Gillman, on behalf of the other magistrates and himself, desired that they put it to the coroner that they ought to be exempt from acting as jurors. He thought it would be somewhat indecent, in case they found an incriminatory verdict, that they should afterwards have to act magisterially on the case.

The coroner said that he could not exempt any gentleman who had been summoned and his position or avocation made no difference in the matter. The law said a man should be tried by his peers, and the coroner saw no more suitable jurors than the gentleman on whose behalf Mr Gillman objected. He then proceeded to swear the jury.

Mr Burke objected on the ground that he was a postmaster and that his authorities would reprimand him.

The coroner replied: "I'll take you as a juror." Mr Burke was then sworn. The following jury was then empanelled: Hebert W Gillman, Albert Beamish, Robert Bowen Colthurst, John G Woodley, Michael Healy, Edmund M Murphy, Patrick Keefe, Paul M Sweeney, David Gregg, John Dwyer, John Murphy, Thomas Sullivan, Edward D Murphy, John Ryan, John Horgan, Timothy Whelan, Jeremiah Buckley, John Dinan, Thomas Carroll, George Colthurst, John Manning Snr, Richard Burke and Michael Sullivan.

The coroner said that they were about to enter a very solemn and grave inquiry in reference to the death of Mrs Cross and perhaps he could do no better than to read the report he had received from the police officer which would explain why they were here:

District Inspector's Office, Ballincollig,
17 July 1887.

Sir – I beg to report for your information the following circumstances in connection with the death of Mrs Cross, wife of Dr PHE Cross, a retired army surgeon of Shandy Hall, near Dripsey. Some time about the middle of last May, Mrs Cross was taken ill and confined to her bed. Her husband treated her himself and called no other doctor, except Dr Godfrey an uncle of his who lives quite close to Shandy Hall. He only called in Dr Godfrey ten days before his wife's death, but Dr Godfrey does not remember the date.

He told Dr Godfrey that his wife was suffering from vomiting and diarrhoea. He went into the sick room and remained with him all the time he was there. Dr Godfrey thought Mrs Cross was suffering from a bilious attack and could see no symptoms whatsoever of fever from this time until her death. He was never called in again, nor was any other doctor.

On one occasion she complained to a lady of intense thirst and said they would give her nothing to drink. Several people who called to see her during her illness were not allowed to go to her room. One of the servants in the house, who was attending on her, states that she was nearly constantly vomiting. He [Dr Cross] gave several different accounts of the illness from which his wife was suffering. To some he said that she had heart disease, to others he said she had angina pectoris.

She died in the early morning of June 2nd and he buried her about 6 a.m. on the morning of June 4th. The day after the funeral he went away. A short time afterwards a lady got a letter saying that Dr Cross had married a Miss Skinner at St James's Church in Piccadilly on June 17th. On the 22nd of June he called at this lady's house and when she taunted him with marrying so soon after his wife's death, he positively denied he was married until she produced the letter. A few days after that, he brought his wife to Shandy Hall.

This Miss Skinner, the girl he had married, had been a governess at his house and went to it in December last and left again about three months afterwards. Mrs Cross was very jealous of her and suspected that there was an intrigue between her and Dr Cross. After she left the place, she and he used to correspond under assumed names.

The day after his wife's death, Dr. Cross went to the District Medical Officer and Registrar Dr Crowley, and registered it as having been caused by typhoid fever.

All the above facts seem to me to be suspicious and I beg to request that you will give the matter your serious consideration and hold an inquest and have a precept for exhumation of the body. There is a very strong feeling in the neighbourhood on the matter and people are very anxious that an inquest should be held.

I remain, sire, your obedient servant
HD Tyacke, DI, RIC

Having received that very full report, the coroner had no alternative but to issue a precept for the exhumation of the body, and summon a jury to hold an inquiry. From the circumstances stated in that report it seemed to him that there was some suspicion about Dr Cross not having treated his wife fairly, and said it was for the jury to inquire what was the cause of the lady's death. They would receive every assistance.

Mr Rice was present on behalf of the Crown and said they would have medical evidence which would throw some light on the cause of death; but they should wait for some days to ascertain the results of Dr Pearson's analysis of the viscera. Mr Rice said that he had little to add to the coroner's statement. He said the jury could readily understand that there were some circumstances of suspicion, to say the least of it – he trusted they would turn out to be only suspicions – but they were deemed sufficient to justify and call for this inquiry and the exhumation of the body. They would not go deeply into the circumstances that day, as the most important part would be the result of the medical examination and analysis.

Acting Sergeant John Gorman was then called. He deposed that he knew the late Mrs Cross and he saw her body this morning, after having been exhumed from the grave at Coachford. He handed a certificate of her death, which had been registered with Dr Crowley and in which the cause of death was stated to have been typhoid fever.

Mrs Theresa Caulfield, wife of Captain Caulfield of Classas deposed: "I knew the late Mrs Cross of Shandy Hall. I went to see her on the 25th of May last. She was then ill; I knew that she had been ill for some time previously. I saw her in bed in the afternoon."

Mr Rice asked: "What did she tell you?"

"Am I bound to answer that?"

"You are."

Mrs Caulfield broke down and began to weep. "She said she was suffering from vomiting, thirst and diarrhoea."

"Did she say she was then thirsty?"

"Yes, but I saw a cup of milk beside her."

"Did she complain of any inattention on the part of anyone?"

"No."

"How long did you stay with her?"

"About three quarters of an hour. There was no one present during that time. That was on Wednesday and I called again on the following Monday. I met the servant at the door and I asked her if Dr Cross was at home, and she replied that he was. I saw Dr Cross in the drawing room. I asked him how Mrs Cross was and he only said 'pretty well'. He asked me if I had seen her and I said no. I then left the house. The interview lasted only five minutes. Mrs Cross died soon after that visit."

"Did you know Miss Skinner who was governess in your family?"

"Yes. She left my employment at the end of last year, having received a month's notice."

"Can you tell where she went from your house?"

"To Shandy Hall, straight. She told me she would not remain after Christmas, and I got rid of her in November or December. [She says elsewhere that Effie left on 29th October.] I think she remained for three months at Shandy Hall. From that she went to a family in the County Carlow, whose name I forget. I don't know how long she remained there, for I lost sight of her until after Mrs Cross's death."

"Soon after the death of Mrs Cross, did you get a letter purporting to come from Mrs Skinner, the mother of Miss Skinner, from Germany?"

"Am I bound to answer that?"

"You are."

"I did get that letter on the 22nd of June."

"What was in the letter?"

"She said in that letter that her daughter had married Dr Cross, in St James's Church Piccadilly. In the afternoon of the day which I received the letter, I had a visit from Dr. Cross. I asked him how Mrs Cross was and he asked me what I meant. I said: 'I simply meant what I say: how is Mrs Cross – Miss Skinner that was,' and then he laughed and said, 'I like a good joke when I hear it' and laughed it off."

"He seemed to be treating the report as a joke?"

"Just so. He asked me who published the report and I said I had a letter informing me that morning, but I did not say from whom. I left the room, he remained behind and I went out driving."

"As a matter of fact, I believe he brought home to Shandy Hall, a few days afterwards, that young lady as his wife?"

"Yes, I am aware that he did."

The witness while under examination was labouring under deep emotion.

Mr Rice said that was all the evidence they needed to take that day, in addition to this lady's was the evidence of the doctors, so there was no possibility of the inquiry closing that day.

Dr Cross said that he wished to have his sister examined, as she could tell all that occurred at the house.

The coroner said he would give Dr Cross every facility he required in the course of the inquiry, and he could examine every person he pleased. This was simply opening the inquiry and they were proceeding in the most convenient way.

Mary Buckley, servant in the employment of Dr Cross as kitchen maid, was then examined. She was in the house during the illness and death of the late Mrs Cross who was ill about three weeks.

Mr Rice: "Who attended her?"

Mary Buckley: "Her sister-in-law [Henrietta Cross] and her husband the doctor. To my knowledge, Dr Godfrey called once. I did not see Mrs Cross very often during her illness, but when I did see her she was complaining of the heart. I did not see any vomiting. She sent down for me four times. The morning before her death she appeared as if she was getting better. I did not hear her complaining of vomiting. Nor did I say to anyone that I did."

"Did you ever tell the sergeant that you pitied her for the way she was vomiting?"

"I might have told him, because Mary Barron, the parlour maid, told me she was vomiting the night before she died."

Mr Cross, who was present, did not ask the witnesses any questions. The coroner and Mr Rice advised him that he should have a solicitor to represent him at the remainder of the inquiry. It would be an advantage to both himself and the Crown.

At this stage of the evidence the doctors were called for, but it was found that they had not concluded their examination and the inquiry was then adjourned until a week hence, the 29th of July.

* * *

The *Cork Examiner* reported that as soon as the inquest was adjourned, Dr Cross drove straight back to Shandy Hall where he immediately went to work, superintending the carting of hay to his haggarth.

The Forensic Scientist

Two doors away in Coachford Courthouse, simultaneously with the inquest, the post-mortem examination was being carried out by Dr Pearson on the body which had been exhumed earlier by two grave-diggers under the supervision of DI Tyacke and members of his force. The examination would naturally take much longer than the inquest.

Dr Charles Yelverton Pearson, despite his youth was a professor and already had an accomplished career as a physician. He was born at Kilworth, County Cork, in 1857, the fourth son of William W Pearson, medical officer of Kilworth. His early years were spent in Carrigaline where his father was transferred. He attended, with his brothers, the Model Schools in Cork.

In 1874 he entered the Arts faculty of Queen's College and the following year took the medical course. After an unusually accomplished academic career, during which each year he won a scholarship and class prizes, he graduated MD MCh. in October 1878. In this final examination, as in others preceding it, he obtained First Class Honours and won a gold medal.

He was appointed Senior Demonstrator of Anatomy in the college. For six years he worked under the distinguished Professor JJ Charles until in 1884 he was appointed Professor of Materia Medica and Lecturer in Medical Jurisprudence (expertise in medical matters in the context of the law and giving evidence as an expert witness), being awarded a gold medal. In 1886 he took a Fellowship of The Royal College of Surgeons in England.

He was also on the surgical staff of a number of Cork hospitals and was medico-legal adviser to the Crown, the reason that brought him to Coachford.

At the graveside the doctor had noted that the grave where Mary Laura Cross had been so hurriedly interred was situated on slightly elevated ground and dug to the usual depth. The soil consisted of ordinary clay of a porous nature. It was quite dry as it was an unusually dry and hot summer. As the coffin was intact the doctor did not take away soil for analysis. The coffin had not been opened. The coffin was made of oak and on the front was a plate with the name and date of death of the deceased.

Present at the opening of the coffin in Coachford Courthouse were Dr Pearson, Dr Crowley, Sgt Gorman and a woman who Dr Pearson did not recognise.

It was nearly seven weeks since the coffin had been interred and in that period of time, with some influence exerted by the depth of burial, the durability of the coffin and the nature of the soil, the body would have passed through post-mortem changes that, whatever the variations in progression, no body could escape.

Putrefaction, as it is called, is the post-mortem destruction of the tissues of the body. The process is caused by a combination of bacteria and breakdown of the cells which produce a lot of gas. The first sign, which occurs within a matter of days, is greenish discolouration of the skin on the abdominal wall which gradually spreads to the shoulders and limbs. The skin colour is transformed from a reddish green to a purple black and the skin on the body begins to slip off. Gas formation in the intestines pushes a bloodstained fluid from the nose, mouth and other orifices. The gas also causes the body to swell. The dusky greenish, purple to black face now appears bloated, with eyelids swollen and tightly closed, lips swollen and pouting and cheeks puffed out, distended tongue protruding from the mouth. The neck, trunk and limbs are massively swollen, giving a false impression of gross obesity. Finally, the gases, which are under pressure, find an escape and the whole mass of decomposing soft tissue collapses. When the putrefactive juices drain away and soft tissues shrink, the speed of decay is slowed down.

Internally putrefaction begins with the stomach and intestine, while liver, kidney and the spleen, usually take longer. While Dr Pearson would have been prepared for any of the stages of decomposition, it was the internal state of the organs that would most concern him, given the suspicions about the cause of Mrs Cross's death.

While the layman might shrink at the prospect, or indeed become weak-kneed at the thought, Dr Charles Yelverton Pearson was in the role of a scientist and his prime concern was to accurately, objectively and fairly establish the cause of death. To say nothing of the fact that he was acting for the Crown.

When the coffin was opened the body outwardly showed the signs of now-settled putrefaction; the awful stage of the explosion of the gases and gross swelling seemed to have occurred or passed in a mild form. It was summer and the temperature and drainage of the soil should have accelerated decomposition. It was an extremely hot summer; in five days' time, the highest temperature ever recorded in Ireland would be recorded at Kilkenny Castle: 91.94 degrees Fahrenheit.

The body was identified as that of Mary Laura Cross. It was "bound in a white garment" according to Pearson, inside which was placed a flannel swathe encircling the abdomen; a white handkerchief was passed around the lower jaw and the top of the head. On the legs there was a pair of blue stockings.

The doctor noted that the body was fairly nourished; the features were drawn; a brownish post-mortem slime was issuing from the nose and mouth. The face and hands were covered in a white mould. Extensive greenish discolouration was present on the stomach, chest, back and left side of the neck. The back of the trunk and limbs showed evidence of the usual ecchymoses or post-mortem bruise-like discolouring. There was slippage of the skin, also usual after death, on the back and on some patches of the limbs.

Having observed these facts, Pearson began the internal examination, assisted by Dr Crowley. Mary Laura Cross had been in the grave for almost seven weeks. The doctor expected and should have been presented with a body in an advanced state of decomposition. But that did not prove to be the case. The irony would not be lost on him. If there was some consolation in the state of preservation of the body whatever the circumstance, he would have been particularly glad of it as a scientist, which was his role.

There was no evidence of violence to the throat or larynx. The lungs were healthy with the usual evidence of blood pooling. The left pleural cavity contained a post-mortem effusion of blood-stained serum, while the right half a smaller quantity. The heart and pericardium were found to be perfectly natural, the right cavities being moderately full of blood, the left being nearly empty.

Examination of the abdominal cavity showed the peritoneum, the membrane that surrounds the cavity, to be quite healthy. The intestines were moderately distended with gas.

Despite the length of the burial, the pathologist was surprised to find that the internal organs, particularly the intestines, were remarkably well preserved. He wrote in his notes: "All the organs were in an excellent state of preservation, the stomach and intestines presenting as fresh an appearance as if the deceased had died but 24 hours previously. The only evidences of putrefaction present in the abdomen were found on the liver, which displayed early putrefactive colour changes and had a considerable portion of its surface covered with small white spots, due to post-mortem deposit of phosphate of calcium; the gall bladder contained a small amount of bile; the spleen and kidneys were healthy; the bladder was empty; the uterus and ovaries presented a healthy appearance."

He and Dr Crowley found nothing peculiar in the mouth. The lower end of the oesophagus contained a number of white particles, the largest being the size of a small pin's head; towards its termination in the stomach, the mucous membrane presented a number of oval abrasions. The membrane was congested throughout.

The stomach contained a small amount of slimy mucous; also a number of hard white particles, some of which were free, others that were partially embedded in the mucous membrane, which itself seemed perfectly healthy. The small intestines were coated in the interior with mucous of a bright yellow colour; a few white particles, similar in appearance, were present in the upper end of the duodenum (the first section of the small intestine).

The large intestines were healthy and there were no faeces present in any portion of the bowel. The condition of the body clearly indicated to Pearson that Mrs Cross had not died of typhoid fever as certified by her husband; the condition of the heart and blood vessels also proved to him the absence of any organic disease that would account for death. The appearance of the intestines, he deduced, must have been a result of the action of an irritant and purging of a bilious character must have preceded death. From the condition of the oesophagus, and the empty state of the stomach he concluded that vomiting of a painful character had existed during life.

The remarkable state of preservation of most of the internal organs of the stomach gave him pause for thought. It was, as he noted, as if the body had been buried just the day before. Given the conditions of the burial, the nature of the topsoil, the weather and the length of the interment, this should certainly not have been the case. He suspected that some external agent was responsible for this exceptional post-mortem circumstance.

From his experience this was most likely to be an irritant poison. He began the removal of the organs and their placement into clean, prepared and specifically uncontaminated vessels. These would be transported to the laboratory in Queen's College where he would spend the next seven days subjecting them to microscopic examination and chemical tests to either confirm or deny his theory about the cause of death.

He made one omission despite its recommendation by Dr Crowley: the removal of the brain for examination. He did this on the basis that Dr Cross, whether innocent or guilty, would have mentioned on the death certificate if there had been a history of problems in that area. There was no evidence of brain affection in the post mortem and even if it did exist the suspected presence of an irritant poison would still remain unexplained.

However, he would have to return to that examination as a result of a discovery during the chemical analysis. Dr Pearson returned to Cork with the organs that he had removed from the body. Apart from the long hours and days he faced in the laboratory and compiling reports, he would have been only too aware of the heavy responsibility that lay on his young shoulders but also the chequered history of the role of toxicology in previous high-profile cases.

Pearson was under a lot of pressure and began the process of examination and testing immediately he returned to the laboratory.

The stomach and attached portion of the small intestine which, along with the lower end of the oesophagus, were contained in a sealed and stoppered glass vessel, were first examined. The stomach contained one drachm of mucus, but no food.

Of the white particles he had already observed on the mucous membrane, some were distinctly hard, others not so. The majority of the particles were smaller than an ordinary pin's head. A few of these were removed, dried over a water bath, and then heated in a subliming cell; they yielded a small crystalline sublimate of arsenious acid. The doctor, and indeed professor, had the first small evidence of the irritant poison: arsenic.

A few other particles were tested and yielded a faint ring of metallic arsenic. Some of the particles were dissolved in distilled water and hydrochloric acid, treated by Reinsch's Process and yielded a deposit of metallic arsenic, which on being sublimed gave crystals of arsenious acid.

The interior of the stomach and duodenum were scraped with glass; these scrapings were dried with a gentle heat over a water bath. Particles similar to those in the stomach were present in the lower end of the gullet and on analysis were found to contain arsenic. Portions of the coats of the stomach and duodenum were separately treated by Reinsch's Process and found to contain arsenic. These were carefully dried and set aside for further analysis.

The liver, spleen and right kidney were contained in a large sealed glass vessel; the bloody fluid contained in this vessel, which had seeped out of the organs, was tested by Reinsch's method and found to contain arsenic in considerable quantity. Portions of the liver, kidney and spleen, were each separately tested by the same method and found to contain arsenic. The largest amount was in the liver, a smaller amount in the kidney and only a trace in the spleen.

The doctor then subjected the same organs to another test called the Stas Process. They gave a small crystalline residue that yielded the colour reaction of strychnine in the most distinct manner and further microscopic crystals of strychnine.

The next set of tests were to establish the quantity of arsenic distributed in the organs of the body. The stomach and the duodenum yielded 1.74 grains. The liver yielded 1.28 grains, the total in the organs examined amounting to 3.02 grains. As this was well beyond a fatal dose, Dr Pearson decided to confine his tests in other parts to a search for strychnine.

To give plenty of notice, Pearson contacted DI Tyacke and informed him of his findings to date so that the detective could plan his actions in advance of the resumption of the inquest, which would of necessity be curtailed when the cause of death was poisoning. He provided Tyacke with more than the justification he needed to make an arrest and provide the resumed inquest with the medical evidence to kick-start a full-blown murder investigation.

The Arrest

Armed with the report of the medical findings, Tyacke wasted no time as the *Cork Examiner* reported in a restrained and undramatic manner:

Cork Examiner,
Friday, 29th July 1887

About four o'clock last evening, Dr Philip Cross of Shandy Hall, Dripsey, was placed under arrest by the police and lodged in the Bridewell. It will be remembered that Coroner Horgan opened an inquest yesterday week into the circumstances of the death of Mrs Cross who died on the 2nd of June last, and whose death, it was suspected, was caused by poisoning. The body was exhumed on the 21st instant and was examined by two doctors.

The analysis of the viscera was entrusted to Professor Pearson, and at the inquest tomorrow the result of his examination will be disclosed. That something of a serious nature has been discovered in connection with the cause of the lady's death is inferred from the arrest of Dr Cross.

He, with his sister, was in town upon their ordinary business when the police, acting on instructions from their authorities, took him into custody. He was brought before Mr Gardiner at the Police Court at five o'clock. Captain Plunkett was also present. Mr Tyacke, DI Ballincollig, made an information upon which Dr Cross will be remanded until tomorrow.

Miss Cross took leave of her brother in the Bridewell, from which afterwards he was taken to the County Gaol.

*   *   *

On his arrest of Dr Cross, the inspector would have been acutely aware that his caution would have to be carefully worded and that he was prohibited from any attempt to extract a statement in the nature of a confession. The Police Code of 1882 laid down in clear terms that it was wrong for an officer to question a person taken into custody or whom he was about to arrest. However, there had been a practice for many years before in Ireland and England that the officer was at liberty to question a suspect for the discovery of other evidence. This was for the procurement of such material evidence and anything of the conversation involved could not be used in a subsequent trial. Henry Tyacke used this practice to an effect whose precise value he did not know at the time. He asked Dr Cross if he had anything on his person, instructed that he be searched and took possession of a photograph, a purse containing a number of papers including a hotel receipt and a bunch of keys.

The photograph was of Dr Cross and his former governess, now his wife.

In it, he is seated, at a slight angle to the camera, facing right. She is standing by his side, her body very slightly turned towards him, her skirts pressing against his right knee, while her head is turned to the right.

The young and highly attractive young woman is wearing a little straw boater on her head, her left hand casually resting on the wrist of her right which is holding, inside the index finger, the handle of an umbrella which rests casually in front of his knee. Her dress is beautifully cut but quite plain and severe, with a high collar about her neck. She has a tiny, buckled waist, lovely eyes, fine features with a well-defined jawline and mouth. Her expression is composed, intelligent and alert. She seems tiny compared to his bulk and obvious height; the impression is that, standing, he would tower over her.

Her companion, with a cigarette dangling from under his heavily moustached mouth, presents the powerful posture of a former military gentleman. His right hand rests over his left which is holding what appears to be a walking stick. His dark well-cut jacket combines well with striped tweed trousers.

While the photograph did not flatter the obviously much older man, it could not have escaped any observer, including the detective, that here was evidence of a couple not only relaxed in each other's presence but also of a relationship in which there was, it would seem, an unusual bond. One which was based on not the fleeting experience of lust but more than likely love.

It is not that DI Tyacke would dwell over the aesthetic quality of the photograph, but it did tell him something in relation to motive, quite apart from the evidential value of the image in the matter of identification – in particular in relation to the hotel receipt on which there were no names linking the couple. The inspector would have also been aware that Effie Skinner, now the spouse of the suspect, was not allowed to give evidence for or against her husband in a criminal trial because of perceived bias. That rule of evidence, based on English common law, said that a man and woman when married become a single person in the eyes of the law

– that person being the husband. A woman had no legal existence. As he was precluded from questioning Dr Cross, he was equally so from his wife. He would have doubted that she had any knowledge of what happened to the former Mrs Cross, given her absence during the events at Shandy Hall at the crucial time. If she did in advance, there was nothing he could do about it, one way or another. He had matters of much more consequence on his mind.

After the suspect had been led away to the cell, DI Tyacke wired the police in Coachford to go directly to Cross's home and begin to preserve whatever was left of the crime scene. He then drove straight to Shandy Hall. A team under the charge of Constable McGovern was there when he arrived. As a matter of procedure, he informed Evelyn Forbes Cross of the exercise and held a brief conversation with her before instructing Acting Sgt Gorman to lock up the room in which Mary Laura Cross had died.

As it was late, the search of the premises was postponed until the following day. The District Inspector returned to Cork, leaving the acting sergeant and one other member of the team to stay in the house overnight. Early the next day, the 29th of July, carrying a green box, a hamper and a smaller box DI Tyacke and his team combed the house. A number of items were taken from a cupboard in the drawing room.

In a small dairy off the kitchen they discovered an array of bottles of medicines, some empty, some full. These were taken and placed in the green box and the other containers with some other items. DI Tyacke took away the green box and instructed Acting Sgt Gorman to lock the dairy, or dispensary as it would later be referred to. The inspector then had to attend the postponed inquest.

The sergeant subsequently delivered the other two containers to the District Inspector. Among the items was a quantity of strychnine, and a parcel labelled dog poison which also contained strychnine. There was a minim glass and a half-filled bottle of Fowler's Solution which was arsenic-based. Interestingly there was no sign of solid arsenic anywhere to be found.

The items were first examined by a chemist, Mr Short, and then sent on for analysis by Dr Pearson.

Subsequently and crucially, Dr Cross's solicitor Deyos came looking for the keys, one of which was for a locked diary, which the inspector opened and retained as evidence. Thus far, the inspector had not put a foot wrong. He would now wait for the conclusion of the second inquest hearing the following morning.

For the former governess and now mistress of Shandy Hall this must have been a shattering experience. Everything in her world and aspirations had been wiped out by a circumstance of which we may assume she had no knowledge. She had been a participant in the affair while Mary Laura Cross was alive, an involvement from which she could have expected some consequence, but not this. She must have been led to believe that her former employer was suffering from a terminal disease and would die, and she had. How else could she have married the widower? He had assured her that everything would be all right and she had no doubt unwittingly pushed him along that road. She loved and trusted him implicitly and looked forward to minding the children with whom she had created a close bond.

Now, instead of overseeing an estate with servants at her command, she had become a virtual prisoner with those same servants more in the role of gaol-keepers. And, even further from her ambitions, a virtual pariah in the neighbourhood. For Evelyn Forbes Cross, her new abode had become a form of hell on earth, from which in the near or distant future there seemed no possibility of escape. Her past had caught up with her in a manner that she must have thought of as intolerable cruelty. It was, however, only the beginning of her suffering. But ultimately little suffering by comparison with her predecessor.

But there was one other reason that added immeasurably to Evelyn's intense pain, which would not be revealed until much later.

Chapter 5

The Second Inquest

Cork Examiner
Saturday, 30th July 1887

The circumstances under which the late Mrs Cross of Shandy Hall, near Dripsey, came by her death on the 1st or 2nd of June last as disclosed by the evidence given at the Coroner's Inquest, which opened on the 21st inst., have produced the most profound and painful sensation, not only in the immediate locality in which the deceased lady resided, but in every place in which they have become known.

For many years past, with the exception of the Sheehan tragedy near Castletownroche, no more startling occurrence took place in the South of Ireland. The deceased lady was 49 years of age and was the mother of six children, the eldest of whom is but sixteen years of age. She was the first wife of Dr Philip HE Cross, ex-army surgeon, and resided with him at Shandy Hall, a nicely situated and commodious house, near the village of Dripsey. The inquest was resumed on the 29th of July at Coachford and the same jury sworn in as at the previous hearing.

The courthouse in which the inquiry was held was crowded by the public. Captain Plunkett drove out from Cork with Mr Thomas Rice SCS who represented the Attorney General in the investigation. There were also present: Mr Tyacke, DI Ballincollig; Capt Caulfield, Classas; Mr Warren Crooke JL; Dr Godfrey JP; Rev Mr Hayes, Rev Canon Jellett JP.

Dr Cross who was committed to the County Gaol on Thursday evening was not present but he was represented by Mr Deyos, solicitor, Cork.

The names of the jury having been called over, the coroner said he wished to have evidence of the death of Mrs Cross.

Mary Buckley, servant at Shandy Hall, who gave evidence on the first day of the inquest as to the state of the late Mrs Cross during her fatal illness, was recalled. She added to her former evidence that she saw Mrs Cross dead on the morning of the 2nd of June. She saw her alive the morning before – Wednesday.

Dr Charles Yelverton Pearson handed in his evidence in writing, which was read out as follows:

"On July 21st, 1887 at 10 a.m. acting on instructions, I proceeded to make a post-mortem examination on an exhumed body, stated to be that of the late Mrs Cross. The coffin was placed in the courthouse at Coachford. I saw that the name of Mrs Cross, her age and the date of her death were marked on the lid.

The coffin was opened in my presence and, the body having been identified, I made a post-mortem examination assisted by Dr T Crowley from Coachford. There was nothing peculiar in the external appearance, but what would correspond to the changes produced by putrefaction. No external marks of violence were visible, though even had they been present at the time of death it is not probable they could be discerned.

The internal examination proved the complete absence of food from the stomach and intestines; the former contained only mucous and some particles of a white substance; the latter contained bile and mucous. There was an absence of excreta from the lower bowel. The liver, spleen and kidney were healthy.

As it was certified that the deceased died from typhoid fever, a special examination was made of the intestines. There was no indication present of the existence of this disease. Owing to the excellent state of the preservation of organs, such indication should have been present if the deceased died of this disease. The upper portion of the small intestine and the lower part of the gullet were congested. There were small abrasions on the lining membrane of the lower end of the gullet and the lining membrane of the upper end of the intestine was thickened and inflamed.

These appearances could only have resulted from the action of an irritant. We examined the heart and found it healthy; the lungs had a venous appearance, but were healthy. A small quantity of bloodstained fluid was found in both sides of the chest. This fluid became coloured after death. There were no natural causes found to account for death, and as the condition of the stomach and intestines corresponded with the action of an irritant, it was not thought necessary to examine the brain.

The gullet, stomach, intestines, liver, spleen and right kidney were removed by me in sealed vessels to the Queen's College, where I made an analysis of them. As a result of that analysis I discovered white arsenic in all these organs, being present in huge quantity in the liver. I also found a small quantity of strychnine in the stomach. The estimate of the quantity of arsenic was made and it shows that it was in sufficient quantity to cause death."

During the reading of the concluding portion there was heard a slight sensation running through the audience.

The coroner asked: "Is it your opinion, Dr Pearson, that the deceased died from poison?"

"Certainly."

"You swear that?"

"I do."

Mr Rice asked: "Where was the strychnine observed?"

"In the stomach."

"And you say that arsenic was found in sufficient quantity to cause death?"

"Yes."

Mr Deyos said that, having regard to the fact that Dr Pearson would be again examined in another inquiry, he would reserve his cross-examination of the witness to that future time.

Dr Pearson said that he had not estimated the quantity of strychnine, and it was only towards the close of the analysis that he estimated the quantity of arsenic found in the stomach. He had not sufficient time to complete the examination of the alkaloids. The strychnine he had found, taken by itself, would not be sufficient to account for death. He had reserved certain portions which he had not yet examined for strychnine.

The foreman of the jury asked: "Is there arsenic in all the organs and strychnine in the stomach?"

"There is."

Mr Deyos asked: "Do you still retain the organs in your possession?"

"I do, except those that underwent the analytical process; they have been destroyed."

Dr Crowley, medical officer of the Dripsey dispensary was next examined and he corroborated the evidence of Dr Pearson, so far as the post-mortem examination was concerned. He had not examined the stomach.

The coroner said that they had gone as far as they could go in order to discharge their function there. Their duty was to find when she had died, where she had died and what was the cause of death. There the duty of the jury ended, and it was for the Crown, of course, to follow the matter up; as they undoubtedly would but there was no necessity for a coroner's jury to go into incriminatory evidence.

He suggested that they should find as their verdict that Mrs Cross died at Shandy Hall and that death resulted from poison, as sworn by Dr Pearson.

The foreman said: "I don't think that there will be much difference of opinion."

The coroner made the point that there would be an inquiry afterwards at which the person who did it would probably be discovered.

The foreman said: "We have only to act on this evidence before us."

After the jury retired to consider their verdict, the foreman returned into the court and said they wished to know whether it was necessary for them to find the exact date of death because there was not sufficient evidence as to the time.

Mr Rice said that they had the evidence of Mary Buckley.

Mary Barron, parlour maid at Shandy Hall, was called, but not sworn. In answer to the coroner she said that she had seen Mrs Cross on the morning of Thursday about nine o'clock, dead. Dr Cross came at six o'clock to her door. He knocked on the bedroom door and said that the mistress was no more since one o'clock in the night.

The jury then retired again and after a quarter of an hour's deliberation, handed in their verdict which was: "That Mary Laura Cross died at Shandy Hall, County Cork, between the morning of the 1st and the morning of the 2nd of June, 1887, and that death was caused by the effects of poison."

The jury was then discharged.

Mr Deyos said that he wanted to say a word. Acting there in the interest of Dr Cross he had examined no witness, produced no witness or commented upon the evidence he saw. He thought the coroner had very properly and judiciously conducted the inquiry to ascertain the cause of death. He had adopted the stance he had taken because he knew from facts that had come to his knowledge that he would have ample opportunity of relieving the cloud which at present surrounded the name of his client. But in the interest of justice he begged to draw the coroner's attention to a paragraph in the *Constitution* of that morning, and he did so while perfectly conscious that, for one reason or another articles might appear in newspapers which might affect or prejudice a case, although such was never intended. In one paragraph in that paper it stated that: "Dr Cross's movements during the day were regarded by the police as rather of a suspicious character," and that "Dr Cross was at the Great Southern and Western railway terminal at the departure of the express train to Dublin, at ten minutes past two and remained in the station until the quarter to three ordinary train left." Now, the only construction that could possibly be put on those words and the only meaning applicable to take was that Dr Cross was at the railway station with a view to avoiding arrest. As a matter of fact, he was there awaiting the arrival of a lady who wired her intention of coming to Cork.

He did not wish to comment on it further, but to say that it was one of those crazy rumours circulated about his client, which when the proper time came, he hoped to be able entirely to disprove. It would be affectation on his part not to see the case at present wore a most serious aspect, but that was the greater reason why comments of a prejudicial character should be abstained from. He hoped similar paragraphs would not appear, and he did so in the interests of the police as well as those of his client. He deemed it his duty to have drawn the coroner's attention to the fact.

The coroner said that Mr Deyos had shown great discretion in the course he had adopted. With regard to the paragraph referred to, it was more for the paper and good management of the paper that such things should be abstained from.

The proceedings then terminated.

Dr Cross's house was yesterday visited by the police who made a thorough examination of every room in the house. The search was directed to the discovery, if possible, of anything that would throw light on the subject of the inquiry. They remained there all day, and if they found anything of which they were in want, it has not been disclosed yet.

The Magisterial Inquiry into the death of Mrs Cross, which was to have commenced in the County Grand Jury Room at 10.30 o'clock on Saturday morning did not come off as anticipated, it having been arranged on Friday evening that Monday would be the better day to fix and consequently the inquiry will commence at half past ten o'clock this Monday morning.

The medical evidence will first be given and it is thought likely that an adjournment will then take place to a future date when the authorities will have all available evidence ready to be presented to the magistrates. As Dr Cross, who has been arrested on suspicion of causing the death of his wife by poison on the 2nd of June, was remanded until today by Mr Gardiner RM, it will be necessary to have him further remanded until Monday and for this purpose a formal remand will be applied for.

At half past three o'clock, Mr Gardiner RM attended the County Gaol for the purpose of hearing an application to have the prisoner remanded. Captain Plunkett DRM and Mr Tyacke DI Ballincollig were in attendance, while Mr R Deyos, solicitor, was present on behalf of the prisoner. The inquiry was held in the warder's room, Dr Cross being in attendance. District Inspector Tyacke applied in affidavit for a remand until Monday August 1st which Mr Gardiner granted.

* * *

Meanwhile Dr Pearson was pushing ahead with his investigations. He was working alone; in another high-profile case, some years before, the Crown in Scotland had no less than four analysts hired for the tests. Not only had he a deadline for this very important analysis, he had other matters to attend to: he was acting as one of the Sectional Secretaries to the British Medical Association and at the same time making arrangements for a much-needed holiday.

The quantitative analysis of the stomach and duodenum had been completed on 27th July, the liver on the 28th. He completed the search for the alkaloids on the 29th, the examination for other metallic poisons on Saturday the 30th. On that night, as well as other writing work, Dr Pearson wrote a full and comprehensive report on the post-mortem examination. The analytical report was completed late into the night of the 31st as it had to be handed in the next morning.

His notes on the quantitative portion of the analysis, on a separate sheet, had been left in his room at the College. He had to trust to memory, and in the midst of his exhaustion made a totally uncharacteristic mistake which would come back to haunt him, even after he had corrected it. The liver was the organ last examined and contained a large portion of poison. He wrote in his report: "This organ which had been specially subjected to quantitative analysis, contained over three grains." It should have read: "The organs which had been specially subjected to quantitative analysis, together contained over three grains."

The arsenic found in the body, he estimated, was taken and administered no longer than four days before the death of Mrs Cross on the 2nd of June but from his knowledge, gleaned from District Inspector Tyacke's preliminary investigation of the length of the victim's illness prior to the date of the death, he concluded that this was a case of slow poisoning.

He made notes of the expected progress of symptoms, which would have to be corroborated by evidence gathered by DI Tyacke as discussed with him in the course of the full investigation that would be the inevitable consequence of his findings. Arsenic administered over a long period of time causes gastroenteritis, inflammation of the stomach and bowels and the symptoms emerge gradually, often with remissions and recurrences as the poison accumulates in the body. The patient may first experience headaches which is later transformed into a sensation of light-headedness and numbness and a tingly feeling in the hands and feet at the onset of poisoning. There is loss of appetite, vomiting, general malaise and diarrhoea. The body mucous membranes become inflamed, causing conjunctivitis, coughing and hoarseness. An abnormal amount of fluid accumulates under the skin and the face and eyelids are particularly affected. Over an extended time, the skin becomes damaged because the arsenic causes blood vessels to dilate.

The natural functioning of the liver and kidney are affected, causing pressure and swelling in the stomach. There follows uncontrollable vomiting and diarrhoea. Vomiting starts after the ingestion of the smallest amount of water and the patient experiences intense thirst and constriction of the throat. Towards the end, the eyesight is affected and painful cramps are felt in the legs. The mind remains clear during all this, intensifying the suffering until delirium, convulsions and severe exhaustion hasten the end.

Pearson suspected that the discovery of strychnine indicated that it was administered to finish off the victim. He could not estimate the quantity given because it is a vegetable poison (derived from the berries of the *nux vomica* tree) and dissolves fairly quickly.

Nonetheless he would have, as a matter of course, made notes of the symptoms of strychnine poison to serve as a comparison with any evidence of the patient's final moments that might arise. Strychnine poisoning produces some of the most dramatic and painful symptoms of any known toxic reaction. Ten to twenty minutes after exposure the body muscles begin to spasm, starting with the head and neck. Sustained spasms of the facial muscles give a grinning look (known as the *risus sardonicus*, also seen in tetanus) and there is inability to open the mouth. The spasms then spread to every muscle in the body with nearly continuous convulsions which get worse at the slightest stimulus. The convulsions progress, increasing in intensity and frequency until the backbone arches continually so that only the heels and top of the head touch the ground. The body temperature elevates dangerously and there is a breakdown of muscle tissue some of which is released into the bloodstream as waste products harmful to the kidneys. This is followed by seizures and altered state of consciousness, drowsiness, confusion and exhaustion. Death comes from asphyxiation caused by paralysis of the neural pathways that control breathing or by exhaustion from convulsions. This usually occurs 2-3 hours after exposure to the poison.

Strychnine was discovered in 1818 and had a history of use for therapeutic purposes. In most cases this use was misguided and potentially dangerous. It has a very bitter taste and so stimulates saliva and gastric secretion which increases appetite and was used to counteract loss of appetite associated with illness. This gave the impression that strychnine had restorative properties.

A book published in 1875 stated that "*Nux vomica* is commonly sold to the public in the form of greyish-brown powder at the price of eight pence an ounce. In this state it may be mistaken for the powders of various medicines." This fact was made use of by various poisoners. "Its properties as a deadly poison have long been known to medical men but they have only within the past twenty years been brought prominently before the public and this alkaloid has now acquired a fatal notoriety."

The young doctor was not just punctilious in his method of work – it was his very nature to leave no medical stone unturned.

He had no agenda other than his innate professional attitude to everything he did. Despite the fact that he was acting as a medical witness for the Crown, he knew that he was not an advocate: his evidence would be assembled and given in a fair and objective manner.

The results of his examinations did not, however, prove who administered the poison. And also, as he was well aware, the presence of the poison would have to match the clinical symptoms experienced by the victim, not only to be accepted by a court but also to withstand a vigorous challenge by the defence.

Dr Pearson suspected there might well be variations in the expression of the symptoms in the case but, in general, they would follow the established pattern fairly accurately. His opinion at this stage was that the cause of death was poisoning by arsenic with the presence of strychnine, a secondary factor due to the small quantity found in the body.

Over the month of August on a weekly basis, during which there were a number of adjournments, the Magisterial Inquiry was held in the Grand Jury room of the courthouse, presided over by Mr Gardiner RM. Stephen Ronan QC acted for the prosecution instructed by Mr Gregg while Mr Deyos acted for the prisoner. A large number of witnesses who would also feature in the trial were examined. On September 5th the magistrate Mr Gardiner acceded to Mr Ronan's request that a trial would proceed.

Mr Deyos did not offer any defence, stating that it would be a waste of time in a preliminary inquiry and would be kept for the trial. Dr Philip Henry Eustace Cross was remanded to the County Gaol until the trial date and venue were set.

Chapter 6

The Poison Detective

On his return from holiday, Dr Pearson set about trying to establish, given the fact that a small amount of strychnine had been found in the stomach, whether it had been administered in a poisonous quantity. He had preserved for further examination portions of the internal organs, not used in his first analysis. He also made an application to the authorities to have the body of Mrs Cross re-exhumed. He based his request on a passage from Alexander Wynter Blyth's *Poisons: their effects and detection* (1895):

"Should search be made for minute portions of strychnine in the tissues, considering the small amount of poison which may produce death, it is absolutely necessary to operate on a very large quantity of material . . . It is only by working on this large scale that there is any probability of detecting absorbed strychnine in those cases where only one or two grains have destroyed life, and even then it is possible to miss the poison."

He was also determined to deal with the widespread misconception that strychnine is a substance that undergoes rapid destruction in dead bodies, which he considered erroneous, and he again relied on the findings of Dr Blyth for his opinion: "At one time it was believed that strychnine might be destroyed by putrefaction, but the question of the decomposition of the poison in putrid bodies may be said to be settled. So far as all evidence goes, strychnine is an extremely settled substance and no amount of putrescence will destroy it."

Having received permission, the body of Mrs Cross was again exhumed on the morning of 23rd August, just over a month after the original exhumation. Dr Pearson removed the heart, lungs, remaining kidney, brain and a large mass of muscle from the thigh. He found that notwithstanding the first exposure, the body presented little additional signs of decomposition. He observed that the flesh from the thigh was a bright red colour, and free from putrefaction as if it had been recently buried.

All the parts preserved, together with those preserved from the previous chemical examination, were carefully treated by a modified form of the Stas Process for the isolation of strychnine, with the result that slightly less than one-hundredth of a grain was found in crystalline form.

The brilliant young doctor knew from both his experience and knowledge of other high-profile cases of murder by poisoning in Victorian England that his role would be subject to great scrutiny by the medical and legal professions, the media and indeed the public. The Coachford Case, the modus operandi and the status and profession of the prime suspect, Dr Cross, fitted into a category that historically had been not only accompanied by huge sensation, gossip presented as fact, but also mired in controversy, recrimination and reconstruction.

Victorian newspapers were notorious for retrying troubling cases in public and condemning what were felt to be improper verdicts. Criminal trials had become occasions for not only huge press exposure but for constant reflection and criticism inspired not in a little part by the fact that Victorian England was fascinated by murders, trials and executions.

Top of the list were cases of murder by poisoning, not surprising as the Victorian era was considered a golden age of poisoners, especially involving middle-class perpetrators and in particular doctors. Any uncertainties surrounding trials resulting from such high-profile cases were greeted with anything but acceptance by the newspapers and the public.

One of the main problems as evidenced in many cases and most notably that of Dr William Palmer, was the presentation of medical evidence and the legal tensions created by both presentation and rebuttal. Like any forensic science in any age, it was playing catch-up both with the guile of the poisoners and with the problems associated with putting forward the evidence in a legal setting, the adversarial cauldron of the court. Just one of which problems was getting prosecuting counsel to properly grasp its principles and another medical expert's diametrically opposed interpretation of those principles.

Developing in conjunction with the rise of poisoning as fashionable murder in the mid-19th century was the field of toxicology. Recognising the weaknesses of current methods of detecting poison, scientists rose to the challenge to develop reliable standards for poison detection.

Among them James Marsh and Hugo Reinsch who, in 1836 and 1841, independently introduced methods of detecting arsenic. Thanks to this research, many poisoners were detected, although not before they had wreaked considerable damage.

The Reinsch test was an initial indicator to detect the presence of one or more of the following heavy metals often used by toxicologists when poisoning is suspected: antimony, arsenic, bismuth, selenium, thalium and mercury. The process involved first dissolving the suspect body fluid or tissue in a hydrochloric acid solution. A copper strip was inserted into the solution. The appearance of a silvery dark coating indicated the presence of poison including arsenic.

The relationship between the dose and its effects on the exposed organism was of high significance in toxicology. The chief criterion regarding the toxicity of the chemical is the dose: the amount of exposure to the substance.

The Marsh test was a highly sensitive method of detection of arsenic especially useful in the field of forensic toxicology when arsenic was used as a poison. White arsenic was then a highly favoured poison, for its odourless, tasteless nature, easily incorporated into food or drink and before the Marsh test untraceable in the body.

In France it became to be known as *poudre de successor* – inheritance powder – and had similar symptoms as cholera, as well as a number of other illnesses at the various stages of progression.

In 1832 in England a man by the name of John Bodle was brought to trial for poisoning his grandfather by lacing his coffee with arsenic. John Marsh, a chemist working for the Royal Arsenal in Norwich, was called in by the prosecution to detect its presence. He performed the standard test by passing hydrogen sulphide through the suspect fluid. While he was able to detect arsenic, by the time it was presented to the jury the sample had deteriorated and Bodle was acquitted. The standard test, not for the first time, was found wanting and a long way from foolproof. Angered and frustrated by the outcome, especially when Bodle later confessed, Marsh decided to devise a better test to detect the presence of arsenic. Taking the previous test as a basis, he constructed a simple glass apparatus, capable of not only detecting minute traces of arsenic but also measuring its quantity.

Marsh combined a sample containing arsenic with sulphuric acid and arsenic-free zinc, resulting in arsine gas. The gas was ignited and it decomposed to pure metallic arsenic. When passed onto a cold surface it appeared as a silvery-black deposit. Thus the most minute quantities of arsenic could be detected.

The first documented use of the test and the first time that evidence of a forensic toxicologist was introduced in a murder case was in 1840 in Tulle, France, in the celebrated and much reported La Farge poisoning case. It was suspected that Charles La Farge, a foundry owner, was poisoned with arsenic by his wife Marie. The circumstantial evidence was compelling. She had bought arsenic from a local chemist, supposedly to kill rats infesting their home. In addition their maid swore that she had mixed a white powder into his drink and food. Although the food was found to be positive, using the old methods of testing, as well as the Marsh test, when the body was exhumed no trace of poison was found.

Mathieu Orfila, the renowned toxicologist, was called in as a referee whose findings both prosecution and defence agreed to be bound by. Born a Spanish subject on the island of Minorca, he studied medicine in Valencia and Barcelona before moving to the Faculté de Médecine de Paris. In 1819 he became a French citizen and was appointed Professor of Medical Jurisprudence. Four years later he became Professor of Medical Chemistry there and in 1831 he was nominated dean of that faculty, a high medical honour in France.

He became the first great 19th-century exponent of forensic medicine, making chemical analysis the basis of his work, and made studies of asphyxiation, the decomposition of bodies and exhumation. He helped develop the presence of blood in a forensic context and was one of the first to use a microscope to assess blood and semen stains.

Orfila performed the Marsh Test again and proved the presence of arsenic in the body and pointed to the fact that the previous testers had not done the job properly.

The wife was sentenced to death, later commuted to life imprisonment. The case was controversial and received huge press coverage. It pushed the science of forensic toxicology on to the centre stage.

Orfila is considered the true founder of toxicology. His most significant discovery was that poisons were absorbed selectively in different organs. If poison was not found in the stomach, it might be present in the liver or kidney or other parts of the body.

The use of poison and its character and the characteristics of the user have remained remarkably consistent throughout all ages. An excerpt from Chaucer's *The Canterbury Tales*, a text that existed sometime in the 14th or 15th century described a killer buying poison from an apothecary to rid himself of a rat infestation, an excuse used for hundreds of years afterwards. Back to the ancients, poisoning has long been a stealthy way of ending life.

The ancients initially used plant substances like curare and aconite to poison their hunting arrows, swords and darts. The word *toxin* is derived from the Greek *toxicon* which refers to poison by an arrow (from *toxon*, a bow). Today, by definition, poison is a substance which causes injury, illness and death to organisms by chemical or molecular activity. This distinguishes it from a toxin, which in the context of biology is a poison of organic origin, especially one stimulating the production of antibodies. These include plant and bacterial substances, such as belladonna and botulinum toxin. However, for the poisoner and toxicologist both terms are synonymous as substances which when administered bring an unnatural end to life.

Many ancient civilisations were intimately acquainted with poisons and their effects. Earliest Egyptian references date back to 3,000 BC. They were the first masters of distillation, knew about classical poisons and could extract them from peach kernels. A papyrus records the preparation of poisonous substances for the purpose of killing.

In 500 BC, Indian physicians were composing the first forensic texts on how to detect poisoners – interestingly, through their personality traits.

Both the Greeks and the Romans were adept at the use of poisons to kill, both to get rid of enemies and family members if necessary and for a time as a form of State execution, a fate suffered by the philosopher Socrates. The widespread use of poison as a killing and as an assassination tool provoked studies among scientists and physicians.

In his treatise, *Materia Medica*, Dioscorides (*ca.* 40–90 AD), a Greek physician, pharmacologist and botanist who practised in Rome at the time of Nero, classified poisons and differentiated their origins and for fifteen centuries, was the authoritative text on the subject.

Whether on the individual, the political, or the financial stage, poison maintained its notoriously high profile in the matter of murder – in the Renaissance, through the medium of the infamous Borgia clan who used the dinner party as an opportunity to practise the nefarious art. In 16th-century Italy a guild was established by a group of alchemists to provide assassinations for a fee.

Despite many efforts over the ages, by Louis XIV, for example, who passed a law preventing apothecaries selling their wares to people not known to them and compelling them to register the purchasers, many poisoners continued to operate without detection.

The Victorian era, the golden age of poisoners, is the period from which many of the world's most notorious hail. While people who killed this way for personal gain were known throughout the ages, now poison was easily available to the man – or woman – in the street. And potential poisoners had a new incentive: the introduction of life insurance.

Poison became such a popular method of murder – being so difficult to detect, so easily administered, and so readily available in various forms for seemingly innocent purposes – that there was a growing demand for legislation in order to impose some measure of control on its sale and distribution. It was hoped that the crime of secret murder could be combated by this means. Legislation, however, was constantly delayed by those who argued that any such attempts at control would be ineffective.

The mystery and infamy of poisoners, which made them popular subjects of both fiction and of creative news-reporting, was increased by their using new, strange and potent poisons from the mysterious East, of which strychnine was perhaps the best-known example.

The system of forensic toxicology dates from the end of the 18th century. It arose as a branch of forensic medicine concerned with the problem of proving deliberate poisoning in criminal cases. It was often difficult to distinguish symptoms produced by many poisonous plants like belladonna (deadly nightshade) and henbane from other diseases.

Medicines often involved the use of poisonous substances and most physicians agreed that a better knowledge of the chemical properties and physiological effects of poisons would aid diagnosis and treatment as well as the search for antidotes. Some physiologists also thought that the ability to trace the passage of poisons throughout the body would offer a new tool for investigating metabolic changes and functions of organs.

All these advances would depend on the development of more

reliable methods of chemical analysis. Chemists like Richard Kirwan of Ireland studied the analysis of minerals and mineral waters while CS Fresnius in Germany, who in 1862 founded the first journal entirely devoted to analytical chemistry, devised the first analytical tables.

In the criminal courts evidence presented by medical witnesses was usually based on clinical and pathological observations interpreted in terms of contemporary notions of the physiological effects of drugs and poisons. The results of chemical analysis were accepted somewhat doubtfully by the courts to clarify the medical evidence when the presence of specific poisons was alleged.

Identification of the mineral acids, alkalis and salts when they were mixed with food and drink presented the analyst with problems that became even more difficult when poison was sought in stomach contents and had been absorbed in tissues or organs.

In 19th-century Britain and Ireland many poisons were regularly available for household use. Rat poison contained arsenic, and other common poisons were on open sale in hardware stores and pharmacies. Opium and its derivatives like laudanum were increasingly given to ease pain and induce sleep.

One of the most useful and widely used, chlorodyne, was invented in the 19th century by Dr John Collis Browne, a doctor in the British Indian army. Its original purpose was for the treatment of cholera. But it also proved an excellent medicine for the effective treatment of diarrhoea, insomnia, neuralgia, and the relief of pain.

The principal ingredients were a mixture of laudanum (alcoholic solution of opium), tincture of cannabis and choloroform. Almost all ethical drugs at the time and up to the early 20th century were generic and not proprietary in nature and this meant that medicines such as chlorodyne were manufactured by nearly all the pharmaceutical companies. This was considered a wonder drug and despite, or in spite of its addictive quality, the heady concoction saved a great many lives, as well as being used as a cover for more nefarious activities. *Nux vomica*, a highly poisonous natural substance, was also prescribed for some nervous diseases.

The fact that poisons could be legitimately obtained increased the difficulty of proving their deliberate use in criminal courts. Laws such as the Arsenic Act 1851 had to be introduced to keep the dissemination of poison under control. This Act ruled, with certain qualifications, that a book be kept by the seller where all the details of the purchaser were entered; that the purchaser must to known to the seller or else known by a witness; that the purchaser must be of "full age"; and that arsenic being sold must be mixed with soot or indigo (to prevent it being mistaken for other white household substances).

An earlier Bill had been introduced in 1819 to regulate the distribution and sale of arsenic. It proposed that certain drugs should not be sold or kept for sale unless labelled 'Poison', and that arsenic and oxalic acid should be mixed with, in the case of arsenic, carbon. The aim was more to prevent accidental ingestion than to prevent deliberate poisoning, as accidents were rife. The Bill was heavily opposed by the Committee of Associated Apothecaries on the grounds that "it was likely to embarrass the dispensing of medicines, and not calculated to effect the object intended". The Bill was withdrawn.

Forensic medicine had been studied in several European countries, notably France, but not in Britain. It was called "medical jurisprudence" or "legal medicine" and included detailed studies of many forms of violent death including poison. In France, *médecine légale* was intensively pursued after the Revolution.

The first university chair in Medical Jurisprudence was established in Edinburgh in 1807. The chair was held from 1822 by Robert Christison. In 1829 he was appointed Medical Adviser to the Crown and for the next 37 years he served as medical witness in almost every important murder case in Scotland.

In 1831 Alfred Swaine Taylor became Lecturer in Medical Jurisprudence at Guy's Hospital in London at 25 years of age and his was the first English course on the subject, which was attended by leading members of the legal profession, including judges. He represented the epitome of the poison detective and his career and writings would have a profound influence on generations of his profession, including Dr Charles Yelverton Pearson.

He identified early on that there were numerous problems in the definition of what constituted poison and in particular a deadly poison, one that was capable of destroying life, a matter complicated by the widespread use of poison in medicines. It was also, as he remarked in his introduction to one of his famous books on the subject, widespread as an instrument of harm and murder. "The crime of poison has been of late so fearlessly on the increase, that it seems essential for the proper administration of justice, and for the security of society, to collect and arrange a convenient form of reference, those important medical facts in relation to death from poison, which while they constitute a safe guide to the barrister and medical practitioner, may prevent the condemnation of the innocent and ensure the conviction of the guilty."

He was driven by a spirit of individuality and conviction. He was lucid in his exposition, conservative in his theories and elaborate and unrelenting in his investigation. He had an ardent and sincere love and respect for the truth which made him incapable of advocating the side he did not believe sincerely to be that of justice. He was the perfect nemesis of the secret poisoner, despite one famous occasion falling foul of the adversarial court play and being the subject of severe public criticism. His public reputation was built on his appearances in court as an expert witness. He was a prolific writer on medical jurisprudence and toxicology and his books became standard texts. From 1845 to 1851 he edited the *London Medical Gazette*, contributed to *The Lancet* and was the leading medical jurist in England.

Writing in 1848 Taylor said:

"Probably there is no branch of medicine in which we meet with a larger assemblage of truths ascertained by observation . . . to the physician, the pathologist and the medical jurist, a knowledge of [toxicology] is of great importance . . . in drawing a clear distinction between changes produced in the body by disease and those caused by poison, [and] in detecting and punishing those . . . guilty of the crime of poisoning."

By the mid-1850's he had been consulted in about 500 medico-legal cases. The controversial trials of Dr William Palmer (1856) and Dr Smethurst (1859) did much to influence his opinions concerning the nature and use of medical evidence in murder trials.

His experience in trials relating to poison led him to conclude that the results of analysis obtained by the imperfect methods of the time provided only a certain degree of probability and where admitted as evidence should be used only to supplement (corroborate) the medical observations.

By examining separately all the organs and fluids of the body, the chances of detecting the presence of poisons was increased. As a form of essential corroboration in criminal trials, the symptoms of poisoning were also essential, as a matter of observation and clinical analysis.

The symptoms, Dr Taylor noted, may be suspended for a time, or slightly modified in their progress – "but sooner or later the poison will affect the healthy and the diseased, the young and the old, with a uniformity in its effects, not to be easily mistaken."

In the 1860s there was concern among British scientists about the role of the expert witness. It did not seem right to them to put the men of science in the role of advocate. Taylor recognised that chemical analysis, no matter how carefully conducted, only provided a certain degree of probability and could never achieve the incontrovertible demonstrations of proof required by the courts.

This was especially true when body tissues and fluids were involved as they usually were in the case of poisoning. Only when chemical analysis identified the same poison in tissues or organs of the body as in food or drink taken by the victim was evidence of poison strengthened. Even the quantity of poison found was crucial.

The expert medical witness was required to provide the court with a quantitative estimate of the amount of poison related to the lethal dose. Counsel could easily undermine the value of scientific and medical evidence. Detail was of the essence and anticipation of legal objections that might be raised.

Taylor distinguished three groups of poisons: irritants, narcotics and narcotico-irritants. Corrosive and irritant substances were identified by effects on the tissues of the mouth, throat and stomach. The signs of poison in such cases were immediately obvious. When there were no such effects, it was harder to detect poison.

Taylor aimed to define chemical and biological poisons in simple terms which could be accepted by jurists. Poison he defined as "a substance which when taken internally is capable of destroying life without acting mechanically on the system." He was well aware that chemical analysis alone could not be relied on to secure a criminal conviction.

His reputation as an expert witness and his contribution to forensic toxicology were based on his shrewdness in recognising what was required by the courts, as well as his skill as a chemical analyst. He was as impartial as possible and had a dislike of "professional witnesses".

He had a remarkable ability to bring scientific evidence into line with the demands of the law: thoroughness, impartiality, love of accuracy and scientific approach to the details of each case. He took account of legal as well as scientific criteria and by diligence in combining the great mass of legal precedents and judicial rulings with chemical and anatomical data he established forensic toxicology as a medical specialism.

This was his main achievement and he was also a prolific writer on the subject. His experiences in criminal courts made him aware of the different perceptions of "proof" in the matter of law. He knew that legal objections were capable of challenging expert evidence which he had found at first hand in a number of high profile cases.

Taylor often cited analytical results supplied by colleagues who were not required to appear in court. But when chemical evidence seemed likely to be crucial in a case, expert witnesses would be called by both sides. This sometimes resulted in controversy in court and outside, most notably in the case of Dr William Palmer, the Rugeley poisoner.

This was a case that caused huge controversy and drew intense critical reaction by the conduct of the trial, criticism that not even the distinguished Dr Taylor would escape. It was a case from which lessons would have prompted great care and caution in Dr Charles

Yelverton Pearson, who as an admirer and disciple of Dr Taylor played the same role as him in Coachford. Dr Philip Henry Eustace Cross would have been equally aware of the Palmer case, given the enormous publicity that surrounded it and the fact that the central character shared his profession and knowledge of even the most fundamental chemistry. Cross was, at the time of the William Palmer sensation, in his thirties and thirteen years away from marrying Mary Laura Marriott. There would be more than one indication in the much distant future that firmly indicated Dr Cross was fully conversant with certain details of this extraordinary case and which he had clearly stored in his subconscious memory. There was another infamous cause célèbre in which the parallels defied the possibility of coincidence, and that was the case involving another member of his own profession, Dr Edmund Pritchard of Sauchiehall Street in Glasgow, a case of equal interest to the chief suspect in the Coachford case as to the poison detective, Dr Pearson in Queen's College, whose knowledge would have been stimulated by the demands of his rapidly developing academic career.

In the very same year of 1887 when Dr Pearson's work would unwittingly receive worldwide media attention, the most famous fictional detective of all time was introduced to the public in serialised form. The author, Dr Arthur Conan Doyle, a young Scottish doctor of Irish extraction had created a consulting detective, Sherlock Holmes, inspired by his college professor, Dr Joseph Bell, but clearly influenced by poison detectives, the chief of which of course was Dr Taylor.

Dr Bell, like Dr Taylor, emphasised the importance of close observation in making a diagnosis. The author's mentor was considered a pioneer in forensic science, forensic pathology in particular, and had a big impact on the creation of Holmes and his trusty sidekick, Dr Watson, a medical man. Something of Holmes' background is given in the first outing *A Study In Scarlet*. The year of the action was set in 1881 and the detective is presented as an independent student of chemistry and has a mini laboratory at his lodgings to conduct experiments. Holmes maintains a strict adherence to scientific methods, and focuses on the powers of logic and observation. He uses a magnifying glass at the scene of the crime and an optical microscope at his Baker St rooms.

The mutual friend who introduces Dr Watson to Holmes informs him before the meeting that he is well up in anatomy and is a first-class chemist. He would be prepared to taste a poison to gauge its effects for the matter of investigation. In fact the friend goes further:

"Holmes is a little too scientific for my tastes – it approaches cold-bloodedness. I could imagine him giving a friend a little pinch of the latest vegetable alkaloid, not out of malevolence, you understand, but simply out of a spirit of inquiry, in order to have an accurate idea of its effects. To do him justice, I think he would take it himself with the same readiness."

Poisons, it would emerge, had a great and special interest for Holmes, and the main murder in *A Study In Scarlet* is carried out by poisoning.

When Watson arrives with the friend to meet Holmes, the detective glances around and springs to his feet:

"I've found it, I've found it!" he shouted to my companion, running towards us with a test tube in his hand, "I have found a re-agent which is precipitated with haemoglobin and by nothing else!"

"It is interesting chemically, no doubt," I answered, "but practically –"

"Why man, it is the most practical medico-legal discovery for years. Don't you see that it gives us an infallible test for bloodstains? Had this test been invented, there are hundreds of men, now walking the earth who would long ago have paid the penalty for all their crimes."

Holmes remarks later that he had to be careful, "for I dabble in poisons a good deal". The detective on the crime scene sniffs the murder victim's lips and detects a sour smell which he deduces was poison and mentions other cases which he says "will occur at once to any toxicologist".

Thus the great detective was thrust upon on the unsuspecting public and world with great powers of observation, deduction and the tools of a forensic expert, test tube, magnifying glass, microscope, laboratory, unlimited access to the dissecting room, intimate knowledge of the tools of the poisoner's trade and a doctor's knowledge of anatomy and chemical analysis.

Holmes embodied the qualities of the forensic scientist, believing that it was a mistake to theorise before all the evidence is gathered, having an infinite capacity for taking pains to collect the evidence to catch the killer and never passing over the smallest clues – "To a great mind, nothing is little." And a passion for definite and exact knowledge.

Without minimising the difficulties of each and every case, Dr Alfred Swaine Taylor and his fellow poison detectives would have agreed with Sherlock Holmes' opinion that, "There is a strong family resemblance about misdeeds; and if you have all the details of a thousand at your finger ends, it is odd that you can't unravel the thousand and first."

Murder by poison, by its nature would involve very strong "family resemblance" and, while unravelling it might seem to be relatively straightforward, testing that unravelling in the laboratory was one thing but in the charged atmosphere of the court an entirely different challenge.

Chapter 7

The Cases of Palmer and Pritchard

Palmer, born in Rugeley, Staffordshire, led an extravagant lifestyle, apart from his medical practices, devoted to wine, women, song and the horses. He was in every aspect of his behaviour a gambler which inevitably led to serious debt. Several people connected to him died in somewhat mysterious circumstances.

These included his mother-in-law and two people to whom he owed money. His wife also died, apparently from the effects of cholera after he had taken out an insurance policy on her life for the then considerable sum of £13,000. He also insured his brother Walter's life for a goodly sum but when he also died soon afterwards, the insurance company refused to pay out. Palmer was now sinking in a mire of increasing debt which had led him to forgery and a line of creditors ready to issue writs against him. He had to get his hands on money and fast.

When, on 13th November 1855, a racing friend who he had accompanied to Shrewsbury races, John Parsons Cook, won a considerable sum from betting on his own horse, Polestar, Palmer accompanied him to the Raven Hotel in the town. Cook, at 28 years old relatively robust despite a bout or two of syphilis, became ill the following evening after drinking brandy given to him by Palmer.

On the 15th, Palmer lost heavily on a horse named The Chicken and he and Cook returned to Rugeley where the latter booked into room Number 10 in the Talbot Arms Hotel. Two days later he was again taken ill at the hotel. On the 19th Palmer travelled to London to collect the indisposed Cook's winnings.

After a number of bouts of violent sickness and intermittent recovery Parson's condition deteriorated rapidly and he died at 10 a.m. on the 21st in his room at the hotel in a manner described as a horrible and painful passing. During that time he had been given medicine by Palmer which seemed to make him worse, followed by treatment from an old and infirm doctor which briefly improved his condition.

An inquest was held and after a post mortem insisted on by the victim's father-in-law, there was no indication that Parsons had died from natural causes. Suspicion fell on Palmer and he was charged on the 15th of December with the murder of his racing companion by poison. The motive was financial gain. The stomach and the intestines of the victim had been sent to London for chemical analysis under the supervision of Dr Taylor.

An act of Parliament had to be passed to have Dr Palmer tried in the Old Bailey as it was deduced that an unbiased jury could not be relied on to be found in Staffordshire, the reasoning for which, apart from the obvious, would be clarified after the trial had ended. Despite the fact of Dr Palmer's desperate financial situation, the clarity of motive and the undoubted circumstance of opportunity the case for the Crown would turn out to be anything but straight-forward. The basis for the prosecution by the very nature of the charge had to rely on medical evidence and from the opening day that seemed to be predicated on very shaky ground.

The trial opened at The Old Bailey on the morning of 14th May 1856, to enormous public interest.

The Times reported:

"The long deferred trial of William Palmer which, owing to the necessity of passing the specific Act Of Parliament to enable it to take place in this court, had been delayed for a period of seven months since the finding of a true bill by the Grand Jury of Staffordshire, commenced today at The Old Bailey, and notwithstanding the interval which has elapsed since this extraordinary case was first brought under the notice of the public, the intense interest and excitement which it then occasioned seem in no degree to have abated.

At a very early hour every entrance to the court was besieged by persons of a respectable appearance who were favoured with cards giving them a right of entrance; without such cards no admittance, could, on any pretence be obtained; and even the fortunate holders of them found they had many difficulties to overcome, and many stern janitors to encounter, before an entrance to the much coveted precincts could be obtained."

The reporter observed among the many distinguished spectators, the Earl Of Derby, The Marquis of Anglesea, Lord Lucan, Lord Denbeigh and Prince Edward of Saxe Weimar. The prisoner was in highly exalted company, a far cry from Rugeley.

The packed courtroom settled and for the next four hours listened to the Attorney General Alexander Cockburn outline the case for the prosecution. Having dealt at length and in minute detail with the troubled financial affairs of the accused and throwing him in a damning light and establishing desperate straits before the trip to Shrewsbury races, he then dealt with the return of the pair to Rugeley.

He recounted the events of the first day and the night when John Parsons Cook showed symptoms of the sudden onset of an unexplained violent illness, followed by a respite and then on the second night a recurrence.

Cook was found in the same condition and with the same symptoms of the night before. Gasping for breath, screaming violently, his body convulsed with cramps and spasms and his neck rigid, Jones raised him and rubbed his neck. When Palmer entered the room, Cook asked him for the same remedy that had relieved him the night before.

'I will run back and fetch it,' said Palmer and darted out of the room. In the passage he met two female servants who remarked that Cook was as 'bad' as he had been last night. 'He is not within fifty times as bad as he was last night; and what a game is this to be at every night,' was Palmer's reply.

In a few minutes he returned with two pills, which he told Jones were ammonia, though I am assured that it is a drug that requires much time in the preparation, and can with difficulty be made into pills. The sick man swallowed these pills but brought them up immediately.

And now ensued a terrible scene. He was suddenly seized with violent convulsions; by degrees his body began to stiffen out; then suffocation commenced. Agonised with pain, he repeatedly entreated to be raised. They tried to raise him. The body had become rigid as iron and it could not be done. He then said: 'Pray turn me over.' They did turn him over on the right side. He gasped for breath but could not utter. No more.

In a few minutes all was tranquil – the tide of life was ebbing fast. Jones leant over him to listen to the action of the heart. Gradually the pulse ceased – all was over, he was dead."

* * *

This was on one level, simply but effectively a powerful evocation of the last terrible moments of a murder victim, all the more horrendous because it was not imagined or exaggerated. It was based on the evidence of those who had witnessed a very particular form of death throes. Ones which it became quickly obvious from the next part of the advocate's speech would stay lodged in the ears, hearts and minds of the jury.

Such was the Attorney General's skill of reconstruction and delivery that it was unlikely that the abundance of evidence and argument that was to follow in the course of the trial would erase the echo of the dreadful demise of John Parsons Cook, a young man with a bright future and everything to live for. The jury would much later be reminded of that, perhaps too well and perhaps not fairly.

The Attorney General then went on to address what in effect was the essential but missing link in the prosecution chain of evidence.

"The body was submitted to analysis and I am bound to say that no trace of strychnine was found. But I am told that although the presence of strychnine may be detected by certain tests, and although indications of its presence lead irresistibly to the conclusion that it was administered; the converse of that proposition does not hold. Sometimes it is found, other times it is not.

It depends on circumstances. A most minute amount will destroy life, from half to three quarters of a grain will lay the strongest man prostrate, but in order to produce that fatal effect, it must be absorbed into the system and the absorption takes place to a greater or lesser period according to the manner in which the poison is presented to the surfaces in which it comes into contact. If it is in a fluid form it is rapidly taken up and soon produces the effect; if not, it requires to be absorbed, and the effects are a longer time in showing themselves. But in either case, there is a difficulty in showing its presence. If it acts only on the nervous system through circulation, an almost infinitesimal dose will be present. And as it is a vegetable poison, the tests which alone can be employed are infinitely more delicate and difficult than those that are applied to other poisons. It is unlike a mineral poison, which soon can be detected and reproduced if the dose has been a large one; death ensues before the whole has been absorbed; and a portion is left in the intestines; but if a minimum dose has been administered a different consequence follows, and the whole is absorbed. Practical experience bears out the theory that I am enunciating.

It has been repeated over and over again that the scientific men employed in this case have come up with the conclusion that the presence of strychnine cannot be detected by any tests known to science. They have been grevously misunderstood. They never made any such assertion. What they have asserted is this – the detection of its presence, where its administration is a matter of certainty, is a matter of the greatest uncertainty. It would indeed be a fatal thing to sanction the notion that strychnine administered for the purpose of taking away life cannot afterwards be detected! Lamentable enough is the uncertainty of detection! Happily, Providence which has placed this fatal agent at the disposition of man, has marked its effects with characteristic symptoms distinguishable from those of all other agents in the eyes of science."

* * *

This last part of the Attorney General's speech, was, of course, if not recognised then but certainly later, an exercise in obfuscation and courtly rhetoric to weave a web of apparent logic which would hardly withstand much examination. A pretty shallow diversionary tactic in an attempt to diminish the unarguable fact that the very instrument that the prosecution contended was responsible for the death of the victim could not be found in the body and therefore not produced in evidence in court. An extraordinary admission by modern standards, but not so in an era where the power of vocal persuasion, of articulate advocacy, of theatrical power of delivery could neutralise the power of evidence and smother logic and in particular reasonable doubt.

The prosecution of the case of Dr Palmer was taken from Staffordshire, by a special Act of Parliament to remove the possibility of bias by a local jury, to London. Which was probably right and proper as long as there was no bias in the prosecution of the case that might unduly influence the Old Bailey jury.

While it was a fact that in the matter of murder from the beginning of time, the dogs in the street know the identity of the perpetrator, particularly in a rural location, what is paramount in the pursuit of justice for the victim is that the killer gets a fair trial. A trial that produces a verdict based on the evidence and the vital consideration of reasonable doubt. In the matter of the trial of Dr William Palmer, the so-called Rugeley Poisoner, that very process was besieged with doubt.

Palmer executed a series of what can only be described as manoeuvres in the days before and after Parson's death which could be interpreted as either blunderingly obvious or cleverly deceptive. In the latter instance, clever enough to seem entirely natural and proper.

He, as a doctor, would have been well aware that in any potential trial, analytical results were allowed in evidence but only

128

to supplement medical observations. Evidence from chemical analysis was always open to criticism and was seldom, if ever, considered conclusive.

Samples could, accidentally or even deliberately, be contaminated. The stomach and intestines of Cook were sent by carrier from Rugeley to London where Taylor and Rees failed to find strychnine, prussic acid or opium present. But they did find antimony.

The circumstances under which the organs to be examined were collected and transported were far from ideal. It appeared that Palmer had made an attempt to contaminate the evidence and persuade the carrier to upset the contents.

Despite the largely negative fact from the prosecution point of view that no strychnine had been discovered in the body of the victim, there was a matter of having their cake and eating it. There was evidence that tartar emetic had been administered but the analysts concluded that it was:

"Impossible to say whether strychnine had or had not been given just before death, but it is quite possible for tartaric emetic to destroy life, if given in repeated doses and as far as we, at present, can form an opinion, in the absence of any natural cause of death, the deceased may have died from antimony."

Note "may" have. This is anything other than conclusive evidence and contradictory to the thrust of the prosecution case outlined in the opening speech. No strychnine had been found so the prosecution would rely on evidence to be established that the victim's symptoms before death were in fact those that could be exclusively assigned to the administration of strychnine and not antimony.

Palmer's defence team had assembled a number of medical experts only too willing to attack Alfred Swaine Taylor's reputation and expertise. The strategy was to put Taylor's expertise and toxicology itself on trial. Counsel for the prisoner showed that the prosecution's chief medical witness had no direct case knowledge of the effects of strychnine on humans, his experience being based on laboratory experiments involving rabbits, some two decades earlier.

The opposing experts for the defence contradicted Taylor's interpretation of the medical symptoms of strychnine poisoning, claiming that they were more suggestive of tetanus. Since poisonous symptoms often mimic natural diseases and no strychnine was found in the body, this represented a real threat to the prosecution case. It was also claimed that Taylor was biased and had made prejudicial statements to the press.

The prosecution countered by claiming that Palmer's tampering with the evidence made thorough chemical analysis impossible and Palmer's medical experience made him a crafty poisoner, knowing exactly how to administer strychnine, lethal in small doses. Being a vegetable poison it is not only hard to trace in a buried body but is also compromised by the process of decomposition.

Despite the evidence being entirely circumstantial, and no strychnine found in the body of Cook, the evidence of the details of his death and the motive was enough to convince the jury of Palmer's guilt. Some 35,000 people turned up at Stafford prison on 14th June 1856 to see Palmer publicly executed.

Dr Edward Pritchard had been profligate in a less spectacular way than his predecessor Palmer, now the occupier of an anonymous prison grave and, according to the opposing points of view, a victim of a miscarriage of justice or a monstrous practitioner of a cowardly art of murder who got his just desserts. They both shared characteristics of selfish, self-obsessed vanity; shallow knowledge and practice of their profession and a propensity to fantasy which led them down a path of ill discipline, indulgence and, ultimately, horror.

Like Dr Cross, Pritchard had led an adventurous life. He served in the Royal Navy as an assistant surgeon with HMS *Victory*, and for another four years served on various other ships in the Pacific and Atlantic, visiting Fiji and South America and gaining knowledge of exotic medicines.

Pritchard occupied a home in Sauchiehall St, Glasgow, with his wife, four of his five children (the eldest girl was living with her maternal grandparents), two servants and two lodgers. He also ran his medical practice from the house which was purchased by a loan from a financial institution and the rest from his mother-in-law, also secured against the property.

Despite the subvention from the lodgers, this was a very expensive household to run and Pritchard was not by nature or inclination industrious. He was overdrawn in two banks, but not alarmingly so. His wife Mary Jane was the daughter of a prosperous retired silk merchant from Edinburgh and her mother had already loaned money to the doctor and was fond of him, so if financial matters got out of hand, there was a safety net.

There was one more apparent complication in the doctor's life. He had seduced a young servant girl Mary McLeod who was only fifteen when she came to the household. He continued to have sexual relations with her and when she became pregnant secured an abortion.

This, it seems, was not the first affair he'd had with a servant girl. In 1863 there was a fire in the bedroom of a young servant girl in the Pritchards' former house in Berkeley Terrace, Glasgow, which burnt the girl in her bed. The likelihood is that she was unconscious, drugged or already dead. The case was looked into but no charges were brought. Pritchard collected a large insurance payout.

In the case of Mary McLeod, one day his wife walked into a bedroom and caught her husband kissing the young maid. Mary went to her mistress afterwards and said she wanted to leave but Mrs Pritchard said she would deal with her husband who she described as "a nasty, dirty man". Whatever the implications, the matter did not become a major issue. In the ordinary course of events such a thing would have caused big conflict. But this was not the outcome. Life in the Pritchard household went on as normal until Mrs Pritchard became ill.

The first manifestation of illness was in October of 1864. The lodgers, two young medical students came in November and at the end of the month Mrs Pritchard went to Edinburgh to visit her relatives and her eldest child. During that time her health improved and continued that way for two weeks after she returned to Glasgow on the 22nd of December.

During the course of her illness, which worsened on 1st February 1865, the repeated symptoms of which were vomiting within a short time after eating, which her husband put down to a gastric fever, she was visited by three other doctors, the first of which was her second cousin who was retired, Dr Cowan, who came from Edinburgh on the invitation of Pritchard. He diagnosed irritation of the stomach and prescribed a mustard poultice and small quantities of champagne and ice.

He stayed the night and, the following morning, finding her better than he expected he returned to Edinburgh. But he was worried enough to contact her mother Mrs Taylor in the same city and recommend that she should go and help nurse her daughter.

But the vomiting accompanied by spasms continued and by her request a Dr Gairdner was called. Her symptoms puzzled him and he got the impression that the patient was intoxicated. He recommended that she be given no medicine and no stimulants and outlined a simple and bland dietary regime. He also was worried about her condition and on the 9th of February wrote to the patient's brother whom he knew well, fellow professional Dr Michael Taylor.

He recommended that Mrs Pritchard be moved to her brother's house and under his care. When Dr Taylor contacted Pritchard he agreed but said that his wife was not fit to travel. The following day Mrs Taylor arrived to nurse her ailing daughter and moved into the same bedroom. Three days later the patient asked for tapioca and it was sent out for and cooked. Mrs Taylor ate some and immediately got sick, remarking with untutored significance that she must be suffering from the same illness as her daughter.

The mother-in-law was a fine, strong attractive woman whose fresh looks belied her seventy-one years. She did suffer from neuralgia, a complaint that she dealt with by taking an opium-based medicine which she bought in a bottle regularly, nothing unusual for the time. She, however, took it in a large but not dangerous quantity, to which she had become immune.

On the 24th of February, Mrs Taylor told a servant who had recently left the house but called back regularly to see the children, that she was very worried about her daughter's condition. She spent the day in the sickroom and went down to tea with Dr Pritchard and the family at seven o'clock. She then wrote some letters and went back up to her daughter's room. A few minutes later the bell rang insistently and when the servants entered the room the old lady was sitting on a chair in a very distressed state and trying to get sick.

Her head then slumped on her chest and she fell unconscious. Dr Pritchard, having been called, sent out for a local doctor who lived quite near. Shortly after ten o'clock Dr Patterson came and was told in the hall by Pritchard that Mrs Taylor had been seized by a fit and "was in the habit of taking a drop", adding that his wife was suffering from gastric fever.

When Dr Patterson entered the room, the stricken woman had been moved to the bed and he immediately realised that she was dying and seemed to be under the influence of a powerful narcotic. He was told by Pritchard that she was in the habit of taking Battley's Solution and probably had taken a good swig of it.

The visiting doctor observed Mrs Pritchard in a state of agitation and distress and it struck him as he would later relate that she was suffering from the effects of poisoning. However, if that was his opinion he neither spoke to the patient or questioned her husband, an omission, if his word was to be accepted, which would cause him much trouble. He left and was called again sometime after midnight but declined to return on the basis that there was nothing he could do.

Just after one o'clock on the morning of 25th of February Mrs Taylor died. Her body was brought back to Edinburgh and buried in the Grange cemetery. Some time afterwards Dr Patterson was visited by the dead woman's husband, Michael Taylor, who said that he had been sent by Dr Pritchard to get a death certificate. Dr Patterson declined.

When the registrar sent him a form to be filled, he also wrote back with a refusal.

Pritchard signed the certificate giving the primary cause of death as paralysis and the secondary apoplexy, duration of the illness – one hour. An example of his flawed medical knowledge – if anything it should have been the other way round with paralysis as the secondary cause.

His wife's ghastly illness continued and worsened during the first two weeks of March. Her husband regularly wrote to her relatives giving accounts of her progress, or lack of it. What he hoped to achieve by this was hard to say, it certainly was not calculated to provide comfort for them. Dr Pritchard was not in the business of giving comfort.

On the 13th of March, Mrs Pritchard had expressed a preference for some cheese. When Mary McLeod brought it to her, she asked her to taste it first. The servant did and got a burning sensation in her throat, followed by a great thirst. The following morning, the cook finding the remains in the pantry ate a small portion, became violently ill and had to go to bed.

On midday of Friday, March the 12th, Mrs Pritchard's bell rang insistently three times. Mary McLeod and Mary Patterson rushed up the stairs, followed by Dr Pritchard. Mary Patterson leaving and returning in a short space of time, found the doctor giving his wife something to drink from a porter glass. As the day went on her condition deteriorated being beset by vomiting, cramps, pain and latterly, delirium.

At 8 o'clock in the evening Dr Patterson was called again and was alarmed by the deterioration in her appearance and condition. He prescribed a sleeping draught and left. Dr Pritchard climbed into the bed beside his wife while Mary McLeod lay on the sofa. At some stage the doctor told the servant to go downstairs and ask Mary Patterson to prepare a mustard poultice. When the servants returned to the room, Mrs Pritchard was dead.

Her husband put on a performance of rambling grief and then went down to his consulting room, wrote some letters and went out to post them. It was the morning of the 18th of March. After months of suffering, the patient was free of pain and suspicion. At one stage of her delirium, she rasped that if her husband cried, he was a hypocrite and they were all hypocrites. This displayed, not a fever-induced paranoia but a very clear assessment of her position.

Later in the day an anonymous letter was delivered to the office and for the attention of the prosecutor fiscal, the man responsible for pursuing criminal prosecutions. It read:

Glasgow, March 18th, 1865.

Sir,
Dr Pritchard's mother-in-law died suddenly and unexpectedly in his house, Sauchiehall Street, Glasgow, under circumstances at least very suspicious. His wife died today also suddenly and unexpectedly. We think it right to draw your attention to the above as the proper person to take action in the matter and see justice done.

Needless to say, the letter was taken seriously, despite its anonymity. It was clear that the sender from the tone of the letter was not a crank and had some knowledge of the events, and the wording was one of an educated person without a hint of over-statement.

There was much speculation later as to the identity of the author and the most intense speculation put it at the hand of Dr Patterson who denied that he'd written it. Considering the fact that he felt that Mrs Pritchard was suffering from poisoning, the speculation might not have been too wide of the mark.

On Monday the 20th of March, Dr Pritchard certified the cause of his wife's death as gastric fever, the duration stated was two months. He accompanied the body to Edinburgh with a view to interment beside that of her recently deceased mother in the Grange cemetery. The coffin was taken to Mr Taylor's house where at Pritchard's request it was opened for viewing for the relatives and servants and during which he kissed the corpse on the lips.

He returned to Glasgow, intending to come back for the funeral which was fixed for Thursday. As soon as he stepped off the train in Queen's station he was arrested by Superintendent McCall on suspicion of having caused his wife's death. As was remarked later: "At last the light was about to be let in upon the dark secrets of the house in Sauchiehall Street."

McCall and his team then did a thorough search of the house and removed a large number of items including the bedclothes and nightdresses worn by Mrs Pritchard at the time immediately preceding her death. A post mortem on the body was conducted by doctors Maclagen and Littlejohn on the 21st of March and they could find nothing to confirm a natural death. Portions of the organs were removed for chemical analysis.

Examination of the books of the local chemist at which Pritchard had an account revealed the purchases of tartarised antimony, aconite and other poisons in quantities that far exceeded the needs of a normal medical practice. The arrest and the progress of the investigation which received widespread newspaper coverage, with leaked fact liberally sprinkled with sensational theories and wild speculation aroused huge public interest in the case.

The prisoner was reported as preserving a calm exterior and expressed confident hopes that he would be proved innocent. The body of his wife was interred in the Grange Cemetery on the 22nd of March. At that juncture neither of his sets of relations believed that Dr Pritchard was guilty. They like the general public or the press or indeed the investigating team could not conceive of a motive for such a crass and brutal act.

But the tide would change after 28th March when the results of chemical analysis revealed the presence of antimony in the organs of the body and the prisoner was committed for trial. Simultaneously, a warrant was obtained by McCall for the exhumation of Mrs Taylor's body and the doctors again found no evidence of a natural death and the chemical results again turned up antimony. On the 21st of April, Dr Pritchard was charged with the death of his mother-in-law.

The press were obsessed with this seeming gentleman and professional who was in essence being accused of being a monster. It almost beggared belief and reporters looked for any, the slightest, sign of the merciless villain who hid behind the handsome, sophisticated countenance with fulsome beard and receding hair. They all agreed that at the preliminary hearings he retained his self-possession and was extraordinarily calm for a man who if things went against him would be facing the scaffold.

But perhaps this was just part of the vanity of the man, who did not want to let the mask slip. That he took pride in his appearance was never in doubt even in the grim surroundings of a Victorian prison. It was reported that he was a little put out that he was not favoured with a supply of pomatum for the trimming of his hair and beard just days after his incarceration. He had always been one out to impress, but to indulge such a triviality in the position he found himself, tells its own tale of denial.

On the 31st of May, the indictment was served on him and stated that he would stand trial on the morning of Monday, 3rd July at The High Court of Justiciary in the criminal court at Edinburgh. Perhaps that served to concentrate his mind on other than matters of appearance, but if it did, it was not manifest. Now he would be subject to the closest examination, not only of the law but also the press who would be at the closest quarter to observe the man and satisfy the huge public appetite for the case.

Every curl of his lip, lift of an eyebrow, change in expression, movement of a hand, veritable twitch, concentration on the proceedings of it would be recorded for the present audience and indeed posterity. Everyone present in court on the opening day was in no doubt that these proceedings would find a prominent place in the annals of crime and that view was quite on the mark. What had happened, was happening and going to happen was without a hint of exaggeration sensational.

The trial opened in the court which was packed to capacity. The countenance chroniclers described his demeanour as cool: "The impression is of mildness, approaching perhaps to effeminacy; he seemed cool and collected." But as the prosecuting counsel lifted the lid on his dark side, there was a change noted in the prisoner's calm exterior. This was observed most notably during the evidence of the servant Mary McLeod, the subject of his illicit passion.

"With the anxiety which had now evidently taken hold of him, a certain vulpine look might be detected, as he keenly fixed his eyes upon the girl's countenance, when under skilful, but gentle questioning for the Crown and of the presiding judge she rent aside the curtain which had hitherto veiled the inner life of that apparently happy home. Throughout the greater part of her protracted examination, a change came over the seducer's features. The mild gentlemanly expression now disappeared, and at times one could almost fancy that traces of malignity could be seen blended with his keen and steady gaze."

Such reporting, compelling it has to be said, was much based on imagination and to satisfy the insatiable hunger of the readers for details other than the simple progress of the trial and of course in a more modern age would be deemed highly prejudicial and lead to contempt proceedings at the very least. The Victorian newspapers operated under no such restraint.

It can be seen from the language of such reporting the inbuilt clues to its status – "one could almost fancy" does not say it is so. "A certain vulpine look might be detected." It might well or equally might not, depending on the point of view of the observer and profession.

Again, when his two children were put in the dock by his defence counsel to affirm the good relationship of the prisoner with their mother, he apparently succumbed to emotion.

"What had the appearance of genuine tears trickled down his cheek. This was the one vulnerable spot in the villain's breast, and the scene altogether was such as none who witnessed would soon forget."

The case itself progressed along expected lines under the skilful legal baton of the Solicitor General. The medical evidence of poisoning was overwhelming and largely left unchallenged by the defence. While it could not be proved that Pritchard administered the poison, the paper trail to the chemist where he purchased the poison and the means and opportunity and the presence of the same poison in the bodies left little room for reasonable doubt about guilt.

The missing link from the chain of evidence was the absence of motive. Why did Dr Pritchard murder his wife?

It would be reasonable to suggest that his mother-in-law had to be got rid of because she was in the way of his main plan. The financial motive, a life rent interest to the extent of two-thirds of a sum of £2,500 in her will would not be a credible incentive, given the risk. As far as his affair with Mary McLeod went, despite a weak promise to marry her if his wife died, there was absolutely no advantage in it to Pritchard, in fact the opposite, and given his track record, he was only using her.

Mrs Taylor was sleeping in the same room as her daughter and looking after her every hour of the day. As long as she was in that position there was an obstacle, apparently in his view insurmountable, of carrying out his fiendish design. There was the added danger of Mrs Taylor's suspicions being aroused about the nature of her daughter's malaise. She was a formidable woman, by all accounts.

The mystery of how, of course, was solved but not the why. Despite being a considerable and important element to be established and accounted for in a criminal trial it unusually did not interfere with the inevitable conclusion of the proceedings. The police had taken possession of a diary kept by the accused which apart from self-serving and hypocritical entries did prove important in confirming the time line of events in the murders.

There was one more mysterious aspect to the case. One that would arouse a considerable deal of controversy and debate. This was centred on the evidence of Dr Patterson who declared that he suspected that Mrs Pritchard was suffering from antimony poisoning on one of his visits and yet did nothing about it, did not consult the patient or question the husband or notify the authorities of his suspicions.

He was criticised by the defence counsel, received the censure of the Lord Justice Clerk in his charge to the jury and the unanimous condemnation of the press. Dr Patterson did defend himself in print in the form of an elaborate apologia. But in the end his evidence was very valuable for the prosecution.

The prosecution occupied three days and by midday on the fourth, the defence finished and the remainder of the day was taken up with counsel final addresses.

On the fifth and last day, Lord Justice Clerk delivered what was generally considered a brilliant summation of the case in his charge to the jury. On the conclusion of the charge at 12.45, the jury retired and returned an hour later with a guilty charge on both charges of murder. At first Pritchard displayed no emotion but then became faint and had to be given water by his guards. He regained his composure for the twenty minutes it took to record the verdict and sentence.

Lord Justice Clerk assumed the black cap and pronounced the sentence of death and the prisoner bowed to the bench and the jury. Outside the court, before being taken away he took off his hat and bowed to the crowd. That was the end of the performance. He was removed to North Prison where reality set in and he lay the following day in his cell in a form of stupor.

On his recovery he was visited regularly by a number of clergymen and took to reading the Bible. On the 19th of July he made the first of three confessions to the murders, only confessing to that of Mrs Taylor on the third. The stipulation was that they would not be made public until after the execution.

On Monday the 27th he was removed to the South Prison and the following day on the green space outside was executed by the public hangman Calcroft in front of a crowd estimated to be in the region of 100,000. It was the last public execution to take place in Scotland. Thus perished Dr Edward Pritchard at the hands of a common hangman.

The great Scottish chronicler of crime William Roughead summed up the case with his usual unequivocal style:

"No criminal career of which we have any record, exhibits a more shocking combination of wickedness, hypocrisy and blasphemy than that of a man, who leaving the deathbed of his murdered wife, methodically entered in his diary a prayer to the Holy Trinity, to welcome her whom his foul hand had, but a moment before, relentlessly done to death."

Roughead would discover sometime later that history, in murder as in all the other dark elements of human behaviour, has an unholy habit of repeating itself, astonishing this great and dedicated chronicler of killing and killers of every shade of blood-letting inclination.

The Glasgow *Evening Citizen* drew a comparison between the doctors Palmer and Pritchard. These men were both educated members of the medical profession. The poisons they made use of

140

were the same, in many respects, inasmuch as antimony was used by both, followed up by vegetable poisons of a more subtle nature – strychnine being employed by Palmer and aconite by Pritchard. The murders by these two wretches were chiefly of near relations and curiously, both destroyed their wives and apparently their wives' mothers.

The psychological peculiarities of these miscreants also admit of a parallel. They both had good professions and many of the graces that make a gentleman, generous in civil and social life and amiable and even beloved in private. Palmer's face and features indicated no ferocity, and nothing abhorrent ever appeared until direful deeds were disclosed. It was the same with Pritchard. After describing his sensitive delicate features, "almost feminine in aspect", the report went on to say: "He seems to have been beloved at home, confided in by his wife, and a witness said he was the idol of his mother-in-law. These soft manners and seeming virtues, of course disarmed their victims of all jealous fears; so much that, under the cover of good public and private reputation, Palmer and Pritchard, for a length of time, practised their diabolical arts without being suspected."

The comparison is well drawn but lacks one very important difference: motive. Palmer's was obvious and unsubtle and common in this regard – financial gain. Pritchard's eluded the investigation and the prosecution, and seemingly his confessions when he faced the retribution of society.

And in a nearby corner of the British Empire, the tide of time was moving inexorably towards the enactment of a tragedy which would in more than one circumstance merit better comparison; that would have not only excited the interest of the Glasgow *Citizen* scribe but made him contemplate the straining of credulity, before applying his pen to paper.

Chapter 8

The Cross Trial

On the 22nd of November Dr Cross's legal team appealed to the Queen's Bench at the Four Courts in Dublin before Chief Justice Lord Plunkett, sitting with Lord O'Brien of Kilfenora, to have the trial transferred to Dublin on the grounds of prejudice against their client that might arise from the trial being held in Cork. The judges heard the application favourably but the following day, when addressed by the Crown Solicitor Gregg, they ruled that the proceedings would be held in Cork.

It was said that a good trial at the Old Bailey would rival the drawing power of any successful London theatre and it could be added that a trial for a capital offence, if there was sufficient accommodation, would empty the very same theatres. High profile hearings were targeted by all classes of society, and just like the popular shows, queues formed outside the courthouses with tickets being issued for admission.

The fact that the tickets were free encouraged, as one observer remarked, sightseers and sensation-mongers who could find time for any business but their own. But, for the less casual members of the courthouse audience, the dramas being played out laid human lives bare in a manner no playwright could hope to achieve, with passion, hatred, greed, revenge, murderous thoughts and plans unmasked and subjected to forensic examination and adversarial argument.

Even though the basis of the plot was written in advance in the book of evidence, it was subjected to all forms of improvisation by the players. While the process closely matched the Aristotelian logic of establishment, conflict and resolution, the script and the plot were full of intentional and unintentional twists and turns.

The atmosphere at a murder trial would be nothing less than electric from start to finish with the shadow of the rope a permanent motif on the backdrop, the unseen black cap of the judge creating a shuddering undercurrent of tension. Upon the outcome depended the life of a human being; no phantom play on a theatre stage could match such a denouement. And that was something that, even though there might be light moments between opposing counsel and the judge, could not be forgotten.

The first act is the necessary reconstruction of all events related to the crime containing examination on behalf of prosecution and defence and cases for both. The second, the speeches on behalf of both. The third, the judge's charge and the verdict.

No backstage trickery could replicate the intensity, the hush, the frightening atmosphere that descended on a court when the jury retires to consider the verdict for a capital felony.

And no art or artifice could replicate the electric anticipation that pervaded the house when the door opened and the jury trooped back to resume their places in advance of the verdict being asked for and given. It had more than once involuntarily caused fainting, shrieking and hysterical collapse, all perhaps set up by the intense drama of the closing speeches and in particular the charge to the jury by the judge.

The dread of the third act was shared by all present, not least the prisoner. Therefore the concluding scene of the second act produced a whirlpool of emotion that sucked in on occasions the most eminent of counsel and the judge himself whose human instinct could not be wholly protected by his lofty position on the bench and his golden robes.

At a famous trial just one year before at the Old Bailey, a young woman, Adelaide Bartlett, was accused of murdering her husband by poisoning him with chloroform, the motive being her affair with a young clergyman who was taken as a witness for the prosecution. There was huge public and press interest in the case, with huge demand for tickets of admission. It seemed to be a cut and dried case.

No one was placed on trial for his or her life without some strong and compelling evidence and so defence counsel were generally from the start fighting against the odds. But those odds could be upset and overturned by a brilliant counsel performing at his best, as became obvious in this instance.

In 1875 French-born Adelaide had married the thirty-year-old wealthy grocer Thomas Edwin Bartlett. Ten years later they met the Reverend George Dyson who became her tutor and the couple's spiritual counsellor. Edwin then made Dyson executor of his will which left his entire estate to Adelaide, on condition that she didn't remarry. Adelaide formed a relationship with Dyson – with the apparent consent of her husband, to the extent of his altering his will to allow her to marry again after his death. Shortly afterwards, Edwin was taken ill and died in the presence of his wife. The doctor certified his death as being caused by an overdose of chloroform. Suspicion fell on her and when it was discovered that she had got the young minister to purchase chloroform both she and Dyson were arrested and charged with murder. She swore that she was innocent and the minister said he had no idea what purpose the chloroform was purchased for. It later did emerge that Bartlett's doctor had prescribed the chloroform at the insistence of his patient.

On the opening day the Crown entered a *nolle prosequi* against the minister, freeing him and allowing him to be used as a witness against the object of his affections. The story of her romance with him was attested by witnesses, while the medical witnesses dealt with the medical evidence. Sir Edward Clarke, a statesman and brilliant lawyer and the chief counsel for the defence, concentrated his attention on the poison experts and subjected them to a withering cross-examination.

He made a stunning closing speech, claiming his client had no motive and the victim had been already suffering from a fatal disease. Sir Edward was so impassioned that he broke down sobbing, explaining that it was due to the nervous tension induced by the six-day trial which required such an emotional release. His efforts succeeded and a Not Guilty verdict was returned.

The result of the Bartlett case must have given Dr Cross some comfort in facing his trial, due to begin on the 14th of December at the Cork Winter Assizes.

Also, throughout the 19th century the protection conferred on the accused by the laws of evidence was substantial. Not only did the law cast the burden of proof as beyond all reasonable doubt, it rigorously excluded hearsay, involuntary confession and evidence of the accused's bad character.

The rules covering indictments were both convoluted and strict. A minor or seemingly inconsequential omission or technical failure to meet the demanding requirements of the indictment could easily result in the collapse of the case. A highly significant proportion of defendants in the 18th and 19th centuries were acquitted at trial. In capital cases there was to be continual warning to the jury that a person's life was at stake.

As a judge warned the jury in a case in 1844: "If you convict while there is any rational doubt, you may commit that foulest of all enormities – murder under the colour of the law."

On the other hand there was considerably less restraint on the judge's charge to the jury. It was accepted that it was the judge's right to tell the jury his opinion of the case. Legal commentators of the day noted that it was rare for an English judge to urge for a conviction, in fact they urged more often for an acquittal, whereas in Ireland judges not infrequently had to urge for a conviction when public justice and safety demanded it. This danger to justice was exacerbated by the fact that there was no proper system of criminal appeal in place. The only one was a motion for a new trial as a remedy against judicial or jury error. But this was not generally available in criminal cases. Where a judge misdirected a jury or wrongly admitted or excluded evidence, his ruling could not be challenged without his consent. The accused was not put into the witness box, as defendants in criminal trials were not allowed to testify on oath. When this was later allowed by the Criminal Evidence

Act of 1898, it was often considered by defence counsel as too great a risk.

However, the prisoner was able to address the court after the verdict was delivered, the object of which was to enable the accused to urge a pardon, an indictment error or anything to effect respite of the judgement. If none was shown, the judge would proceed to sentence.

The royal prerogative of mercy was in the hands of the Home Secretary in Britain and the Lord Lieutenant in Ireland. If new evidence was presented in a petition, the judge would be asked to comment on it. This route was considered to be as favourable an appeal procedure as could exist at the time. But ultimately there was one inescapable fact relating to any trial for a capital offence: that the biggest stake at issue was the life of the prisoner. This fact excited the attention of the greatest writers of the century including Dostoevsky, who was in a particularly privileged position (if that is the right description) because he had been condemned to death and escaped the consequence. He had in common with many others an unequivocal opinion of the subject:

"To kill for murder is a punishment incomparably worse that the crime itself. Murder by legal sentence is immeasurably more terrible than murder by brigands. Anyone murdered by brigands whose throat is cut at night in a wood, or something of that sort, must surely hope to escape till the last minute. There have been instances when a man has still hoped for escape, running or begging for mercy after his throat was cut.

But in the other case, all that last hope, which makes dying ten times as easy, is taken away for certain. There is the sentence, and the whole awful torture lies in the fact that there is certainly no escape, and there is no torture in the world more terrible. You may lead a soldier out and set him facing the cannon in battle and fire at him and he'll still hope; but read a sentence of certain death over that same soldier, and he'll go out of his mind or burst into tears. Who can tell whether human nature is able to bear this without madness?"

It was a sentiment with which Dr Philip Henry Eustace Cross, having constantly faced death in the heat of combat would have been in agreement – if he had any doubt about the outcome. Perhaps, on the other hand, it never entered into his thoughts at that juncture, for he had made no confession and, like every accused man, would take his chances and hope that his defence counsel were capable of setting him free to continue to live without the ultimate blemish. It had happened before and why not again? A person who might resort to murder, after all, is the biggest of risk-takers.

The Castletownroche murders had attracted considerable newspaper coverage but excited much less interest than the Shandy Hall murder, more than likely because it might have been considered the aberrant and savage behaviour of a member of the lower social orders, a strata which more generally as a result of poverty, deprivation, ignorance and desperation was responsible for crime. This emanated within the privileged class, where such things were not supposed to happen and shook the foundation of belief in what that class supposedly represented: utter respectability and honour that should inspire deference and respect and not degeneracy, immorality and cold-blooded horror. It also might have raised an expectation that a member of that class might not be subject to the ordinary and accepted rigours of the law as applied to lesser mortals.

The already ventilated salacious aspect of the case, the affair between the accused and the young governess, would of course have attracted considerable attention, as well as the prospect of the revelations about life behind the previously closed doors of Shandy Hall – the lid of the life of the gentry uncovered. What might previously have been the subject of gossip would now inevitably be entered into the public domain.

Effie's Secret

There was one other matter that, although it must have been widely known at this stage, would not be allowed into the court proceedings – no doubt a source of disappointment to those who revelled in sensation. The former governess and now mistress of Shandy Hall, Evelyn Forbes Cross, was, as the trial was about to begin, in an advanced state of pregnancy. As a matter of prejudice to the accused, it was apparently excluded from evidence. The newspapers were silent on this most newsworthy matter and so must have been warned with the threat of contempt to make no mention of it before or during the trial.

She would give birth to a son on the 23rd of December and therefore it is more than likely that she conceived during the time the couple were away together in March. Obviously this put the doctor under far more pressure than the affair itself would have done. So it was a situation that he had to face up to with his wife Mary Laura still very much in his personal equation. He was an ageing man who would not have the same mental energy to work out such a dilemma, facing, as he did, not just the prospect of social destruction but also the danger of the financial destruction of his estate.

This may have provided a powerful motivation for his alleged action, but one which would not come into play in the legal arena that would be the judge of the path he had seemingly walked upon. While he occupied a cell in Cork Gaol, the object of his passion and now his wife was virtually a prisoner in his former home.

The absent young woman would, like a ghost, cast her presence on proceedings in an unrelenting manner. She might not have been in the body of the court, but she was always in the mind and imagination of those present as every procedural cut was made to her reputation without the possibility of reply on her behalf. For the former Effie Skinner, behind the closed windows of Shandy Hall, hell itself could not have offered such torture.

It can be only imagined what was going through her mind, surrounded by servants of her former mistress, all going to give evidence in the trial about matters of which she had no knowledge. Awful might have been a way to describe her situation. She was waiting with no sense of an outcome that might give her any comfort.

The Cast Assembles

Nonetheless, despite the pregnancy being kept secret, the trial of Dr Cross would not lose its status as the case of the century in

Ireland, with reporters not just in Cork and the country but also in many parts of the world sharpening their pens and editors their minds for coverage and leaders after the outcome would become known.

The drama of reconstruction was about to begin with the resolution as yet unscripted. The cast was already chosen.

Accused:
Dr Philip Henry Eustace Cross

Judge:
Lord Justice Murphy

Prosecution Counsel:
The Attorney General Mr John Gibson QC MP;
George Wright QC; Stephen Ronan

Solicitor:
GV Gregg.

Defence Counsel:
John Atkinson QC; Richard Adams QC

Solicitor: Robert Deyos

The opposing counsel were highly qualified and brilliant advocates with glittering careers, destined to reach the height of their chosen profession. Neither the Crown nor Dr Cross could complain that they were not ably represented.

The Attorney General

John George Gibson, Irish lawyer and Conservative politician, was the youngest son of William Gibson of Merrion Square, Dublin, and Rockforest, Co Tipperary. Educated at Trinity College, he was called to the Bar at King's Inns, Dublin, in 1870. He was made an Irish QC in 1880 and third Serjeant-at-Law in 1885.

The same year he was elected MP for Liverpool Walton and appointed Solicitor General for Ireland from November 1885 to

January 1886 and Attorney General for Ireland from 1887 to 1888. He married Anna Hare in 1871 and lived at 38, Fitzwilliam Square, Dublin. Aged 41.

Defence Counsel

John Atkinson was born in Drogheda, County Louth, the eldest son of Edward Atkinson a prominent physician of Glenwilliam Castle, Co Limerick and Skea House, Enniskillen, Co Fermanagh. He was educated at Queen's College, Galway, where he excelled at science and maths, and was awarded a first class honours degree from the Faculty of Arts.

He moved into law and graduated with a first class LLB in 1865, the same year that he was called to the Bar, and was appointed a QC in 1879 at the young age of 35. He practised on the Munster Circuit and was elected Bencher of the Kings Inns in June 1885. Aged 43.

Witnesses for the Prosecution

1. Mr Colthurst, neighbour.
2. Mrs Caulfield, friend, neighbour, previous employer of Effie Skinner.
3. Capt Caulfield, neighbour.
4. Dr Godfrey, relative of the accused.
5. Miss Mervynia Jefferson, old school friend of victim.
6. Jane Leahy, servant.
7. Mary McGrath, servant.
8. Mary Buckley, servant.
9. Mary Barron, servant.
10. Hotelkeeper William Poole.
11. Beatrice Handcock, hotel bookkeeper.

12. Mary Smythe, chambermaid, hotel.

13. Arthur Johnson, hotel porter.

14. Dennis Griffin, postmaster, Dripsey.

15. Cornelius McCarthy, post messenger, Shandy Hall.

16. District Inspector Tyacke, investigating officer.

17. Sergeant Higgins.

18. Mr Short, chemist.

19. Mr Kiloh, Gouldings.

20. Mrs Isabelle Madras.

21. Dr C Yelverton Pearson, pathologist.

22. Dr Crowley.

23. William Tyndall, brother-in-law of accused.

24. Humphrey Marriott, brother of victim.

25. Mr Squires, Official, Registrar General's office.

Witness for the Defence

Henrietta Maria Cross, sister of accused.

The First Day

Thursday 15th December 1887

The *Cork Examiner* began its "minute-to-minute" account of the proceedings, as follows:

"The trial of Dr Philip Eustace Henry Cross of Shandy Hall, Dripsey, on the charge of having poisoned his wife on 2nd June last, was commenced in the City Court this morning before Lord Justice Murphy and a special jury. Owing to the great anxiety of the public to hear the details, and to get a look at the accused, it was deemed necessary by the Sheriff to regulate admission to the court by ticket.

Notwithstanding this, what between jurors, witnesses, pressmen and spectators, almost every available inch of space was fully occupied long before the proceedings commenced. A number of ladies were present.

The prisoner was brought down from the gaol in the ordinary prison van at quarter to ten o'clock and as only a few persons were outside the court at the time, the prisoner passed through the door leading to the dock cells almost unobserved. Miss Cross, a sister of the prisoner, occupied a seat in court throughout the proceedings.

The prisoner seemed none the worse of his imprisonment and when called as to plead, he answered, "Not guilty" with a firm voice.

The arrangements for admission to court were excellent and Mr Meehan, Sheriff's Officer, superintended them in the most competent manner. The same arrangements will exist throughout the trial.

Amongst the spectators in the court were: Mrs PJ Forde and Miss Forde; Mrs and Miss Gilbert; the Misses Simpson; Miss Fitzgerald; Miss White; Miss Mack; the Misses Gregg; the Misses Rogers; Mrs O'Brien (North Wall); Miss Burke; Mrs Murphy (John Street); Mrs O'Callaghan (Great Georges St); Mrs George Lamkin.

Counsel for the Crown: The Right Hon, The Attorney General, Mr John Gibson MP; Mr George Wright QC; and Mr Stephen Ronan instructed by Mr WV Gregg, Crown Solicitor.

The Counsel for the prisoner: Mr John Atkinson QC and Mr Richard Adams instructed by Mr Robert Deyos, solicitor.

The names of the gentlemen summoned on the special jury were first called over and the greater number answered. The prisoner was formally arraigned by Mr O Keefe, Clerk of the Crown and Peace.

The following jury was then sworn:

Carlton R Palmer, Lower Glanmire (foreman); Robert Thomas Alexander, Grand Parade; Joseph Milligan, 92 Patrick Street; Wm George Moore, 5 Morrisons Quay; RM Moncaster, 66 Patrick Street; David Barry, Cornmarket Street; John Hughes, Marlboro Street; Christopher Cook; John Grimes, 16 Blarney Street; Thomas Farrar, 14 Grand Parade; and Benjamin Atkins, South Terrace.

The jurors who were asked to stand by for the Crown were: Timothy Callaghan, 1 Waterview; Wm Morris, 34 Grand Parade; John Fitzgerald, 18 Union Quay; WD Harris, Adelaide Lodge; David Healy, Shandon Street; Daniel Harrington, Ballyhooly Road; William Ahearn, 19 Barrack Street and Edmund Carrol, 7 Princes Street.

Challenged for the prisoner [objected to by prisoner's legal team]: John Daly, 11 Great Georges Street; Patrick Abury, Grand Parade; John Murphy, Morrison's Island; James Murphy, Morrison's Island; J Ashlin, Lappis Quay; L Tivey, Beaumont, Blackrock; John Daly, 41 Leitrim Street."

* * *

The Attorney General's Statement

Amid the hush and the silence that falls over the court on such occasions, in which hardly a breath could be heard in the room, the Attorney General rose and proceeded to open the case for the Crown. He said that the duty evolved upon him, with the learned friend for the Crown, to state there before the jury as clearly and as simply as he could the case upon which the Crown relied, to fix upon the prisoner at the bar the responsibility for having murdered the late Mary Laura Cross, his own wife, by poison in his own house, Shandy Hall on the 2nd June last.

The circumstances of the case were painful and unusual, and if the jury were satisfied of the prisoner's guilt, he had been guilty of one of the most brutal and cowardly murders which had disgraced their common humanity. The prisoner at the bar, Surgeon Major Philip Cross, was a gentleman of means and he resided at a place called Shandy Hall, Dripsey, in the County of Cork.

He married many years ago a lady of good social position, Mary Laura Marriott, an English lady and one of a well-known family. Apparently at that time he was on active service in the army, and the Marriott family was not able to accept the alliance. But finally that girl's love for the man overcame any resistance which the father might be disposed to offer and on the 17th of August 1869, in St James's Church, Piccadilly, the prisoner at the bar became her husband and was bound to cherish and love her by the obligations he took in the church.

Shortly after, the couple went to Canada where the 53rd regiment in which the prisoner was then serving was stationed. Sometime afterwards, he left the army and set up in Shandy Hall. No settlement was made on this lady's marriage. She was about forty-six years at the time of her death. Therefore she was eight and twenty when she married the prisoner, who now was past sixty years, somewhere between sixty-three and sixty-four.

But on her father's death in the following year, 1870, her fortune, amounting to [something over] a sum of £5,000 became payable, and paid it was, he understood, into the hands of the defendant. [This seems at odds with later statements by H Marriott and Cross.] Of that marriage there were born five children, three girls and two sons. The eldest girl was about seventeen years old; her name would again be mentioned by him before he closed. Two of the girls were unfortunately not strong in their minds, and one of them at all events was the subject of epileptic attacks. Husband and wife lived in Shandy Hall in a comfortable position, having four servants in their employment, received and visited by the surrounding gentry up to the time of this unfortunate lady's death on the 2nd June, 1887.

The jury would see when the evidence was before them that the love the prisoner had for his wife cooled into indifference and that indifference, certainly, in the beginning of the year 1887, under an influence of which they would not find it hard to estimate the force, into dislike and a willingness to be free from a burden – a hated and intolerable burden.

There lived almost two miles from Shandy Hall, a gentleman and lady by the name of Mr and Mrs Caulfield and they had in their employment in the year 1886 a lady as a governess, Miss Skinner. That lady left Mr and Mrs Caulfield's employment on 29th October 1886, and as they would be able to collect from the evidence she went from Mrs Caulfield's house to the house of Surgeon-Major Cross of which she remained an inmate for three months.

The exact cause she left the house was not distinctly stated in evidence, but it appeared that she was with the Crosses and that he would infer in the capacity of governess for three months and she left for Scotland in the month of January. In January, later, Miss Skinner went to the County of Carlow to take up a new engagement as governess.

He thought that the most convenient way of dealing with the case would be to follow accurately the order of time and they, the jury, would see how important it was to hear the different period of times in their minds in estimating the overwhelming force of the case against the prisoner.

Miss Skinner was lost sight of until 29th March when they found her coming to the London and North Western Hotel on the North Wall, Dublin, in company with the prisoner and where they occupied the same bedroom as a married couple. Did that young lady come up that day from the County Carlow to throw herself at the defendant's head? Was it the reckless impulse of a young and foolish girl that brought her accidentally to town? It would appear from the evidence that would be laid before them that during Miss Skinner's stay under the prisoner's roof there had been a marked change for the worse in the demeanour of the prisoner towards his wife. He threatened her, cursed her and wrote letters after Miss Skinner left his house.

These letters he used to deliver himself to the messenger who carried the letter bag to the post and on one occasion, the prisoner went to Mr Griffin the postmaster at Dripsey to get a letter which in the ordinary course of things would have been sent to his own residence. Dr Cross kept a diary, which would be produced, under lock and key and in it was an entry under the head of the 28th of March: "Started for Punchestown Races."

And the race he was going on was a race with Miss Skinner, who came as a married woman to spend the evening with him at the North Wall hotel in Dublin. It was for the jury to say this guilty and most wicked intrigue had not commenced actually in the prisoner's own house under the roof which sheltered his weak and ailing wife.

On the following morning, they left the hotel and nothing more of them was known until the 21st April when they appeared again at the same hotel and asked to have the same bedroom they had occupied on the former occasion. The interval corresponded with the time usually allowed by our custom and observances for what is called honeymoon.

On the first occasion, no name was given. On the 21st April the bedroom was occupied by a 'Mr Osborne". They [the jury] would have little doubt that the prisoner must have made arrangements as to how Miss Skinner would be disposed, for on the 22nd April he went home after his tour and lived at Shandy Hall with his wife and family, going through the outward appearances of an ordinary married man up to his wife's death on the 2nd of June.

Mrs Cross was delicate, but in the month of April, when the first chapter of this scandalous intrigue was closing, they would be able to prove by the evidence of Mr Bowen Colthurst that she was apparently able to walk about and was not suffering from any acute form of malady. Mr Bowen Colthurst lived some five miles away, and the distance of his residence would be a matter they would have to take into their consideration in a few moments. In the month of April, he happened to be not far from Shandy Hall, and he saw a lady in a field, a short distance away, who came towards him. It was Mrs Cross and they had an interview, but he did not observe any signs of weakness or anything that would lead him to believe she had only a short time to live.

On the 29th of April, there came to her house an old school friend to spend a long visit with her, a lady whose evidence in the case would be of enormous value. A Miss Jefferson on the 29th April became an inmate of the house. She was wanted to stay until the middle of August; she said she could only stay until the middle of June. But she was present during the last fatal illness of her old school friend and it was much upon the circumstance of her presence that they [the jury] would be able to find some very valuable evidence in the case. The lady kept a diary, and of course the servants in the house would not be able to give the same accurate statement of different periods of time, so he would proceed shortly to lay that diary before them. On the 8th May, Mrs

Cross was at church; on the 9th she was out visiting and the 10th of May was the first day on which she was attacked with the symptoms of the fatal illness under which she was to succumb in three weeks.

Vomiting, diarrhoea and thirst – the fatal symptoms of arsenical poisoning – were present on that day. On the 11th she was still ill in bed suffering from the same symptoms. The next entry was the 13th and the same observations were made. The 14th was the next entry and Miss Jefferson was able to fix accurately the incidents of that day.

On the 14th Mrs Cross was not that well; and on the 17th she was not well. On the 18th it would appear, by this entry, that the effects of the preliminary dose were wearing away. The first dose may have only been a tentative experiment which a person might rely upon afterwards, as the results of natural infirmity and natural disease.

On the 18th, Mary Cross was much better, so that she was able to get up and walk halfway to Coachford and on Thursday, Ascension Day, she was at church. And on the 20th May she again was attacked by the same symptoms – these symptoms from which she was never able to shake herself free. On the 21st she was ill in bed – and what he was now telling the jury would be important for them to carry into their box when they would decide the enormous issue in this case, and it would be for them to say whether the prisoner was not operating on his wife.

And not by one large fatal dose of poison – but by small doses, which in her enfeebled organisation might extinguish the flickering sparks of life that would be left. On the 22nd, she was a little better, and she crept into the garden to breathe in the fresh air and to hear the birds sing for the last time. She never again went out of the house until she went out as an unhonoured and neglected corpse under circumstances which surpassed belief.

On the 23rd she was now coming to the crisis of her fate – after her little walk in the garden, she was again in bed and never again was able to rise from it. On the 24th of May the unfortunate lady was very ill, the same symptoms presenting themselves.

There was living in the next house to Dr Cross, a relative of his own called Dr Godfrey. Dr Godfrey had married Dr Cross's aunt and had attended Mary Laura Cross upon previous occasions. The last preceding occasion on which he had seen Mrs Cross was two months before.

On this occasion, Dr Cross asked his relative Dr Godfrey to see his wife. He did not say to attend her for a fatal or critical illness and, on Dr Godfrey's asking what was the matter with her, he said diarrhoea.

Dr Godfrey went to see the unhappy lady. He saw her in her own bedroom, Dr Cross being present during the interview. She then had a wet cloth on her forehead – he supposed to cool her aching brain – and Dr Godfrey thought she was suffering from a bilious attack. On going away he told Dr Cross he ought to give his wife some doses of calomel – treating the case as one of simple character, not a case of fatal malady and not as he [Cross] would inform them, a case of typhoid fever.

Away the doctor went and, although living next door, in the hours of the woman's death agony (prolonged for some days), he was never asked to visit her again. The last time and the first time Mrs Cross was seen by a doctor was on the 24th of May. And on that occasion the prisoner represented her as suffering from diarrhoea, but he never told his relative again that it was necessary for him to give his professional assistance in the death struggle of the poor woman.

It seemed as if there was a special type of providence in this case, because they were able to fix days and facts by the coming of the school friend, Miss Jefferson, to Shandy Hall – dates and facts that would be the most decisive evidence against the prisoner.

On the 25th, Mr and Mrs Caulfield visited the house, having heard, he supposed, of Mrs Cross's illness. Mrs Caulfield went upstairs and saw Mrs Cross. She was very weak. There was a cup of milk beside her on the table. And it would appear that she was unable to take solid food. She was seen by another friend Miss Kirchoffer, and also by the Rev Mr Hayes, her clergyman. These three persons saw her then, for the last time, and they would describe the symptoms, because the poor woman was then, no doubt, in a very critical state.

On the 26th, Miss Jefferson described her as being in a very dangerous position and on the 27th symptoms showed themselves which were the well-known marks of gradual or chronic arsenical poisoning; her eyes became inflamed, she could neither read nor write, and her letters had to be written for her, as would be proved by Miss Jefferson.

There could be no doubt in the mind of an ordinary husband, who had a heart, that this poor creature in her bed, racked with constant vomiting and diarrhoea, was in a state that demanded all the attention of her most devoted friends. On the 29th, Sunday, Miss Jefferson had a conversation with Dr Cross on the subject of her leaving the house. She was willing to stop with the dying lady, though the time of her visit was up, but Dr Cross said that he himself would look after his wife, and under those circumstances, Miss Jefferson arranged to go on the Thursday morning, 2nd June.

On the 30th, Monday, Mrs Caulfield called. At this time there could be no doubt that the poor woman was in a dying state, but Dr Cross told Mrs Caulfield that his wife was pretty well. The Rev Mr Hayes called on the same day, he was the clergyman of her own religion, and in the woman's state it would be decent and right for her to receive a visit from her pastor. He was told that Mrs Cross would be better left quiet.

Rev Mr Hayes would have called the following day, the 31st, when he returned from Cork, but when he got to his house he found Miss Jefferson and Miss Cross were there before him. Miss Cross said something to him and he did not go to visit Mrs Cross. A long round of visits was paid by Miss Cross and Miss Jefferson on this day, and on the following day visiting still went on. There was nothing to convey to the outer world that Shandy Hall had within it the wife of Surgeon Major Cross in her death agony. On that day, Miss Kirchoffer came to Shandy Hall to pay a visit and was told by Dr Cross that his wife was as bad as could be and that it was typhoid fever she was suffering from, though Miss Kirchoffer would tell them she never observed any symptoms of that disorder.

The learned counsel said he now came to the time, every moment of which must be scanned by the jury. The 1st of June was the day preceding Mrs Cross's death. When she died, Counsel could not say, for she died away from the presence of any living being except the prisoner. On the 1st of June, the day being Wednesday, Miss Jefferson who was going away the following morning, went out for a drive in the direction of Ryecourt with Miss Cross.

There were in the house, besides the children, Dr Cross and his dying wife, Miss Cross his sister, Miss Jefferson and four servants. First there was Jane Leahy the cook, there was the kitchen maid Mary Buckley, the housemaid Mary McGrath and the parlour maid Mary Barron. During her illness, it would appear, she was unable to take solid food. The milk and corn flour – two articles of nourishment they would have to bear in mind when he [the AG] was giving scientific evidence – the milk, corn flour and chicken broth were prepared by the cook and used to be brought to her by Dr Cross sometimes and sometimes by his sister and the medicine, at all events, the administration of it, whether it was chlorodyne or any other remedy that be administered, were given under the control and disposition of her medical gentleman, Dr Cross.

This poor woman's sufferings were witnessed to a large extent by those servants and it would be described to them [the jury] how she used to vomit – this poor, weak, fragile body. Mary Buckley saw her and she seemed to be somewhat better. She had no nourishment taken. There was no woman in her room. Dr Cross slept in the same apartment, occupied a bed in the same room with his dying wife. Her night watches were not attended by the loving kindness of a woman. Her husband took the responsibility for her medical treatment upon himself. Between five o'clock and six o'clock that evening she was seen by Mary Barron and during the time she was near her she appeared to have done nothing but retch and vomit. When her body was examined on the 21st July, there were no particles of solid food in her stomach or excreta in the lower bowels.

Miss Cross had taken Miss Jefferson out for a drive. Miss Jefferson saw Mrs Cross on her return and Miss Jefferson saw her for the last time sometime about ten o'clock that night.

She [Mrs Cross] awakened Mary Buckley that night; she heard

for four minutes her mistress's screams. She had never heard her scream before. She went off to sleep again, having no doubt the husband would call her if there was any necessity for a woman's help – they would have been called from their repose.

The following morning – the girls used to get up between six and seven o'clock – the master called them: "Girls, get up, the mistress is gone since one o'clock last night." Why not call up Miss Jefferson, the old school friend, those women servants, his sister, why not give an explanation to those women of the four minutes of screaming that awakened Mary Buckley at that hour of the night?

The cook came late in the morning when the master was at his breakfast and why not give an explanation to his own retainer Jane Leahy? When she remarked about the sad end of her mistress to the prisoner, she got no answer, any more than she was speaking to a stick or stone. Miss Jefferson heard the news that morning and saw the body of her friend, lying on the bed, not stretched out in the last rites which are given to the dead, but lying across the bed. She heard nothing.

She breakfasted with Dr Cross that morning and did not see Dr Cross again until the 14th June, when for the first time he gave her an explanation of how her friend, in this strange, shocking manner had died in the middle of the night, without a friend near her.

Dr Cross, the moment she had died, proceeded to register her death. It was necessary to get a medical certificate, as to the cause of death. And had an independent doctor been in attendance upon this lady, having regard to the mysterious circumstances attending her departure, he would have insisted upon an inquest having been held. However, there was no inquest held under his [Dr Cross's] direction.

Dr Cross was the only medical man in attendance upon his unfortunate wife, and he gave the necessary medical certificate, in which he stated the cause of death was typhoid fever. Every line of that certificate was written by Dr Cross in person and the cause of death had been changed from diarrhoea which was the cause he told his uncle.

How or when she died it was impossible to explain except from Mary Buckley and a statement in the diary [of Dr Cross] in which it was written that she died on the morning of the 2nd of June at one o'clock and was buried on Saturday 4th of June. None of the servants were at her funeral and nothing was known of it, except what was disclosed in the statement of the kitchen maid, Mary Buckley, who said that she saw through the window three persons: Dr Cross, whom the Crown said was the murderer, Griffin, a publican, and the man who drove the hearse.

Thus, the unhappy lady who died in the presence of her husband was taken away to her last resting place without any apparent public intimation, without any decent support of sorrowing friends.

The doctor, during those days, was not idle with his pen. On the 29th he wrote a letter to his wife's brother Humphrey Marriott who lived in England and who received the letter a few days before his sister's death.

The next letter was written on the day of Mary Laura Cross's death and in this he mentioned his sorrow for the manner in which some of the children had taken the death of their mother. He [the AG] should say it was something for the father, regretting the absence of tears from his children. But it would be for the jury to say whether the prisoner himself shed a tear and whether there was a decent particle of regret for this poor woman and whether there was nothing but a hideous, cowardly and disgraceful hypocrisy in the whole letter.

Continuing the reading of the letter, he said that the prisoner wrote that he grieved that his daughters – Bess and Etta – did not realise the situation, and as for the others, the children at school, he did not know how to break it to them. He had written, informing of them of their mother's illness and thought he should run across and tell them of her death. God help those children. He [the AG] did not think there was one in court, in deciding that case, who could forget the most painful incident in the whole of the miserable tragedy: the disgrace and sorrow that should hang over those innocent beings.

On the day of the funeral, the 4th of June, he wrote another letter to his brother-in-law, commenting, "My dear Marriott" and stating that the last rites were duly carried out that morning in Magourney graveyard, the family vault at Carrigrohane being filled and he added that he should lie, side by side in Magourney with her, whom he had loved. He also wrote that he would go over the next week and see the children.

Did he go with that object? He thought none of them would have a doubt when he stated it was not to comfort his poor children at the loss of their mother he went to England but to renew his intimacy with his paramour and make her mistress of Shandy Hall in the place of his wife.

In reply to a communication from Mr Humphrey Marriott, Dr Cross wrote on the 4th of June stating that Mrs Cross was buried at 6 a.m. Now, he had certified in his medical certificate that his wife had died from typhoid fever, but in his letter he had come on a new account and wrote: "In fact spasm of the heart, as you may see was the immediate cause of death." Spasm of the heart might account for the screams heard by the girl Buckley during the night. Continuing, he referred to the frequent attacks she had and said Henrietta Cross and himself had agreed that the last attack she had received at the breakfast table was the worst and they only kept her alive by administering brandy, mustard and ammonia. He also wrote that "Jim and Gussie" [Mary Laura's younger sister Augusta] had broken the news to his son Harry who had written to him stating that as Bob, his brother, was ill, he had not told him. And he concluded the letter by again stating that Bess and Etta did not seem to realise their situation.

He then read the following letter, which he said had but lately come into their possession. It was to a Mr Tyndall [William, husband of Augusta, an East India Merchant born in Ireland] and ran as follows:

Dear Mr Tyndall – you will be very sorry to hear that poor Laura passed away at 1 a.m. Typhoid fever debilitated the poor dear, and I wonder how she ever lasted so long. Pray break this to her pet Gussie. It will be hard for me to do the same to those little ones at school.
P.H.E.

PS Owing to Sunday being the Papist day, I am sorry I must bury her on Saturday.

There were two things about those letters which would strike the gentlemen of the jury – one was the letter gave no statement as to the duration of the illness, or as to the symptoms she was suffering from, a disorder that was rife in the neighbourhood!

For a fortnight she had been racked by constant vomiting and the only medical attendant she had was the prisoner at the bar and again they would be struck by the fact that those letters were bound up in expressions of affection for the poor woman who lay in her grave and he expressed his intention to go to England and break the news of the mother's loss to the little ones at school.

On the 6th of June the prisoner wrote a postcard to a gentleman named Woodley to come to lunch with him. He told that gentleman that his wife died of fever or disease of the heart – angina pectoris – of which, he supposed they the jury would hear a good deal from his learned friends, the counsel for the prisoner. Not very much bore on that interview and now that he had read those letters, he would again refer to the diary kept by the prisoner. The last neighbour or acquaintance whom the prisoner apparently saw, as far as the Crown case went, was on Monday the 6th.

On the following Wednesday or Thursday he left Shandy Hall to go to England. He should ask them, the jury, to bear in mind the following entries which were made by the prisoner in the diary.

On the 2nd he wrote: *"Mary Laura Cross departed this life. May she go to Heaven is my prayer. Buried on the 4th."*

On the 5th, he wrote: *"James Cross, funeral and Ac."* Which he [the AG] supposed was the name of the undertaker and from that entry it appeared that the funeral was disposed of for the modest sum of five guineas.

Next entry was: *"R and H Hall, five tons of maize, £3 10s."*

And after that on the 9th: *"Started for London this Thursday."*

What he did after he got to London, he could not state but there was found on Dr Cross, when he was arrested, a purse which had got some entries in it – some pencil jottings, amongst others, some referring to the North Western Hotel; there was, in that purse, a bill of his for the 10th, 11th, 12th and 13th of June and at Euston where he had stayed.

He went from his own home, darkened by the sorrow of a recent dead wife. There was a bill of his in that purse for the dates he had mentioned, to which there was no name but it was a bill for two persons. That wretched man, who had cohabited with that woman for three weeks, as on a kind of a honeymoon, had, in the presence of his dying wife, determined to make her his bride, but before he could raise her to that position of honour, he could not spare her from his lust, for even a few moments preceding his wedding.

The next time the prisoner was seen was the 14th June when he visited Miss Jefferson in Piccadilly, where she was living with her mother. He paid her a visit of condolence as one who had been in the house on a very painful occasion and for the first time said how his wife had died. She had, he said, woken up in pain. She then dozed off and died straight away.

Well, the next thing they had was an entry in his diary, stating that he married Miss Skinner in St James's Church, Piccadilly, on the 17th of June, and whom he announced to the world a fitting representative for the place of the woman who had gone. On the 17th August 1869, in that same church he had led to the altar on the selfsame day of the month of June, a woman who had put herself in his power.

On the 19th of June, he went again to the North Western Hotel with [the new] Mrs Cross and remained there until the 21st and resided there not under the name of Philip Henry Eustace Cross but under the name of Mr Onslow. He went away on the 21st but his new wife did not accompany him; on the 22nd he paid a visit to the Caulfields.

That morning Mrs Caulfield had received a letter from Miss Skinner's mother in Germany and when Dr Cross came in she said to him, "How was Mrs Cross?" He asked what she meant and she replied: "Miss Skinner, that was." He began to laugh and said that was a good joke and would like to know who put it in circulation.

On the 21st they both left the North Western Hotel, but only Dr Cross went to Cork. On the 24th they both arrived there again and it was plain that she must have met the prisoner on the way up. That was on Friday, and on the following Sunday a telegram was sent to Coachford by the prisoner, but as the telegram office was shut, it could not be despatched and was sent back to the accused.

On the 26th they both went down to the country, and then for the first time, the servants at Shandy Hall learnt that they had a new mistress.

It was not likely that a man in the prisoner's social position would be suspected of the crime of murder, and the murder, above all, of his own wife. But the police having got some information, the body was exhumed on the 21st of July and Dr Cross was later arrested by an officer named Tyacke. He said, when arrested, told the charge and cautioned: "My God, my God, to think that a man at my time of life should commit murder. There is a God above who will see the villainy of this."

He asked might he talk to his sister but he was told not. Subsequently a Sergeant Higgins was placed in charge of the accused and on the 1st of August, notwithstanding the officer's prohibition, the prisoner did converse with his sister. Dr Cross asked had she seen the two bottles about the length of his finger with some white powder. She said, yes and she had destroyed them with some other things.

When such a conversation passed to the defiance of the officer's prohibition, it was evident that both the prisoner and his sister attached considerable importance to it and there must be a strong motive to cause him to violate injunctions of the constabulary officer.

Before closing with the evidence of the analyst, there was one matter he wished to state. On the 2nd of September 1886, Dr Cross had bought a pound of white arsenic at Gouldings in Cork, for the purpose, so he said, of sheep dipping. But whether it was with that arsenic this crime was accomplished, there could be no man in the defendant's position would have any difficulty in arming himself with any amount of this poison, necessary to accomplish this hideous crime.

On the 21st July, seven days before the arrest, the body of Mrs Cross was exhumed in the presence of Dr Crowley, the dispensary doctor who assisted in verifying the identity of the deceased and also in the examination. She was wrapped up in a white shroud, a flannel swathe was around the abdomen, a white handkerchief under the jaw and blue stockings on her feet and legs.

She was straightened for the coffin and apparelled in her death garment by Mary McGrath, Mary Barron and the prisoner and certainly the funeral habiliments hardly corresponded with the melancholy raiment that was put around a lady in her coffin – the white shroud, the bandage of flannel and blue stockings.

The face appeared drawn and from the length of time the body was in the grave there was an appearance of slime and exudation coming from the nostrils. The analyst's examination disclosed symptoms of arsenical poisoning. The lower part of the gullet leading into the stomach was inflamed and upbraided and Dr Pearson would give the details. No food was found in the stomach, but slimy, yellow bile. There were white patches in the gullet and white patches studded the liver. From the appearance of the body, Dr Pearson would tell the jury that there must either have been no food administered before death or violent vomiting or purging would get rid of the food. The doctor would also tell that there was no appearance of heart disease or of typhoid fever.

The doctor found small particles of a white substance over the mucous lining membrane. He heated them in a subliming cell and they yielded a small quantity of arsenic. He subjected the others to the Reinsch process and they also yielded crystals of arsenic. Dr Pearson then divided the stomach and portions of the intestines into two portions.

One portion he subjected to Marsh's process and he obtained arsenic. The doctor also proceeded to make an independent inquiry as to whether some other poison had been applied in order to hasten death and he got a small quantity of strychnine. He examined the particles on the stomach by Reinsch's process and found they contained arsenic. He took the liver, the right kidney and spleen and subjected them to an independent process of analysis.

The total quantity of arsenic found by the doctor was 3.2 grains; 1.74 grains was found in the organs other than the liver. Dr Pearson had found traces of strychnine, which was a poison that is very readily absorbed; a very small quantity was a killing dose. And it had often happened that when a man had been poisoned by strychnine and that the body was subjected to tests, practically an infinitesimal trace only was found in the tissues.

The doctor in order to find whether an appreciable quantity of the poison had been employed for the purpose of finishing off this unfortunate woman, proceeded to make a second examination on the 23rd of August. He found a small quantity of strychnine. Dr Pearson would tell the jury that strychnine is a non-cumulative poison – it does not stay in the body and if the patient survives the dose, all traces of poison have disappeared in a fortnight.

The purging and vomiting of Mrs Cross would account for the disappearance of large quantities of poison [the arsenic], if it had been administered. From the quantity of poison found in the liver, the poison must have been administered two or three days before death. The poison, producing vomiting, was what is described as mineral irritant poison; it was entirely different from the poison of strychnine and the symptoms which were produced by this mineral irritant poison were: vomiting, purging, soreness of the eyes and irritation of the lower part of the stomach.

This woman had all the symptoms which were found in arsenical poisoning, or at least the symptoms which most provoke attention. Apparently, the last day of her life was spent in miserable and torturing retching, unable to take solid food and every attempt was made to give her nourishment, having the effect of exciting contraction of the stomach, which must have distracted the unfortunate creature until she was within the jaws of death.

The other poison, strychnine, was not a matter they would expect to find in the body of a woman who had been treated in the ordinary way. There was an appreciable quantity of that type of poison found in her but whether it was used as the doctor thought, to expedite her departure, it would be for the jury to say.

In conclusion, the Attorney General said:

"It may be that the doctor employed this strychnine, but whether that be so or not, the question for your determination is to decide, calmly, firmly and with a sense of responsibility. Your duty in this case is to decide whether or not this woman's body had been made a receptacle of murderous poison, destroying her life with slow torture, from day to day, and whether that poison was or not administered by her own husband.

The first question for you is: was this woman Mary Laura Cross, married in St James's Church, Piccadilly, in 1869, the daughter of a good family, a lady of good fortune, murdered in Shandy Hall, Dripsey? If she was murdered, who murdered her?

It is often said, and rightly said, by the prisoner's counsel that human nature itself shrinks in horror from the crime that is charged against the prisoner. The crime of patricide, the murder of a father by the fruits of his own body, the murder of a wife by her husband and of a husband by a wife, all these are things which a prisoner's counsel may fairly say should be proven by evidence, more conclusive and more demonstrative than is usually sufficient to convict in case of larceny or the ordinary moonlighting case.

But in this case, such appeals by my learned friend are wasted breath, for the prisoner at the bar has told us by his actions that he was labouring under the influence of a motive, the most powerful in a man's heart – to draw him into a crime we all know. He loved a woman, a woman younger than himself, a woman that was a partner of his adultery, and the partner of his crime and late to whose arms he rushed frantically from the corpse of the woman who had come to her death on the 2nd of June.

Was this story the prisoner at the bar had told the true account of her death and last illness? Who was the only doctor who was called in? The doctor who would not have charged a fee, coming to visit his niece-in-law, the doctor who ought to have called to see his former patient, the doctor who was left unnoticed and unsummoned, up to the very last?

Was it typhoid fever? Was it heart disease that killed this woman or was it poison administered by her husband?

Upon you, gentlemen, rests the duty of determining this case. I have attempted to state it as clearly and distinctly as I could. It divides itself into two broad parts. First the history of the defendant's conduct during the last fatal illness of his wife, in his own house and in order to fly back to the woman whom he had seduced, in order to place her in a position of replacement – a combination of horrors, that is not I believe to be found in the history of our criminal law.

If you are satisfied from the evidence which the Crown will produce of the guilt of the prisoner, I ask you to do your duty. If you are not satisfied, your duty is quite clear. But, gentlemen, I am satisfied in that verdict which you will pronounce in this case. You will not consider any circumstance, whatever, except your obligation to decide as between the state of society on the one side and the prisoner on the other, upon the evidence and upon the inference which that evidence coerces you to draw."

The Attorney General concluded his evidence at quarter past one, having spoken for two hours.

Case for the Prosecution

Mr Bowen Colthurst's Evidence

Mr Robert Bowen Colthurst was the first witness called. In reply to Mr Wright, he said he knew Mrs and Dr Cross for the last 12 years. On a day at the end of April he saw Mrs Cross in a field on the road. She asked how his wife was and then he asked how she was and she said, "Well". She was looking well. Dr Cross was not at home then. Then a week before her death he saw Dr Cross and asked him how his wife was, Dr Cross replied that he, Mr Colthurst, should not be surprised if he heard of her death at any moment.

Cross-examined by Mr Atkinson, he said: "I heard of Mrs Cross's death the morning it occurred."

Mrs Caulfield's Evidence

Mrs Caulfield, in reply to Mr Ronan, deposed:

"I live at Classas about two miles from Shandy Hall. Miss Skinner came to me as a governess on the 22nd of June, 1886, and remained until the 29th of October when she went to Shandy Hall as governess. There were five children in Shandy Hall, three girls and two boys. [The boys, in fact, were away at school. An example of vagueness from all quarters during the trial about the number of children and their whereabouts.] While Miss Skinner was in my house, Dr Cross used to see her when he visited my house.

On the 25th of May I visited Mrs Cross and she was in bed. It was in the afternoon between three and four o'clock that I called. I had a conversation with Mrs Cross. She spoke of her illness. I noticed a cup of milk on the table. On the following Monday, the 30th May, I called at Shandy Hall but I did not see Mrs Cross on that day. I saw Dr Cross and I asked how his wife was, he answered, 'Pretty well.' I did not call again during the life of Mrs Cross. After her death I heard of Dr Cross leaving Shandy Hall.

On the 22nd of June I got a letter from Germany [from Miss Skinner's mother] and Dr Cross came to my home that day. I said to him: 'How is Mrs Cross?' He said, 'What do you mean?' I said, 'I mean what I say. How is Mrs Cross?' 'What do you mean?' he said, and I said, 'Miss Skinner that was.' He said, 'Ha, ha, I like a good joke when I hear one.' I said it was no use denying it as I had got a letter that morning. He treated it as a joke and then left. I was told that a few days after that he brought Miss Skinner as his wife. Miss Skinner went to County Carlow when she left Dr Cross's after being governess in my house."

Cross-examined by Mr Atkinson, Mrs Caulfield said that she was one of Mrs Cross's best friends. She was on intimate terms with her. On the evening she called in she was with her for three quarters of an hour, on the first occasion. Mrs Caulfield added that she made no complaint of any want of attention or not being given what she required.

Captain Caulfield's Evidence

Captain Caulfield stated, in reply to the Attorney General, that Dr Cross called to his home on the 22nd of June. His wife came in and asked how Cross's wife was. He pooh-poohed this whole matter.

After his wife went out, Dr Cross said, "Who is spreading those absurd rumours?"

Captain Caulfield said, "There is no use in denying it. I know you are married and murder will out." He said that he did not mean anything by the latter part of his expression.

On the 25th of May, he and his wife called to see Dr Cross. While he was in the house the Rev Mr Hayes was announced. Dr Cross said, "Damn Hayes." He did not say why.

In reply to Mr Adam's cross-examination he said that Dr Cross was with him while his wife was upstairs and there was no objection to his wife seeing Mrs Cross.

Rev Mr Hayes's Evidence

Rev Richard Thomas Hayes was then called and, in answer to Mr Wright QC, he said that on the 25th May he went to see Mrs Cross. She was in bed and seemed to be poorly and weak. She said nothing particular about her health. The interview lasted about a half an hour. On Monday 30th, he called again and told Dr Cross that he wished to see his wife. Dr Cross replied that she had better be kept quiet and he acquiesced and went away.

On the 31st he was in Cork and came home earlier than he intended for the purpose of seeing Mrs Cross. He first went to his own house and found Miss Cross and Miss Jefferson there and in consequence of a conversation with Miss Cross, on that occasion, he did not go to Shandy Hall, as he had intended. During Mrs Cross's last illness, he was never asked by Dr Cross to go to see her.

Cross-examined by Mr Atkinson, for the defence, he deposed: "Before I went upstairs on the 25th May, I saw Dr Cross. He placed no obstacle in my way of seeing his wife. It was Miss Jefferson who showed me upstairs. I was on intimate terms with Mrs Cross."

Mr Wright resumed questioning the witness.

In response he [Rev Hayes] said: "It was the conversation I had with Miss Cross that prevented me going on the 31st May. I was at the funeral – it took place towards 7 o'clock in the morning. Dr Cross, Mr Cross, the undertaker, another Mr Cross from Waterford, two gentlemen named Mr Fitzgibbon and Mr Griffin, Dr Godfrey and some others I don't know were present."

Mr Wright asked: "Then it would be quite untrue to say that Griffin only attended it."

The Attorney General said: "I was only stating what was seen by Mary Buckley." Mr Atkinson asked if the evidence of this witness was in possession of the Crown.

Attorney General answered: "It is not."

Lord Justice Murphy asked the witness if he had spoken to Dr Cross about the funeral arrangements.

"He made arrangements to have the funeral at six o'clock on Saturday morning. That was on Friday the 3rd."

Mr Atkinson: "Did you know whether Dr Cross was boycotted at this time?"

"No, I think not."

The Attorney General said he wanted his learned friend to explain how this affected the question of Mrs Cross's death. Mr Atkinson replied that he had a successful answer to the question which he would give at the proper time.

In conclusion the Rev Mr Hayes said he could not tell the names of the other people at the funeral.

MISS KIRCHOFFER'S EVIDENCE

Miss Caroline Kirchoffer said that she lived at Dripsey House at the time of Mrs Cross's death. She knew the latter intimately and had lunch with her on the 25th of May. Mrs Cross was in bed when she visited her. She was looking very bad and stated that she had been suffering from diarrhoea. She said, "Phil tells me that I have disease of the heart", and that she could get no one in her room at night except Dr Cross who slept in a bed at the other side of the room and could not hear her when she called.

Miss Kirchoffer called on the 31st at Shandy Hall and spoke to Dr Cross. He said Mrs Cross was as bad as could be from typhoid fever. She asked him whether Mrs Cross had a nurse, and Dr Cross replied, "No, we are all nurses here and Miss Jefferson is a professional nurse."

In reply to Mr Adams the witness said that during her visit on the 25th of May, Dr Cross told her that his wife was suffering from a gastric attack but when asked by Mr Ronan on what sort of terms she observed he lived with Mrs Cross, Mr Atkinson objected strenuously but was overruled by Lord Justice Murphy.

Mr Ronan said: "I did not ask if Mrs Cross complained but what the terms were you saw they were living on. Did they live as happy people?

Mr Atkinson: "I object to that."

Miss Kirchoffer told Mr Ronan that she saw them living on friendly terms, but very rarely saw them together: "In fact I could almost count the times." She had been in the area for five years.

Cross-examined by Mr Adams for the defence, the witness said that Dr Cross showed her upstairs on the 25th and asked her not to stay long and she remained for half an hour. Mrs Cross complained that she had no one staying in her room to look after her but she had not requested a nurse.

The court then adjourned for luncheon. After the resumption and when the court had settled, the next witness for the prosecution, Dr Godfrey, was called to the stand. He was an elderly man of eighty years but without any physical infirmity and clear and bright in his mind.

Dr Godfrey's Evidence

Dr Thomas Godfrey, in reply to the Attorney General, said that he lived in the next house to Shandy Hall and had always been acquainted with the Crosses. He was married to Dr Cross's aunt. He did not recall the time that Mrs Cross came to live at Shandy Hall, but he supposed it was a dozen years. He had on some very trifling occasions seen her. He had recollected seeing her at her last illness and about eight or ten days previously.

"Dr Cross called on me and asked me to see her. He told me that she had diarrhoea." He did go to see her and was with her for about 15 minutes, during which time Dr Cross was present in the bedroom, shook hands with him and thanked him for his visit. He said he was very sorry to see her ill, felt her pulse and asked her the usual questions as a medical man would.

He was, at the time, of the opinion that Mrs Cross was suffering from a bilious attack. She did not say that she had a headache, nor did she describe her illness but she had a wet cloth around her head, which he asked the reason for but got no reply. He suggested that Mrs Cross should get three or four grains of calomel and an aperient [laxative] the following morning.

He was told by Dr Cross that morning that the vomiting and diarrhoea were much better and she did not appear to be in any danger. He never saw Mrs Cross afterwards and was never asked to see her. The date of the visit was the 24th and previous to that time he had frequently visited Mrs Cross for trifling matters. She presented no symptoms of typhoid fever.

Cross-examined by Mr Atkinson for the defence, Dr Godfrey stated that Mrs Cross had a dread that she had heart disease and he told her that she had no reason to fear; but she never complained to him of irregular action of the heart. He could not recollect whether he swore on the 22nd of August that Mrs Cross complained of palpitation. He promised to examine her but she did not come to him, and a short time afterwards, when he saw her, she said that she was quite well.

Mr Atkinson asked: "Did you ever hear that Mrs Cross got epileptic fits?"

"No, but she had two fits of hysteria. I examined her carefully on that day and she did not complain of any pain. She did not, of herself, explain what the symptoms were."

Dr Godfrey went on to say that he had asked her if she had a headache and she said no and he next asked her why she had the wet cloth on her head and he got no answer. If one was given, he did not hear it. Subsequently Dr Cross told him that the vomiting and diarrhoea were better. He felt her pulse the day he saw her but he did not test her temperature with any instrument. He said that he had extensive experience of typhoid fever as a young doctor and was in active medical practice until eight years ago after which he retired.

Pressed by Mr Atkinson, he said that he saw no signs of typhoid fever in Mrs Cross and described the early symptoms as heaviness, abdominal pain and a tendency to derangement. And it could be attended by vomiting and diarrhoea.

Lord Justice Murphy asked the witness if typhoid fever could be mistaken at first for a simple bilious or gastric attack.

Dr Godfrey agreed that it could but after four to five days it would be able to be definitely determined that the patient was suffering from typhoid fever. He had not been told on his visit to Mrs Cross how long she had been ill.

Lord Justice Murphy intervened: "As it was, you concluded that it was not typhoid fever?"

"Yes."

"Supposing you had been told she was showing the same symptoms for a fortnight before. If it was typhoid fever would it be fully manifest?"

"Certainly, yes; fully developed."

Mr Atkinson resumed and asked if Dr Godfrey meant to say that he did not ask the lady herself how long she was ill. The witness said that to the best of his recollection he did not.

Dr Godfrey then stood down.

MISS JEFFERSON'S EVIDENCE

Miss Jefferson was then called to the stand and examined by the Attorney General.

She confirmed that she had been at school with Mrs Cross and was an Associate of a religious organisation by the name of The Sisters of The Church. She firmly denied the suggestion that she was a professional nurse and added that it was quite false to say so. While on her visit to Shandy Hall she occupied a room next to Mrs Cross but without any connecting door and spent a considerable portion of the day in her company.

When she first arrived her friend was in good health. She had been depressed for a time, but generally was in good spirits. It was a fortnight after she came there that Mrs Cross got her first bout of illness. Miss Jefferson kept a diary at the time which was a great aid to her recollection of events.

The Attorney General enquired into the nature of the attack. She answered: "She seemed to have an attack of spasms of the heart with cramps, sickness, vomiting and diarrhoea."

"Looking at your diary, can you say how Mrs Cross was for several days – for instance, take Sunday the 8th?"

"She went to church that morning."

"On the 9th?"

"She paid some visits with me in the afternoon."

"What day was she first attacked?"

"The 10th of May."

"Are you able to state how she was on the 11th, 12th, 13th, 14th?"

"She was in bed."

"Suffering from the same complaint?"

"Yes."

Miss Jefferson went on to tell the court of the progress of the illness with the same symptoms and then brief remission on three occasions when Mrs Cross was able to go to church, sit down to dinner and go out to the garden. But then the illness returned, during which it was noted that she became drowsy. The Attorney General enquired when she became really alarmed by the worsening condition.

"I began to be alarmed about her on the 26th, but I don't remember thinking she might die, until the following Sunday. I had a conversation with Dr Cross on the 29th. I suggested leaving but he said that he did not want to hurry me. I did not recollect making any observation as to who would look after Mrs Cross. I offered to remain and look after my old schoolfellow but I did not make this offer to Dr Cross. On Monday morning I proposed leaving the following Saturday. Dr Cross suggested leaving on Thursday instead, so I did."

Miss Jefferson went on to say that Dr Cross spoke of his wife's illness as gastric or bilious attacks and hinted at typhoid fever. She had seen one or two cases of typhoid fever but, in reply to the Attorney General's question if she could discern any symptoms of typhoid fever, the witness attested that she could not.

The chief prosecution Counsel went on to press the advantage by asking if she had observed any addition to her symptoms on the 27th and 28th.

"Her eyes were irritated and inflamed and she complained that she could not see things at a distance distinctly or could not see the paper or write."

"Did you write a letter for her, to her sister?"

"Yes, on the 28th."

"On the 29th was her strength holding out or was she weaker?"

"She was getting weaker, but it did not strike me that she was perceptibly weaker."

"Was she bright or was she drowsy?"

"She was drowsy."

The witness recalled that at lunch on Monday the 30th of May, Dr Cross suggested that she should go visiting in the neighbourhood with his sister Miss Cross. After lunch they went out and returned to Shandy Hall at 6 p.m. On the following day they were out between 2.30 p.m. and 5 p.m. and on the Wednesday for two hours in the direction of Ryecourt.

During her illness, Mrs Cross was attended by Dr Cross, his sister Henrietta and the servants Mary Barron and Mary McGrath, the last mentioned being the one who brought her food and drink.

* * *

The Attorney General must have been well pleased with the assured tone of his witness and her straightforward and clear responses to his questioning. If all witnesses were so accomplished, his job would be a lot easier. What pleased him even more was the obvious credibility of her evidence. She was an upright woman, an Associate of a Sisterhood, thus incapable in the eyes of any rational jury of false or even exaggerated testimony.

As a highly experienced counsel he was more than aware of the uncertainties of the trial process and how both his and his witnesses' performance in court were vital to the success of the prosecution. He also knew the danger of over-examination which could confuse the jury. There was no question of that in this instance.

* * *

The examination continued:

The Attorney General asked: "Did you see Mrs Cross get any food or drink from her husband?"

"No, not that I remember."

"Was he very much in the room with her?"

"He was in and out."

"Did you see him give her medicine, at all?"

"Once or twice."

Miss Jefferson told the court that while she was aware that Mrs Cross was constantly sick at this time, she had never acted the part of nurse to her. She was vomiting. The last time that she saw Mrs Cross was at ten o'clock on the Wednesday night and the patient was in bed.

"I don't remember distinctly seeing Dr Cross in the room, I think he was, but I am not quite certain. Mrs Cross had to have her head supported when she was receiving nutriment. Her head seemed clear and she was quite intelligent. She was able to express her wishes and give orders and describe her state. I slept in the room next to that of Mrs Cross and woke naturally about six on the following morning. About quarter past six I was told by Mary Barron of Mrs Cross's death.

I went into her room about seven o'clock or soon after and I left Shandy Hall soon after nine o'clock. Before leaving, I saw Dr Cross in the passage outside my room. I said how grieved I was to hear of Mrs Cross's death. Dr Cross said nothing special to me; he said something at breakfast about burying her. He spoke about the funeral and he said that Saturday was too soon and Monday was too late."

"Did he make any statement about the circumstances of his wife's death or what she had died of?"

"He did not."

The Counsel for the prosecution then changed tack and went back in time. Miss Jefferson testified that Mrs Cross had received gentian early on in her illness and this made her sick. She saw Dr Cross giving her chlorodyne which made her drowsy and had the effect of stupefying her. When she left Shandy Hall and went to London she stayed with her mother in Dover Street. She had received a letter from Dr Cross which she passed on to the police. Dr Cross came to visit her on the 14th of June.

The Attorney General enquired if she had asked him anything of the circumstances of his wife's death, and the witness confirmed that he had asked the question.

"What did he say?"

"He said she died screaming, and that she dozed off and died straight away."

"Did she say what she died of?"

"To the best of my recollection he said she died of a disease of the heart. His visit on that occasion was a very short one, lasting a quarter of an hour."

The witness said that Dr Cross had not told her why he was in London and when Counsel asked if he had mentioned that he was to get married to Miss Skinner three days later, Mr Atkinson objected and the matter was dropped.

She had been present when Rev Hayes called to Shandy Hall on the 30th when Mrs Cross was extremely ill and, while he did not see her, there was nothing as far as the witness knew to prevent him seeing the patient.

Finally, she said she had never seen anyone other than mentioned give Mrs Cross medicine.

*　*　*

The Attorney General took his seat. There must have been one line reverberating in the minds of the spectators to the unfolding drama and this related to the last moments of the victim recounted by the witness. By the account of the man who was now in the dock she "died screaming". A matter of fact, told factually and apparently without the least display of emotion. It must have sent a shudder up the spine of every man and woman present – the sheer expression of it even without any interpretation attached.

Mr Atkinson rose to his feet and began the cross-examination, knowing that it would take the best of his professional experience to shake the confidence of the witness in the box.

He began by asking how long Miss Jefferson knew the victim to which the witness said they had been in school together. She had also been on a previous visit to Shandy Hall to see her. She had never heard that Mrs Cross had epileptic attacks and never witnessed a fit. When she had referred to cramps she meant spasms of the heart. Mrs Cross complained of spasms of the heart, vomiting and diarrhoea. The servants had access to her at all times. She had given her sal volatile at an early stage of her illness. Mrs Cross had never called for her at night. The defence counsel asked her what she meant by cramps.

"A sort of convulsion of the limbs with chattering of the teeth."

"Have you been speaking to anyone about this case since you made your first information?"

"Yes, to different people."

"Have you had any conversations since then about the symptoms of arsenical poisoning?"

"Yes."

"Were you told since then that cramp was one of the symptoms?"

"No, I was not."

"Or about the chattering of the teeth?"

"No, I was not."

Mr Atkinson continued to press the witness about symptoms she had mentioned in her statement to the authorities and she confirmed that she had been asked to detail them but did not mention chattering of the teeth and cramps of the limbs because they did not strike her as important at the time. She was too busy trying to recollect other symptoms. Nor had she mentioned them in her diary.

The defence counsel then concentrated on another matter. He elicited the fact that Miss Jefferson had consulted a book about the effects of arsenical poisoning at a later date, she claimed, than when she had given her statement on the 5th of September. She said that she had picked it up in a second-hand bookshop, looked at a particular page about arsenical poisoning and then put it down. She did not remember the name of it. Asked if she had any conversation with any person about the symptoms of the poisoning she said no, no one had told her anything about it. None, she added, from which she had any information.

Mr Atkinson pressed the witness.

"Had you any conversation, Miss Jefferson?"

"Yes."

"With whom?"

"I told one or two of our Sisters what the symptoms were as I understood them."

"Did you say anything about the cramp?"

"I did not."

"Since you read the book have you had any conversation with any person as to the symptoms the lady suffered from?"

"Yes."

"Who was it?"

"I told one or two of the Sisters about it."

Lord Justice Murphy intervened: "Had you any conversation with any person from whom you derived any information about the symptoms of arsenical poisoning?"

The defence counsel repeated the question and was told: "Nothing that gave me any information."

"And the only explanation you can give for leaving out about the cramp and chattering of the teeth was that you were not asked the question?"

"Yes."

"You said that you were talking to some doctor?"

"Yes."

"Will you give me his name?"

"Dr White."

"About arsenical poisoning?"

"Not exactly, but he is my brother-in-law and we naturally spoke on the subject."

"And you said nothing about the symptoms of poisoning?"

"As far as I remember I did not."

"Did you say anything about chattering teeth?"

"I can't say I did."

* * *

Now this extraordinary passage of evidence, while skilfully brought about by Mr Atkinson, was unaccountably not pushed to the limit of examination which could have seriously dented the credibility of Miss Jefferson's previous testimony to the court. She admitted not mentioning symptoms of convulsion of the limbs and chattering of the teeth in her statement. Her excuse was simply incredible. She had consulted a book which she had picked up in a shop, the name of which she could not remember, opened a section on the effects of arsenical poisoning and left it down.

How is it possible that she could not remember the title which was the only way she could have known what the book contained? Clearly Miss Jefferson was being economical with the truth, and it was most unlikely she got the information at all in this manner. She had a conversation, she testified, with her brother-in-law, a Doctor White, on the subject during which the symptoms of arsenical poisoning or cramps or chattering of the teeth were not mentioned. Not only highly unlikely but beyond belief. Whatever the reason, Mr Atkinson lost a golden opportunity to both profit from his own skill and make a much-needed point on behalf of his client. Instead he moved on. The witness had been left off the hook.

* * *

Miss Jefferson said she had suggested her date of leaving Shandy Hall, not Dr Cross. He had mooted Thursday the 2nd of June but she had suggested Saturday the 4th. She could not go into the particulars of typhoid fever because she was not a nurse.

At the beginning of her testimony to the defence, Miss Jefferson had said she had never seen Mrs Cross suffer from fits and yet when Mr Atkinson asked her if she saw her faint more than once she answered:

"Yes."

"Did you ever give her anything to revive her?"

"I never gave her anything but sal volatile."

"Did she not frequently complain to you of action of the heart?"

"Yes, it seemed very weak."

"On those occasions used she faint away?"

"I never saw her absolutely faint away but once."

"Did she tell you that she used to faint?"

"Yes."

"When did you see her faint?"

"On Tuesday the 10th of May."

"Did she tell you she had fainted previously?"

"I don't remember."

"She told you she had been suffering from weak action of the heart?"

"Yes."

"When?"

"I don't know."

She said in response to the continued examination that Mrs Cross had experienced dimness of eyesight on the 27th and 28th of May. She said that she had made no remonstrance with Dr Cross after his suggestion that she go visiting. On the morning of Mrs Cross's death she met the doctor at 8.30 and sympathised with him on her death. Mr Atkinson asked her what she had said to him.

"I told him how grieved I was at Mrs Cross's death. He went towards the door as if to show me in, but I told him that I had been there before. I had heard previously from Miss Cross that Mrs Cross had woken up screaming, and that he [Dr Cross] had got her some brandy; and she dozed off and died straight away."

"Did you see her as she lay on the bed?"

"Yes, she was laid out quite straight."

"Was there any sign of rigidity as if her limbs were fixed, or as if she had tetanus?"

"I know that she was laid very straight."

On re-examination by the Attorney General, she said that she had the conversation with her brother-in-law Dr White on the 13th of September. When he asked what went on between them, Mr Atkinson objected and this was upheld. She had a conversation with Miss [Henrietta] Cross on the morning of the death in Miss Cross's bedroom. Cross's sister was up but not dressed. In reply to Lord Justice Murphy, she said that the first time she saw Mrs Cross faint was on the 10th of May. There had never been any talk of a night nurse. Mrs Cross had complained of a pain in her heart. Asked by Mr Atkinson if it was like a knife, she said she could not be sure.

Miss Jefferson then stood down.

JANE LEAHY'S EVIDENCE

Jane Leahy said that she lived near Shandy Hall, and had been in the employment of the Cross family for a great many years, since 1839; she knew the late Mrs Cross and remembered her last illness. During that time she was in her room, she could not say how long before her death. When she spoke to her on one occasion, she said that she had a cold; and on another that she had a fever. She remembered the day Dr Godfrey called.

It was before that Mrs Cross said she had a fever. She went to see her three times altogether, and on the second occasion which was about four days before her death, she complained of her sight being bad and she was not able to see the paper. When she visited her the third time, two days before her death, she was very bad and lay on her right side and had her hand on her heart. She, however, did not complain of her heart.

Mr Wright for the prosecution examined the witness.

"Who used to take food to Mrs Cross?"

"Mary McGrath and Miss Cross."

"Used the doctor?"

"On one occasion the doctor did give her a wineglass of chicken broth."

"About what time did she get that chicken broth?"

"I could not tell but she was bad and in bed at the time."

Lord Justice Murphy asked: "Was it before the second or third visit that she got the chicken broth?"

"It was after my third visit."

In further examination by Mr Wright, the witness stated that on the morning of Mrs Cross's death she went into her bedroom, and the body was lying on the bed. She saw Dr Cross at breakfast and said to him: "The mistress is no more," but he made no reply and walked away.

"When did the second Mrs Cross arrive at Shandy Hall?"

"I don't know. I am not sure whether she arrived in the same month as the late Mrs Cross died."

The witness stated that she was in the present employment of the second Mrs Cross.

In reply to Mr Adams cross-examining for the defence, Miss Leahy said that the late Mrs Cross was a delicate woman. She often saw her suffering from fits. She sometimes complained of her heart as if she was going to faint. "I saw her get one of these attacks, about six weeks before her death; she used to get them once a month."

"Did you ever see her suffering from the falling sickness?"

"No. I asked her what was the cause of her sickness and she said it was spasms. She used complain of her heart. There was only one child born since the late Mrs Cross and the doctor returned to Shandy Hall."

Under questioning, the witness further stated that it was the doctor who attended her in her confinement, and there was no other medical man present. She had seen the corpse on the morning of the death and it looked like any other corpse would.

In reply to Lord Justice Murphy she said that the deceased many times got into the condition she described, but never stopped in bed for a day or two on account of it, though she often remained there until twelve o'clock in the day. She only saw the face of the corpse, so she was not able to say the condition it was in.

MARY BUCKLEY'S EVIDENCE

Mary Buckley, the kitchen maid in the employment of the house, was then sworn in and examined. She said that Mrs Cross was sick about three weeks before she died. Mary McGrath and the doctor used to take things up to her while she was sick. She saw the doctor take her up, on one occasion, chicken broth in a wineglass and some sago. She saw Miss Cross take up some toast and bread and milk.

She did not hear Mrs Cross make any complaints to her as to what was the matter with her. Some time after ten o'clock on the night that Mrs Cross died, she heard screams coming from her room as if she was in a little pain. It lasted four or five minutes, but she made nothing of it. At six o'clock the next morning, Dr Cross came to the room where she and two other servants slept and, knocking at the door, told them to get up, that their mistress was no more since one o'clock that night.

At nine o'clock she went to the room where the deceased lay. She saw the bed and did not think it was tossed. However, Mrs Cross was in it as she had died in it. She saw the funeral [cortege] from the window. She saw five people at it.

Cross-examined by Mr Adams, she said that she often saw Mrs Cross get fainting fits, but she never heard her scream, except on the night she died. She always complained of her heart and used always press her hand to her side when going up the stairs, as if her heart were panting.

Mary McGrath's Evidence

Mary McGrath was sworn in and said that she was housemaid at Shandy Hall at the time of the death of Mrs Cross. She was still in service there. She attended the late Mrs Cross during her illness. She saw Dr Cross give his wife chlorodyne once, about three days before her death. Mrs Cross used to get chicken broth, corn flour and sago. During her last illness, the witness did not see her get any solid food. The chlorodyne made Mrs Cross vomit and she said she wished she had not seen it.

For three days before her death Mrs Cross was vomiting continually. The vomit was of a yellowish green colour. One morning when she took her letters to Mrs Cross, the mistress could not read them. About eight days before her death, Mrs Cross told her that Dr Cross had informed her that she had typhoid fever. Mrs Cross suffered from biliousness, diarrhoea and her heart used to affect her. After being informed about six o'clock on the morning of the 2nd June by Dr Cross that her mistress had died the previous night, she went to Miss Jefferson's room, and afterwards, with Miss Jefferson went to Mrs Cross's room.

The corpse was on the bed, with a sheet thrown over it, the face alone being exposed. Dr Cross, Mary Barron and herself dressed the corpse for the grave. The body was buried on the following Saturday. She recollected Dr Cross going away from home after the funeral and when afterwards he came home for a day or two, he was not accompanied by anyone.

The Attorney General then said that he proposed to hand in a photograph of the prisoner and the present Mrs Cross.

Mr Atkinson said: "I object, My Lord, to it's being handed in."

The Attorney General stated: "It is the only way we can prove the identity of this lady, who is not in court."

Lord Justice Murphy asked: "What is the objection? If I thought there was any objection to it, I would have Mrs Cross produced in court."

Mr Atkinson said: "I don't see how it arises, unless to account for the fact that he married a second lady."

Lord Justice Murphy replied: "I can't shut my ears to the Attorney General's statement. He says, now he wants to prove the identity of this lady, and I suppose he wants to prove facts previously with respect to the prisoner. The Attorney General said in his statement that sometime in the month of June the prisoner and a lady, whom he will prove to be the present Mrs Cross were married –"

Mr Atkinson interrupted: "If that is the purpose for which the photograph is handed in then I have no objection."

The Attorney General said: "That is the purpose. I am not going to hand it in as a work of art."

This was an extraordinary objection on behalf of the defence. Naturally given the advanced state of the pregnancy of the accused's wife, she could not have been brought into court. The judge's threat was more than enough to make him retreat, but why Atkinson even contemplated the objection is not just mysterious but incompetent. He must have known that on any level it could not succeed.

The photograph was then handed to the witness and she stated that it was a photograph of the prisoner and the present Mrs Cross. On further examination she said that she did not know Dr Cross had got married for a second time until he brought home his second wife.

The witness was then cross-examined by Mr Atkinson for the defence.

Miss McGrath testified that she had been employed for two months before the victim's death and had seen her get fits three times before her illness. During the fits she would faint and her hands and feet would get stiff and her teeth would chatter. Mrs Cross complained of her heart, which she thought was weak but said she had strong nerves. She would fall down during the fits.

The witness and Mary Barron brought the patient corn flour and sago during her illness which was prepared by the cook Jane Leahy.

She saw Dr Cross administer chlorodyne from a bottle which was kept on the chimneypiece. Dr Cross also gave the patient chicken tea which was made by the cook.

"Were you in the lady's room when you saw him getting it?"

"I had to come down to the kitchen and I saw him getting it in a wineglass out of the pantry."

"Did you observe anything in the glass before he put the chicken broth into it.?"

"No, I did not."

"Were you up in the room before he came back from the kitchen?"

"Yes, I was in the room when Mrs Cross was getting the chicken broth. Before I left the kitchen, I saw Dr Cross get a glass in the pantry and go to get the chicken tea. I went up to Mrs Cross's room before him and he gave her the chicken tea in my presence. He put the glass aside and I took it away. It was not washed by Dr Cross before I took it away. I looked after the room in the usual way; I noticed signs of vomiting sometimes when I came up in the morning. The principal discharge used to be during the daytime."

She had seen the body of Mrs Cross about half past six in the morning and the body had been laid out. She, Dr Cross and Mary Barron were present. Dr Cross washed the body. In reply to re-examination by the Attorney General, she said that her mistress's lips were open but she could not say that her teeth were open. She had been vomiting continually for three days beforehand.

She stayed for ten minutes in the room after Mrs Cross had been given the chicken broth.

"Was it not your business to bring the glass downstairs and have it washed?"

"Yes."

"Used you do that immediately?"

"Not always."

The witness was not able to say how long before her mistress's death it was that Dr Cross brought up the wineglass; she could not say whether it was within the last three days of her life.

Mr Atkinson objected to the examination.

Mr Justice Murphy thought that it was important to fix the date as the witness Leahy had said it was after her third visit, which was three days before her mistress's death that Dr Cross had taken the chicken broth to his wife's room.

The Attorney General said that he had a particular reason to test the witness.

Examination was then continued and the witness further stated that the last time she saw the wineglass was when the police took it; it was broken at the time. The witness thought that there was a bit out of the side of it. Miss McGrath could not state when the wineglass was broken, or whether it was in the same condition when the police got it as it was when Dr Cross administered the chlorodyne from it.

In reply to Lord Justice Murphy she said there was a small piece out of the side of it; the bottle of chlorodyne was not quite full and she could not state whether previous to this she had seen the chlorodyne bottle in the room.

Examination continued.

She could not say whether her mistress had been in the habit of taking chlorodyne. The fits her mistress used to get would last eight to ten minutes and she would be all right in ten minutes more. Before her last illness she had never seen Mrs Cross vomiting.

In answer to further questions from Mr Atkinson, the witness said that the wineglass was on the chimneypiece the day after it was used, but she did not see the police take it away.

In reply to Mr Justice Murphy, Miss McGrath said she thought the wineglass of chicken broth was given before the chlorodyne was administered. She had not known chlorodyne before that day, but saw it labelled on the bottle. It was the doctor who proposed that Mrs Cross should get the chlorodyne, but she did not recollect what she said. Dr Cross was in the room when Mr Cross complained about the chlorodyne making her sick to her stomach but he made no reply to that remark.

Lord Justice Murphy: "When did you read the word 'chlorodyne' on the bottle?"

"I can't exactly say but it may have been the day before her death, but I can't say exactly when."

"Used she often take the chicken broth?"

"She only took it twice as far as I know. Dr Cross gave it to her once and I gave her some in a teacup on another occasion."

The hearing was adjourned until the following morning at half past ten.

The court rose at quarter to six and the jury was conveyed to the Imperial Hotel, where they were sequestered for the night.

* * *

While the reporters went off to file their copy and the opposing counsel retired, no doubt to contemplate the first day's proceedings over a good repast and fine drinks, none could claim that the results were anything but inconclusive.

From the earlier period of the 19th century, when the prosecutor was considered as a zealous and partisan advocate whose single purpose was to secure the conviction of the accused, things had changed and he was now perceived to have a wider role as a minister for justice who was to seek the truth of the case and promote the course of justice. His duty was to see that every piece of evidence relevant and admissible was presented in due order, without fear or favour and not to regard the question at issue as one of professional superiority and pre-eminence of skill.

The defence counsel was supposedly more accessible, the defender of the underdog and somewhat of a more noble calling.

But yet as the first day's proceedings illustrated, those noble expectations did not preclude an adversarial game of cat and mouse. The arbiter of that game was the judge whose interventions were crucial.

In that regard there should never be allowed any personal attack on the accused outside the matter of evidence. While the Attorney General had played his part in examination properly, in his address he called the accused a wretched man who could not spare his mistress from his lust and made other incriminatory remarks on the prisoner and his "paramour". This should have been roundly challenged by the judge when he had finished his speech, but was left, astoundingly, without comment from the bench.

Such lapses on the part of the judge would come back to haunt him. His checking, when necessary, should have been entirely impartial; in time it would be perceived not to be so.

The Defence Counsel would then, it seemed, have to be a lot more vigilant as the trial entered into the second day. The business of the Crown was fairly and impartially to exhibit all the facts to the jury. It was the business of the Defence Counsel to make sure that was done.

Already they had missed an opportunity to vigorously challenge one of the prosecution's strongest witnesses, Miss Jefferson. If Dr Cross was to have any chance of contesting the case against him, his counsel would have to perform to the heights of their ability, despite the inconclusive nature of the opening day's evidence. Whatever his view of the proceedings, thus far, the fact was his life was at stake.

The Second Day

Friday, 16th December

The trial was resumed in the City Court at half past ten before Lord Justice Murphy. As on the first day, admission to the court was by ticket, but the room was not as crowded in the earlier part of the proceedings as it was the previous day. This was changed utterly in the afternoon with the court packed to the rafters with even standing room at a premium.

The *Cork Examiner* reporter noted that there were fewer ladies present than on the opening day, then listed the notables present in court:

Captain Stokes RM; Dr H Corby; WT Hungerford TC; WH Babington, solicitor; Thomas Babington Snr; Thomas Babington Jnr; Thomas Winder; H Cooke, solicitor; Martin Beattie; Alderman Madden; Dr R Callaghan; Dr Moriarty; Dr Harty; Dr Riordan, Cloyne; Dr Curran, Killeagh; Dr JP Golding; DL Sandford; RM Hennessey; T Jones; S Grehan; RA Powell, B.L; W McMahon, solicitor, Fermoy; W Scollard; RM Hennessey, BL; M Murphy, BL; Miss Cross, sister of the prisoner.

District Inspector Kerin of Youghal had charge of the police arrangements.

At the sitting of the court, all the names of the jury having been called and answered, the foreman, Mr Palmer, made a request that the witnesses should be removed from the court and called in one by one. The Attorney General asked if the observation of the juror applied to medical witnesses and Mr Palmer replied that it did not.

The Attorney General said that as it applied to all the unexamined witnesses with the exception mentioned, the witnesses for the defendant should be kept in a separate room from the Crown witnesses.

Lord Justice Murphy gave directions acceding to both applications.

MARY MCGRATH RESUMES

Mary McGrath who was under examination when the court adjourned the previous day was called and in reply to Mr Atkinson said that the minim glass produced was like the one out of which the chlorodyne was administered. As far as the witness could remember it was in the same condition when she last saw it.

The chlorodyne bottle was then produced but the witness did not think it was the bottle in which the chlorodyne was kept.

"Do I understand you to say that from the time you saw the glass first to the last you saw no change in it?"

"I think it was the same."

She was re-examined by the Attorney General: "Did you say last night that you could not recollect whether the glass was the same or not when the police got it, as it was when the chlorodyne was administered to Mrs Cross?

"I think I said I could not tell until I saw it."

"What has become of the chlorodyne bottle that is different from the one produced?"

"I think it was taken by the police."

"Did you see a bottle of the shape produced in your mistress's room?"

"No, I don't think it was a bottle that shape. I only saw the one I described to you."

Lord Justice Murphy asked: "Was the bottle you describe larger and one in which you could see the medicine?"

"Yes."

In reply to further questions from the judge she said that she herself, Mary Barron, Dr Cross and Miss Cross brought food to the patient. No person in particular attended, it was a matter of chance and who was available. She did not spend much time in the bedroom.

The witness further stated that she used to go into the room at ten o'clock every night; drink was left for the mistress on the table every night, sometimes toast and water; they used to be left on the table in the middle of the room.

Mrs Cross asked her to answer the bell at night if she rang it. She answered her ring on three occasions. She couldn't exactly remember when but thought it was about a week before her death.

"On those occasions I would give her a drink and settle the cloth on her forehead. No milk would be left in her room at night, but sometimes during the day. I gave her a drink whenever she wanted it, usually a half a cup at a time."

Miss McGrath said that her mistress's bed was not made every day. When it was, as it was the previous day to her death, she and

Shandy Hall as it is today

The humble cottage in which
Rev John Skinner lived for most of his life

Rev John Skinner: poet and songwriter
(1721–1807)

Bishop John Skinner (1744–1816)
Primus of Scotland from 1788 to 1816

Marriage record of PHE Cross and Mary Laura Marriott (17th August 1869)

Marriage record of PHE Cross and Evelyn Forbes Skinner (17th June 1887)

Mary Laura Marriott (1840–1887), pictured at Yarmouth 1867
Reproduced by courtesy of Essex Record Office

Henrietta Cross, sister of Dr Cross: reluctant witness

Bob Cross, eldest son of Dr Cross

Henry Eustace Cross, British Army vet,
son of Dr Cross

Effie Skinner and Dr Cross pictured before their wedding (1887)

Alfred Swaine Taylor: father of British forensic
medicine (1806–1880)

CHARLES YELVERTON PEARSON
M.D., M.CH., DIP. MED., F.R.C.S.
PROFESSOR OF MATERIA MEDICA 1884–1900
PROFESSOR OF SURGERY 1900–1927

Dr Charles Yelverton Pearson: doctor of
brilliance, man of integrity (1857–1947)

Baron John Atkinson: Law Lord (1844–1932)

James Berry: executioner with a conscience
(1852–1913)

Birth record of John Eustace Cross, son of Dr Cross and Effie Skinner, born December 1887

Marriage record of Evelyn Forbes Cross and Patrick James Robertson, 1898

Death record of Evelyn Forbes Robertson, 1937

Magourney Old Church and Graveyard, County Cork
Photo by Anthony Greene, Coachford historian

The tomb of Mary Laura Cross, buried 1887: note the more modern inscription
Photo by Anthony Greene, Coachford historian

Mary Barron would take hold of her arms and move her over to the other bed where she lay while her own bed was being made up.

MARY BARRON'S EVIDENCE

Mary Barron who was employed as a parlour maid at Shandy Hall was next witness for the prosecution called and said in reply to the Attorney General: "I was in Dr Cross's employment at Shandy Hall. I left it about three months ago. I was about seven months in his employment altogether, I came there on the 2nd of March. Dr Cross was absent in the month of March for about five weeks. I was not very long in his employment then. I recollect the late Mrs Cross getting ill. She was about a fortnight ill before she died. It was after Dr Cross came home that she got ill – almost six weeks or two months afterwards.

Miss Cross, Mary McGrath, Dr Cross and myself used to attend on Mrs Cross while she was sick. I used to make the bed for her. It was always made at night during her illness. Sometimes she used to object to it being made, and she used to say that she did not like getting out of bed. She did not like being lifted out of it. The bed was made three or four days before she died. Miss Jefferson used to sit in the room sometimes with Mrs Cross. The doctor used to be up and down in the room. No one used to sit regularly in the room. I used to go into the room regularly at half past four or five when she used to ring the bell. She did not get drinks from me very often. I didn't see her drink much. There was drink alongside her bed – lemonade and water and milk. I saw toast and water in the room the first time she got ill, and I also think I saw toast and water during the last days of her illness."

The witness said that the mistress did not complain to her of thirst. She would go to her room when the bell rang and this was usually because Mrs Cross had been sick. She brought her drinks but only once food, some corn flour. The bell rang about 5 p.m. the day before Mrs Cross died and she went to the room. It was in broad daylight. During the hour or more that she spent in the room, Mrs Cross was continually sick and in distress.

She tried to comfort the sick woman at whose suggestion she dipped a cloth in water and put it to her head. She also held her head and tried to settle her in the bed. It seemed to her that Mrs Cross was very weak. After she had stopped vomiting, Miss Cross, who had been out visiting in the afternoon came to the room, stayed a short time and left before her.

Before that she had seen a bottle of chlorodyne in the room but she could not say exactly when. She had seen Dr Cross in the room but had never seen her mistress take medicine. She was with Mary McGrath and Mary Buckley the morning Mrs Cross died. Dr Cross told them that they should get up as their mistress was no more since one o'clock that night. Miss Barron told the judge that Dr Cross had called the housemaid to go and she, the witness, went with her. The body had not been laid out at that time. The witness confirmed that the portmanteau used by the prisoner was yellow with a white cross.

Letters were brought to the post office which was only a short distance away by one of the workmen in an open leather bag. A staff member or sometimes the postmaster Mr Griffin used to deliver letters to the house which were received by the housemaid. She was cross-examined by Mr Adams for the defence: "The doctor was away in April?"

"I said March, I think."

"He then returned to the house?"

"Yes."

"You saw Mrs Cross in a fit in her last illness?"

"Yes."

"Did you ever see her in a fit before?"

"Yes, I think I did."

In reply to further examination by Mr Adams, the witness described her mistress as going off in a weakness, getting quite stiff and closing her mouth when she was having a fit. She complained of the action of her heart when she went up the stairs but never described a knife-like pain. She and whoever was in the room at the time helped the patient to walk across the room by holding her arms. There was a wardrobe at the head of the room about two feet

196

away from the bed. It belonged to Mrs Cross and she used keep the keys to it.

She had seen Mrs Cross at half past eight the night before she died.

There then followed a bizarre exchange introduced by the Defence Counsel on the subject of a long narrow piece of macaroni which Mary McGrath, who was referred to as "Annie" as there were three servants by the name of Mary in the house, discovered under Mrs Cross's pillow. It was uncooked and dry.

Mary Barron went on to explain to the judge that Mrs Cross used to eat it before she became ill. The macaroni was dry and thick. Two or three pieces were found under the pillow. Herself and Mary McGrath, while making up the bed, had never found it before. She said that it was not under the pillow as she remembered but under the tick [mattress cover]. When they made the bed, generally they did not turn up the tick. The purpose of the discussion was not revealed or indeed the significance of the presence of dried and uncooked macaroni in the bed. The witness could not account for its appearance two days after she had last changed the bed. Whether it mattered a whit, no one could say.

* * *

Perhaps the mysterious macaroni provided some small and merciful relief from the unrelenting intensity of the court process, trying for both the spectators and the witnesses who, it has to be said, were conducting themselves in a very assured manner given the nervous tension of being placed centre stage of a major and, whatever the result, tragic drama.

But apparently there was a particular steeliness and steadfastness displayed by Irish witnesses in court proceedings of the time, as noted by Timothy Healy's brother Maurice, also a lawyer, in his excellent book *The Old Munster Circuit (1939)*: "The vast majority go to give their evidence as a cricketer who walks to the wicket. Each is confident that he will not be bowled out until he has knocked up a good score."

* * *

Mr Adams moved on to an issue of more importance as far as the case was concerned.

"Had you ever seen a corpse before?"

"Yes, but not like I saw Mrs Cross."

"When you went to look at the lady did you notice any particular stiffness about it?"

"No, it was like any other corpse."

"This chlorodyne bottle, was it always on the chimneypiece?"

"Yes."

"It was there before her illness?"

"Yes."

"And after her illness?"

"Yes."

The Attorney General started his re-examination.

The witness said that she had never seen Mrs Cross sick in her stomach before her last illness. The wardrobe in the room was not open and it was on the far side of the room from the bed; she never saw it open. She never told Dr Cross about the macaroni, she never told anyone until that day, the day her mistress died. It was about twelve o'clock when she found it. Afterwards they laid it on the table at the right-hand side of the bed.

She had never seen macaroni brought to Mrs Cross but knew that she had eaten it and it was prepared by boiling it in milk.

She addressed the judge: "It was not after the body was removed for burial that the macaroni was found but when it was removed to the other bed to have it dressed. I believe that it was Mary McGrath who first observed the macaroni. When I saw Mrs Cross eat macaroni, it was out of a store room."

"What hour of the day was it when you and Mary McGrath were called up to the room for the purpose of dressing the body?"

"At about eleven o'clock."

"When you came into the room, Dr Cross was there?"

"Yes."

"What did he say?

"He told me to pour out some water and I did so and held the basin close to the body, when Dr Cross got a sponge and sponged it and at that time there was nothing tying the chin, but the mouth was partly open."

"Was there anything else directed to be done?"

"Dr Cross asked for a clean nightdress and the housemaid brought it to him."

"Who put it on?"

"Dr Cross put it on her head and we helped to put it on then."

"Was there anything else on her?"

"Yes, a flannel vest she had on some time before her death."

"Was any handkerchief put round the chin?"

"Yes."

"By whom?"

"By Dr Cross, I think."

"Was anything done by you or anyone there to the limbs of the body?"

"No."

The foreman of the jury asked the witness about whose responsibility it was to bring Mrs Cross her breakfast and she said either herself or the housemaid. This usually consisted of tea and toast up to a week before the death. After that she could not even take tea. In reply to Mr Adams she said the patient got whatever she wanted and was treated kindly and attentively. Mary Barron then stood down.

FRANCIS WOODLEY'S EVIDENCE

Francis William Woodley was the next witness called and under examination stated that he lived about seven miles from Shandy Hall and on the 5th of June he got a postcard from Dr Cross, inviting him to lunch on the following day, Monday the 6th, and saying he wanted his advice about some colts. Miss Cross and the two girls were also present. After the lunch was over he had a conversation with the doctor while they were alone.

"What was the conversation?"

"I asked Dr Cross what Mrs Cross had died of and he said she had fever and that the immediate cause of her death was heart disease. I mentioned the word 'angina pectoris', and he said 'Yes' or words to that effect. I could not swear to the exact words. He led me to believe that heart disease was the immediate cause of death."

He told Mr Atkinson he was relying on his memory of the conversation and had not taken any notes of it and told the judge that he had given a similar account of the conversation at the Magisterial Inquiry in August. He then stood down.

* * *

The prosecution's looking into the inner workings of the house and events at Shandy Hall during the illness of Mary Laura Cross was an effort to prove that the accused had the opportunity to carry out the crime, given his special place as the constant medical attendant and his control over the flow of visitors to the patient. The Attorney General and his team now turned their attention to the motive: the illicit affair with the young governess, the communication after her departure from the house and change in the behaviour of the accused then, especially to his wife, and the attempt to cover up their identities while consummating their passion.

The curious everywhere inside and outside the court would have naturally been salivating throughout the ventilation of the facts of the highly dangerous liaison between the retired army surgeon in the dock and the beautiful young governess. He, who was viewing the proceedings, unmoved and fixed in attitude, as if he also was a spectator – and she, now the permanent inhabitant of the scene of the crime and yet ever present in the minds of the counsel, the witnesses, the spectators and in some manner in the mind of the prisoner, now a third party to the recollection of their passionate encounters.

EVIDENCE OF THE DUBLIN HOTEL STAFF

Four witnesses, members of the staff of the London and North Western Hotel situated in the North Wall of Dublin Port were next to be added to the burgeoning prosecution parade. They were humble and slightly nervous, first of their surroundings and secondly in discussing in public the comings and goings of hotel customers who previously would have been held by them in a mixture of awe, deference and respect.

First in the box was William Poole who deposed to the Attorney General that he was the manager of the North Western Hotel in Dublin. He was handed a photograph of Dr Cross and the then Effie Skinner and identified them as having stayed at the hotel in the month of March. The man in the photograph, he pointed, was present as the prisoner in the dock, the woman his companion of that time.

The couple arrived at about six or seven in the evening of, he thought, 29th March, certainly the end of the month. He noticed that the man carried a portmanteau which had a P and a cross on it and which looked relatively new. They occupied room Number 3 and as far as he could recall they left the next day by boat to England.

He saw them again in June. They arrived by Sunday's mail boat at half past six and occupied room Number 12. They departed the following Tuesday and returned again on the Friday, late in the evening, having needed to be let in by the night porter Edward Stafford. They left again on Sunday evening. The witness was not cross-examined.

Miss Handcock the bookkeeper was next directed to the stand and examined by Mr Wright for the prosecution. He handed her a book, which she confirmed was the one she kept in the hotel in Dublin and that entries were also in her handwriting. She identified the persons in the photograph given to her, one being the prisoner, the other his companion with whom she had seen him twice at the hotel. She had seen them first on the 29th of March. They both had come to the window at which she sat. The gentleman asked for a bedroom and was given the key to Number 3.

Mr Wright paused and seemed to be re-arranging his papers. It was a ploy, a successful one, often used to catch the attention of the room in general and the jury in particular. The spectators leaned forward, a question no doubt in their minds as to what was counsel going to come up with next. They could not wait; all this had been previously the subject of speculative rumour. Now they were getting chapter and verse, right this minute from a small and unprepossessing bookkeeper.

Mr Wright continued: "If he gave a name, did you catch it?"

"I did not hear any name."

"What entry have you in your book for Number 3?"

"Mr and Mrs - - - "

"There is no name."

"No."

"Was that the entry you made?"

"Yes, as far as I can remember."

"How long did they remain in the hotel?"

"They went by the Holyhead boat the next morning."

"They were marked off in the book as having left then?"

"Yes."

"That was the 'Mrs and Mrs' that were in the hotel the night before?"

"Yes."

"In the following month, did they again come to the hotel?"

"Yes."

"Look at your book. Then turn to 21st of April. Did the same lady and gentleman arrive on the evening of the 21st of April?"

"Yes."

"Did you see either or both of them on that occasion?"

"I saw both."

"Did the gentleman, the prisoner in the dock, ask for anything?"

"He asked for the same bedroom as they had before."

"Did they get that room?"

"Yes."

"Did they occupy it that night?"

"Yes."

"Did he give a name on the occasion when asking for the same room?"

"Yes, I think I took it as Osborne."

"As well as you could catch it, was that the name given to you?"

"Yes."

"And you have it so entered in the book?"

"Yes."

"What time did they arrive that evening?"

"They came by boat from Holyhead at the North Wall at about nine o'clock in the evening."

"And they stayed in the hotel that night?"

"Yes."

"When did they leave?"

"The next morning."

"By the train to the south?"

"Yes."

"Did you see them again?"

"I did not."

"Is the Number 3 room one with a bed in it?"

"Yes."

"And is that a bed for two?"

"Yes."

The witness was not cross-examined.

Mary Smythe under examination said that she was chambermaid in the London and North Western Hotel. On the 20th of March last the persons in the photograph stayed in the hotel and occupied the same room; a large room with one bed; she afterwards saw them in the hotel.

The witness was not cross-examined.

Arthur Johnston was then called to the stand and under examination from the Attorney General said that he was a porter in the London and North Western Hotel. On seeing the photograph, he said he remembered that those persons, one of whom was the prisoner, stayed at the hotel at the latter end of March.

He saw them again in the month of April, when they came over on the boat at six o'clock and left the next morning at five minutes to seven. He noticed the gentleman's portmanteau which had a white cross on it. The lady had a small hand basket. He saw them again in June. He was asked to send a telegram on the Sunday morning but because the local office was not open he had to bring it back to the gentleman.

"Where was Dr Cross then?"

"In the coffee room."

"Do you know what was in the telegram?"

"I think it was telling a servant to meet him at the train."

"By himself or with a vehicle?"

"With a vehicle at two o'clock in the morning."

"While you were in the house did you hear the prisoner being called by any name?"

"No."

"Was there a name on the telegram?"

"I don't recollect there was."

The witness was not cross-examined.

* * *

Compounding the previous evidence, that of the hotel workers presented confirmation of the illicit affair with the young governess and the blatant attempt to cover up the subsequent marriage.

* * *

Dennis Griffin's Evidence

Dennis Griffin the postmaster was then called to the witness stand and examined by Mr Wright for the prosecution. As a man who had received a lot of business from the accused over the years, he probably found himself in an invidious position in regard to giving evidence which would be detrimental to his near neighbour. And also to have to discuss the matter of letters which would have been anathema to any self-respecting postmaster. He did indeed prove to be a brittle and somewhat reluctant witness who would try Mr Wright's patience.

In reply to counsel he said that letters were delivered to Shandy Hall between seven and half past in the morning. When asked did that apply to the present year up to the month of June, he said he could not tell the time. He said that two letters were marked "To be left to be called for" – the last, he thought, in June – he could not remember the time of arrival of the one before that as he did not keep an account. He thought it was in the present year but he could not be sure.

When Mr Wright suggested that it was before June, he received no answer. Dr Cross had received the letters but the witness had no conversation with him on the subject. He confirmed that there were initials on them. He remembered Miss Skinner but when asked when she had left he replied that he did not remember anything about her. He thought that she had left when the letters came.

Dr Cross had come over one day and asked was there a letter in the post office marked "To be left to be called for" and he gave it to him.

For the prosecuting counsel it must have seemed that his examination was more akin to an activity reserved for the dental as opposed to the legal profession.

Lord Justice Murphy was bound to intervene and he did: "I am not asking you for the dates. It was a thing that had never occurred before and it must have struck you."

"Indeed, My Lord, I could not tell you what time it was."

Mr Wright asked: "How many weeks or months after Miss Skinner left was it?"

"I could not tell you."

Lord Justice Murphy took over again: "Can you remember even the year it occurred?"

"I can."

"Was it this year?"

"It was."

"Can you recollect what month in the year?"

"I can't recollect."

Mr Wright resumed examination: "Was the second letter in June?"

"I think it was."

"Who gave it to him?"

"He took it himself."

"He walked in and looked at the letters?"

"He did not look through them at all; he only took this one."

"Do you remember if the day he got the letter was after or before the funeral?"

"I could not tell you."

At this Lord Justice Murphy lost patience: "Come now, Griffin, think! Recollect where you are."

Mr Wright took up the baton again and elicited the fact that the letter came after the funeral and before Dr Cross went away. He did not notice anything about the postmark and made no reply to counsel's question as to what had made him remember when the letter had arrived. Under cross-examination by Mr Adams for the Defence he said that he had attended the funeral and others included Dr Godfrey, Rev Hayes, John and Edward Roche and the Fitzgibbons, and members of the local gentry who lived two miles from Shandy Hall.

After brief questions from the judge which added nothing to what he had already testified, the postmaster stepped down.

*   *   *

Given the potential seriousness of his evidence and his memory, which could justifiably have been viewed as unnecessarily defective, the postmaster had been let off relatively lightly. The judge's admonishment that it was an unusual occurrence to have post collected in that manner and must have struck him, and the reminder that Mr Griffin ought to remember he was in a court had some effect. The evidence most important and damaging to the prisoner was the fact that the second letter arrived after the funeral, indicating that Dr Cross's attention was elsewhere other than on the apparently tragic event of his wife's awful illness and death.

The evidence of the next witness would attempt to copperfasten the prosecution's establishment of motive.

CORNELIUS MCCARTHY'S EVIDENCE

Cornelius McCarthy was examined by Mr Ronan for the prosecution and stated that he carried the letters from Shandy Hall to the post office.

"How were they given to you?"

"In a bag."

"How far is it from the house to the post office?"

"About four or five hundred yards."

"On your way to the post office used you to meet Dr Cross?"

"Yes."

"Used he to give you any letters?"

"Yes."

"To whom were they addressed?"

" To: Miss Skinner, Tullow, Killanure, County Carlow."

"How many of them did you get from him?"

"About fifteen."

"Were these on different days?"

"Yes."

"You remember Miss Skinner being at Shandy Hall?"

"Yes."

"Was it after she left she got these letters?"

"Yes."

"How long were you at Shandy Hall?"

"Five years and over."

"Are you still there?"

"No, I left on 25th March last."

"After Miss Skinner came did you ever hear Dr Cross arguing with his wife?"

"I did."

"Tell what you heard him say."

"On one occasion I was in the workshop. Dr Cross and Mrs Cross were in the schoolroom. There is a doorway from one into the other and the door was open. I heard them scold and I heard him say loudly he wished the devil would come and sweep her out of the house."

There was what could be described as a collective intake and exhalation of breath in the court and a good deal of quiet muttering in reaction to the alleged brutality of the accused towards his wife. When it died out fairly quickly, Counsel pressed on with his examination.

"Did you remember one day Mrs Cross being in the yard and Dr Cross saying anything to her?"

"He said, go in and if she did not, may the devil crack her neck or her legs."

"Besides this, did you hear Dr Cross saying anything rough to his wife?"

"Not that I remember."

Mr Atkinson cross-examined for the defence.

"Dr Cross had stopped 5 shillings from you and more if it was known?"

"He stopped 6 shillings from me for a wrench. I had no quarrel with Dr Cross."

"Do you remember whether he gave a choice to the devil to break her neck or her legs?"

"I don't say which he mentioned. I remember he said the devil crack her neck or her legs."

"When was that?"

"I kept no day or date."

"You don't know when it happened?"

"No. It happened in the yard."

"Do you remember the words?"

"Yes."

"When was it?"

"It was before Miss Skinner left Shandy Hall."

"Where was Dr Cross and his wife when you heard them talking about this?"

"They were in the yard, but I could not tell what they were talking about, as Mrs Cross spoke very low." Cornelius then addressed Lord Justice Murphy: "I left Dr Cross of my own accord."

* * *

Incrementally but now upping the pace, the Attorney General and his team were tightening the prosecution screw, focusing on more and more damaging revelations about Dr Cross, as in the instance of the witness McCarthy whose account of the vile attack on Mary Laura Cross was even more significant in the placement of time – before the young governess left Shandy Hall. The only meaningful challenge the Defence could make was that the witness might have had a bias against the prisoner, and there was not a good fist made of that.

* * *

EVIDENCE OF DISTRICT INSPECTOR TYACKE

District Inspector Henry D Tyacke took the stand and was sworn in and, in reply to the Attorney General, stated that he arrested Dr Cross on the 28th of July. When he arrested him, he cautioned him and told him what he was being charged with.

"I charged him with the murder of his wife, Mary Laura Cross. He said 'My God, my God' and a short time afterwards he said: 'Think of a man of my time of life to commit a murder.' A short time after that again, he said: 'There's a God above who will see the villainy of this.' He asked me if he could talk to his sister, and I said he could talk to no one except in the presence of a policeman and his solicitor."

On the 2nd of August he had placed Sergeant Higgins in charge of the prisoner at the Magisterial Inquiry and he retrieved a letter from the prisoner who asked him to pass it on to the press.

"I said I could not do it, and if he wanted to write anything he should do it through the Governor of the gaol."

The Attorney General then read the letter to the court as follows:

Sirs – In your impression of the 29th, commenting on Dr Cross and the charges against him, relative to his late wife, I beg to inform you the statement that "the prisoner attended his wife during her illness and allowed nobody to attend her or attend the funeral" is not quite the fact. She was also attended and prescribed for by Dr Godfrey, uncle to the prisoner. She was nursed and cared for during her illness by an old schoolfellow and friend, Miss Jefferson, Mercy Orphanage, Kilburn, a guest in the house for weeks before her death, at whose suggestion and that of Dr Godfrey, the funeral took place before 7 a.m. instead of 11 a.m. that day.

For this reason, as the funeral was advertised privately, being held at 11 would make it appear as if it was not intended to be so. Any friend who wished to see her during her illness had free access to her room, and her funeral was attended by several neighbours. As your article had the unintentional effect of creating a prejudice against the prisoner, may I trouble you to insert this.

Mr Atkinson said that he had not got a copy of this letter, but one which was handed to him by the Crown when he made the complaint.

Under examination, Inspector Tyacke stated that immediately after he had arrested the prisoner, he proceeded to Shandy Hall and he got there the contents of the green box then in court. He found the minim glass on the mantelpiece in Mrs Cross's bedroom. He found a paper labelled strychnine, wrapped in brown paper in a cupboard and in the same place he found a parcel labelled "dog poison", supposed to be strychnine.

The other matters contained in the box he also got in the house, the broken measure glass he found in the bedroom. He gave the green box and its contents to Dr Pearson, for analysis. The small box and hamper also contained some articles found in the house by Sergeant Gorman and were also brought in by him, but they were not considered worth examining.

Dr Cross's diary came into his possession through Mr Deyos. The book was locked. He had the key, having taken a bundle of keys from the prisoner when he arrested him amongst which it was. Mr Deyos came to him for the key and it was by that means it came into his possession.

The diary was then handed in as evidence.

The Attorney General next produced a purse which was found on the prisoner and questioned the witness in regard to it.

He had been given it when Dr Cross had been searched in his presence, along with a photograph of the prisoner and Miss Skinner.

In the purse there was a number of papers including a bill from a Euston Hotel dated from the 10th to the 13th of June. He was cross-examined by Mr Adams for the Defence.

"Were you at the inquest into the body of Mrs Cross on the 21st of July?"

"I was."

"Was Dr Cross present?"

"He was."

"Was it stated in his presence that this body had been exhumed?"

"He walked in and saw the body after it had been exhumed. I arrested him on the 28th."

"And you found either upon his person or in the house, the various articles you have mentioned?"

"Yes."

"From the 21st to the 28th was Dr Cross residing at his house in Shandy Hall?"

"Yes."

"And during that time he was under no kind of arrest?"

"Yes, he was not under arrest."

"And he had full control over his house and all that was in it during that week?"

"Yes."

"You have seen that diary that was produced here?"

"Yes. I knew nothing of the diary until Mr Deyos asked me for the key for it."

The witness then stood down.

* * *

Given the intensity and depth of DI Tyacke's investigation, it was obvious from the shallowness of his cross-examination by the defence that he had not put a foot wrong in its execution or left himself or the prosecution open to any manner of inappropriate behaviour. He had played his part, from start to finish entirely by the book. An approach he had also clearly instilled in his team.

However, here was the small reference, not dwelled upon for good reason in the legal setting, to the accused walking into the room where the post mortem was taking place, indicative of the informal nature of location of post mortems of the time. It is reminiscent of Dr Palmer's appearance at the post mortem of John Parsons Cook. But the fact that Dr Cross would feel it necessary to view the body of his exhumed wife is bizarre to say the least. It spoke of something of the impulsive nature of Dr Cross, and also reminds us that he had become over long years of war inured to death and putrefaction. Or perhaps that by nature he was coldly insensitive. Or is a poisoner irresistibly drawn to the evidence of his skill and power?

Perhaps, however, he was trying to achieve the opposite effect and prove he felt no guilt? Certainly, the visitation would neither intimidate or inhibit the chief Crown medical witness in the exercise of his duty – if indeed that was the purpose.

* * *

EVIDENCE OF SERGEANT HIGGINS

Sergeant J Higgins RIC was then examined by Mr Wright for the prosecution. He stated: "I was pressed the first day of the magisterial inquiry into this case. It was on Monday the 1st of August. I was put in charge of Dr Cross by District Inspector Tyacke. Himself and his sister were speaking together and Mr Tyacke told me to take a note of any conversation I heard. I took a note of a conversation I heard, and I have kept the note of it. Shortly after I had received instructions from Mr Tyacke, I heard Dr Cross ask Miss Cross: 'Did you see the two little bottles about the length of my finger?' Miss Cross replied: 'Yes, yes, I destroyed them with the other things.'

He asked her secondly about the two little bottles, the length of his finger, and he added 'with the white powder in them' and I heard her answer: 'Yes, yes, I destroyed them with the other things.'

I saw the letter in his possession and I said, 'I must have that.' I then took it from him and afterwards gave it to Mr Tyacke."

Mr Atkinson cross-examined.

"How did you take the letter from him?"

"He was handing it to some person who was sitting beside him in the County Grand Jury Room."

"You took it before the party got it?"

"I did."

"Who was the party?"

"I cannot say. I know his brother Ben Cross and his sister Miss Cross were present and there were several others sitting to the right of him in the room, but I did not take any particular notice who they were."

Dr Cross had never been handed back the letter and it had not been given to the Press. On the morning of the opening of the Magisterial Inquiry Sergeant Higgins brought Dr Cross from the gaol and when he came to the Grand Jury Room he was greeted by friends but no conversation took place between them. There was further conversation with Miss Cross, of about a half a minute's duration, but nothing which he considered had any bearing on the case.

He had heard no mention being made of Dr Pearson's evidence at the inquest, which he had not attended but about which he had read a newspaper report.

Sergeant Higgins then stood down.

Mr Short's Evidence

Mr John S Short, in reply to Mr Ronan, for the prosecution, said that he was a pharmaceutical chemist and he remembered receiving from Mr Tyacke, a green box, a small box and a hamper containing certain articles. And he had made an inventory of the contents.

Sergeant Gorman's Evidence

Sergeant John Gorman then took the stand and after being sworn in, he stated, in reply to the Attorney General examining, that he went to Shandy Hall on the 28th of July and locked up various rooms and took possession of the dispensary. He took the articles away in a small hamper and a box. And delivered them to Mr Short who examined them. They had been since under his care. The green box had been passed on to Dr Pearson who after analysis of the contents returned the box. When asked, he described Shandy Hall as an ordinary country gentleman's house. The stairs were very low.

MR KILOH'S EVIDENCE.

Mr James Kiloh was the next witness and in reply to Mr Wright, for the prosecution stated: "I am in the employment of Messrs Goulding of Patrick Street [Cork]. On the 2nd of September, 1886, I was present in the shop. On that day Dr Cross came in and bought one pound of arsenic. He said that he wanted it for sheep dipping and I made an entry in the book: *2/9/86. Name of the purchaser, Dr Cross; address of the purchaser: Shandy Hall, Dripsey. Name and quantity of poison sold: Arsenic, 1lb. Purpose for which required: Sheep dipping. Signature of the purchaser: Philip HE Cross, Surgeon."*

Under cross-examination by Mr Adams, Mr Kiloh could not say that the arsenic was pure. It did not have to be mixed when sold to a medical man and in this case there was no need to sign for it, but he took the precaution anyway. He had removed the arsenic from a cask. Mixing usually took place at the counter. In reply to the judge he said that he had known Dr Cross from before.

Mr Kiloh stood down.

Mr Atkinson said he should apply for Miss Jefferson's diary, as on the previous day she had not given any dates, but there were entries which enabled her to fix dates with other matters. Inasmuch as she was not examined till the 5th of September, three months after the death of Mrs Cross.

Mr Justice Murphy said that at any time it would be necessary, Miss Jefferson could be recalled.

The Attorney General said that he was sure Miss Jefferson would have no objection to allow her diary to be looked over.

Miss Jefferson said that she would not have the least objection.

The court then rose and adjourned for luncheon.

MRS MADRAS'S EVIDENCE

On the resumption Mrs Isabella Madras was examined by the Attorney General and deposed that she lived about two miles from Shandy Hall and knew Dr Cross and his late wife whom she described as an "intimate acquaintance". She was away from home when Miss Skinner went to the Crosses but remembered her when she resided with the Caulfields. She used to call into the Crosses in passing.

"Do you recollect seeing Dr Cross in town in January of the present year?"

"Yes."

"Did you ask him how Mrs Cross was?"

"I did."

"What did he say?"

"He said that she was so poorly that he would not be surprised if she was dead when he got home."

Lord Justice Murphy: "What date was that?"

Mrs Madras: "About the end of January."

In reply to the Attorney General, the witness said that she had been staying in Cork and did not see Mrs Cross until the end of May at her brother's house and she looked ill. The next time was at church on Ascension Thursday and while Mrs Cross said that she felt much better, she thought that Mrs Cross looked worse than she had last seen her. She called to Shandy Hall twice afterwards. She had heard about the illness but was not aware how serious it was.

"Did you call again?"

"Yes, on the evening before she died and I walked from the gate to the house, as I thought any vehicle would make too much noise. Dr Cross and Miss Cross came to the door to meet me."

"Did you say anything?"

"Yes, I asked how Mrs Cross was. They said she was very ill and either the doctor or Miss Cross said she was suffering from vomiting, and that she was very weak."

"Did you make any suggestion?"

"I said I thought champagne should be tried, as I gave it successfully in cases of vomiting."

"Did you make any offer?"

"Yes, I offered to take a messenger with me to my brother's house and give him some champagne."

"Did Dr Cross say anything?"

"Yes. He said it was no use."

Mrs Madras further testified that she had seen Mrs Cross about the middle of November in her own house and she seemed in very good health. When she expressed concern after meeting Dr Cross in January he said his wife was suffering from "an attack of the heart".

The defence had little of consequence to ask the witness and she stood down.

THE EVIDENCE OF DR CHARLES YELVERTON PEARSON

Dr Charles Yelverton Pearson was then sworn in and examined by the Attorney General for the prosecution.

"What are your qualifications, Dr Pearson?"

"Doctor Of Medicine, Master Of Surgery; Licentiate Of Midwifery; Fellow Of The Royal College Of Surgeons, England; Professor of Materia Medica at the Queen's College and lecturer in Medical Jurisprudence."

"Have you considerable experience in analysis?"

"Yes."

"Were you present at the Courthouse in Coachford on the 21st of July for the purpose of making a post-mortem examination on Mary Laura Cross?"

"Yes."

"Had the coffin been opened before you saw it?"

"No, it was in the same state as when taken out of the grave."

"Who was present at the time that the coffin was opened?"

"Dr Crowley, Acting Sergeant Gorman and there was a woman present whose name I did not know. The coffin was an oak one and on it was a plate giving the name and death of the deceased."

"Was the coffin opened in your presence?"

"Yes, and the body taken out. It was bound in a white garment. A flannel swathe was around the abdomen and a white handkerchief was about the chin and blue stockings on the feet."

"Did you notice the features?"

"Yes, the features were drawn and there was slime on the face and about the mouth and nostrils. There was a white mould on it also and the scarf or superficial skin was separated in some parts, particularly on the back and limbs from the real skin. There were livid marks on the back and discolouration on the abdomen; the results of post mortem changes; the green marks in certain parts due to putrefaction."

"Did you then proceed to make an internal examination of the body?"

"Yes, along with Dr Crowley."

"When you opened the abdominal cavity were the lining membranes healthy or diseased?"

"Healthy."

"Were the organs in the interior of the body well preserved?"

"Remarkably so."

"Does that observation apply to any particular part of the body?"

"It applies especially to the stomach and intestines, and more especially to the small intestines."

"Were there any traces of putrefaction at all in the intestines and stomach?"

"No."

"Now, may I ask you, has arsenic an effect in preserving the stomach and the intestines?"

"Yes, it has a very great effect. Arsenic is used, as in medical preparations, for preserving bodies for dissection. It was more likely to preserve than any other poison, but there are some other poisons such as corrosive sublimate, which preserve very well, also."

"If a body without any chemical injection but in its natural state, was put into a grave in the summer on the 4th of June and if it was taken up on the 21st July, would you expect the stomach have presented positive appearances of advanced putrefaction?"

"I am quite certain of it; in the absence of arsenic or any other preservative."

"As a matter of fact; in the ordinary human body what are the first parts to putrefy?"

"The soft parts."

"For instance: take three parts – the stomach, the liver and the ordinary muscles – which of these would putrefy first?"

"The muscles of certain parts."

"But of the liver or stomach, which would putrefy first?"

"That would depend on the condition of the stomach at the time of death."

"Suppose the stomach was empty?"

"The liver would likely putrefy first."

"Did you examine the intestines to see if there was any solid substance, such as food in them?"

"I did."

"Was there any food in them?"

"No."

"Was there in any other part of the intestines any traces of excreta?"

"No, except bile."

"What did you do on the first day you saw the body?"

"I first viewed the general appearances of the various organs without disturbing them, and then I began examining for traces of typhoid fever."

"Tell the jury what are the evidences of typhoid fever?"

"There is a peculiar inflammation of the intestines, particularly the lower portion of the small intestines and also the adjoining portion of the large intestine."

"Well, now, what is the appearance which the small intestine and the upper part of the large intestine present when the patient has suffered from typhoid fever?"

"It would depend on the stage of the disease. In the first week there would be evidence of these patches, and they would be elevated beyond the surrounding surfaces of the bowel. Later on, sometime in the second week, portions of the patches would be sloping; and still later portions would be cast off; and probably leave ulcers on the bowel."

"Is the bowel perforated from these ulcerations?"

"Sometimes."

"Are these appearances the well known and recognised results of typhoid fever?"

"Yes."

"Did you find any such appearances?"

"No."

Over a long sequence of examination during which Dr Pearson was at all times assured and forthright in his testimony, he retraced the process of removing the internal organs of the body and placing them in rigorously cleaned vessels before bringing them to his laboratory in Queen's College, Cork for analysis. This process began the day following the initial post mortem in Coachford and would last for seven days.

The professor found no evidence whatsoever of typhoid fever or heart disease. There was no sign of illness in the stomach but he found particles attached to it. Having subjected these particles to three independent processes of analysis and when examined under microscope they were found to be minute crystals of arsenic. They were of a very defined character, in this instance, crystals of white arsenic.

They were subjected to further tests which confirmed the original finding. There was no probability of mistake unless any of the tests proved contradictory, and they did not. The analysis for quantity resulted in 1.74 grains of arsenic in the stomach. A minute quantity of strychnine, one hundredth of a grain, was also discovered. The witness tasted the sample which he said was intensely bitter.

Traces of arsenic were also discovered in the liver, kidney and spleen, the largest amount in the liver amounting to 1.28 grains. He said in response to questioning that two grains of arsenic had been known to destroy life.

"From the appearance this lady presented were you able to discover any natural cause of death?"

"No. And further I will state that the quantity of arsenic present was quite sufficient to cause death, along with the appearances discovered."

"And in a case of arsenical poisoning it is possible to go beyond what you stated – that there is no appearance of natural causes of death and there is arsenic sufficient to cause death?"

"I don't think so."

"In case of death by arsenic, and on examining the body after death, do you expect to find the entire quantity that may have been administered?"

"Most certainly you will not find it if vomiting takes place."

"And you can form no certain estimate of the amount that has been given?"

"From the quantity I have found I am able to swear that a poisonous dose must have been administered or taken."

The Attorney General then moved on to the equally vital matter of the symptoms of arsenical poisoning which would of necessity have to match the evidence of witnesses to the symptoms that Mary Laura Cross experienced during her long and painful illness.

Dr Pearson said that a poisonous dose of arsenic would produce a pain in the upper part of the stomach which could be confused with a pain in the heart and the pain would be very acute and severe followed by "purging and vomiting; vomiting usually precedes the purging. Thirst is usually an early symptom, with a tightness in the throat as if something was being tied there. There is a burning feel also in the throat and later on, if the person lives long enough, there are cramps in the limbs, particularly in the calves of the legs; and possibly there may be a pain referred to the forehead, with suffusion of the eyes; and that is more usual if there is a lingering death."

"In slow poisoning?"

"Yes."

"What is the colour of the vomit when there is a poisonous dose delivered?"

"It would depend on the kind of arsenic given. If white arsenic were given, the vomit would be yellow or green; or possibly a yellowish green."

"Has this vomiting and purging which you have described, as a direct result of arsenic, a great effect in weakening the vital powers?"

"Yes."

"Could you explain the exact way in which it destroys life – does it destroy by exhaustion or affection of the body?"

"If a large dose has been taken and death comes early it may be caused by shock but it is usually caused by nervous exhaustion and finally failure of the heart's action would probably be the immediate cause of death. In some cases it affects the nervous system alone and kills more like a narcotic poison, but that is a rare case. The membrane of the eyelids may become congested and this may be the case especially in chronic poisoning, even after one dose. In consequence, persons are not able to see things, especially near them."

"From your examination of the liver in this case (1.28 grains) could you say what time before death the poison was administered, to be found in such quantity?"

"To be found in that quantity it must have been administered within three or four days before death – certainly no longer than four."

"Now, doctor, as a result of your post-mortem examination of this body and your analysis, are you able to state what in your opinion was the cause of death?"

"I am."

"Be good enough to inform the jury what, in your opinion, was the cause of Mrs Cross's death."

"I believe that the death was due to arsenical poisoning, but having found a small quantity of strychnine, I would not undertake to say that it may not have been accelerated by strychnine."

Dr Pearson further stated that he had been in court for the whole of the proceedings and heard the witness evidence of the symptoms of the victim, in particular Miss Jefferson whose evidence he had taken down in notes and confirmed his own opinion gleaned from both the post mortem and the analysis. He had no doubt that the victim had not died from the effects of typhoid fever. He had examined the contents of the green box and found pure strychnine in three packages and traces of chlorodyne on the broken minim glass. The symptoms of strychnine poisoning come on very soon and the person generally dies within two hours. He could form no medical opinion on the cause of the screaming of the victim before her death.

Dr Pearson was then cross-examined by Mr Atkinson for the defence and subjected to an intense attack on his professional status, possibly to his surprise, but under which he stood his ground. The defence was quite aware that if the medical witness's evidence could be undermined, to the extent of reasonable doubt, then their case could be considerably strengthened.

Mr Atkinson went for the jugular straight away.

"Do you know anything practical whatsoever about what you have been talking about for the last hour?"

"Yes, I do."

"Did you ever attend a person who was killed by poisoning from arsenic?"

"I attended a person who was suffering from arsenical poisoning."

"Did you ever analyse the contents of the stomach of anybody who was killed by arsenical poisoning?"

"Not a human being."

"Did you ever make a post mortem examination upon anybody who had been killed by arsenic?"

"No, except in this instance."

"Is this your first attempt at either analysis or post mortem on a person who died from arsenic?"

"It is not my first attempt at analysis, and I have attended a person afflicted with arsenical poisoning."

"Have you ever performed an analysis on the contents of any human being?"

"Yes."

"When?"

"I could not give you the exact date, but it is not very long ago when a young man in the city died from poison – about two years ago."

"Who assisted you?"

"Nobody."

"And this was the only case?"

"Yes."

"Are these your sources of information?" – pointing to the books on the table.

"No."

"Are these your books?"

"Not all of them."

"And are these your sources of information; or are they brought here by you as your testimonials?"

"No, they are not."

The Attorney General voiced a protest.

Mr Atkinson responded: "I beg your pardon; I know just as much about it as he does; for I have read it also. Have you any practical experience of poisoning by arsenic on the human being?"

"There are cases of mine that are suffering from chronic arsenical poisoning."

The Defence Counsel then grilled the witness regarding the mistake that he had made in his evidence to the Grand Jury in relation to the amount of arsenic discovered in the liver, the record of which Dr Pearson subsequently corrected. Despite the witness's excellent qualifications, in the eyes of the court and the jury he would have been viewed as a young man, who possibly may not have had the life experience of his position. The mistake of attributing the total amount of poison found in the body to the liver could prove a very damaging error for the prosecution. How damaging would depend on the effectiveness of Mr Atkinson's cross-examination.

"Did you ever swear twice it was three grains?"

"I don't think so."

"Was your deposition read over to you?"

"It was."

"Did you not make two depositions, in the first of which you state the biggest portion of arsenic was in the liver, at the inquest. Don't you know?"

"I cannot quite remember what I swore."

Mr Atkinson read: "'As the result of my examination, I discovered white arsenic in all these organs, being present in the highest quantities in the liver.' You swore your first information on the 28th of July and did you not swear you had your analysis complete?"

"I don't know that I did, but I believe it was."

"You came again to make an information on the 1st of August before the magistrates?"

"Yes."

"Had you your report before you?"

"No."

Mr Atkinson read: "'*A portion of the liver was examined by quantitative analysis and an estimate made of the quantity present. The quantity was poisonous and the liver contained three grains.*'"

"I believe I did, but I was mistaken. I'd like to explain very fully. A portion of my notes in quantitative analysis was distinct from the other parts and were not with me when I was writing my report for the examination of which you ask. It was locked up in the College with some other notes, and I was not able to obtain it and the quantity that most impressed my mind was three grains in the organs. That was my intention to convey. I had not this particular report with me. I had no notes before the magistrate."

"Were you so very correct?"

"I thought I was correct."

"Are you not aware that if you died that these depositions you made would be evidence against the accused?"

"Yes, but you had my notes also."

Mr Atkinson continued to press the point, claiming that there was no authority for three grains ever having been found in the liver. The witness replied that it was not so much a matter of the amount alone but the distribution throughout the body. He was questioned about the process used in the analysis to which the doctor said he had ensured there was no possibilities of impurities present in his use of the testing apparatus.

Mr Atkinson went down every avenue to cast doubt on the credibility of the witness, a tactic which, while understandable, surely might have been better employed by the medical expert retained by the defence who was sitting in the body of the court. Under the circumstance he was labouring against Dr Pearson's unflappable demeanour in the box. In exasperation he claimed that here was a man who had never examined the contents of a human body which prompted the intervention of the judge to refute counsel's incorrect statement.

Mr Atkinson suggested that strychnine might be confused with something else by the decomposition process but the doctor said not by the test process he had employed. It was now clear that the tide was somewhat turning against the counsel, who was displaying his frustration in not being able to rattle the witness by becoming intemperate in his examination.

"Now, look at your Taylor *On Poisons* and tell me if you agree with it?"

The Attorney General objected. He stated that it was very inconvenient to be reading parts from different authors and asking the doctor if he agreed with it. It was merely throwing books at his head.

Mr Atkinson answered smartly: "That is what he has done to me."

Lord Justice Murphy responded: "No, no, he did not certainly."

Mr Atkinson resumed after this rebuke from the bench, addressing the witness: "Do you agree that strychnine may be mistaken for cadaver alkaloid?"

"Not if applied in the way I did it."

Lord Justice Murphy asked: "Were the tests you applied strictly accurate?"

"They were perfectly satisfactory to me. The test, in the way I applied it, could not be confounded at all."

Mr Atkinson asked: "Will you show me a case where it cannot?"

Dr Pearson replied: "Will you show me a case where it can?"

There was laughter in the court.

Lord Justice Murphy: "It is a shame for any person, while such a case as this is on, to indulge in laughter. It is a scandal."

* * *

While the judge was correct on that matter, the reaction was not to a smart answer from a man who would not naturally indulge himself that way, but to the over-aggressive stance the Defence Counsel was adopting which, if the spectators' response was to be measured, would be in the favour of the man in the box as opposed to his interrogator.

* * *

The Defence Counsel, his personal affront on the witness seemingly spent, moved on to the subject of symptoms of arsenical poisoning which Dr Pearson conceded could have a number of variations, sometimes no thirst or vomiting or purging and other times complete absence of pain.

He stated that there were some affections of the heart that might not be detected in a post mortem but a weak or defective heart was not one of them. Then, in relation to strychnine poisoning, he said the body is usually stiff immediately after death.

"The whole body quite rigid?"

"Yes."

"In the lower animals is the head drawn back?"

"In some of the lower animals, yes."

"The head drawn back at right angles to the body?"

"Not quite that."

"But the whole body is stiff and that is almost immediately after death?"

"Yes."

After one or two more perfunctory questions, Mr Atkinson announced the end of his cross-examination and the Attorney General made a brief re-examination to clarify a few issues in which the witness testified that vomiting could further weaken a defective heart and that it would be highly improbable that a person would die from angina pectoris.

He also explained that he removed the brain after the second exhumation to determine if he could find more traces of strychnine. In reply to the judge, he said that strychnine takes effect immediately.

Dr Pearson then stood down from the witness stand.

* * *

The Crown Prosecution team would have been well pleased with the performance of the state analyst who had maintained his professional dignity during what he himself would later describe as abuse at the hands of the defence. But quite apart from his resistance to the goading of Mr Atkinson, Dr Pearson had given evidence of a scientific nature which was not only not capable of interpretation or misrepresentation but would have stayed long in the minds of those in court and more pertinently the jurors.

His revelation of the fact that arsenic was used for the preservation of bodies for dissection, tied in to the state in which he found the body of Mary Laura Cross which should have been more ravaged, must have made a powerful impression. The stomach should have shown signs of advanced putrefaction; and the fact that the liver only had small signs of the same was extraordinary, as a soft organs are the first to fall to the process of decomposition.

The very poison that the doctor proved beyond all doubt was present in the body had, in an astounding chemical process, helped to preserve the evidence. And this evidence had been adduced by rigorous testing that did not allow for the introduction of impurities or the possibility of mistakes.

And most tellingly as Dr Pearson pointed out to DI Tyacke very early on in the investigation, he was not an advocate and delivered his evidence in a very objective manner, refusing to be drawn for example, to speculate about the cause of the victim's screams before she died. Above all he demonstrated that he knew his jurisprudence just as well as his medicine.

DR TIMOTHY CROWLEY'S EVIDENCE

The next witness was Dr Timothy Crowley.

"I am dispensary doctor at Coachford and live almost a mile from the place. On the 2nd of June Dr Cross came to me for the purpose of regulating his wife's death. I asked him the cause of death and he said typhoid fever. I told him to come to the dispensary the next day and he did. The entry in the registry on 3rd of June is his except the third column."

Mr Wright, for the prosecution, read the entry:

"*Mary Laura Cross; female, married aged 49, lady; certified cause of death: typhoid fever. Duration of illness: fourteen days. Signature, address and qualification of informant: P.H.E. Cross, widower of the deceased; occupier of Shandy Hall.*"

"Did you ever attend Mrs Cross?"

"No."

"Was there much fever in the neighbourhood during the month of May?"

"Not a case at all."

"Were you able to form an opinion on whether the deceased had died of natural causes?"

"I was. She did not die from natural causes."

"Were you and the Crosses on good terms?"

"We were not unfriendly."

"Were you ever in the house?"

"I was there a short time before her death when I saw Dr Cross about some oats."

"Have you examined many persons poisoned by arsenic or strychnine?"

"No."

"Where did you get your experience of arsenical poisoning?"

"From books."

"Did you make it a special subject of study?"

"No."

"You are not an experienced toxicologist?"

"No."

"You know that rigidity occurs after strychnine poisoning; if the mouth of a corpse is found wide open five or six hours after death, is it not inconsistent with poisoning?"

"It may or may not be."

Lord Justice Murphy asked: "When had you typhoid fever prevalent in your neighbourhood?"

"April 1st."

"When had you it before that?"

"I can't remember it was so long ago."

The witness stood down and the Court adjourned until half past ten the following morning. The Attorney General stated that the Crown would close its case early.

The Third Day

Saturday, 17th December

The trial resumed at half past ten. The names of the jurors were called out and proceedings got under way.

The first witness called was Mr Tyndall.

MR TYNDALL'S EVIDENCE

In reply to the Attorney General, Mr Tyndall stated that he was married to a Miss Marriott and was brother-in-law of the prisoner, Dr Cross. He knew Dr Cross very well, having often seen him in England.

"Did you know his handwriting?"

"Yes, I had corresponded with him, and knew it perfectly well."

"Did you get this letter from Dr Cross?"

"Yes, dated the 2nd of June."

"Was that the only letter you got in reference to his wife's illness?"

"Yes."

"When last before you got this letter had you seen Dr Cross?"

"In the summer of '86."

"Did you see him after getting the letter?"

"Yes, on the 17th of June about 9 o'clock in the evening at my own home."

Mr Atkinson said that as far as his experience went, when a witness was about to be examined where a deposition had not been made, some note of some kind was given of his evidence to the Counsel for the prisoner. This witness was simply brought to identify a letter.

The Attorney General said: "It was only a few moments before the court sat that I heard he had seen Dr Cross."

Lord Justice Murphy said that if there was any material fact to be established by a witness, some intimation should certainly be given. There was no real point in this and unless he concluded that the Crown had possession of the evidence and withheld it, he could not disallow it.

The Attorney General resumed the examination: "It was in a conversation with Mr Tyacke that this came out. What conversation took place between you and Dr Cross?"

"I commenced by expressing sympathy for his loss, and he did not say very much. I did not pursue the conversation because my wife was present. I asked some particulars of his wife's last illness and he said, or I understood him to say, at the last she died of angina pectoris. I did not afterwards get an opportunity to pursue the conversation."

"How long did the interview last?"

"He was in the house about an hour."

"Did your wife say anything?"

"She bade him goodbye and kissed him when coming in."

Lord Justice Murphy: "You say you understood that you heard angina pectoris at the last – who mentioned it?"

"Dr Cross."

He was then cross-examined by Mr Atkinson for the defence.

"Would you give us the whole of the conversation as to the cause of death?"

"I said I was very sorry to hear that there was typhoid fever in the neighbourhood, and then I understood him to say angina pectoris was the last [cause]."

HUMPHREY MARRIOTT'S EVIDENCE

Mr Humphrey Marriott, brother of Mrs Cross, was then called and examined by Mr Wright QC for the prosecution.

"Do you remember the date of her marriage to the prisoner?"

"The 17th of August, 1869, to my belief."

"Where were they married?"

"At St James's Church, Piccadilly."

"Was there any settlement in the marriage?"

"No."

"What fortune had your sister?"

"She had, on the death of my father, something over £5,000."

"Do you know Dr Cross?"

"Very well."

"Have you corresponded with him?"

"Yes."

Mr Wright addressed the judge: "This is the letter of the 29th of May; it has already been read, My Lord." He turned to the witness: "Had you also that letter from him?" He handed the witness the letter.

"I had."

Mr Wright continued: "This, My Lord, is the letter of the 2nd of June from the prisoner to the witness." He enquired of the witness:

"On receipt of the letter of the 29th of May, did you write a letter in reply?"

"I did."

Mr Wright proceeded to read the letter aloud: "The following is the letter of the 29th of May:

My dear Marriott – I am sorry to inform you that poor dear Laura is very ill with fever (typhoid) for the last week. If anything, she is rather better, with less fever, but so very weak and prostrated, that with her weak heart I should be very much afraid if she got any faintness it would be most dangerous. We must hope for the best, and with kind regards, truly yours,

P.H.E. Cross.

Poor Bob is laid up at the infirmary at Epsom, with something like diphtheria. It is really a very trying season. Any number of persons have gone off about this neighbourhood. There is a lot of fever about and the medical men say that they have an unusual lot to do.

The following is the letter of the 2nd of June:

I had wired the sad news about poor dear Laura ere I got yours today. The poor thing was taken ill last Friday week with a slight feverish attack attended with much bilious derangement.

This gradually went into continued fever; which is rather rife all about and finally the poor weak heart failed from exhaustion, as I felt sure it would, many a long day ago.

I only wonder how it carried her along for such a length of time, as even running up the stairs made it beat so hard that she could rarely get to the end of the passage without halting to recover herself. We must have the funeral on Saturday morning, in consequence of Sunday being the day the Papist select, if possible, for a funeral; and Monday would be too long for the poor body, much as I should wish to do so.

Still we must protect as much as we can the living. I was much shocked when I took Bess and Etta to see their poor mother this morning after breakfast. I would not allow them to see her until they had eaten, fearing their feelings might have been too much; but no, they never shed a tear, I grieve to relate. I don't think even now (noon) they realise the situation. It is hard to be the father of two such children; as for the others at school in England, I don't know how to break it to them – their little hearts will nearly burst in twain.

I have written informing them of their mother's illness, and wrote today to their masters saying she was very bad. I think I must run across and tell the poor little things all about it; they need someone to give them a little comfort in their time of trouble. Miss Jefferson left us this morning for England, having arranged to go some days before. She was a great nurse to poor L, in a quiet way, and very kindly offered to remain a few days longer, if she could be of use, but to tell the truth, both my sister and myself thought we should not wish for any intruders on our sorrow; and indeed I don't feel very inclined to be loquacious just now, but that silence is much trouble to her; it is strongly enforced in her sisterhood. I don't know Emmy's [Mary Laura's unmarried sister Emmeline's] address or I would drop her a line – she shall know the bad news too soon.

Best regards from,

P.H.E.X.

Mr Wright addressed the witness: "Where do you live, Mr Marriott?"

"Abbots Hall, Essex."

"What was the purport of your reply to the letter of the 29th of May?"

"I expressed regret at her illness and asked him to let me have an immediate reply as to how she was going on."

"What was the wire you got?"

"Something to the effect that Mary Laura had passed away."

"Did you get this letter of the 4th of June?" (He handed the witness the letter.)

"I did."

"Was the letter of the 29th of May the first information you got from Dr Cross that your sister was ill?"

"Yes, the first. I heard before that she was unwell."

"From whom?"

"My wife heard she was unwell from family correspondence."

"When?"

"The week before, I think. The letter of the 29th of May was the first I got from him of any serious illness."

He was cross-examined by Mr Atkinson for the defence.

"Did you get letters from Shandy Hall from persons residing in the house?"

"I myself did not but my wife had a letter from Mrs Cross which was written for her by Miss Jefferson."

"How many days before the 29th of May was that?"

"I cannot remember."

"In addition to the sum of £5,000 did Mrs Cross get £50 from you?"

"Yes. I gave her £50 a year."

"In addition to that was there a legacy left her by one of your family?"

"No."

"Did your sister Miss Marriott leave her everything?"

"That is only hearsay, I know nothing about it."

The Attorney General asked: "Is your sister Miss Marriott alive?"

"She is."

Mr Atkinson said: "That's no matter. I have a right to ask the witness in cross-examination what he was told."

Humphrey Marriott stated: "I know nothing about it."

Lord Justice Murphy asked: "How is it evidence?"

Mr Atkinson said: "To show pecuniary loss."

Lord Justice Murphy asked: "How can a statement made by this gentleman be evidence for or against the prisoner?"

"Very well, my lord."

Lord Justice Murphy addressed Humphrey Marriott: "Was there any other person in the house in the habit of corresponding with your wife? Used Mrs Cross to do so?"

"Yes, very frequently."

"Did any other member of the Cross family correspond with any members of yours?"

"The children used to correspond."

Mr Atkinson: "Did not Miss Jefferson correspond?"

"Miss Jefferson was not acquainted with my wife, but she used to write letters to my wife for Mrs Cross."

"Miss Jefferson mentioned that she wrote a letter for Mrs Cross on the 28th of May."

The prisoner's diary was handed to the witness and he identified the handwriting as being that of Dr Cross.

The Prosecution Case Ends

Mr Squires, officer in the General Registry of Births, Marriages and Deaths confirmed that the entry of Mrs Cross's death in Dr Crowley's book reached him in the ordinary course of the event.

Dr Crowley was recalled and stated that he sent the entry to his superintendent.

Mr Ronan, handing Dr Crowley a document, asked him whose handwriting was in the manuscript portion and the witness replied that it was in the handwriting of Dr Cross. Mr Ronan then read the document which was the medical certificate of the cause of death as given by the prisoner: *"I hereby certify to the death of Mary Laura Cross whose age was stated to be 49, and last saw her on the 2nd of June 1887 at Shandy Hall, that she died on the 2nd of June at Shandy Hall, Dripsey, and to the best of my knowledge and belief, the cause of death and duration of illness were as here under written – cause of death; primary: typhoid fever; secondary - - - . Duration of illness, fourteen days. Witness, my hand, this 3rd day of June 1887. Signature: P.H.E. Cross, Surgeon Major (major scratched off) Residence: Shandy Hall, Dripsey.* The document was then signed by Dr Crowley."

Mr Marriott was recalled by Mr Wright and stated: "At the time of her death, she was forty-six and nine months. Her birthday was the 21st of August 1840."

The Attorney General: "May it please your Lordship – that is the case for the Crown."

Lord Justice Murphy suggested that evidence should be given as to the identity of the corpse. Dr Crowley was then recalled and in answer to the Attorney General said that the corpse he found in the coffin was the corpse of Mrs Cross. The case for the Crown then closed.

The Case for the Defence

Mr Atkinson QC opened the case for the defence. He said that he could say without any affectation that he never rose to address a jury without a greater sense of responsibility and a greater sense of his own inadequacy to discharge the duty that devolved upon him. It was not that this was a capital case and that the life of a human being hung upon the result of deliberations to which they must all bear their respective parts. It was not on account of the weight of evidence, rightly considered, but it was because these deliberations were carried on there in an atmosphere charged with rumours and reports about the prisoner which could not be proved there and which had not been proved there – false as he was instructed, as the Father of Lies himself, but yet for all he knew may have been the means of bringing them into the box, with minds prepared to hear the worst of him; with indignations so aroused against him that when they came to the solemn task of deciding upon his guilt they would be hurried along over doubts that ought to arrest them; and a verdict might be given not of their minds but of their passions.

It had pleased those entrusted with the administration of the criminal law in this country to send the prisoner for trial before a jury so placed; and that was why he felt an over-whelming responsibility. He knew a Cork jury too well to think for one moment that they would deliberately allow these rumours to warp their judgement; but their unconscious effect, the unknown bias these rumours might give, were perilous. Not so much to the life of his client, but to the administration of right and justice between man and man; and perilous to the great interests which the jurors had, as individuals on that occasion, when placed in the highest position that men could be – namely by their word and their art to determine whether a human being (after the decent delay the law allows him to make his peace with the God he had offended) was to be hurried into His presence to account for his actions here.

He could not tell the jury what these rumours were. He could not combat them, they were not mentioned there. But he knew the air was thick with them; and he implored and begged of them, as they valued justice to examine their hearts and conscience as to whether they had heard these reports and rumours, which it was scarcely possible to doubt, and by that exercise endeavour to drive their minds away from these reports, so as to bring their unclouded intelligence to bear on the task they had to discharge, namely to satisfy themselves whether the prisoner did commit this crime. Which if he did, he [counsel] would be the first man to describe it in words used by the Attorney General: that it was one of the worst and most brutal murders that ever disgraced their common humanity.

Thus far, for the influences without the court.

Now, for the influences within the court.

The Attorney General rightly disclosed to the jury the transactions in Dublin in April. That was necessary and proper for the purpose of showing a motive for this crime. This showed that there was a wicked and criminal intrigue going on between these parties during this woman's unhappy life.

It also showed how this man got married to his present wife; but where was the necessity to fall back on the hotel bill that was produced and ask the jury to conclude that this man rushed from the grave of his wife into the lustful embrace of the woman that they were told he was about to make one [a wife]?

What was the necessity of producing evidence to show that Mrs Tyndall kissed her brother-in-law? He did not accuse the Crown of doing this for illegitimate purpose; but it was unnecessary and calculated to have its effect in determining the question whether the prisoner was a murderer inasmuch he had had an intrigue with and married this governess. It was calculated to raise their indignation and hatred against the prisoner.

Black and horrid as was the crime charged against the prisoner, a crime as dangerous, if not so revolting would be done to society by a jury who allowed themselves to be swayed by anything like disgust or hatred in coming to a conclusion; and he called upon them to decide upon the question they had to try only upon testimony and proof and not upon prejudice and passion.

Although each link in the chain of evidence was weak, the Crown contention was that Cross was a libertine, a hypocrite and a liar; anything was good enough for him. Banish him forever. Drive him from the world. He was false to his wife, and told lies of her disease. It was said if he was not guilty of murder, he was guilty of things equally as bad. He appealed to them not to be influenced by such feelings as these. It was on account of the unconscious influence that might be operating upon their minds, and he appealed to them with all the power of which he was capable, for the sake of justice, for the sake of their own character, to banish such feelings and influences from their minds.

His learned friend, the Attorney General, had introduced the question of immorality into this case. He, himself, was not there to defend the prisoner's infidelity to his wife, but he should say that such things should not be allowed to influence their minds. They were not there to pass sentence on him for these things. They were outside this inquiry to a great degree.

Passing on, however to the next question, he submitted at the beginning that if he was a criminal, if he had committed those acts, he must be a lunatic, not responsible for his actions, he must be mad. From the beginning to the end of this case, there was not a single instance, not a single matter proved that would create in the minds of those around him the least suspicion that he was a guilty man.

Everything he did agreed with the actions of an innocent man. It would not do for him, counsel, to say that there was no suspicion in this case, and of course there was suspicion but he would show them that there was nothing about the case that would justify them in saying that his guilt was clearly established. The evidence was entirely circumstantial. They were told circumstances never erred. In one sense that was true, but in another equally false and misleading. Colouring can be given to circumstances which should be entirely neutral. Circumstantial evidence may be likened to a number of bricks placed one upon another; or to links of a small chain; if the bricks were well poised or balanced the structure may be a permanent one. But if there were a few rotten or entirely non-finished bricks in this structure that had been built up, the whole must be looked upon as weak and fragile.

But so it was exactly with the evidence raised up against the prisoner at the bar: the Crown urged against him, as motive, lust. The Attorney General said that he was compelled because of his unsatisfied lust to sacrifice this lady, his wife, because she stood in his way. That might, indeed, be very strong evidence if this lady's existence did stand in his way. But it was proved all through the case that it was no impediment to him whatever.

They had met in Dublin in the month of March; they had spent what the Attorney General called their honeymoon of lust without hindrance. The lady he had since made his wife did not appear to have refused the offer; as far as the fear of the existence of his former wife went, it was of no concern, whatever. He had already gratified himself. He was free to gratify himself further.

If it was proved that she had refused to yield to him in the capacity of wife, then the Crown could rightly say that that they had proved a motive for the crime. It seldom occurred that a man was willing to commit murder to get rid of a woman that was no impediment to him. It would have been a different matter if it had been proved that the lady had said: "No, I shall never be a victim of your desires, until you are my affirmed husband."

His learned friend might comment on it with tremendous force but it came with no force under the circumstances detailed there. The interview in Dublin in March, the three weeks "honeymoon" in April, unfortunately and unlawfully true, showed conclusively that the prisoner's wife's existence imposed no impediment and put no difficulty in the way. It could not be supposed for a moment – it was impossible to suppose – that the prisoner at the bar could have ever imagined that he could have got rid of his wife without tremendous danger; and it was for the jury to say if the Crown had shown any adequate motive for the commission of such a terrific and terrible crime.

What, he asked, were the probabilities of the prisoner acting in a guilty way? They should remember that he was a doctor and that he should have known the effects of poison and how suspicion would be aroused by his wife's sudden removal and by his marriage in hurried haste. Such a suspicion would have placed him at the mercy of the skills of proper experts if their skills were brought to bear on the traces of poison left behind.

How was the prisoner surrounded in Shandy Hall? Was there any faithful servant to act on his confidence? No, everything was done in the presence of persons who had not served him for a longer period than twelve months. He was in the house in April, after his visit to Dublin, waited, on the Crown evidence, for the presence of witnesses for his crime, and who was the witness he waited for?

His wife's old friend, an intelligent lady, and a trained nurse – Miss Jefferson – a lady who had attended persons suffering from typhoid fever. If necessary, before her arrival he had plenty of time to operate, but he waited until her arrival and until she was in daily intercourse with her friend, his wife, and until she occupied the next bedroom and within call.

He, according to the evidence of the girl, Mary Barron, administered the poisons in the presence of everyone who could have easily listened to any complaint the deceased might choose to have made.

The closing part of the proceedings seemed to him to be the most incredible. It was attempted to have proved that the prisoner suggested that Miss Jefferson leave, but such was not proved. Proof was conclusively given that he told her not to hurry herself.

It was arranged that she should leave on the 2nd of June, and the suggestion of the Crown was that the prisoner lest he might not have an audience for the closing bloody scene poisoned his wife with strychnine in a room next to that in which Miss Jefferson was. Let the prisoner be false to his wife as ever a man was, let him be the greatest hypocrite, the greatest liar that ever breathed, but he was not the fool, idiot or man as he would be if he had acted as stated.

Was he such an idiot, or was he possessed by some fiendish desire to forward his diabolical work before the world? If the prisoner at the bar concocted the murder, and committed it, he must have known, of course, the mode in which it would operate. If he resolved to poison his wife slowly, he must have known the way in which it would operate and would have taken the measures, accordingly.

But as they had seen, he took no steps to secrete the vomit in any way, but on the contrary, left it there, to be seen by anyone who happened to come in there. During the three long weeks that Mrs Cross was ill, she but once said that the medicine she was getting made her sick on one occasion. If she believed that was what was making her sick, was it humanly possible that she would not have said so? But, no, she accepted her illness as a natural one.

It had been sought to make out that persons were denied access to Mrs Cross during her illness.

Here the Attorney General interposed and denied that he had said any such thing. He never said that access was denied to her.

Mr Atkinson said that he did not state that the Attorney General had said so, but that was the drift and object of it. It meant that Dr Cross was anxious that no one should have access to the woman. But where in this case had he denied access to her? Where was the proof of it? Did he deny Mrs Caulfield, Mr Hayes or Miss Kirchoffer access to her?

Why, if he was the crafty murderer that it had been sought to be made out, he would be only too anxious to have persons brought in. In January last he had stated to Mrs Madras that his wife was suffering from a weak heart, and she might not be alive when he got home. What conclusion were they then to come to? Why, that so early in the month of January, he had resolved upon committing this crime, and was getting proof of his innocence, and was putting forward that false statement.

Having called the jury's attention to the fact of Dr Godfrey being called in, he proceeded to refer to what had been sought to be made out a secret funeral and to the contention of the Crown that the body of Mrs Cross had been hurried away out of sight and with indecent haste. But where was the evidence of that?

The clergyman was there, numbers of people were there. It took place at seven o'clock in the morning; and to say that there was any secrecy or haste about that funeral was, he submitted, a subversion of the evidence. He next dealt with the fact that on the morning of Mrs Cross's death, the prisoner did not call the servants until six o'clock, but if he were a guilty man, would he not have done quite the contrary, and would he not have at once aroused up his servants and shed sham tears of sorrow over the woman he had murdered?

No doubt that the prisoner married. Well, it was not his duty to defend that marriage, from a moral or delicacy point of view, but if there was one thing or another to set people's tongues wagging, and raise suspicion it was that marriage. It was the one thing a criminal, under the circumstances, would have avoided. It was folly and nonsense to say the accused thought it necessary, from a moral point of view. The time spent in the Euston Hotel before the marriage disposed of that suggestion.

It was proved that the accused purchased a pound of arsenic in September 1886 and was it to be suggested that even then Dr Cross had determined, before Miss Skinner came to Shandy Hall, or to the country at all, he believed to do away with his wife's life?

And what was the poison used? Arsenic which had a preservative effect, and which according to the analyst Dr Pearson, could be afterwards discovered in particles as one thousand part of an inch. One would imagine that a good narcotic would be the best poison to use for a person of an admittedly weak heart. As to the conversation overheard by Sergeant Higgins about the destruction of the two small bottles, which it was said took place between Dr Cross and Miss Cross, he would show by the evidence of Miss Cross that the two bottles were destroyed. But where were they found? They were found in Mrs Cross's own wardrobe under lock and key, to which no one had access but herself and one contained rouge and another a white powder, and they were the only things to which that conversation referred. If destruction was in his mind – if getting rid of evidence of guilt was on his mind, he had from the inquest on the 21st until the 28th to destroy and remove every trace of poison from the household.

What was the result? Had he destroyed it? On the contrary, they would have a list produced, a list of a dozen poisons, strychnine among the number, the very thing that had been deposed to and which he must have known. If this lady died from strychnine it would form the most conclusive case for his guilt.

He [counsel] should next draw attention to the fact, that though they on the part of the prisoner had been supplied with a most elaborate report from Dr Pearson to prove that a white powder labelled strychnine, was strychnine, they had no report until the last instant on the alleged fact that the body contained strychnine. He could understand it. While he did not mean to impute anything to his learned friends, a report of that nature would have enabled them to go through Dr Pearson's analysis, step by step, and see how far his unskilled efforts were a safe guide.

Counsel then referred to the symptoms shown by the deceased lady for the fortnight before her death, and said that it was absurd to say arsenic would not have produced its well-known symptoms, and one symptom would be most certainly a pain in the stomach, which the late Mrs Cross, in reply to Dr Godfrey, said she did not suffer from.

Next as to strychnine. How did strychnine kill? It invariably produced stiffness, plainly observable. The jury should not to allow the Crown to patch up their case. Was the prisoner a medical man? Did he not know the inevitable symptoms of poisoning by strychnine, which never could kill unless it stiffened? He came now to the evidence of Dr Pearson. What was his evidence? His evidence was that never in his life before did he perform a post mortem on a person killed from arsenic – never before in his life did he perform a post mortem on one who died from typhoid in the early stages.

The Attorney General interrupted: "The opposite is the case."

Mr Atkinson said: "My learned friends are looking at the papers and they are misleading."

Lord Justice Murphy said: "I have my note here anyway; but I think you are in error."

The judge read the note, from which it appeared that Mr Atkinson was in error. Mr Atkinson said that the doctor had never performed a post mortem on a human body. They cared not for his skill on the lower animals – they cared not for his skill outside this case – he might be the best in the world and he might be the worst in the world. It was not for the jury, by their verdict, to take away a human life on the testimony of that gentleman with the inexperience he admitted. Invariably that "cram" or book knowledge was accompanied by confidence and a knowledge that was not tried by experience. That gentleman was the merest tyro [novice] with a confidence of the most distinguished ornaments of his profession, but practically ignorant of what he deposed to.

He came now to his evidence about the liver absorbing three grains. They heard a great deal about that being a mistake – his notes were at College – the fact was that he was completely ignorant of the subject he was dealing with and that his book had altogether failed him.

That gentleman might yet rise to eminence in his profession, but he should ask the jury in the name of justice and humanity not to allow his experiment with human lives. The whole case depended mainly on the evidence of Dr Pearson, and if it were disregarded the whole thing would fall to the ground like a house of cards.

In concluding the counsel said: "I appeal to you, is there any man bold enough to pronounce a verdict which will have the effect of strangling out of life a human being like yourselves upon the testimony of that tyro? I have done now. My anxiety to pass over nothing is the only excuse for having detained you at such length."

The judge said that there need be no apology on the part of counsel for detaining the jury in consideration of a case like the present one.

Several jurors responded, "No, no."

Mr Atkinson continued: "I should have called your attention to the fact that the bottle containing the chlorodyne proved that it contained something else and was nearly full. I leave the case in your hands, subject to any remarks that will be addressed to you by my learned friends. You can have a little sympathy and we can have a little sympathy as anybody else with the accused, but gentlemen it is your duty – a duty which you have discharged before and I know you will discharge again – fearlessly to follow where your conscience and your judgement lead you, but beyond where they lead you, treading on the solid ground of established proof and satisfactory evidence, the same sacred duty committed you to hold.

Go where your conscience and judgement lead you, so long as you feel the ground beneath your feet; but hark back so you do not unjustly sacrifice a human being if reasonable or rational doubt stand up before you. Gentlemen, I beg you not to disgrace and prostitute the position in which you are placed by showing any antipathy for the man's conduct or any prejudice by passion to hurry forward that course, which otherwise you would hesitate to follow."

Mr Atkinson, the counsel for the defence, resumed his seat after speaking for two hours and there was a muted outbreak of applause among the public spectators, which considering the seriousness of the charge, was a highly inappropriate reaction. It did however, prove that despite the defence efforts to have the trial heard in Dublin on the grounds of bias against their client that the prisoner had in fact considerable support at the proceedings.

Lord Justice Murphy addressed the officer in charge of the court: "If you see any persons manifesting the slightest attempt at applause or the opposite expression of feeling, you will at once bring him before me and I will remove him from court to some place of which he should be an inmate."

The Attorney General added, "It is hardly a case for applause."

The judge said that such exhibitions displayed an utter disregard of propriety and decency.

Witness Evidence for the Defence was then introduced.

THE EVIDENCE OF MR DEYOS

Mr Robert Deyos was the first witness called and, in answer to Mr Adams for the defence, deposed: "I am solicitor for Dr Cross and have been since the commencement of these proceedings. I attended the inquest in Coachford on the second day; that was Friday, July the 28th. Dr Pearson on that occasion verified on oath his report which was read. I communicated with Dr Cross at the County Court and told him what had passed at the inquest."

HENRIETTA CROSS'S EVIDENCE

Miss Henrietta Cross was then called to be examined by Mr Adams. What would follow would be a very strange passage of evidence with points that were mostly overlooked for both tactical and evidential reasons. It would also be shown in no uncertain fashion that the spinster sister of the prisoner, who had been resident at Shandy Hall for over two years before the awful event, put family loyalty before the legal and moral imperatives of the truth.

* * *

"Are you the sister of the accused?"

"I am."

"How long were your brother and the late Mrs Cross residing at Shandy Hall?"

"About twelve years."

"At the beginning of that period did you reside with them for a while?"

"Yes, for about three months."

"After that did you go about amongst your friends in England and Scotland for a series of years?"

"I did."

"How long before the death of the late Mrs Cross did you return to Shandy Hall?"

"I am at present almost two and a half years there."

"What terms did Dr and Mrs Cross live on?"

"Pretty good terms."

Asked what condition of health her sister-in-law was in before the month of May, Miss Cross said that she always considered her a delicate little lady who had a very delicate stomach and suffered from attacks of the heart during which "she would get quite giddy and lose all strength; she would sometimes fall down and suffer very great pain; she told me that she sometimes felt as if a knife was plunging into her heart; and she said she knew she would die of these attacks." Her stomach was affected by disagreeable smells and she would discharge her stomach. She could not remember whether food affected her.

"Did Mrs Cross leave Shandy Hall for visits in England?"

"Yes."

"What time before her death?"

"She went in July 1886."

"In what condition were her spirits?"

"She was in very low spirits, and she mourned over having to live in Ireland."

Miss Cross testified that she attended her sister-in-law from the commencement of her illness and mainly brought her drinks. She brought her sago the evening before she died. Mary McGrath was present. The sago was left in the room for a minute while she went out. Nobody entered during that time and no one touched or interfered with the sago. She gave the patient a whole saucerful. That night she had gone to her own room about half past ten and went straight to bed.

She was roused some time later by a little scream from Mr Cross's room. She then heard two or three more screams. Her own bedroom door was open. She then heard her brother going downstairs. There was then another little scream or cry from Mrs Cross's room. She heard Dr Cross coming back up the stairs and re-enter the room. He then came to her room. From the time she heard the first scream until that point was about three or four minutes.

She then rose immediately and went back to the bedroom with the doctor. She went to the bed where Mrs Cross was lying quite still with her head on one side, and her hand as if she had it on her heart.

Mr Adams: "Was she alive or dead?"

"I think she must have just passed away."

"Did Dr Cross do anything?"

"He put his ear down to her mouth and heart and felt her pulse."

"Did you do anything yourself?"

"I went to my room for the hot water tin, thinking the heat would restore her and put it on her hands, but found it was no use – that she was dead."

* * *

Now what was strange to say the least was Miss Cross's reaction to the screams coming from the bedroom. Whether her brother was there or not the natural thing would have been to go to the assistance of a woman who was obviously in extreme distress and who she had attended since the start of her illness. Instead she stayed stuck to the bed listening to her brother's footsteps go up and down the stairs.

The retrieval of the hot water tin was even more bizarre, since she had been in bed by her own account somewhere in the region of two and a half hours before. There might have been some warmth retained but hardly enough to revive an absolutely still woman who Miss Cross somehow, again strangely, had the impression contained some vestige of life. There was no mention of upset on her or her brother's part, her recollection of life's most final and poignant events was marked by a total absence of emotion. Never mind that it had been the painful and pitiful end of a very close relation.

She told Mr Adams that she stayed quite a while in the room and then returned to her own room and lay down on the bed. She rose about seven and saw and had a conversation with Miss Jefferson. She had seen her father dead and thought that Mrs Cross's corpse was the reverse of rigid: "Her head was on one side as if she was asleep."

Nothing of that description, set against everything that had been already ventilated in the court about the nature of illness and the last sufferings of Mary Laura Cross, rang true. Her brother had told Miss Jefferson on his visit to London that his wife had died screaming. It is a prelude to death that every human being contemplating mortality would most dread.

The proved administration of strychnine would have brought convulsions, great pain and the inevitable post-mortem rigidity. Miss Cross heard the cacophony of pain, did nothing and then tells the court that the woman who succumbed to those brutal and inescapable symptoms, lay there as if she had fallen asleep. It was as likely as someone being shot through the heart and suffering no blood loss.

*   *   *

In reply to Mr Adams Miss Cross said she was in the room the following week with Dr Cross. There was a press near Mrs Cross's bed, the keys for which had always been in the possession of the mistress of the house. She went through it that day and among clothes and articles found three or four bottles. One contained rouge and the other white powder. It was a little round bottle and after showing it to her brother she threw its contents into a grate with other rubbish.

She placed the bottle on the chimney-piece and later sent it downstairs to be washed. The other bottle remained there for a long time and it and some other bottles were washed after Dr Cross came home. There had been chlorodyne in the house in two bottles and a minim glass on the chimney-piece.

After Mr Adams finished his examination, Miss Cross was examined by the Attorney General for the prosecution.

"Now, did you observe any harshness or roughness in the conduct of your brother towards his late wife?"

"He used to be hasty sometimes."

"Do you remember when Miss Skinner came?"

"Yes."

"When did you first find out that your brother was going to marry Miss Skinner?"

"He never told me."

"From whom did you learn it?"

"When I received a telegram, no, I think I heard it first from Mrs Caulfield."

"Do you recollect him coming from Dublin on the morning of the 22nd of June by himself?"

"I do, well."

"Did he tell you what brought him down on that occasion?"

"No."

"Did he tell you that he had been visiting Mrs Caulfield?"

"He did."

"You heard from Mrs Caulfield that your brother had been married to Miss Skinner?"

"Yes. I heard that after church on Sunday previous to his coming home. It was the evening of the 21st I think he came home."

"When he arrived that evening was there any quarrel in the house between you and him?"

"No."

"Did he say anything to you or you to him in reference to the marriage about which you had learned about on that preceding Sunday?"

"No."

*   *   *

There were a number of questionable responses to counsel's examination by Miss Cross who was very close and no doubt a confidante of her brother. She was the first person he asked to see after he was arrested and the first he came to after his wife died which of course suited his purposes in more ways than one. His trust in her and her reciprocal and unquestioning devotion was crystal clear by her willingness to get rid of potentially damaging evidence.

Therefore it was very hard to believe that she was not the first to know about his marriage to Effie Skinner. So when the enquiry is made, she first says she heard about it when she received a telegram and then quickly changes it to hearing it from Mrs Caulfield on the 19th – Mrs Caulfield who told the court that she heard about on the 22nd.

And quite incredibly there then had been no mention of the marriage between herself and Dr Cross when he returned from Dublin on the evening of the 21st. The row that counsel referred to more than likely occurred on the night of the 22nd which he originally referred to as the day that Cross returned – and the same evening after Cross had been confronted and exposed as attempting to hide the marriage by the Caulfields. Perhaps he thought that his sister Henrietta had told Mrs Caulfield after receiving a telegram from him and this prompted a conflict. If so, it had no impact on her loyalty to him – no matter what he did.

* * *

Miss Cross admitted that she had been aware that he went away at the end of January and stayed for three days in the Hibernian Hotel in Dublin with Miss Skinner. She said that it did not excite any suspicion in her mind. She never heard Mrs Cross make any complaint about the matter. She was aware that Miss Skinner was going to Killanure in Carlow, said that she had corresponded with her but did not know that her brother was also doing the same.

She said that Dr Cross had gone to Ventnor to visit his brother at Easter where he also brought his children. He had not gone there before because the children were always at home.

The Attorney General went on to the subject of the illness of the patient.

"When was Mrs Cross sick last?"

"She had a gastric attack and vomiting when my brother was in England."

"Do you remember during the two and a half years you were in your brother's house how often was Mrs Cross confined to bed?"

"One day."

"Was she ever confined in any illness?"

Miss Cross hesitated, then answered: "She was confined in a gastric attack."

"When last before her illness?"

"I don't remember the time."

"Was it two or three years?"

"A shorter time than that, I think."

"When was it?"

No answer.

Attorney General asked: "Did you give evidence to Mr Deyos, solicitor?"

Miss Cross: "Yes."

"Did you ever say your sister-in-law got gastric attacks which used to make her vomit?"

"I don't know."

"Come, answer, did you mention it?"

Miss Cross hesitated, then answered: "If I was asked it. I don't think there was any mention of it."

"If you were not asked it, why did you not mention it?"

No answer.

"And did you not think it a matter of importance, Mrs Cross having gastric attacks accompanied by vomiting?"

No answer.

"When did you think your sister-in-law was in danger?"

"I didn't think she was in danger."

"Did you think she was in danger up to the end?"

"No."

"Though he was telling people five miles away that she may be dead at any moment, he never told you. Did he ever speak to you about his wife's dangerous condition?"

After some hesitation, Miss Cross said: "I have often heard him say she might pass away from her heart; that was not during her last illness."

"Had he ever had any conversation with you on the subject of his wife's terrific and painful agony; you being an inmate two and a half years?"

"Of course we knew she was very ill."

Miss Cross said that she had seen her brother mix chlorodyne and water for his wife and she did not see him mix any other medicines. There were one and a half bottles of chlorodyne used. She also received sal volatile and ether. Both of them would give ether. She was in and out of the sick room and didn't remember any medicine bottles there. The gentian was kept downstairs in the cellarette. She also saw her sister-in-law being given sweet spirits of nitre and external applications of mustard poultice on her stomach and breast.

Mary McGrath applied one of these two days before her death and she had been given drinks almost every night. On the Wednesday after she had been out visiting she went to the sick room. Her sister-in-law told her that she had been very sick and she put her arms around her and said she was sorry for her suffering. She was not aware that she had vomited the sago as she left the room afterwards.

She could not say exactly how long she had been in the room after she died, a bit more than a quarter of an hour. She did not know where her brother was after she left the room and went back to her own bedroom. Her brother had not been in bed when she left the room and she did not hear him go down to the servants in the morning. She did not have a fire on that night. She said that the water tin was still sufficiently warm to restore a person.

She agreed that people who were visiting during the illness were not present at the funeral. She did not go to the funeral. She did not attach any importance to the emptying of the bottles, one of which contained white powder. Her brother had asked if it was labelled, she replied no and he said she had better throw it away. He did not see her throw it away as he was reading letters at the time.

She did not believe that the bottle contained arsenic and never said that there were two bottles with white powder. In reply to the judge who asked if she at any time thought it might contain arsenic she replied that she had thought since that it might have.

Lord Justice Murphy then asked: "Did you think then your sister-in-law might have taken it?"

"I have since thought she might have taken it for her great delicacy."

The Attorney General said: "Did you say to Mr Tyacke: 'Poor Laura was always vain, and if arsenic was found in her, she must have taken it for her complexion.'?"

"Possibly I did."

"Now when you said you thought she took it for delicacy what form of delicacy did you think arsenic would be a good remedy for?"

"It is taken for fits."

"Do you think it was possible that your sister-in-law was taking arsenic as a remedy for fits?"

"I thought it since her death."

"When first did you think there had been arsenic in this bottle?"

"At the conversation between my brother and myself after one of the inquiries."

"Was that before he was arrested?"

"No, it was after he was arrested at the Police Office."

Lord Justice Murphy asked: "Was that conversation between your brother and yourself?"

"Yes."

The Attorney General said: "Was that the time Sergeant Higgins referred to?"

"Yes."

"What was it you said or your brother said to you about arsenic on that occasion?"

"He said: 'Do you remember the two little bottles with some white powder that was amongst the rubbish – amongst the old clothes?'"

"Now, was it rubbish or old clothes?"

"Well, there were all kinds of clothes there."

"What did you say to that?"

"I said, 'I do'. And then he said: 'Is it possible that could have been arsenic?'"

Lord Justice Murphy asked: "What reply did you give to that?"

"I don't remember. I did not know what was in the bottle."

"But what answer did you make to it?"

"I don't know."

"Did you say 'I destroyed them'?"

"Perhaps I did."

The Attorney General asked: "Were you a great deal startled at your brother suggesting that arsenic might be in that bottle?"

"Well, yes, I was."

"Did you know the charge against your brother at that time was that he killed his wife by arsenic?"

"Yes."

"Were you a great deal startled by his observation to you?"

"I was astonished."

"Do you recollect the answer you made?"

"I said I emptied the bottle amongst the rubbish."

"Will you say that what you said was that you destroyed them?"

"I think that is what I did say."

"Did he intimate to you what kind they were?"

"He said about the length of his finger."

"Did your brother ever say anything to you about arsenic being a remedy for fits the day you had a conversation about the two bottles being destroyed?"

"No."

"Had you ever a conversation with him that 'Poor, dear Laura' might have taken it as a remedy for fits?"

"I don't think I had."

"How did you get it into your mind that one of the things that arsenic might be used for was for medical purposes?"

"I read it."

"When did you read it?"

"I read it recently."

"What book?"

"One of my brother's books."

"What was the name of it?"

"I forget."

"Has he got a book about arsenical poisoning?"

"Yes."

"Was it in that book that you read about arsenic being a remedy for fits?"

"Yes, in that book."

"What was the name of the book?"

Miss Cross hesitated.

"It must have made a painful impression on your mind. When did you read it?"

"Within the last two months, but I cannot think of the author's name."

"Was your only reason for accepting that arsenic might be used for medical purposes what you learned from the book?"

"I think I heard my niece got it."

"When did you form the suspicion that Mrs Cross might have taken it for her complexion?"

"Not until the bottles were found."

"Was it immediately after the bottles were found?"

"Yes."

"How soon after the bottles were found did you come to believe that they contained arsenic for Mary Laura Cross's complexion?"

No answer.

"When did you form the opinion that arsenic was used to gratify people's vanity?"

"I don't know."

"Was it before the inquest?"

"I cannot say."

"Do you recollect the inquest?"

"Yes."

"Did you know that the examination was for the purpose of finding out whether you sister-in-law had been murdered?"

"Yes."

"Are you able to say whether it was before your sister-in-law's body was exhumed that it was found that she died of arsenic that you formed the opinion that the arsenic in the bottle was used for the purpose of the complexion?"

Miss Cross hesitated and had not replied after a couple of minutes.

Lord Justice Murphy: "Well, Miss Cross?"

"The subject never gave me a thought."

Attorney General: "Did it not give you a thought that you believed two bottles contained arsenic?"

"I don't believe they contained arsenic, I never analysed them."

"You have no idea as to how white arsenic could have got into the house?"

"No."

"You never heard Dr Cross say he used to give it to his wife as a medicine against fits?"

"No."

"Did you ever hear he gave her any medicine?"

"No, except in her last illness."

"What did he give her?"

"A diaphontic medicine."

"What is that?"

"A medicine to produce perspiration; sweet spirits of ether, I think."

"Do you know whether Dr Godfrey's prescription was carried out – the three grains of calomel?"

"Yes, she told me she got it."

"What happened to the rouge bottle?"

"I think it is at home."

"Did your sister-in-law go out in the last year of her life?"

"Yes, she went to Mrs Caulfield's."

"Did you ever see her rouge herself up?"

"I have seen two very bright spots on her cheeks."

Mr Justice Murphy asked: "Do you recollect in the morning after your sister-in-law's death, did Miss Jefferson go into your room, or you to hers?"

"She came into my room."

"Do you recollect the conversation you had with her then?"

"I told her that Laura passed away in the night and that I heard her cry."

"Did you tell her at all that you had gone into the room?"

"Yes, I did."

"And saw her dead?"

"And saw her dead."

"When your brother came into your room had he his night dress on?"

"He hadn't taken his things off at all."

"Were her eyes closed or open when you went into the room?"

"They were open."

"Was there any announcement sent out that the funeral was intended to take place?"

"No, she said she would like to be buried very quietly."

"How far was Dr Godfrey's house from Shandy Hall?"

"A few fields."

After this Miss Cross stepped down from the box.

* * *

The Attorney General had demonstrated his professional mettle in his cross-examination of a clearly hostile witness whose evidence to the defence counsel had contained not only contradictions but efforts to cover up and transgress truths in relation to her brother's behaviour. His questions had elicited far more doubts than if he had confronted those earlier contradictions. He had ignored the obvious bond between the brother and sister and by sticking to the facts shown that, short of being a willing accomplice to the accused's action, Miss Cross's misguided loyalty made her at best an unreliable witness to events leading up to and after Mary Laura's ghastly death.

Her behaviour in the face of that event came across as not just bizarre but reprehensible. Within walking distance of the unmistakeable sounds of the final suffering of her sister-in-law she had remained stuck to her bed, despite her gratuitous effort in hugging her earlier when it was so obvious that the poor woman was literally expiring. A fact that she averred she had no idea about.

She then claimed that a body that would have displayed every last sign of its death throes showed nothing but peace and calm.

The eyes were open, she told the judge, but yet she had employed the use of a lukewarm tin in a so-called attempt to revive a person whose previous and last pain must have been abundantly obvious. She returned to the comfort of her own bed and never heard her brother going down to announce the death of their mistress to the servants.

She had supported the illusion that the poor little delicate woman as she described might have succumbed to the effects of arsenical poison on the mere matter of vanity, evidenced in her view by two red spots on her cheeks when she might have gone visiting. She had read such twaddle by reference to a book in her brother's library on the subject of arsenical poisoning.

She could not remember the name of the book but if this was a case of selective reading there could be no better example of it.

* * *

At this stage, the clock falling at three o'clock, the court adjourned for half an hour for luncheon.

On resumption, Mr David Barry, a juror, told Lord Justice Murphy that the jury would like to have a copy of Dr Pearson's report of his analysis. The Attorney General said that they would produce the original notes of anything that was wanted. It would be satisfactory if the notes were examined.

Mr Adams said that he would not like to say anything until Mr Atkinson came into the court. Mr Atkinson then entered the court and said he was given to understand that the jury would like to see the notes of Dr Pearson. Counsel for the defence had no opportunity of seeing them. They were not evidence in this case and he would not consent to them being given to the jury.

Mr Grimes (juror): "If this is an application emanating from the jury, I presume it would be made through the foreman. It is an application from an individual."

Mr Barry answered: "The foreman gave me permission."

Lord Justice Murphy said that Mr Atkinson, on behalf of the

prisoner had objected to those notes being given, and he could not furnish them, but he would give the jury when he was charging them all the evidence as succinctly as he could. If he was to give them the evidence then, it should be taken from newspaper reports, or some such other source. He was perfectly confident that the newspaper reports, as taken, were accurate but he could not give them to the jury as evidence.

Dr Pearson had put those notes in his hand the previous day, but only to give the counsel for the defence a means of testing his accuracy.

Mr Atkinson said: "At all events, they were never furnished to us."

The Attorney General replied: "They were never asked for."

"We did not know they existed."

Mr Adams' Address to the Jury

Mr Adams then addressed the jury on behalf of the prisoner.

He said that before night fell – certainly before night fell tomorrow – the jury would in their room perform the most lawful duty that citizens could be called on to perform: to pass between the Crown and the prisoner on the great issue of life or death – not guilty, let him go free; guilty, let him die. There were only two issues in the case: "Did Mary Laura Cross die of poison? Did Philip Henry Eustace Cross, the prisoner at the bar, administer that poison to her?"

He would grant that in his old age and grey hairs, the prisoner might have seduced the young girl, perhaps in his own house. He granted that the prisoner had led her to the marriage altar, within fourteen days of the death of his wife. But the worse man the prisoner proved himself to be, the greater reason there was for the jury not to be led away from the two great issues by anything they had heard outside the box.

Had the Crown fully satisfied them beyond reasonable doubt? Had it been proved, by the evidence, that Philip Henry Eustace Cross mixed up these poisons and with his own hand, given them to his wife? If they were not so satisfied, then the prisoner was entitled to their verdict of acquittal. Had the evidence done aught but raise a cloud of suspicion against the prisoner – a case of "vehement suspicion" as the lawyers called it? However dark might be the doings of the prisoner, unless there was absolute evidence of guilt, the jury must acquit him.

They had called for the defence the only person in Shandy Hall who had not been called by the Crown. They called Miss Cross, the sister of the prisoner; they had heard the able cross-examination of her by the Attorney General; and if they were not convinced of his guilt before, was there anything in her evidence to convince them of his guilt? It was shown by the evidence that Mrs Cross used to vomit when an unpleasant smell was put before her; but at a period long antecedent to her last fatal illness she had upon her a terrible disorder pointing to serious illness in the most important organ of her body, and pointing to her early death: her heart was diseased.

Miss Cross also proved to the fits and weakness of Mrs Cross and if the Crown case meant anything, it meant that if the brother was guilty, so also was the sister. The jury might find motive for Philip Cross's conduct, but where was the motive for Henrietta Cross? Referring to the finding of strychnine and arsenic at Shandy Hall, counsel said that the prisoner knew that the body of his wife had been exhumed on the 21st, and although seven days intervened between that and the inquest – seven days in which Dr Cross was master of Shandy Hall and free to do as he liked – yet he did not destroy the evidence of his guilt as the Crown alleged.

Dr Cross had not been in practice as a doctor for many years; and because the prisoner, a thick and inexperienced man, said to the registrar of deaths that his wife died of typhoid fever, instead of gastric fever, which it was very much alike, he was to be adjudged guilty of murder, and he must die the death.

If that poor lady, going upstairs, suffering as she was from gastric affections, became faint and passed away, was there any more reasonable and natural explanation of death? Referring to the symptoms of arsenical poisoning, counsel said that there were three symptoms that had come to be accepted as general by the common knowledge of mankind. There was devouring, tormenting, consuming thirst. They had no evidence that Mrs Cross suffered from this awful affliction. Then the stomach could not be pressed; for it would produce great pain, yet Dr Godfrey had told them how he pressed Mrs Cross's stomach, and she felt no pain. Again, the person being poisoned by arsenic would be afflicted with cramps. Yet they never had a word about them until they came to the third division of Miss Jefferson's evidence. Referring to the evidence of Dr Pearson, Mr Adams said that they were asked to hang Dr Cross, in order to set up Dr Pearson. If in his evidence he had made a mistake, then the whole case was at an end. The system of government under which they lived had often been abused and stones thrown at Dublin Castle, and indeed he thought they often spent money in many ways to no avail; but they might have spent a few guineas in procuring an analyst for Dr Pearson, who could tell him something of the effects of arsenic in poisoning on a human being.

This young man wanted to try his practice on the unfortunate man in the dock, when he had never before experimented on a human being who died by arsenic or strychnine. Agreeing she had died by poisoning, it had not been proved that the old man in the dock, who extended his hand for nothing but bare justice, had administered it. It was easy for him to suggest, to imagine many things, to set up various theories.

Here was this old woman, Jane Leahy. What obscure quarrel may not have occurred between her and Mrs Cross? May not she have administered the poison in her food? Then they could say she committed suicide, but no, he rejected all those ideas and maintained that if the poison was found in the unfortunate woman – which he did not believe – it had never been administered by the prisoner at the bar.

Concluding, Mr Adams said that he only asked bare justice for the man in the dock, the same justice they would extend to the noblest of their fellow citizens, and in asking for that, he believed he would pass out of the court a free man. He admitted that the prisoner had sinned against the heart and affection. Whatever mis-fortunes, sufferings, difficulties and differences there were amongst

261

Irishmen, amongst all classes, there was no lack of family love or affection, the devotion of the husband for the wife, the wife for the husband, for it existed to a degree unknown in any other country.

Because of the holy vow that this man had sinned against, because he was found wanting in Christian love and truth, and the noble qualities of husband according to their notions and customs, he asked them in God's name not to blind their eyes to the great and important question they were called upon to decide. It would be an awful thing if they were tempted into passing some verdict, that perhaps at some future day when the mysteries of Shandy Hall would be cleared away, would cause them to bear in all time to come a most bitter conscience: the conscience of having convicted an innocent man.

*   *   *

The last sentiments and words "an innocent man", from Mr Adams, had a powerful effect, whether true or not, and rang in the ears of every last person in the court. It was as if a bell had rung and the weight of the proceedings hung heavily over all the participants. The trial was approaching the end game but nothing yet was decided. There are moments of deadened gloom in every trial, that is the nature of the process and this was definitely one of them.

Mr Wright's Address to the Jury

The silence was broken as Mr Wright QC rose from behind the space occupied by the prosecution and shuffled a few papers before beginning his address.

"I entirely agree," he started, "with the observations of Mr Adams and Mr Atkinson that the jury were not to mind rumours. If rumours there had been, none were known to me or my colleagues. But if they were known to the jury, I ask them to banish them from their minds and try the case as we have been trying it, on the evidence that has been laid before you. And what you have to find is this: did or did not the circumstances point in the one direction and one conclusion, namely that Mary Laura Cross died by poison and the hand that gave her the poison was that of her husband, Philip Henry Eustace Cross?

The case for the Crown has been unassailed up to now, and the only question for you, the jury, to consider is: has it been proved to your satisfaction? It has been said that the case for the Crown depends on the evidence of Dr Pearson, and no one else examined the body after death. It has been said that Dr Pearson was inexperienced and that no experienced toxicologist had examined the body. I ask you, where in Ireland would you get an experienced toxicologist? For whatever crimes are committed, poisoning is rarely among them.

Dr Pearson's mistake has been commented upon more than once by the prisoner's counsel, but I should ask, are you satisfied of this: that Dr Pearson, in the analysis, that took him several days to complete, found arsenic in the body in what he considers a poisonous quantity? I have been very troubled for the past two days, and I have fifteen years' experience, as to what the case for the defence would be. Whether it would be suicide or not.

Dr Pearson has also been charged with not having properly cleaned the vessels which he used, and that arsenic might have been in them, but his evidence on that point stood without contradiction and unassailed. In relation to Mrs Cross's last illness, if Dr Cross was not an experienced physician why did he not send to Cork for a physician? Or was Dr Crowley not good enough to prescribe for an inmate of Shandy Hall?

There was no one in the room attending this poor lady, but the man himself, and the poor lady according to the evidence of one of the servants had said: 'If I ring at night, will you answer my ring?' This was a most dreadful request; it was as if the wretched lady in her own room, with that callous fellow, who, with his own hands laid her out in the room after her death, and who had already entered into a guilty intrigue with her own governess – it was as if she knew she could not call on her husband for assistance.

If the unfortunate Mrs Cross died of poison, whose was the hand that administered it? No one under that roof had any object in getting rid of her except the man who was tired of her, and who was determined to put another in her place. There is now the matter of the conversation between the prisoner and his sister deposed on by Sgt Higgins regarding the two small bottles with the white powder and the reply of Miss Cross that she had destroyed them with the other things.

Dr Pearson has given evidence that the poison was white arsenic; and I ask you, the jury, to believe from the evidence of Miss Cross that day when Dr Cross spoke to her about the small bottle with the white powder in it; she knew it was a bottle with white arsenic. In fact, Miss Cross's theory, from her evidence, was that poor Mrs Cross either used arsenic for her complexion or was experimenting on herself for fits. These were the theories of the defence – the doubts upon which the counsel for the defence asked the jury to avoid, if they could in finding a verdict.

These were the suggestions which the counsel for the defence made in naturally and properly asking the jury to keep away from the irresistible logic of fact, which I asked them to approach. What were these facts? That the prisoner was tired of his wife; that he was a harsh husband to her; that he was engaged in an intrigue with the governess to the knowledge of his wife; that he lived with the governess for a month; that his wife was immured and shut off from life by him from the world; that she died unseen by any friendly eye; that all the symptoms of poisoning by arsenic were present in her case; that when the body was exhumed traces of the poison were found; and that the prisoner gave different accounts of her death, all which were contradicted by the appearance of the body after death.

There was not one fact in the case to contradict the theory for the Crown; and they all pointed cogently and conclusively to the inference which the Crown asked the jury to draw, and that was that Mary Laura Cross was done to her death by her husband, who saw her die and that she was done to death by him to make room for his paramour. The further facts were that accounts he gave subsequent to his wife's death were as lying and hypocritical as the letters he wrote to her brother in England; that the true Dr Cross was not the loving husband his letters made him out to be but the callous brute that saw his wife die at night, and prepared her for the grave the next morning; and hastened off on that day week to make love to another – the other that he had been living with before; and the hand that administered the poison that was found in the unhappy woman's intestines was the hand of the man who had vowed to love, honour and cherish her.

In conclusion, I ask you, the jury, to say that the evidence against the prisoner is overwhelming, and pointed clearly to his guilt. There should be no shirking of your duty, no temerity in coming to a resolve. You owe a duty to the prisoner and to your fellow countrymen. If you believe the evidence that has been produced, it is your duty to declare the prisoner guilty of the crime laid to his charge."

Mr Wright QC took his seat.

Mary McGrath was recalled and Lord Justice Murphy examined her.

"What kind of bell had your mistress for making her wants known? Was it a hand bell or used she ring by the ordinary bell?"

"It was a bell pull."

"Did it communicate with the kitchen?"

"It could be heard all over the house."

"Was it in the kitchen it hung or did it hang in the hall?"

"It hung in the hall."

"Did it go into the room where the servants slept?"

"Yes, it went all through the hall."

Lord Justice Murphy was asked by the foreman of the jury if they could be supplied with a photograph of Miss Skinner and His Lordship replied that he could find no objection to the request.

Mrs Caulfield was recalled and in reply to His Lordship stated that Miss Skinner's age was about twenty-one.

It being six o'clock, the court rose, the case was adjourned to the morning when Lord Justice Murphy said his intention was to begin his charge to the jury at eleven o'clock.

The Fourth Day

Saturday, 17th December 1887

Before the hour of eleven o'clock, the courtroom was packed and the atmosphere was one of tension and expectancy.

The greatest influx of people to the court was reserved for the fourth and expected final day of the trial on Saturday, when it was known that the case would terminate in some way or another so far as the then empanelled jury was concerned.

Counsel for the Crown, The Right Honourable the Attorney General; John Gibson, QC, MP; Mr George Wright QC; Mr Stephen Ronan and solicitor Mr VW Gregg took their seats as did the counsel for the prisoner Mr John Atkinson QC; Mr Richard Adams and solicitor Robert Deyos.

The jury then filed into their seats led by the foreman Carlton Palmer. Robert Alexander, Joseph Milligan, Robert Moncaster, William Moore, David Barry, John Highet, Peter Allen, Christopher Woods, John Grimes, Thomas Farrar and Benjamin Atkins. It would be fair to comment they would never forget this morning for the rest of their lives and the heavy responsibility that burdened their collective shoulders: to decide, after the charge to them by Lord Justice Murphy, whether the prisoner at the bar would live or die. That was just a little over four hours away.

At eleven o'clock Lord Justice Murphy entered the court. All stood and resumed their seats when his Lordship was seated and began his charge.

The Judge's Charge to the Jury

He began by stating that this was a very serious case and one that had occupied the jury's undivided attention for three days, and that time was necessarily occupied with statements by the Attorney General, statements for the defence by Mr Atkinson and replies made by Mr Adams and Mr Wright, as well as the evidence, which of course was necessarily given with all the accurate details that are requisite in very serious criminal cases, but most of all in a case where the charge was one such as in this case.

He was sure that the jury had devoted to the case during the time it had been before them their utmost attention, and that they had fixed on the evidence, on the statements made by counsel, all the attention it was possible for them to do. The duty was now devolved upon him of presenting to them, as accurately as possible, and in the form and shape that he thought might best aid them in arriving at a just conclusion, the evidence that had been placed before them; and observations on different parts of the evidence.

Whatever comments or observations he did make would be only such as suggested themselves to him by his own knowledge and experience, and these he would lay before them for their clear and purified judgement. Clear and purified their judgement should be from everything like prejudice and perfectly free and unoccupied with anything they might have heard before they came into that box, and applied their knowledge and experience merely to the evidence that had been placed before them in court.

Now, notwithstanding what might be said in many cases, he did not think that any jury – any honest jury – going into a box to try a serious criminal case, and especially one of a capital nature, could have any difficulty in freeing their minds or casting away out of their minds anything they might have heard about the case before they came into the box. No man with anything like a fairly constituted mind, when weighing the evidence that had been given in this case, could bring into it anything he might have heard in current gossip or conversation before he came into that box, and he should solemnly implore of them to cast out of consideration everything they had heard of and read connected with this case and to consider solely the charge on the evidence that had been adduced before them in court.

When he had closed his observations to them, then would devolve on them the serious duty and responsibility of deciding what verdict they would return. If it was a verdict of guilty, then the prisoner's life must be forfeited to the law for the crime of which he has been found guilty. If it were a verdict of not guilty, he would leave the dock and the court a free man. The duty and responsibility was very great and serious for them, but if they returned a true and honest verdict, according to the evidence, laid before them, then they would have done their duty and discharged the responsibility thrown on them.

They would have freed their conscience, with whatever might be the consequences of their verdict. Now then, considering the case, he thought it would be well if the jury in the first place took all the circumstances of it into consideration prior to the 21st of July, the day on which the body of the deceased lady was exhumed.

It had been said and rightly said, by both eminent counsels who had, with such conspicuous ability discharged their duty in the case, that the jury was not trying the prisoner Cross here on a charge of immorality; that they were not trying him here for being an unfaithful husband or a cruel father; they were trying him here solely on the charge whether or not he hastened the death of his first wife Mary Laura Cross.

That was quite true; but it was impossible that the jury could consider that charge without taking into serious consideration all the circumstances connected with the relations between the prisoner and his former and present wives prior to the death of the lady Mary Laura Cross. It was impossible but that circumstance which might otherwise have no guilty complexion must acquire a guilty character and complexion when viewed by the terrible light that was thrown on them by those relations.

But before they came to the consideration of the circumstances that appeared in the body exhumed on the 21st of July, they must with the light of facts that had been made, approach the consideration of what was then, according to the evidence of Dr Pearson, brought to light. It was impossible that it should be otherwise. If a crime was committed one of the first considerations that would present itself to the officers of justice who were looking after the crime was, for whose benefit could that crime have been committed? And one of the first things that would be proved in a criminal case, if it could be proved, was to show that the party charged was the party – and if possible to show that he was the only party – that could have obtained his end by the commission of that crime which was laid in his charge.

It appeared that the late Mrs Cross had been married in the year '69. She was the mother of at least four children – perhaps it was five – two sons and several daughters, the sons being at school; the daughters being at home. It appeared, as far as the evidence went, that she had been a good and faithful wife. She had been a woman, undoubtedly from the evidence, of delicate formation, or constitution, spoken of by the woman Jane Leahy and by Dr Godfrey as a smart little woman subject to attacks of illness, and if any illness could be spoken of as threatening her with any danger, it was said to be some affection of the heart.

To Dr Godfrey, who was her connection by marriage, she complained about the affection of her heart. The doctor, without making any examination, used to tell her not to trouble herself about any danger, it was not serious at all. On one occasion he said, "If you like, I will examine you carefully if you come tomorrow or the next day." She did not come and some time afterwards, when he saw her he asked how she was. She said that she was all right, and he made no further allusion to the affection of her heart.

It appeared that in the month of May last she was taken ill, and after a while the signs of a usual character began very speedily to acquire a serious character, but still she blamed it on whatever complaint she had about the affection of her heart; she had some fainting fits which the doctor did not look upon as very serious. It had been said by witnesses that she was very sensitive as to smell, and that her stomach was easily affected.

The first witness examined was Mr Colthurst, who knew her for about twelve years; that on April last he saw her coming on briskly towards him, 150 yards away. She came at a smart pace. He asked her how she was, and she said better. This was about the last week in April. Dr Cross called at his house a week before her death. He asked him how his wife was and he said to him: "Don't be surprised if you hear of her death at any moment."

On cross-examination he said again that she had said "Better,

better". He heard of her death the morning after she died. Now a week before her death the prisoner told that gentleman, in answer to his inquiry how his wife was, "Do not be surprised if you hear of her death at any moment." Sometime in January previous he said substantially the same thing to Mrs Madras. According to that witness, Dr Cross was then alarmed about the condition of his wife, whether from heart disease pure and simple or from the development of heart disease increased by illness open and patent from which she had been suffering for, according to the evidence, nearly a fortnight before her death.

He must have been, according to those words, if an anxious and fond husband, greatly alarmed at the condition of his wife.

Mrs Caulfield, who was the next witness, stated that a lady named Miss Skinner came to her on the 22nd of June '86 – that she left on the 29th of October in order to take the same place in the house of Dr and Mrs Cross; that she was intimate with Mrs Cross and family; that she saw Mrs Cross in bed on the 25th of May about three or four o'clock; that she told her that she had vomiting and diarrhoea and thirst. Now that was exactly a week before her death – seven or eight days, perhaps; that she saw milk at her side; that she called again on the 30th and saw the doctor, but not Mrs Cross; that she asked for her and that he said: "Pretty well" and that she did not call again during her life.

Dr Cross called to her house on the 22nd of June, and she having previously received a letter, communicating what was to her a very startling fact, and seeing him, and having ascertained that her old friend's place was so soon filled up, as they might say, assailed him with the salutation:

"How is Mrs Cross?"

"What do you mean?"

"I mean what I say – Miss Skinner."

"I like a good joke, when I hear it."

"No use in denying it. I had a letter."

She stated in cross-examination she was one of Mrs Cross's friends and on the 25th Miss Jefferson showed her upstairs to Mrs Cross, with whom she remained three quarters of an hour. She called on the 30th and saw Dr Cross, but he did not ask her upstairs to see Mrs Cross.

Mr Caulfield had been there on the 22nd. He heard his wife's challenge to Dr Cross, and on their going out, Dr Cross said: "Caulfield, who gave rise to this rumour?"

"There is no use in denying it; murder will out, you know."

They then parted.

Mr Hayes was the next witness. He was with Mrs Cross for half an hour; he again called on the 30th, but was told it was better that she was kept quiet. He did not call on the 31st, and was from home on the 1st of June. Observations were made on the visit of Mr Hayes and Mrs Caulfield on the 31st that Dr Cross did not ask Mrs Caulfield up to see her, and he did not permit her for the reasons he stated to Mr Hayes on the same day.

It was said by counsel, prosecuting for the people and the Crown, that this was for the purpose of keeping persons from her who might make too close inquiries into her illness; that she was not to that condition in which the visit of a friend must be burdensome; that the nature of her illness was not such as to render the presence of an old friend, a clergyman, a disturbing element to her.

On the other hand, it was argued for the defence that if she was so seriously ill as it was proved she was on the 30th, that there were enough of persons in the house to see her, and it would not be wise or judicious to allow friends, not to say strangers from outside, into her bedroom. In considering that, the jury would have to consider the whole circumstances of the relationship of Dr Cross and Mrs Cross at the time. They would have to consider whether or not these two persons, lady and gentleman, who might be expected to visit this old friend of one and parishioner of the other, whether these two were obstructed in seeing her because of the watchful anxiety of the husband about her.

"Was it anxious consideration for her then condition – was it apprehension that their presence would advance her illness or the symptoms of fever if there were any? Counsel for the Crown says so. How idle to talk of love, affection and regard for the health –

271

tender regard for the health and comfort of the woman who was then in such a dangerous illness – when you look at the state of things that existed before that and immediately after the woman was placed in her grave.

You must have regard of these facts to say whether or not Counsel for the Crown are right; for it is of considerable importance to the case. They asked tender consideration for her condition – anxiety lest her symptoms or her illness would be increasing – an unwillingness lest her quiet should be disturbed; but what terror was there exhibited to show that the invalid was in such a dangerous illness as it was pronounced prior to that by Dr Cross; why was she not kept under the quiet and considerate attention of some nurses, or in such an illness as that why was not a second doctor sent for from Cork?

Dr Godfrey was invited on the 24th, but never after that did he see her, notwithstanding the fact that she was so bad with retching, vomiting and diarrhoea, and the tenderness and anxiety about her quiet was so great – her condition was so alarming – that Mrs Caulfield and the Rev Mr Hayes had to be refused admission to her room.

In considering this, you are to consider that she was the mother in that house; that here under ordinary circumstances, was the life on which most care, most anxiety and most attention should have been lavished and bestowed; no trouble should have been omitted to care and preserve the life of the head of the house. Why was it done, you should ask yourselves. Did it arise from want of means? No. Did it arise from ignorance? No. Did it arise from an over-confidence in her condition and in her strength and staying powers? No. A woman with a delicate heart had been for nearly three weeks suffering from what to a person with a delicate heart must have been a terrible and dangerous affliction. Constant vomiting and diarrhoea that by exhaustion might have worn out a strong and lusty frame.

Supposing nothing turned up afterwards as to the previous relations of Dr Cross with this person Skinner and supposing nothing turned up after the death of Mrs Cross, which has been given in evidence here – hearing the evidence given by that lady, hearing the evidence being given by the servants, and the whole of the circumstances attending that illness, if one of you were a relative of that unfortunate lady and heard it all, would you say that she got, in battling against her illness, a fair chance for life? Did she?

Was it right to leave the mistress of the house – she appeared to be an uncomplaining creature, she seemed to have been a person not given much to insisting, so to speak, on her rights – was it right to leave her in this condition, pronounced by Dr Cross himself to be so eminently and imminently perilous? Was it right to leave her to the casual attendance of the servants who ran up or down and in and out as they liked?

Three days before the death, Miss Cross and Miss Jefferson were out visiting. Miss Jefferson was no professional nurse and she did not, as a visitor to the house, feel herself ready to intrude on them. She was in no respect at all nursing Mrs Cross. The cook, Leahy, was not nursing Mrs Cross; the kitchen maid Buckley was not; Mary Barron used to come up to her room when her work was over, about three or four o'clock in the day.

If there was any disease that required constant nursing and constant attention and constant watchfulness, it is that of typhoid fever or gastric attacks which might end in typhoid fever, or end fatally. The servant was to come to Mrs Cross if she rang the bell. Would a mother allow her child to be so treated? Would a father allow a son or a daughter; and should a husband allow a wife to be so attended? Well, it has been said and rightly that the jury was not trying the prisoner for neglect or disregard of his wife during her illness.

No, they were not; but you are bound to see whether or not certain acts were done from disregard or dislike or whether the evidence carries you to the conclusion that they were not mere acts of omission but acts of commission towards this woman. You will have to ask yourselves this.

Dr Godfrey was the next witness examined. He lived in an adjoining place or house. The last time he saw her the vomiting and diarrhoea were better. He never saw her again, and he was never asked to see her. It was said that when the stomach was probed there should have been pain. Dr Godfrey undoubtedly said she complained to him of a pain that day. [In fact, Dr Godfrey said in evidence that she felt no pain.]

The next witness, Miss Jefferson, was a very important witness. She took us through the history of the case and gave many details. Her evidence was established by other witnesses putting their evidence together. Now, from Miss Jefferson's evidence, it has been made clear that this poor lady had been suffering some malady manifested by vomiting, diarrhoea, and it was said, thirst. Now, did this alarm Dr Cross or did it not? If it did not alarm him it should have alarmed him.

Was there any member among you, who, having a delicate wife of eighteen years or more their companion, that they should love and cherish, the mother of their children, which of them who were there, and seeing her afflicted for fourteen days prior to the 25th with illness of this character, and know that she was a woman of delicate constitution, though what some might call a wiry, smart little woman, subject also to complaints about the heart, and not feel great alarm for her condition and security?

Was any conscious effort made to ascertain what was the cause of that constant vomiting, diarrhoea and thirst? Was it not a wonder a woman of delicate constitution could have lasted such an attack for fourteen days? Two days of an attack of that kind, and I suppose hopeless nights, how weak and exhausted would it not make strong persons – vomiting, diarrhoea and pain, great pain combined – was it not a strong person, man or woman who would endure it for three or four days without being terribly prostrated?

Well, Dr Godfrey was asked to see her on the 24th, and you will have to ask yourselves was it merely accident, carelessness or thoughtlessness that no physician was summoned out from Cork, only twelve miles distant? Why was no physician brought out from Cork to say whether some remedy should be prescribed to stay the vomiting and diarrhoea that were wasting away the life-blood of the woman?

You must ask yourselves why it was not done, and you must say, looking at the facts that have come to light, and which have been established beyond all contradiction – whether, looking at those facts, you could hesitate about giving an answer why it was not done. Was there shown in this case, fond kindness counterfeiting absent love? If you are able [to judge] by what has been proved in the case your judgement is inevitably forced to come to the conclusion as to the cause of that omission."

Lord Justice Murphy then read extracts from the evidence of Miss Jefferson and proceeded with his charge to the jury.

"Counsel asked the question if the doctor was a skilled practitioner and Counsel for the Defence said that he was only a doctor in name. He had left the army and was retired from practice for many years since. As I said before and should say again, why was there not something done to procure from skilled persons, some remedy for these, and why was not some person told to watch her, and why was there not some person to sleep in her room at night?

I grant that there might be husbands so lavish in their tenderness, so anxious about the condition of their wife – and I have seen such – so careful and watchful that perhaps they were imprudently attentive and would never depart from the bed of their sick wife, and who scarcely allowed any other person to give them food or drink and who had spent wearisome days and sleepless nights in attending, perhaps, and ministering to their wife in illness. If the love of Dr Cross was of this character, it might possibly be said to account for this, but it was not; and there the lurid light was thrown.

Why, the adulterous relations that existed with Skinner before that, and which must have been then continuing? From which of these two causes did this state of things arise? With respect to the condition of that poor suffering lady, what was a protracted – looking at it utterly independently, if the body was never exhumed from the earth – and agonising illness, was also a neglected one.

Taking the evidence of the three servants, excepting the cook,

Jane Leahy, what were the facts? She had a bell pull by her in her room, but she had no one sleeping there these nights. The servant Mary Barron was rung for by the poor lady, and she went into the room and did something to allay her suffering. The anxious husband who had undertaken himself the responsibility of nursing and attending his wife, was, so far as Mary Barron saw, asleep at the other end of the room during the time she came in to answer the summons of the bell and to minister to the wants of the suffering patient.

Well, she also gave an account of that scene at an early hour of the morning, that scene that I should call an appalling scene. Screams were heard at one o'clock in the morning; the husband was up and about, and according to his sister's account, he brought up a brandy bottle. In a few moments all was over – the wife of eighteen years and more was dead – the wife that was attended chiefly or altogether at night by her husband. If he was not a loving husband, he had no right to be there.

I should say that he had no right to be there if his love had turned to indifference, or indifference to hate. This person should have not have been left to care her – she should have been left to the touch, even of a stranger's careless hands who would have watched over her for the last moments of her suffering and wronged life.

The sister goes back to her room. He was dressed according to her account.

In the morning he calls the servants; no hustle, no alarm, no sound of wailing or grief for the calamity that had befallen the house. There were two girls there, said not to be strong in mind. Perhaps they particularly required a mother's watchful care. Two young boys away at school. No sound of lamentation, no appearance of grief for the departure of the wife, who was released from torture and suffering.

It is usual when that inevitable death visits a house that those who were familiar with the deceased were summoned to the house to pay last decent attention to the lifeless frame. Some there might be so constant and affectionate as not to allow a friend too near the body from which life had gone. Was that the case here? The servants are called in, the lifeless frame is raised and something like washing takes place, a servant holding the basin of water.

These are scant rites – none others are observed – a flannel swathe, a clean nightdress, and a pair of stockings, and subsequently a handkerchief tied around the chin; and that was all that was done in preparation for the funeral of poor Mary Laura Cross, preparatory to her being placed in the grave.

All that has a most important bearing on the case. As Mr Atkinson and Mr Adams said you were not trying the prisoner for it; you were not trying him for his adultery or for his callous indifference to the deceased that might have been observed at the time.

No, you are not. Still you cannot help asking yourselves what produced that? Was her death a surprise to him? Was there any act of grief or sorrow on his part? The two eminent counsel for the prisoner, as they were bound to do, put forward everything that their intellect and power could suggest to his defence and spared no person who was examined in the case if they thought that any cross-examination or reference to them would serve their client. There were certain limits within which they would confine themselves, but they could not pretend to urge to the jury, that in all these circumstances, antecedent to her death, and what occurred on the night or morning of her death there was any vestige of sorrow on the part of the husband for the wife who was taken away on that night from some illness or another."

His Lordship then read Mary Barron's evidence and commented on the fact that there had not been a paid nurse obtained for Mrs Cross, a medical man called and an honest inquiry made to discover what was wrong with her. He then reviewed the evidence of Captain Woodley, Mr Paul, Miss Handcock, Mary Magrath and Mr Johnson, two of whom he remarked came from the London and North Western Hotel, in order to establish, as it had been, beyond all question, that in the March previous to the woman's death, an adulterous intercourse existed between the prisoner and this woman – this young girl.

It had been proved by Miss Handcock that on the 29th of March they were in the hotel and appeared again on the 21st of April. Where he had been between those two dates, no one knew. It had been said by Miss Cross that he had left for Ventnor to take his boys away to spend their Easter vacation with his brother-in-law but this at least had been established beyond all matter of doubt that he had been there on the 20th of March, occupying the same room with the girl Skinner again on the 21st of April.

His Lordship then referred to the evidence of the postmaster Mr Griffin and the man Cornelius McCarthy, who had during his time taken fifteen letters addressed to a place where the girl Skinner was staying after she left Shandy Hall.

"It was said that this establishes a terrible motive. It was said by the eminent counsel for the defence, what motive, why rush into a crime to enjoy what he already enjoyed? While Laura Cross was living as his wife at Shandy Hall, he might have had the girl Skinner as his mistress in some other country or place, but he could not have her raised to the rank of wife. Whether she wished for it, whether or not she had expected that elevation of her position. He could not have placed her in the position of Mrs Cross of Shandy Hall until the old companion of eighteen years was removed out of the way and left the place empty to be supplied by another.

Was that the mode of acting? How was it proved? It was proved by the fact that after the house was made empty for the new occupant, the marriage – if marriage it ought to be called – was celebrated with as much speed as it could possibly be. Notice, I suppose, for marriages must be given, a week or ten days, or whatever was the time; but some notice must be given in the place where the parties resided – where the marriage was to be celebrated, unless under very special circumstances.

And a week after, the girl Skinner was made Mrs Cross of Shandy Hall, with indecent haste; or wicked speed, it might be called. But there was some terrible impelling motive. It could not be supposed that the adulterous intercourse could be carried on with the same satisfaction to him and the girl Skinner if the wife was still living; who though she might have heard of the occurrence January or February when there was something about escorting Miss Skinner to Dublin and might have had some little exception or jealousy aroused in her mind then, seemed to have at least concealed from her anything that subsequently occurred.

Even the correspondence was kept concealed from her. The visit to Dublin in August, the going to Ventnor to see the boys, which if she had heard of it she would, with whatever little energy or life had been left to her, have been loud in proclaiming the wrongs done to her and to the children whom she bore to the prisoner. Griffin told him that two letters came with the extraordinary directions, merely 'to be called for' at the Post Office.

Some initials were on the envelope – the same on both. Dr Cross came down for the first to the Post Office, which was only a few hundred yards away from the house and Griffin gave it to him. When the second letter was delivered this extraordinary coincidence took place – it was in or about the day of the funeral.

From whom was it? Have you, the jury, any doubt? What did it refer to? There were a great number of letters sent to this person and they came in the hands of this man McCarthy. The master of the house could only conceal some guilty correspondence in that way, made arrangements for letters of this kind. This second letter came about the time of the funeral. Had the tidings of the illness been conveyed to Skinner?

Were the glad tidings welcome, or was it some appalling news that should awaken him and her to the wrong that had been done this lady – the wrong that had been manifestly done by the adulterous connection. Well, now, as to these angry expressions, sworn to by McCarthy, as having been used by the accused – if it stood there alone it would have very little importance, but it became very serious when it happened during the time the person Skinner was there and it was noticed by this man, McCarthy, and evidently there was some anticipation of what subsequently developed.

The accused left home on the 9th, was later was at Euston with a companion, occupying the same room. On the 17th, he went through the ceremony of marriage, and strange enough in the same church and on the same day of the month as he had been married to his first wife."

His Lordship then revisited the evidence of Mrs Madras and referring to her offer of champagne on the 30th for the weak and dying Mrs Cross and questioned why the offer had not been availed of; and if not, why was not something done.

Why was a messenger not sent to Cork for a physician; or was it that the prisoner had too much confidence in his medical skill? Was Shandy Hall such an out of the way place – was it deserted – or was she in such a position of life that in what proved to be the last hours of her death pangs, at least her last evening on earth, she could not procure the services of the physician Dr Godfrey in whom she had some confidence? Anything like that was not done and all those circumstances you should take into your consideration in your inquiry into the cause of death of Mary Laura Cross.

Did she meet with fair play or foul play? From whom did she receive it? Now before you approach the evidence of Dr Pearson and Dr Crowley, both of whom gave very important evidence, it is as well to look at what took place immediately after the death.

On the 29th of May he had written to her brother, Mr Marriott, who appeared to have been a very affectionate and friendly brother, stating that she was ill from typhoid fever.

I should ask why if she was ill with typhoid fever, no medical man was called to see her? Twelve miles from Cork, an hour and a half's drive in to see and bring out a doctor to see the poor invalid who was so racked with the terrible purging and vomiting? In this letter he wrote to Mr Marriott, he stated: 'The medical men say here they have an unusual lot to do.' Was that true or false?

Dr Crowley, the medical officer of the neighbourhood, stated that some time in the end of March or beginning of April there was one case of typhoid fever in the adjoining parish, six miles off, and not a single case after that. Was he one of the medical men who had a lot to do? Now, was the statement true or false? It was proved by Dr Crowley that it was false; there was no evidence that it was true. If it was false why was it stated in the letter, written to

England preparing for the death of Laura Cross – a terrible question according to the answer that you find yourselves compelled to give.

Again in a second letter to England, he states that her heart 'failed from exhaustion, as he knew it would, many a long day ago'. But even supposing that it did not fail from exhaustion, there still remained the question, what produced that exhaustion? Counsel for the Defence had said no matter how false in affecting a sorrow that second letter from the prisoner might be, it did not show that Laura Cross died from foul play.

No, it did not; and until you find that proved, you should find a verdict of not guilty against the prisoner. But did the letter affect the prisoner when taken into account with other facts in the case? Be the grief sincere or affected, genuine or false, what was the reason of the false statement outside that with respect to the prevalence of fever to account for the death of Laura Cross? Real or affected grief did not require that statement to be made. In the third letter, fever disappeared altogether and it was stated that spasms of the heart caused her death.

On the 3rd of June the prisoner went to Dr Crowley to tell him that he wished to register the death of his wife. In the form to be filled up there was a column for primary cause and secondary cause, and in it, the primary cause was set down as typhoid fever; the duration of the illness fourteen days; but the heart was not put down as primary or secondary. In the letter to Mr Marriott, fever is put in as the disease. In the third letter there is some complaint of the heart mentioned.

Now, it would occur to you that if a person had a plain and simple story to tell, it would be consistent and uniform, but you should take this into consideration; to the man who had anything to conceal from his fellow men, if it was not permitted to let the entire truth be known, then would the story be told of any transaction that concerned or affected him to be uniform or consistent?"

His Lordship then referred to letters written by the prisoner for publication, stating that some particulars in their reports were not accurate. After the death of Mrs Cross, it was perfectly plain what took place. The moment the knowledge came to the ears of any friend of Mrs Cross or her family, the moment it came to Mrs Caulfield, everyone commenced talking and inquiring into the antecedents connected with Laura Cross's illness, which made manifest to the public eye and ear that this marriage that took place on the 17th of June, must have been in the source of preparation prior to the death of Laura Cross; everyone must have been driven to this and no other conclusion.

"Mr Atkinson said that they hurried persons to a conclusion without proof. But circumstances were evidence, very important and vital evidence. They could not establish legal proofs, but they must be taken into account as circumstances leading up to proof. So long as they might create a prejudice in your minds before you went into the box, you must cast them out of your minds; but when in that box, you must allow your judgement to be affected by all those circumstances, because if a body was exhumed from any other chance directing it and if that was the body of a wife who had been snatched away from a manifestly fond and affectionate husband, and a man who had clearly and manifestly exhibited the natural grief of a husband on the death of his wife – a man who had been known to be faithful and a loving husband and was the person who would have suffered most by the terrible divorce that took place by death – if such a body was exhumed and found to have met with a foul death by poisoning, the last person in life on whom guilt could be attached by inquiry would be the fond and loving husband. Human nature, instinct, proof of life together, affection, love, devotion, the mother of the children – all that would repel almost any proof that could be given.

But when the facts had been proved in this case beyond all doubt of question, and made known and manifest, both what occurred before her death and what took place after it – if foul work was done and any person in connection with the lady whose death was the subject of investigation, the person on whom the guilt should attach would be the man who had acted as the prisoner was proved to have acted.

Against the inhabitants of Shandy Hall no breath of suspicion could lurk in the mind of any mortal. Mr Adams, as he was bound to do, said that even if there was poisoning, others could have done it. There was this servant, or that servant; the sister, Miss Jefferson and all. Now, you can put that out of the question altogether. Any man who meant to do his duty would not for a moment dwell on that. Let you not cast a single mental glance at it. If Mary Laura Cross's death was hastened, whether by suspended action of the heart produced by any foul drug administered, or by actual poisoning solely or entirely, if her death was caused by it, who now on earth could have poisoned her if not the prisoner?

Let you put arsenic for the complexion and arsenic to ease pain out of the question. The idea of a poor lady of her age, with her two afflicted daughters, using arsenic for her complexion – and then as to the use of arsenic to ease pain, was it ever heard of since the world was established?

Now it has been properly said that the jury should not find Cross guilty to set up or establish Dr Pearson's reputation. It was hardly necessary to make such a suggestion as that to any juror; but you need not in order to set up or establish a reputation for Dr Pearson – if he needed any – be swayed in your verdict, yet you are not to suppose, without evidence and without proof that Dr Pearson, a medical man of established reputation, chosen for his high office because of his high repute, that he without any evidence, he was supposed to be an ignorant pretender in subjects of which he knew nothing.

He told you of his degrees, of his professorship of Material Medica in Queen's College. He succeeded a man of known eminence, an established chemist, the late Dr O'Keeffe. He was established there and when called on to perform this matter he knew that it was a matter of life and death; so far as the evidence might aid, and was bound by every means to use the utmost care, attention and watchfulness, in any experiments he might make.

Now, it was said and very properly that he never made an experiment or analysis on the body of any human being who died from arsenical poisoning. If that were necessary to be established in every case where a witness was brought forward to prove that in an examination of a human body he had got poison, I am afraid they would have to search for a long time, all over Ireland. I have myself been a long time at the bar and cannot recollect much more than one case of the proof in court of analysis of a human body after arsenical poisoning.

This was not the way in which the science of chemistry or any other science was established, and if he was not to have a knowledge of science until he had experimented on a number of people who had died by poisoning, it would be a long time before he had any experience. There were great chemists, who in their laboratory could get certain results of substances put before them that they had never seen before. In the process of analysis, if carefully done by a careful man, circumstances come about where they cannot be mistaken.

It has been said and of course it appeared to them in their practical ignorance as absurd, that they as Mr Adams had said, found it necessary to work on an infinitesimal portion. It was not a matter of one trial with a chemist, for he got one result with one experiment and another by another, and another by a third experiment, and if the results arrived at were not contradictory they were able to come to an inevitable conclusion.

Dr Pearson came here fortified with certain books; he had a certain array of books against him also. Quite right that both should be prepared. He said 'I will tell you what I have done; I have here my report showing how I did it; produce any authority to me to show that it was not the right way to do it. Produce any medical man here and let him listen to me, and then let him come forward and say that in anything I have said that there is any such thing as ignorance displayed in what I have scientific knowledge of and proved by demonstration.'

No such thing was done. There was a slight mistake made and Mr Atkinson, with the great vigour of his intellect seized on the fact, that in his information, Dr Pearson said that there were three grains of arsenic in the liver, which could not be. A man might be as good an analyst as ever worked on a subject of this kind; he may have done all that could be done, but the analysis never could be made unless a vast amount of comparisons could be made.

He may not have turned his attention to the fact that the liver could only assimilate with itself a certain quantity of arsenic. Dr Pearson might say he had not known that, but that would not affect the question at all, as to his finding it there. He made an analysis and compared it to the way mentioned. He found 1.28 grains of arsenic in the liver, which he wrote down in his report, and in the other organs analysed 1.76 grains, and the two together made 3.02 grains. That what was in his mind, when he stated so at first, without having his notes by him, but when he looked at his report, he saw the error and had it corrected.

Dr Pearson might not have known how much arsenic the liver would contain; but that would not affect his knowledge and his power of distinguishing whether arsenic was present there. Both doctors swore, in the first instance, that they saw no trace whatsoever of typhoid fever, and they saw no trace whatsoever of disease of the heart – lungs sound and other organs. Professor Pearson had a laboratory under his charge in the Queen's College. He had considerable experience in analyses, and if that were true, he must have experience that would enable him to discover certain particles minute though they might be, that he would recognise to be of this or that substance.

Dr Crowley said that he found in certain organs signs of preservation that could not have existed unless there was something in those organs that prevented putrefaction from setting in, and that was a most important piece of evidence. Though you are not to foreswear one hair's breadth for the sake of the reputation of Dr Pearson, still, on the other hand, when an accomplished physician of established reputation, selected for a high office by reason of his known experience and ability, who comes into the box and challenges contradiction of his knowledge – and he could have been contradicted if there was anything that he described inaccurately – you cannot set aside his evidence without great and sufficient reason.

He came into the box and challenged contradiction by the eminent counsel for the defence, who had at their disposal any amount of eminent medical testimony to set aside the evidence of Dr Pearson, if it was possible to overthrow it. When he came into the box and gave evidence you cannot look at it as a mere matter of conjecture. In speaking to you of many things, Dr Pearson had spoken of his own work done by his own hands entirely, and in his own words he has given you the results of that work.

Unless there was evidence to show that there was something false or deceptive, or some traces or vestige of ignorance, you are not to displace or cast aside his evidence. That could not be done at all. Now I have told you of the processes he went through. Was there any proof from any book that might be produced against him that the processes he had adopted and the tests he had applied by three different methods, were not the tests that could be applied by any known chemist or analyst; not a particle.

It was said that in such and such a process might not a mistake be made? Yes, but he had guarded against that. And then could the suggestion be made – and it was made – that the learned gentleman, whose excellence was marked by ability, an earnest desire to tell the truth, and as far as I can see, a great deal of modesty; would give you a false account of any respect that he had not adopted the methods, which he swore he had adopted; and the results he said he saw with his own eyes, did not appear to me such a thing could not be suggested. He produced for you the particles he found, and any of you by the aid of a microscope, could see them, if you wished.

He had told you how he had adopted the best known and best recognised process in use in order to obtain the result of those analyses and then proceeded to describe those processes. Let any medical man, and analyst, any man accustomed to use a microscope, come here and he would see them. When or how did he get them? He did not put them here himself to convict Dr Cross! That would make him a worse criminal than the man alleged to be guilty of the crime charged against him.

He told you that he also found strychnine. That was quicker in its deadly work. Where did he get it? Dr Pearson swore he got it in the body. He is able to say that they are tests that could not err, and by them he had established the presence of strychnine and arsenic in the dead body of Laura Cross who died on the night of the 1st or morning of the 2nd, terminating her suffering in death. He may have commenced from small applications of it, and if that were so, of course the power of resistance to another application would be less. He said the way in which arsenic kills is frequently that you cannot say the size of the dose administered."

His lordship then read most of the medical evidence and completed his comments on the case for the Crown.

"You have been pressed by Mr Atkinson as to general matters, which, he said would have manifested the greatest follies on the part of the prisoner, and unless he was a great fool or a lunatic, he would not have chosen such operations or such a time if he wished to get rid of his wife. That criminals who were about to commit crime were always on their guard, and were very foreseeing, was not the case, for in all the great crimes that had been detected, it was always said, 'What folly to have done this, or what madness to have done this?' and as far as my experience went, it had never been advanced that criminals had acted with a common sense or prudence, but on the contrary in a manner that any man with common sense would consider most foolish.

Now, after the arrest, Dr Cross was prohibited from speaking to anyone except in the presence of some constable or police officer. Higgins stationed himself behind Dr Cross and heard him use those words, which have been given in evidence. It was said, for the defence, would Dr Cross be so foolish in the presence of Higgins to say this; but if Higgins had down what Miss Cross swore he said on this occasion, it would only be said Cross was mad.

She stated that he said: 'My God, is it possible that it could have contained arsenic?' If Higgins heard the word arsenic used at that time, do you not think, so sure as he heard anything, so sure he would write it down to establish the use of the vial and important word, 'arsenic'? Did he hear it? What testimony from that poor lady – for he should call her so – would satisfy you that Higgins heard any such words? Was the prisoner speaking at the time to his sister on what he thought was a matter of vital importance? Wherefore, did he, under such circumstances, break the silence that was imposed on him?

Miss Cross's evidence was the same, as that given before as to the circumstances as tending to the death of Mrs Cross. It was idle inquiry to try and conjecture what manner poison may have been administered, but there could be no doubt, that there was ample opportunity of doing so, morning, noon and night.

The question had arisen as to whether there was one or two bottles containing arsenic found in the press in Mrs Cross's room; but it was at least clear that a pound of arsenic had been brought into the house in the course of a year, and if the thought came into the head of the prisoner, it was very easy for him to take several bottles of it and put it away. In the matter of the prisoner's question to his sister about destroying the bottles, in the presence of the constable, this piece of evidence should have your careful consideration.

I cannot see how that conversation points towards innocence. It is for you to ask did it? It was said it was the act of a man who felt he was innocent, and who when he heard that arsenic had been found in the body of his dead wife that the thought suddenly flashed upon him that she could have committed suicide and that he feared the bottles containing arsenic had been destroyed. It is for you to decide that question. As I have said before and will now repeat for the last time, you are bound by law if you do not believe the evidence to bring in a verdict of not guilty against the prisoner, unless you are satisfied of the proofs that have been given; that these proofs were not consistent with his innocence.

It is your duty to look about and see if you can find any reasonable explanations to give, as rational men, to the facts that have been proved entirely consistent with the prisoner's guilt. If, in your consciences, you could find out that it was consistent with his innocence, if you could find a rational and reasonable doubt, as suggested on close observation and examination, you ought to give him the benefit of such a doubt, or such want of satisfactory proof, and to find him, 'not guilty'.

But, if, on the other hand, you think you could apply it to lead to the conclusion that Laura Cross met foul play, during that fortnight, and particularly on the night of the 1st or morning of the 2nd of June, at the hands of the husband, who was bound to protect her, then a foul and hideous crime had been committed, and you without hesitation must find that the prisoner is guilty. No timid faltering in your duty, no exertions to strive to avoid doing your duty, no belying of your own reason and judgement and conscience by conjuring up fancies or wild conjectures must allow you to turn aside from the direct path in the performance of the duty you owe to God, to their conscience – which was the God within you – and to your country.

That Mary Laura Cross was wronged by foul adultery, which must have been at least concealed by the husband under her own roof, with a young girl who was brought there as instructress of the prisoner's children – that was proved beyond doubt. That in the city of Dublin at an hotel there he consorted with that unhappy, if we may call her so, creature, was proved beyond all doubt; that its commencement and existence was proved beyond all doubt; that an unholy correspondence was, in terrible close proximity with the death of that unfortunate lady; that heartless and callous indifference was exhibited on the occasion of her death; that after the very scant funeral rites were performed he left the roof where his poor girls were to join that creature again; that on the 9th and 10th they were at the Euston Hotel again; that going to see the poor boys was a sham and a mockery; that giving notice as soon as it could be possibly given, he hurried with wicked speed to replace the faithful wife, that was then in the grave, has been proved without doubt.

Was he pleased at her death? Did it bring him one pang of sorrow, or did it bring him exultation, at the opportunity given to him to gratify his passion? Could any man who was not a loving husband or who counterfeited love by kindness – who was not a kind husband – could he have permitted that lady, his wedded wife to have been in the state she was from the 10th of May to the 2nd of June, without any doctor or without any of the ordinary attention that should have been paid to her? Was it from regard to her that she said herself she would not have a nurse to sit up with her, that Phil preferred it himself?

Was it from love or affection that he kept himself in the room as guardian – should I say guardian – to his poor sick wife? Was it with the thought that no hand would minister with such attention as he, or was it that he desired to have her under his own control not as a guardian but as a keeper? Was it lest she should be disturbed? Was that the reason that Mrs Caulfield and Mr Hayes were not allowed to see her? Was it from excessive watchfulness that he went down himself to the kitchen for a wineglass full of chicken broth?

Wherefore in the letter was there introduced the statements about typhoid fever? Wherefore was it changed and altered to disease of the heart? Wherefore was that not mentioned in the certificate of the 3rd of June or why was in not mentioned in the subsequent certificate it was necessary to send to Dublin?

Wherefore was it necessary to state that Miss Jefferson was a nurse and a professional nurse which she was not? Wherefore were the facts about the prevalence of fever invented and wherefore was there such a careful abstaining from summoning any medical attendant to the side of the poor lady? Was there anxiety at her presence becoming lonesome and anxiety to get rid of Mary Laura Cross? Was there a substitute provided? That a substitute had been provided had been proved; that a cause existed, no question of doubt could be raised. Were there bottles kept in the room? Was there a desire for the removal of the little bottles? If not, what was the use of the conversation subsequently?

She was put quietly into the grave, and nothing was said to inform anyone that he had been guilty of being married until Mrs Caulfield got the letter and Miss Skinner appeared, translated into Mrs Cross. Was that conversation about the bottles foolish or wise? What of the testimony sworn to by Dr Crowley and Dr Pearson? What of the positive evidence sworn to by Dr Pearson, a competent medical man established in the position you know he occupies – not one that was gained as Mr Adams had said, but by his merit and qualifications.

What did he swear? 'I saw arsenic extracted from the body; I tested it by all the tests that could be applied to it by any scientific man.' He also stated that they could see no trace of typhoid fever. Ask yourselves those questions, gentlemen, and ask yourselves was Mary Laura Cross done to death by poison. If you believe she was – then you must find the prisoner guilty."

His Lordship who was deeply affected at several points in his charge then concluded. The able and exhaustive charge of the judge lasted some four hours and a half. As His Lordship, speaking with deep emotion referred to the treatment by the prisoner of his late wife, the relatives and friends of the lady were deeply affected. The prisoner presented the greatest coolness throughout; and never for a moment was his face seen to blanch, or a quiver observed in the muscles of his powerful and well-knit frame.

The judge's charge finished at half past three o'clock, and although the concluding words – "If you believe that Mary Laura Cross died of poison then you must find the prisoner guilty" – sounded like the death knell of the accused to many present, Dr Cross went down the steps of the dock as firmly as ever and the only remark he made to his custodian was that the judge was very hard on him.

The jury retired to consider their verdict at half past three. At ten minutes past four the foreman Mr Palmer returned to the court and asked His Lordship if the jury could ask Dr Pearson a question.

Lord Justice Murphy said: "Certainly. I will be of any assistance I can for you. Call out the jury."

The jury again entered the box, and His Lordship directed Dr Pearson to come to the table.

The foreman asked: "Dr Pearson, had you any assistance when you were examining the body?"

"Examining the body; yes, but not at the analysis."

"That is all we wanted."

"If you want to know if there was anyone present –"

Mr Atkinson intervened: "Now, now."

Dr Pearson said: "I had the entire thing in my own hands."

Lord Justice Murphy asked: "Had you any assistance whatsoever?"

Dr Pearson replied: "Not performing the analysis. I had an assistant to bring things when I wanted them from a distance. If I required a glass rod, or anything of that kind, my own assistant would hand it to me. He was never out of my sight in the room, and whatever I employed I invariably –"

291

Mr Atkinson interrupted: "Now I beg your pardon!"

Lord Justice Murphy said: "He can say that."

Mr Alexander (juror) asked: "Have you the slightest doubt upon your mind that Mrs Cross died of poison?"

Dr Pearson answered: "Not the slightest."

The Verdict

After a deliberation, in all of fifty minutes, the jury returned to the court and the foreman Mr Palmer handed the issue-paper to the Clerk of The Peace, Mr William O'Keeffe.

Mr O'Keeffe: "Have you reached your verdict, gentlemen?"

The foreman: "Yes."

Mr O'Keeffe then called out the names of the jury. All answered.

Mr O'Keeffe: "Philip Henry Eustace Cross, you heretofore stood indicted for that you, on the 2nd of June, 1887, feloniously, wilfully and of malice aforethought, did kill and murder one, Mary Laura Cross. To that indictment you pleaded not guilty, and for trial put yourself on God and your country, which country has found you guilty. What have you now to say why sentence of death should not be awarded against you, according to the law?"

The prisoner who bore up in the most firm manner throughout, showing only slight emotion at one portion of his speech, then said: "I am perfectly innocent of the crime laid to my charge, and I will give you my reasons, if I am allowed. May I speak, sir?"

Lord Justice Murphy: "Yes, you may speak now."

The speech was delivered from notes he had in a book, and with one arm resting on the edge of the dock he held the book up to the light of the gas jet in order to read. He got through the trying ordeal without betraying the least emotion except when on the first occasion he protested it was not likely he would commit such a crime; if not for his own sake, for the sake of his poor children.

The Prisoner's Speech

It is very hard for me to say much after being in gaol in solitary confinement for the last five months, without access to my friends, or books or memoranda or anything. I have just taken a few notes here. And I will say what I can in defence of myself. Well, in the first place, gentlemen, I have not seen a grain of arsenic since September last year since I dipped those sheep.

I have never seen it, to my knowledge, directly or indirectly. I never gave my wife arsenic. It was not found in the house; I purchased on that occasion a pound of arsenic; a pound of arsenic is the allowance to dip fifty sheep, and I had forty-eight, and it was not likely that I would go and put a little bit of arsenic away, to poison my wife, for the sake of Miss Skinner, a lady that did not come into my house until the 28th or 29th of October following and the sheep were dipped before the 20th – in or about the 14th or 15th of September.

Then there is my previous history. I have been all over the world; I have always been on good terms with my wife; I have always had the greatest regard for my children and family; I did my best for them, from six or seven in the morning until six or seven at night and often later. It was not likely, that even, for my own sake alone, but for theirs, I would go and make away with that lady. I am sixty-three years of age; I know what the consequences are. Even it if were not for myself alone, but for my poor children, do you think I would commit murder?

I may knock down a man but I am no murderer. I poisoned a dog once and I felt ashamed for doing it. That dog came up to me, and he took the poison out of my hand, and when I saw him die, I could not but cry, and I said to my family I would never do the like again. After that do you think I would do the same to my wife? I never did it. Phil Cross never did it. Comparatively speaking I have never told a lie in my life. It is well known I am as truthful a man as there is in Great Britain.

I lose £40 a year that her brother was good enough to give to me. He gave it as part and parcel of the £2,000. I expected that money when he [Mary Laura's father] died. I expected it to be given by him to my wife. I was led to expect that and a third share of the £6,000. Why should I risk that and my half-pay of £200 a year for the sake of that girl? It is not likely, gentlemen, not likely. [The sums quoted and financial arrangements referred to here by Cross seem at odds with those given by Humphrey Marriott and the Attorney General.]

If I wanted to make away with her – this lady was subject to fits and fainting attacks for the last dozen years, more or less, and what was to prevent me any day or any moment to make away with her; why could I not have put a handkerchief over her mouth, and who would have found it out? No one would be the bit wiser.

I do not know what to say exactly. I have been pitched into it by three of the greatest men in Britain. According to them, everything I did was wrong. His Lordship said, comparatively speaking, that I starved her, neglected her, did not give her any food, didn't attend her or watch her. He says also she was ill and vomiting all day long – the usual talk of servants. Is it likely that if she was vomiting, her intimate friend of twenty or thirty years standing, who was in the house, would not have made some remarks to me? Is it likely she would go out driving three days before my wife's death – she and my sister? – to go out and leave my wife, and she vomiting and suffering from diarrhoea, and everything else? No, it is not likely; and then to say I would select the time that lady was in the house to go and commit murder? Well, as Mr Atkinson said, I must be a madman to do such a thing. Is it likely I would select arsenic – a poison that of all others would be found ten years after in her body; and if not in her body, in the earth beside her. Is it likely I would do that? I don't suppose such a thing ever happened as a medical man doing so. If he did so he would be the most ignorant man on the face of the known globe. Is it likely that I would go and use strychnine at the same time? Not likely. Well, in some of those medicine chests, there ought to be a bottle of quack medicine and there is strychnine in it. I am not going to say whether or not it was found in her body. I don't know as I wasn't there. But the quantity of strychnine was very small – the hundredth part of a grain, Dr

Pearson says, and I daresay he is right. I have not been speaking to anybody so long that I hardly know what I am talking about.

There's a process, what's this they call it? – the ptomaine process and you are very likely to make a mistake in that. You can find it in any one of our bodies if we died tomorrow; and if dried it will show three different colours when tested by the bichromate of potass test. He doesn't say he got hold of a frog and injected it into it, and then he could ascertain whether it was strychnine or not. If he injected it into the leg of a frog, he would see the convulsions. He doesn't state that he did so. It was stated by one of the counsel that strychnine is an alkaloid, that is a poison that passes rapidly away and that accounts for the small amount found.

With all due respect to the Attorney General, that able gentleman, I beg to differ with him, and I would say it is the contrary; I don't know if things are different now; but when I was learning I understood that strychnine was a poison that remained in the body for ever so long. I think there may be some little doubt about it.

Well, is it likely that having poisoned my wife, I would go and marry another young woman? When it was reported all over the country before I married Miss Skinner, I had poisoned my wife, why did Mrs Caulfield, turn to me and say, "Mind you don't poison her" and she said to my sister, "Take care he doesn't poison her."

Look at the reports circulated about the country about me. I am a boycotted man for the last six years, boycotted since I went to gaol [for assault on farmer?]. All sorts of extraordinary reports were put about concerning me – that I had pulled the coffin down the stairs, that I pulled brasses off the coffin, that I had her taken out of the coffin, and filled it with stones, and that I had burned her. These were the rumours, I don't know where they came from or who put them into circulation. Whatever I did was wrong, nothing I did was right.

I would wish you, Mr Deyos, to show me the prescription written by Dr Corby and Dr Townsend, which my little girls were taking, and in which arsenic and strychnine were both combined, and which were applicable to my wife's case. Whether she was taking them or not, I can't say. In this case where her bottles were kept, there was a bottle of stuff containing strychnine. The learned judge, comparatively speaking, says I starved her, that she was suffering from vomiting and diarrhoea always, and all treatment I gave her was wrong. Well, I did not see that, and I am not aware of it, and with all respect to his lordship I don't believe it. I don't believe it.

Why did not the Government offer a reward of £50 or £100 to prove that I had purchased arsenic within the past twelve months? But they did not do that. Give a man a chance, I only want fair play. Mr Deyos handed to the prisoner the prescriptions he had previously mentioned. There is a prescription" [holding it up] "made by Dr Townsend, written by me at his dictation. That was in the house. I can't tell whether my wife took that or not. Here is another prescription made out by Dr Corby, which suited her and there is both arsenic and strychnine in it. These medicines were in the house. Her room, comparatively speaking, was an apothecary's shop. Show that to any doctor here and tell him whether it is the case, or not.

It was stated that Mrs Cross had vomiting, purging and diarrhoea all day long. Mrs Cross was a lady of very delicate stomach. If she went into the kitchen, it made her ill – even the smell of an egg would sometimes make her ill, and she should get up at breakfast and run away out. She was at this time suffering from certain diseases that ladies suffer from every month. This was also the cause of her vomiting. I must say, as far as I am concerned, I never feared the lady's life was in any danger. She had a feverish attack, which commenced with a cold, which went on for a time, with a sort of low, nasty typhoid fever, but she would recover from that.

The day before she died, she got up and walked around her room. When Miss Jefferson saw her she told her she was better. It was afterwards, when she got the fainting fit, that she died of that fit. I slept in the room with her, and my bed was within two yards of hers, and when she got this bad attack, though for the moment, I did not deem it so – I jumped up, got into a pair of trousers, and thinking she might want brandy, I ran downstairs and got a bottle of brandy and then I called my sister, but the poor lady had passed away.

Few moments occurred when all this was taking place; few moments, I suppose, it is very hard to judge of intervals of time on such an occasion. Dr Crowley says I only registered her disease as typhoid fever. I went to Dr Crowley and the following conversation took place: I said: "My wife is dead." He said he was very sorry for it. I said it was a sort of nasty, low, insidious fever. He said: "What sort of fever is it?" I said: "Every sort of fever is typhoid, these times, and you had better put it down, typhoid; it is the easiest way and the simplest way." Then he spoke to me about the secondary disease and I said that it did not matter.

I was blamed during the hearing of this case for being solely my wife's medical man. I am her husband, and she was perfectly satisfied with me, and desired no other doctor. I attended her in every confinement for the last seventeen or eighteen years. Dr Godfrey never was her medical attendant. I have not very much more to say. Then it is spoken about Miss Jefferson going to church and I staying at home. I could not easily detain a guest to remain at home to mind my wife, while I was at church, so that was the reason Miss Jefferson went to church and I remained at home, to take care of her. Everything I did seemed to be wrong.

There's a great deal of fuss made about me giving her a glass of chicken broth – I quite forgot that altogether. I knew when she was in the habit of getting drinks, to drink a large quantity and I directed that she should not get more than a small quantity at a time. There's macaroni alluded to. My wife was always eating macaroni. She had it in her pockets and in her press. Wherever she went she had macaroni. She was more fond of blancmange and cornflour than anything else.

Now this talk of me washing this lady after she died – I don't think anyone had a greater right to wash her than I had – I washed her when she was alive, and why not wash her when she was dead? Old Jane Leahy tied up her face. My wife had everything she desired, chicken broth, eggs and brandy, corn flour. It was the greatest difficulty to get her to eat meat. I was constantly rowing with her about it. All these things she had if she wished for them. There is no doubt, I think, that I allowed everyone to have access to her. Mrs Caulfield called on the 25th of May. She stopped three quarters of an hour. She got medicine from Dr Godfrey when she was suffering from vomiting. She was better after that dose of medicine.

Miss Kirchoffer came the same day, and she told her she was vomiting. She stopped a long time with her and Mr Hayes was there the same day also. On the 30th of the month, my wife was in bed; I don't know whether Miss Kirchoffer wanted to go up to see her or not; you can't have people going into a sick room and stopping there as long as they like. Dr Godfrey says that on the 24th she had no fever; I don't think she had either; she might be getting the fever for all I know; it takes three or four days to say whether it is coming on or not. She had low fever; that is quite certain, but she got the better of it; Miss Jefferson came to us on the last day of April, and she went after being with us about a fortnight. While she was with us Mrs Cross was taken ill.

On the 6th of the month, she went to church. On the 16th which was Ascension Day, though she was seedy, she went to church and on the 18th, she was so far recovered as to be able to walk halfway to Old Coachford – two miles, that is a good deal. On the 22nd she was up and able to walk about. I don't think she had very much typhoid fever; I was not certain she had any low fever until about the 26th. Well, these girls described her as having fits during her illness. Mary Buckley said so, and Mary Barron said the same thing. If I wanted to make away with this lady; it was very easy when she had one of those attacks to make away with her.

It was said what made me go to Dublin in January with Miss Skinner. I went up to attend a meeting of the Property Defence Association. On the 11th of January, Miss Skinner was going to her situation. It was a coincidence we stayed at the same hotel. We occupied different rooms. I stayed there two days, not three days as was asserted.

It has been stated very truly, but very wrongly, that I met Miss Skinner after the Punchestown races where I had been on the 28th and 29th, and went over to England, together. I went to my brother's place – I don't know whether he is in court or not. I was there a week and I was in my brother-in-law's place another week. It is stated I was with Miss Skinner there three weeks, but there is not a word of truth in it. I apologise to those gentlemen for saying so, but it is not true, however.

I met Mrs Madras after my wife had an attack; she asked me how my wife was. I said, she may pass away any day, and indeed how she got out of it I don't know. It is asserted by Con McCarthy, that I sent seventeen letters to Miss Skinner. He was in my employment more or less about five years, and I don't think he took the letter bag to the post office fifteen times; that is very extraordinary. If he took those letters, he must have gone there every second day. What he stated was not true – that was the long and short of it.

It is stated that I wrote to Mr Marriott to say that there was typhoid fever about. Well, now, four fields from my house, Mrs Jerry Riordan died. I think Dr Crowley was attending her. Riordan was in my employment. Though she belonged to the other side of the Lee, I am pretty certain that Dr Crowley was attending her. I went to see the poor woman but she died very shortly afterwards – the same day, I believe. She died of fever. This was in the month of May. I believe I am sure it was. All her children went to the Macroom Infirmary with fever. The family opposite him, Con Sullivan's – Jack, Jack of the Quarry, also went into the hospital about the same time.

So there was typhoid fever about there. At Coachford, two people died of fever – a butcher and a publican. I believe he was the publican. The judge says that my letters to my brother-in-law were all cram, but I suppose people's minds get imbued with these sorts of things, and when they hear a man abused, he is put down as doing everything wrong. We now come to the most important thing in the whole case, and what I think was the cause of my wife's death.

There are two bottles on which his lordship laid great stress, and very properly. When I was arrested every single bit of medicine I had was taken possession of. There was no concealment. There was a lot of poisons there, horse poisons, such as you will have about a farm. There was no attempt at concealment. Shortly after Miss Skinner came to us, I remarked at the time that my wife began to ask her all sorts of questions about arsenic. It was the topic of conversation every day. Miss Skinner had travelled a long time in Germany, Switzerland and knocked about a good deal with her father; she knew a lot about those things.

Mrs Cross was always asking about this arsenic and how it should be used to improve the complexion. As soon as I heard there was arsenic in her body, I was perfectly convinced my wife had taken arsenic. I had forgotten all about it. After the first day that Dr Pearson gave his evidence at Coachford, he stated that there was arsenic found in her body. I was simply horror stricken. I could not account for it; I could not believe it. Mr Deyos will tell you what took place. I could not help going on my knees and saying: "God strike me dead if I know anything about it."

Well, I was simply horror-stricken and thought and thought and thought, and I said this accounts for it – here's my wife always talking about arsenic. She did not say she wanted to take it, but it was taken before by other people, and it struck me immediately, it was perfectly possible she took it. Well, a few days after my sister and I went to her room to tidy up the place, and in her press found four bottles – two little bottles, his lordship said – with white powders – a bottle of rouge puff powders and that sort of thing, in the corner of the press. There it was. Henrietta said to me: "Look at these bottles, what is in them?" I said: "Is there a label on them?" She said: "There is not." And I said: "Throw them away."

My impression is that these bottles were taken away with a lot of smashed-up crockery and were thrown out in a yard – a passage where all sorts of broken glass was thrown away. The next time I met my sister at one of the inquiries, I said: "Have you any recollection of seeing a couple of bottles in Laura's press when we were looking at it after her death?" "Yes, I did," said she. "What did you do with them?" [I asked.]

Whatever conversation we had was very much on the quiet, because we were told we were not to converse, except in the presence of a policeman, or Mr Deyos, or something like that. I suppose it was on this occasion I asked her about the bottles. I said I wonder could they have held arsenic. My impression was that there was arsenic in those bottles. If I had a notion that there was arsenic in her body while I was free, I had access to the press and what would have been easier for me to put arsenic in there, and call a coroner's inquest, and say she poisoned herself?

I did no wrong to her and a chain of evidence is wound around me – it is brought by the ablest men in Great Britain. It is sworn everything I did was wrong. Sleeping in the room at night, I was too stupid, too deaf or lazy to get up and attend to her. Every transaction in my life is tortured and twisted against me. When there is such ability against me as I see here now before me, there is not a man in this room, in this house tonight, against whom the same charge could not be brought as against me.

I married her [Effie Skinner] – I did wrong to her, but I think I did the honest thing, I might say, to repair that wrong. If I had not done wrong do you think I would have married her? No fear – nothing of the sort.

She was wanted in the house to look after those poor children – those poor unfortunate girls – and Sophia, to teach her. She was wanted in the house. I had no more intention of marrying her, when I met her, than I had of doing anything else. I did so and see what it has brought me to?

All I can say is this, though Mrs Cross is stated to have been constantly vomiting, such is not the fact. It was stated that I know nothing about my profession. Perhaps not. I won't say whether I do or not. She was quite satisfied with me, and I can certainly state from the bottom of my heart that I had no more notion of my wife dying that night than I have that I am going to die tonight. I have no more to say, but I have stated the whole truth and nothing but the truth.

The prisoner was speaking for three quarters of an hour, and never faltered during his address. When he had concluded, he remained standing in the corner of the dock and listened attentively while his lordship addressed him.

The Sentence

Lord Justice Murphy, who came close to breaking down, so emotionally was he affected by his now solemn and dark duty, said:

"Philip Henry Eustace Cross, on very clear and convincing evidence, you have been found guilty by a jury of this crime of murder. That jury, I am bound to say, devoted the utmost care and attention to very circumstance that appeared in evidence, during the trial. No jury of intelligence that has any regard for the discharge of the duty they were sworn to discharge could have found any other verdict than that which the jury that tried you have found. The evidence demanded it from them and that verdict has been given, finding you guilty of this foul and terrible crime, by which you – by the slow torture of lingering death – deprived of life one who appears to have been fond and true to you for eighteen years.

Having regard to the terrible nature of the sentence that I must pass upon you, it would not be seemly for me to address any exhortations to you. They would come from me to you, as only from one who discharges a terrible duty of having to try you, and having to pronounce the inevitable sentence on you – the sentence you must undergo. Others, whose sacred office may qualify them better to speak some words of comfort and consolation to you, may more seemly discharge that duty, and I hope that their words will be addressed to ears that may profit from them.

I discharge my duty now, and pronounce upon you, the sentence attached by law to this terrible crime and the sentence of the court on you, Philip Henry Eustace Cross, is and I do adjudge and order that you be taken from the bar of the court where you now stand, to the prison where you were last confined, and that on Tuesday the 10th of January next, in the year of Our Lord one thousand eight hundred and eighty-eight, you to be taken to the common place of execution, within the walls of the prison in which you shall then be confined, and that you shall be there and then be hanged by the neck until you are dead, and that your body be buried within the precincts of the prison in which you shall be last confined after your conviction, and may the Lord have mercy on your soul."

When the judge pronounced the terrible words which would consign Dr Cross to the executioner on the 10th of January, the prisoner's firmness did not forsake him. He beckoned to his solicitor Mr Deyos, held a few minutes' conversation with him over the side of the dock, after which he disappeared down the steps of the dock from the public gaze.

He was removed almost immediately to the gaol in the ordinary prison van, three policemen, entering it with him, and an escort of mounted police following. As the van was being driven off some hooting was indulged in by a crowd which had assembled outside.

*   *   *

The greatest chronicler of crime and punishment in the Victorian era Charles Dickens, having attended a number capital trials and executions was a passionate opponent of capital punishment captured brilliantly the moments in court that accompanied the verdict of execution:

"I know the solemn pause before the verdict. The hush and stifling of the fever in the court, the solitary figure brought back to the bar, and standing there, observed of all the outstretched heads and gleaming eyes, to be next minute, stricken dead, as one may say, among them. I know the thrill that goes round when the black cap is put on; and how there will be shrieks among the women; and taking out of someone in a swoon; and when the judge's faltering voice delivers the sentence, how awfully the prisoner and he confront each other; two mere men, destined one day, however far removed from one another at this time; to stand alike as suppliants at the bar of God."

Chapter 9

The Interval

On Monday morning when Dr Cross was contemplating his fate and a number of his supporters were planning a petition or, as it was termed, memorial in an attempt to secure a reprieve, the judge was back on the bench of the City Court as were members of the prosecuting team, Mr Wright, Mr Ronan and the solicitor Gregg, for consideration of matters that might have seemed more mundane, though not to those indicted, as compared with the intense drama of the trial the previous week.

First up at the ten thirty sitting was John O'Neill who was in custody charged with the robbery of £27 and who was given bail. There was a discussion about when the Christmas break would be taken by the court and fixed for Thursday, when Mr Wright remarked that if it sat day and night the list would not be completed in time. A murder trial was marked into the list for commencement.

Mr Wright applied for a bench warrant for an apparently insane woman, Margaret Twomey, who was charged with cutting her husband's throat. Robert Milne, a private in the Argyll and Southern Highlanders pleaded guilty to and apologised to the court for stealing a suit of clothes, two shirts, a hat and £5 and 16 shillings, the property of one, Timothy Sullivan. However, his colour sergeant Alfred Robinson deposed that the soldier's character was bad during his five months in the regiment and Milne received a year in prison with hard labour for his crime.

Patrick Tobin, a bailiff, was indicted for firing a revolver at Garrett Casey near Mitchelstown on 1st August with intent to kill. He pleaded self-defence. Mr Wright and Mr Ronan instructed by Mr Gregg were prosecuting, Mr Lawrence defending. According to the evidence, Tobin was laughed at by a number of young men including Casey when he rode past on his horse.

He dismounted, drew his pistol and threatened them, which after some of them ran away he discharged at Casey who had apparently first thrown a rock at him, wounding him in the hip. Casey told the court that he had never heard that there was a notice posted calling his attacker, "Tobin the Hang Gallows Rogue." Mr Lawrence referred to the general unpopularity of bailiffs and the state of things in Mitchelstown as provocation and mitigating factors. The jury found Tobin not guilty and he was free to go.

Thomas McCormac was arraigned for having indecently assaulted Bridget Donoghue in County Clare. When he was asked how he was pleading, he told the judge that he was ready to marry the woman. His lordship's humour had returned after the emotional burden of the Cross trial and said that the court could not be turned into a tribunal for establishing marriage contracts. "I cannot interfere with ecclesiastical privilege, my good man," he told the accused who promptly pleaded guilty, somewhat more than belying his intention for nuptials. The prisoner was put back for sentencing.

There followed cases of horse stealing and one in which a good-looking servant girl was indicted for robbing her employer of £10 and clothes. She had been arrested in Queenstown as she was about to take passage to America, instead she ended up in gaol for a year with hard labour. It was her first offence.

Kate Collins was charged with stealing 40 lbs of butter, worth £2 2s 6d. She had already spent 17 years of her life in prison and was sent back for seven years' penal servitude, an incredibly harsh sentence.

Two days later in the "Letters to The Editor" space in the *Cork Examiner* on Thursday the 22nd December the following letter in

306

relation to the case appeared which hugely undermined a central contention in Dr Cross's speech to the court in his defence.

62 South Mall, Cork
21st December 1887

Dear Sir
As several of my friends have spoken to me about a prescription, which I was understood to have written for the late Mrs Cross, and as much misconception exists on the whole subject, I will thank you to allow me explain what actually occurred. In the first place, I never at any time prescribed for the late Mrs Cross. In March 1886, Dr Cross brought one of his daughters into my study and requested me to prescribe for her. I did so and heard nothing more of the young lady or the prescription until about a month prior to the present assizes, when a lady called on me and informed me she was the sister of Dr Cross and asked me if I remembered prescribing for Dr Cross's daughter. I said I did. She then handed me a copy of the prescription which had been compounded at Messrs Harrington and asked me if I could recollect whether that was an exact copy of my prescription.

I said it probably was, but after such as lapse of time I did not feel certain, and if I saw the original as a matter of course, I could identify my handwriting. The prescription contained arsenic and strychnine in the ordinary minute medical doses. Dr Cross, in his speech after mentioning that Dr Townsend had also prescribed arsenic for some members of his family, said my prescription for his daughter "was applicable for my wife's case". And what he apparently wished to convey was at times, Mrs Cross had been complaining in the same way as her daughter, and that she may have procured similar medicines in large quantities. But if Mrs Cross happened to take the whole of my mixture together, it could not possibly produce fatal results.

I am sincerely yours,
Henry Corby, MD

This was a huge blow for the credibility of any effort for a so-called reprieve on behalf of the prisoner as Dr Corby's relating of the facts showed that Cross had falsely in a highly exaggerated manner connected this innocent prescription to his wife's death. It did not deter his supporters and another medical man who clearly had fewer scruples than his profession should have demanded. A surgeon dentist, Mr Butterfield of Cork, joined the campaign on the basis that Mrs Cross used to attend him for dental treatment and had asked him about the use of arsenic for the complexion as late as a visit on 6th April.

In the edition of the influential *British Medical Journal* published on Saturday 24th of December there was a truncated report of the trial followed by commentary on the outcome, some portion of which could have provided comfort for Dr Cross and his supporters if the conclusion could have been passed over. This read:

The defence made was singularly weak; perhaps it was the best that could be urged. The judge's charge was against the prisoner and in drawing a picture of the dying wife, he is reported to have shed tears. Touching as an incident of this kind may be in its proper place, it is not desirable that it should occur in a judge's charge. It may be suitable that a counsel should weep, but a judge should be superior to emotion of this sort. The judgement of a weak or doubting juryman may be influenced in a way prejudicial to the prisoner, and the prisoner is entitled to the benefit of any doubt.

In this present case, protestation of innocence may be true. Immoral the convict was, but some other hand may have administered the poison. It was left to the unhappy man himself to show that his wife had been ordered arsenic and strychnine on a bona fide prescription; it was suggested from her conversations that her mind was directed to the use of the drug for cosmetic purposes. Or there is the possibility that knowing her husband was too attentive to Miss Skinner, the poison may have been taken by herself."

It was also remarked that even though Professor MacNamara was present throughout the trial on behalf of the prisoner, he was not called on the stand as a medical witness.

However the report concluded that it was difficult to see, on the whole, how the jury could have come to any other conclusion, and the tide of popular feeling was running against the prisoner, it was not likely that there would be any modification of the sentence. Nonetheless, there were serious issues raised about the manner of the judge's charge and indeed doubts ventilated about the commission of the murder that might have given Dr Cross hope that he might have a chance of escaping the looming shadow of the noose.

Apart from the inherent evil displayed by Cross in the murder of his wife and the merits or de-merits of the appeal for clemency and commutation of the sentence, it could be said that the murderer, when it came to the statistics of wife murder in the country should have stood a reasonable chance. But tempering that fact with the reality that every case was considered on its own particular circumstances. Over a hundred men killed their wives between 1838 and 1887 and around the same number killed other female relatives.

Only a minority of men sentenced to death were executed. The Lord Lieutenant showed greater compassion to women who were sentenced to death with only three going to the gallows in the second half of the century. Only men who were regarded as having committed the most serious of murders ended up going to the scaffold. The Maamtrasna, Castletownroche and the Phoenix Park murders were examples of a crime for which clemency would have never been entertained.

Most sentenced to death had the sentence reduced to penal servitude for life after appealing to the Lord Lieutenant. And it seemed from the circumstances that clemency was granted in cases where the killings were not premeditated, deliberate or carried out in a cruel manner.

In that context and despite the fact that the courts were generally extremely tough in the matter of poisoning because of the premeditation involved and the terrible suffering visited on the victims and as a result of the widespread use of poison as a method of killing, there were some signs of comfort for Cross. Over the previous three and a half decades six men had been convicted of the murder of their wives and sentenced to death. All sentences were reduced to penal servitude for life. Two of those crimes involved poison. As did a case just three years before, in this instance one of a woman poisoning her husband. All death sentences were commuted.

David Dripps a farmer from Londonderry was sentenced to death for poisoning his seventy-five-year-old wife in 1873, as was Thomas Price, a labourer from Co Tyrone who killed his sixty-six-year-old wife using arsenic in 1878.

The same sentence was passed on Catherine Delaney from County Tipperary who also used arsenic to kill her fifty-three-year-old husband, also a farmer. Catherine, a mother of four and a farmer's wife from Co Tipperary poisoned her husband in April 1884. Michael Delany, a farmer and builder, died from the effects of arsenic poisoning, administered by his wife, who it was alleged wanted to get rid of him to marry someone else. Her trial was delayed, as was her execution. At the conclusion of her trial in 1885, she was found guilty and sentenced to be hanged on 18th July. The execution was postponed for a month, allowing her counsel more time to prepare and present an appeal. Though the RIC report showed that she had a lover, nobody else was arrested for the crime, so maybe there was some doubt about the motive for killing her husband. The petition for mercy was successful and her sentence was reduced to penal servitude for life but she served only thirteen years.

However, the Cross case, given the huge coverage, not just locally but internationally, would be paid very close attention by the Lord Lieutenant, not just for that reason but because of the individual characteristics of the murder and indeed the profession and social status of the condemned man. The modus operandi would be significant and the similarities with other cases taken into account.

The comparison with Dr Pritchard would have presented immediately. Both were involved in sexual relationships with women who were considerably younger and of which the wives were aware. They utilised two principal poisons, Pritchard antimony and aconite, Cross arsenic and strychnine. They were the sole medical carers and called in a retired doctor to attend, gave misleading and false diagnoses and falsified the death certificates.

They employed slow poisoning to give the impression of a prolonged illness and thus imposed a passage of immense suffering for the victims. And as William Roughead observed: "But perhaps the most extraordinary parallel of all is the fact that each, upon the consummation of the crime, forthwith proceeded to enter into his diary, in similar and shocking terms, a blasphemous and hypocritical prayer for the repose of the soul of the departed victim."

Ultimately, with a little prompting, Pritchard accepted the justice of his fate. And made a confession, which though self-serving and not showing much remorse for his victims, was some-thing to be said in his favour – all the more so since it was not going to make any difference to his sentence. There was no sign of Dr Cross following the footsteps of his infamous counterpart in this regard.

While in Cork County Gaol Cross's behaviour had echoes of another serial poisoner, Thomas Wainewright, whom Dickens and some companions happened to visit while he was incarcerated in Newgate prison. He boasted: "I will tell you one thing in which I have succeeded to the last. I have been determined through my life to hold the position of a gentleman. I have always done so and I do still. It is the custom of this place that each of the inmates of a cell shall take his morning sweeping. I occupy a cell with a bricklayer and a sweep but they never offer me the broom."

This display of rather tragic dignity provides an insight into the mind of the upper-class murderer, determined to maintain their status in a prison community. Breeding was breeding and the fact that they had fallen from grace did not in any way diminish their stuffy self-regard.

This vain, silly, venal aspect of character would be of less concern to the Lord Lieutenant. Rather, his concern would be the cold heart and resolve of steel with which the crime was carried out and the cruel indifference to the suffering of the victim.

In the majority of high-profile cases of poisoning among the privileged classes, the motive was lust or gain or a combination of both.

This form of murder was marked out from others, as the ghost in Hamlet describes it:

"Murder most foul, as in the best it is,
But this most foul, strange and unnatural."

The chances of mitigation in the Coachford Poisoning must have been slim at best.

During the following week the requisition to the Lord Lieutenant for the respite of the death sentence was brought about the city for signature and an attending reporter wrote that the short time the memorial was taken around amongst the people, a good number affixed their signatures. This is what they were signing up to:

To His Excellency, the Most Noble Charles Marquis of Londonderry, Lord Lieutenant of Ireland.

The memorial of the undersigned humbly sheweth:

That Philip H.E. Cross, a retired surgeon major in Her Majesty's service was on the 17th day of December, 1887 found guilty of the murder of his wife, Mary Laura Cross and sentenced to be hanged on the 10th day of January 1888.

That grave doubts are entertained of the justice of the conviction, arising from the fact that the analyst had not previously examined the body of a person supposed to have died from arsenical poisoning.
There was no direct evidence to connect the accused with the alleged crime.
The evidence was entirely circumstantial.
That a most important piece of evidence had turned up since the trial as embodied in the statutory declaration annexed herewith made on the 28th of December by Mr John Chas Westropp Butterfield, of the city of Cork, dental surgeon to the effect that the late Mary Laura Cross had, on two

occasions alluded to poison in his study, asked him if he could procure it for her, and inquired if he had heard that arsenic was good for the complexion, and one of which occasions was as recent as 6th day of April last.

That the said P.H.E. Cross was very unpopular with masses of the people of Cork and its neighbourhood; had been boycotted and subjected to many signs of popular indignation.

That he has served her Majesty for many years in Europe, Asia, Africa, and America; amongst others was engaged in the Indian Mutiny, at the Crimea, the China campaign and received three medals.

Your petitioners humbly implore your Excellency to mitigate the capital sentence passed on the said Philip H.E. Cross and your petitioners will, as in duty bound, pray.

The petition was sent to the Lord Lieutenant and also to the judge, Murphy, who had tried the case. Now while pleas on behalf of a condemned prisoner were as a matter of course sent to the Lord Lieutenant for a commutation of the death sentence to what would inevitably be life imprisonment and sometimes had a reasonable chance of success, this petition, despite the grovelling at the start and end was in effect an arrogant and largely baseless and erroneous challenge to the findings of the court.

Whatever the shortcomings of some parts of the judge's charge he had dealt more than adequately with the matter of Dr Pearson's experience as a chemical analyst and his testing process. The first point was entirely moot. The second was ludicrous – nobody saw Dr Cross administer the poison, nor could they – throughout the ages that is precisely why it was chosen as a weapon. The third point was ignoring the fact that the evidence most responsible for conviction was forensic – the discovery and proof that poison was found in the body and responsible for death.

Judge Sir Henry Hawkins, who presided over a poisoning case in Huntingdon a decade later, which as usual provoked some debate after the fact of conviction of the only candidate for the guilty party, had this to say about circumstantial evidence:

"It is actually almost the only evidence obtainable in all great crimes, and it is the best and most reliable. You may draw wrong impressions from it, I grant, but so you may from evidence of witnesses where it is doubtful; but you cannot fail to draw the right ones where the facts are not doubtful. If it capable of a wrong inference, a judge should be absolutely positive in his direction, to the jury, not to draw it.

I have witnessed many great trials for murder, but do not remember one where there was an eye witness to the deed. How is it possible then to bring home the charge to the culprit, unless you rely on circumstantial evidence? Circumstantial evidence is the evidence of circumstances – facts that speak for themselves and that cannot be contradicted. Circumstances have no motive to deceive, while human testimony is too often the product of every kind of motive."

The statement of the dentist was evidence that proved absolutely nothing other than what had been ventilated in the court and added little to the evidence of Miss Cross. Arsenic for the complexion is normally in a solution, not in the solid crystal form found in the body. Dr Cross's unpopularity, highly exaggerated in the petition, was likely to be as a result of his own behaviour and local, and unlikely in any event to influence the jury and certainly a lot less than his behaviour with Miss Skinner, the possible prejudice of which was strongly urged by both the defence counsel and the judge to be put aside by the jury.

While the condemned man's military record might well have been admirable, the status of it would have been sullied and diminished by his crime as was his profession as a doctor.

The document and the campaign, if it could be called that, smacked of a section of the gentry and professional class looking for special treatment for a member of its ranks and at the same time an attack on the judicial process, points that would not be lost on the Lord Lieutenant. To say that it was a dangerous and counter-productive move would be understating this effort on behalf of a man whose demeanour had seemingly not been changed by incarceration, though somewhat according to some reports modified by the sentence of death.

Also it would probably have the effect of giving the prisoner hope of a reprieve and that would strengthen his misguided resolve to maintain his innocence and obviate any doubts he might have entertained in the immediate aftermath of his sentence.

The "new evidence" in addition, apart from being vacuous was also a heartless slur on the victim Mary Laura Cross, giving the impression that she was some sort of vain arsenic addict, a contention that there was no proof and was nothing but conjecture, referred to by Miss Cross whose action in destroying the bottles, demeanour in court and action in seeking the prescription from Dr Corby provided ample demonstration of where her loyalties lay.

On 27th December at seven o'clock Dr Cross was for the first time since his conviction visited by members of his family. His five children were the visitors for almost an hour and one can only imagine the scene which was briefly reported in the *Cork Examiner* like this: "The interview while it lasted was of a most painful character; the tearful agony of the children contrasting with the cool indifference of the father, who, it must at the same time be said, did his best to assuage their grief."

In the 4th January 1888 of the *Examiner*, a letter from a supporter of the petition was published in response to an article of 31st December in relation to the same subject. It provided an interesting aspect to the efforts being made on Dr Cross's behalf, all the more so as the author claimed to have approached members of the jury.

Sir
I trust that you will allow me to make some comment upon the article of your issue of the 31st of December, criticising the petition in the course of signature through the city in the case of the prisoner Dr Cross.

With the spirit of your critique I fully concur, and I would heartily endorse your conclusion, if I could but adopt your premise, but unfortunately, for your argument, the former are utterly invalid.

The petition was, I believe, wholly drafted by the prisoner's solicitor, who is neither a Protestant not Freemason, an Orangeman, not a member of the Property Defence Association; and I, being as strongly opposed to the wording of certain parts of it, as yourself, took the precaution of expressing my dissent therefrom to everyone whose signature I solicited.

I personally canvassed five of the jurymen on Friday the 23rd of December, and obtained from all of them, promises to sign a petition for a reprieve pending further investigation of the case by the law advisers of the Crown, in consequence of the most unfortunate, though unintentional misdirection of the judge on the point that completely cut the ground from under the prisoner's feet in the only available line of defence, viz, as regards arsenic as a remedy for angina pectoris, and for the complexion, and more especially in consequence of the wholly new evidence of Mr J.C. Butterfield, corroborating in the most circumstantial manner the prisoner's own defence from the dock, and it was with surprise and regret that I first saw the actual wording of the present petition when it was too late to ask the gentleman who drafted it to alter it, and no course remained but to make the best of it. Its defects therefore do not lie at the door of the very objectionable classes who you have gibbeted. I can positively answer for those who signed the copy I took round the district of Passage and Monkstown, that they, one and all, adopted it solely on the ground, which you so properly put forward as the sole legitimate one, viz, "reasonable doubt as to the sufficiency of the evidence against the accused" and were in no way influenced by the objectionable and out of place clauses referring to the prisoner's unpopularity, age, military service etc, and I am convinced that the same explanation holds true as regards the very numerous signatories in the city and other districts.

As regards your most strongly expressed opinion on the judge's charge, I may say that it seems to me to be endorsed by the whole community; I have conversed with hundreds of intelligent men of all ranks and classes, including many of the leading solicitors in the city, and have not yet met with one single dissentient and I think with you "that it should have been called in question by the memorialists" and extracts from it appended to the petition.

James Ridings M.D.
Glenbrook, 2nd January

Cork Examiner:
Thursday, 5th January, 1888

Tomorrow the fate of Dr Cross under sentence of death for the murder of his wife will be decided. The Lord Lieutenant has received the petition and additional evidence, all of which was submitted to Judge Murphy, who tried the case. Further papers arrived yesterday morning and those have been sent to Cork for the judge's opinion. From what I can learn there is little probability of a reprieve being granted.

Friday, 6th January

There was no change in the demeanour and attitude of Dr Cross. He still derived comfort from the hope of a reprieve and from the exertions of his friends, who are assiduously attempting to save the wretched man from the gallows. We understand that a memorial sent by Dr Cross to the Lord Lieutenant has been turned down. No response to the one prepared by his friends is expected until the next day or two.

Meanwhile prison officials have completed all arrangements for the execution which will take place at eight o'clock on Tuesday morning, if the death sentence is not commuted. Members of the press will not be allowed at the execution but will be allowed to view the scene immediately afterwards.

Monday, 9th January

It is understood that the official notification that the Lord Lieutenant has declined to accede to the petition for a respite of the sentence on Dr Cross, which he did on Saturday, came yesterday for Mr Deyos, the prisoner's solicitor. There has been a good deal of discussion of the right to Dr Cross to make a will and distribute his property. Dr Cross has made a will in which he has considered all the claims of his relatives. He also made a will before he was convicted. It is stated that he is possessed of £20,000 out of which he demised £5,000 to the present Mrs Cross and Shandy Hall farm to the eldest son.

The Protestant chaplain Rev Mr Connolly visited the gaol at two o'clock on Saturday and informed the condemned man of the decision of the LL in his case. The convict enquired if there was no possibility it was only a rumour but the Rev assured him that this was not the case. And this was backed up by the official statement of the Deputy Governor. When the condemned man saw that his last hope had vanished, he gave way to visible emotion and since then his manner has not been so stern as it was. Later he was even more critical than ever of the way his food was cooked.

The chaplain made several visits yesterday. Berry the executioner will arrive in Cork today and take up his quarters in the gaol. The execution will take place at eight o'clock tomorrow morning in the presence only of the sheriff, doctor, governor, warders. Only after the bolt has been drawn will a member of the press be admitted to the scene of the execution.

Tuesday, 10th January

Dr Cross is thoroughly resigned to the terrible doom that awaits him. He was visited yesterday by the Bishop of Cork and Rev Connolly the Protestant chaplain of the gaol saw him several times during the day. Rev Mr Hayes who gave evidence in the trial also visited and he and the chaplain gave the Sacrament to the prisoner.

Dr Cross is reported to be much changed in appearance and has completely broken down since the decision of the Lord Lieutenant. The present Mrs Cross has declined to visit her condemned husband. When a visit was suggested to her, she replied that she did not see what good it would do and had not a good word to say of her husband.

Berry the executioner arrived at two o'clock yesterday and inspected the gallows and tested the apparatus before retiring to his accommodation. [This is no doubt an error. The Home Office insisted that hangmen booked into a gaol two days in advance of an execution, first to do the job properly and secondly "to avoid the temptations of drink".]

Chapter 10

The Hangman

The execution of Dr Edward Pritchard had been fixed for the 29th of July 1866 and the man assigned for the job was the long serving and notorious hangman William Calcraft, who began his career in 1829 and, as well as a stipend from the City of London plus a fee for every hanging, was also a hired and paid hand for executions all over Britain. He had a poor technique and obviously cared little for the victims. A great many because of the short drop employed on the scaffold, strangled to death.

Despite the awful deeds of many murderers who went to the gallows over time before public executions lost their appeal as a spectator sport and were eventually banned, the tide began to turn against the hangman and the perception of his role as the last line of legal retribution was diminished and replaced by private and public distaste and he rather than the prisoner was cast in the role of villain.

An eye-witness to one of his hangings said that he would never forget "that ghoul of a Calcraft, with his disreputable grey hair, his disreputable undertaker's suit of black, and a million dirty pinpricks which marked every pore of the skin of his face".

On the 13th of November 1849, Calcraft hanged George Manning and his wife Maria, who had murdered her lover, on the roof of Horsemonger Lane gaol. A husband and wife condemned to be executed was a rare occurrence and attracted a crowd estimated at 40,000 when execution was at its height as a form of grotesque public entertainment. Charles Dickens was present on a nearby rooftop and recoiled with distinctive horror at the event, as he relayed in a letter to *The Times* (14th November 1849):

"I believe that a sight so inconceivably awful as the wickedness and levity of the immense crowd collected at that execution this morning could be imagined by no man, and could be presented in no heathen land under the sun. The horrors of the gibbet and of the crime which brought the wretched murderers to it, faded in my mind before the atrocious bearing, looks and language of the assembled spectators. When I came upon the scene at midnight, the shrillness of the cries and howls that were raised from time to time, denoting that they came from a concourse of boys and girls already in the best places, made my blood run cold. . . .

"When the two miserable creatures who attracted all this ghastly sight about them were turned quivering in the air, there was no more emotion, no more pity, no more thought that two immortal souls had gone to judgment, no more restraint in any of the previous obscenities, than if the name of Christ had never been heard in this world and there was no belief among men but that they had perished like the beasts."

Dickens, brilliantly and presciently identified an ambivalence towards the murderers that in a matter of a decade or slightly more would be shared by the spectators whose behaviour he had heaped such criticism upon and also by the authorities and personages who by law had to be ultimately the last spectators behind the prison walls.

As Dickens expressed, when it came to the act of execution the crudeness and barbarity of this piece of fatal theatre would have the conscious effect of moving the horrors of the perpetrator's crime backstage, so to speak, and transform the so-called monster character into an object of pity and sympathy while the executioner, beforehand a man of power and mystery, became a target of hate and derision.

Seventeen years after Calcraft despatched the Mannings he was in Scotland to deal with the hitherto notorious Dr Pritchard who had himself without a thought by poison confined his wife and mother-in-law to the grave. The report in the Edinburgh *Evening Courant* of Saturday, 29th July 1866 was a perfect example of how attitudes had changed to the public execution and the main players. It was fitting that it was to be the last public execution in Scotland:

"About two o'clock the scaffold was brought from a shed in Clydesdale, a short distance from the goal. And its appearance caused great sensation. The erection of the scaffold, which has been in use for the last fifty years, was watched with much interest. On the rope being fastened to the beam, a thrill of horror ran through the crowd. Underneath the scaffold, as usual, a coffin was placed. It was plain black, shell [a light coffin] and appeared scarcely long enough for the body it was to contain.

About half past seven o'clock, Calcraft appeared on the scaffold and looked about for a minute. He was soon recognised by the assemblage, who greeted him with cheers and hisses. After satisfying himself that the apparatus was in proper condition, he withdrew. At five minutes past eight, the prisoner was pinioned and prayers offered by the clergymen as the melancholy procession was moving from the condemned cell.

Dr Pritchard walked firmly up the scaffold, and stood quite erect while he was being handled by the executioner. When he appeared on the scaffold, a great commotion prevailed.

He slightly stumbled on coming to the drop, which he struck against with his foot, but promptly recovered himself and stood firm without moving a muscle.

Mr Oldham read a short written prayer while Calcraft put aside the long hair and beard to allow the rope to be tightly placed and tied the legs. Calcraft after putting the rope around the prisoner's neck and drawing the cap over his face, steadied the wretched man by placing his hands behind his back and on his breast. On a signal given by the culprit, the bolt was drawn, and at ten minutes past eight o'clock, he was launched into eternity."

The reporter went on to note that as soon as the body was seen dangling from the rope, a loud shriek arose from the crowd and many turned their heads away from the horrid spectacle. People around the scaffold began to move away; some of them were crying. There was no screen around the scaffold as there had been in previous executions.

It was the opinion of the writer that Pritchard suffered a good deal, as his shoulders shrugged more than six times, his head shook, the whole body trembled and swung round and round. There was no manifestation of feeling against the prisoner while the pockmarked Calcraft, observed to be wearing a faded rose in his buttonhole, was met with hooting when coming down the scaffold.

It was as if the hangman was not human, not possessed by jealousy, greed, cruelty, lust as motive for the taking of human life. Just ice-cold retribution, not revenge which involved emotion, a killer that takes life as a retribution but faces none himself. And does so, not once, twice, three times but, dozens, hundreds. There was something at the heart of this so-called occupation that evinced revulsion, not latterly just among the masses but also intelligent professional observers and participants in the process of punishment like governors, guards, clergymen, doctors, reporters who felt guilty and demoralised and corrupted by association.

In 1868, an Act of Parliament banned public executions and from that time on the hangings would take place inside the prisons with a selected small number of spectators including for a long time, reporters. There were also changes in the methods of execution. On the retirement of the money-grubbing and incompetent and finally much detested Calcraft in 1874, in his seventies, the job went to William Marwood.

He took a great interest in the art of his job which combined with the authorities' demands for more efficient and humane execution. He introduced the long drop of six to ten feet and combined with weight and the noose properly positioned should bring about instantaneous death. It was designed to remove the gruesome struggling and convulsing on the rope, common in his predecessor's reign.

Marwood travelled to Ireland frequently and had the job on the 14th of May 1883 of executing Joe Brady and four of the Invincible gang who murdered Lord Frederick Cavendish and Thomas Henry Burke in the Phoenix Park. The following year he was succeeded by his protégé James Berry who was assigned the job of executing Dr Philip Henry Eustace Cross and two years earlier had hanged William Sheehan, the Castletownroche triple killer in Cork Gaol.

For a number of reasons in the heritage of executioners, James Berry was a horse of a different colour, who in the future would be given reason to remember among the hundred and more people he led to the scaffold, one more than the many – Dr Cross of Shandy Hall.

James Berry's most important contribution to the science of hanging, if one could, but with the greatest hesitation, call it that, was the refinement of the long drop developed by his mentor William Marwood whom he succeeded. His improvements were designed to diminish the mental and physical suffering of the condemned and some of them remained standard practice until the abolishment of hanging for capital murder.

He considered his role as the last link in what he called "the chain of legal retribution".

He was the thirteenth of eighteen children. In 1874 he joined the West Riding police force and settled in Bradford with his wife Sarah Ackroyd. During his time as a constable a mutual friend introduced him to William Marwood, a cobbler and part-time executioner. Berry had always had an interest in hanging and spent many hours discussing the scientific principles.

Marwood told him that it was essential to give the prisoner confidence and assure him or her that the end would be swift. Berry retired from the police in 1882 and went through a number of jobs and was getting into debt. After Marwood died in 1883 he applied to the City Of London for the vacant position of executioner.

There were 1,400 applications and when the Sheriffs weeded out the vast majority of the unsuitable candidates there was a shortlist of twenty. Berry was not successful; Bartholomew Binns got the job. But Berry did not give up and got an opportunity when he offered his services to magistrates in Edinburgh. After a rigorous interview with the prison governor he was given the job of executing two men.

Despite being haunted by the possibilities of what could go wrong Berry carried out the hangings perfectly and the men died instantaneously. He got an excellent recommendation and when Binns' time was up Berry was appointed. He entered a new era when hangings no longer took place in public and later the press were only allowed in after the event.

For a long time before his elevation to the role of executioner there had been efforts made to make the grisly business more efficient. The long drop had been introduced based on a concept devised by doctors in Ireland to hasten the death of the condemned by breaking of the neck as opposed to asphyxiation by strangling.

However, such vital elements such as the rope and its condition and the length of the drop related to the weight of the prisoner were left to the discretion of the hangman and thus subject to human error.

Berry set himself two tasks. First to reduce the preparation time so that the prisoner's ordeal would be over sooner, and secondly to produce instant death by dislocation. Not strangulation. He improved on Marwood's rough table of drops by practising with nags of cement and pressing for standardisation of gallows and trapdoors.

But despite his best efforts, some executions would go disastrously wrong.

Just over a year before he was assigned to despatch Dr Philip Cross, Berry was sent to Norwich for the execution of Robert Goodall on

30th November 1885. His calculation deemed a drop of 5 ft 8 ins as sufficient. His report tells what happened:

"The whole of the arrangements were carried out in the usual manner and when I pulled the lever, the drop fell properly and the prisoner dropped out of sight. We were horrified, however to see that the rope jerked upwards, and for an instant, I thought the noose had slipped from the culprit's head, or that the rope had broken. But it was worse than that, for the jerk had severed the head entirely from the body, and both had fallen together to the bottom of the pit. Of course death was instantaneous, so that the poor fellow had not suffered in any way; but it was terrible to think that such a revolting thing should have occurred."

Berry declared the inquest was a trying ordeal for all concerned. In the opinion of the popular Victorian novelist and regular prison visitor Felicia Mary Skene, the manner in which Berry treated the matter at the inquest was not calculated to allay the universal indignation aroused by the event: "He spoke of it with careless unconcern, as a little accident which was likely to happen often on these occasions, and which simply could not be helped."

It was likely that the hangman was being defensive as he was wont, as a professional, to take pride in his expertise even if he hid his personal feelings about his role until he could eventually conceal them no more.

That year was a bad one for the executioner. Another hanging was botched in an entirely different manner and even more famous and injurious to the executioner's reputation. But this time more merciful to the prisoner.

The previous February he led a young man John Lee to the scaffold as punishment for the vicious murder of his employer, an elderly woman who was battered to death and then set on fire. Three times Berry pulled the lever and each time the trapdoor failed to open. In the intervals between the execution attempts there were adjustments made to the trapdoor apparatus and when tested worked perfectly but when the prisoner was brought back it failed again. A Home Office investigation found that incorrect assembly of the gallows mechanism allowed the trapdoor hinges to rest upon an eighth of an inch of drawbar, preventing the trapdoor from opening when the doors were weighted. Eventually the prisoner was led back to his cell and on the instructions of the Home Secretary his sentence was commuted to life imprisonment.

Berry carried out 130 hangings in eight years including those of five women. He was the first executioner in Britain to write his memoirs: *My Experiences As An Executioner* (1892).

He was a hangman who unlike most of his kind kept an extensive diary that included his feelings. Justin Atholl wrote a book in 1956 based on this diary. He was also one of the few executioners who gave up his work because he did not like it. After giving up the job he said that it was an awful business and spent the rest of his life campaigning for an end to hanging.

With the end of public executions in 1868 and, even more, with the later exclusion of the press from the scaffold, a change took place. The executioner became more a man of mystery and his methods and personality a subject for speculation. A different type of man became eligible for the role. It is doubtful whether in 1883 if the hangman had still been required to operate in public under the gaze of thousands of spectators that James Berry would have offered his services.

Unlike many of his fellow executioners, Berry was an articulate, sensitive and intelligent man. There is no way, if one was to judge from his photograph, that anyone could possibly guess his occupation. His rounded face and likeable eyes portray anything but a harbinger of ultimate doom.

He had a typical Yorkshire frankness and openness but his wife said that even though she had been living with him for nineteen years that she still did not know him thoroughly. She added that his strongest point was his tender-heartedness.

His period in the role was relatively short, but with more than a measure of drama, a lot of it both disturbing and unsettling, not just for the public and the authorities, but also for the man who considered his job one to be carried out with an exactitude and a certainty that a scientist would not expect.

Hanging by the new method of the long drop with the objective of achieving instant death was undeveloped and it was during his reign that it was recognised and scientifically studied for the first time.

However, the act began to fill him full of nervousness and anxiety and what amounted to depression.

He may well have agreed with Charles Dickens' assessment of his profession: "The executioner has done nothing more criminal than nature may do tomorrow for the judge, and will certainly do in her own good time for judge and jury, counsel and witnesses, turnkeys, hangman and all. I learn from newspaper accounts of every execution, how Mr So and So, and Mrs Somebody Else, and Mr So-Forth shook hands with the culprit, but I never find them shaking hands with the hangman. All kinds of attention and consideration are lavished on the one, but the other is universally avoided, like a pestilence."

Like a lot of hangmen, Berry kept souvenirs, photographs, albums and relics of all kinds from ropes to personal possessions of the people he executed. The photographs were selective: they were of executions where there had been no foul-ups or where the hanged man or woman was of particular public interest.

There was a popular perception that there was something special about the face of a murderer. But like people from any walk of life, they came in all shapes and sizes. Berry thought this a fallacy and agreed with Shakespeare's dictum that there was no art to find the mind's construction in the face. He was well qualified to judge, he had looked into the eyes of a very large number and cross-section of murderers before he drew the hood over their heads.

The collecting of photographs and memorabilia of the executed seems a bizarre act, as if an executioner would need constant reminders of his grotesque trade. As evidenced in the era of public executions there was huge interest in the act of capital punishment as there was in the more sensational murder trials. Like murder, execution was a dramatic human ritual, shrouded in a mysterious and mystical aura.

It could on the other hand, be a form of affirmation, that the job he carried out was a real one and should not be a matter of shame and like other professions, where photographs provide memories, he was just doing as any other person was doing, keeping a photographic record in albums, of their life and achievements.

But one would have to be of a particularly dull mental character to continue to believe that such records were ordinary in any way and not a chronicle of a particular form of human horror and cruelty. Berry was not of that mind-set so in time the albums would present a form of haunting.

There was every likelihood that at the natural end of his career, James Berry could sell his collection at a very good price. But it was hardly profit alone that motivated the soon-to-become-reluctant executioner. When Berry was at the height of his powers, he viewed them as a powerful reminder of the dark art of his trade and evidence of the pride he took in his work when everything was carried off swiftly and satisfactorily.

Each successful execution was in itself, a conquest, a victory over the myriad of circumstances that could lead to a botched hanging, unnecessary suffering for the victim, strangulation as opposed to asphyxiation, an inevitable inquiry and the possibility of bad light being thrown on Berry's professionalism.

Ironically, for such a barbaric act of legal retribution, the authorities were very focused on the necessity for a swift and painless, a humane – if that is a way to describe it – death for the condemned. Unfortunately the method of execution did not lend itself easily to such hoped-for results. When hanging went wrong, it was usually horribly wrong. And Berry was on the wrong end of the rope, figuratively speaking, a number of times when there was such an awful occurrence.

Berry began to suffer from what he recognised was irrational anxiety about the job. What he possibly did not realise was that when such conflict enters the mind, the greater part of anxiety is irrational. He had to stay two nights in the prison before the execution, insisted by the authorities to minimise the temptation to drink and allow for an efficient performance of the job in hand.

On one occasion while preparing for a double execution, he was beset by insecurities:

"On Saturday night I was very restless and I did not feel very refreshed from my night's sleep, as I was thinking of the poor creatures who were slumbering their hours away in the prison cell, just beyond where I was laid, thinking of the dreadful fate that awaited them, in such a short space of time, two men in full bloom, and had to come to such an untimely end, leaving wives and large families.

"I retired at ten on Sunday night, but only cat naps all night, one eye shut and the other open thinking and fancying things that will never be and which are impossible. I fancied the ropes breaking, I fancied I was trembling, and could not do it; I fancied I fell sick at the last push. I was frantic in my mind, but I never let them know."

When revulsion set in one of the first things he did was to throw out of his house of everything that reminded him of his past hangings as they had become a source of mental torture. His rationale was that these things brought him "bad luck". Reminders of a past that weighed heavily on him. Getting rid of the reminders was for him like laying a ghost. He could not erase from his mind his victims or the details of their end. He was no longer proud of his role. "It was a different house when they were gone. I found that I could sleep and no longer had an uncanny feeling when I entered a room where they were kept. The evil influences of my victims, clinging to those relics."

After a hundred hangings, signs began to appear that Berry's nerves were being affected. He had been a teetotaller when he started. He then took to the drink – like all late vocations, a dangerous thing. He became emotional and bad-tempered. His nights were sleepless and agitated. When he slept he was plagued by dreams – the replaying by shadowy figures of real scenes that needed no embellishment from a troubled mind to make them nightmares.

One such was Joseph Lawson, whom he hanged early in his career and who laughed at Berry when he pinioned him and kept up a stream of invective as he was led to the scaffold. When the hangman put him in position and pulled down the white cap, the prisoner let out a stream of foul language. Berry was seized by what undoubtedly was a panic attack and everything went into a state of slow motion. It seemed forever before he could pull the lever and the drop opened, it seemed that the evil Lawson would never be despatched. Sweat sprouted out his brow and his breath came in gasps. He finally realised the job was done but had to lean against the wall to quell the rising tide of his panic.

He was bedevilled by thoughts of the families and dependents his victims left behind. The fact that the killers had no thought for them before they committed the crimes did not provide consolation for the hangman, so fraught had he become with his fears and anxieties. He had become a mirror for the paralysing fright that gripped many of the condemned men and women.

There was one, MacDonald who, when Berry arrived in his cell, was shaking from head to foot and not able to stand. He tried to help the fear-crazed prisoner to relax but only managed to absorb himself some of the communicated horror. He could not wait for the drop, which he knew would bring the only relief to himself and the condemned man.

Such scenes not only impacted on Berry but also made him question the ritual of the procession of officials to the scaffold, some in full regalia, while the very object of the exercise was the shivering epitome of human trepidation on the cusp of eternity. All of this weighed heavily on Berry, a burden that was becoming intolerable in both his waking and sleeping states.

"I may not live to see the capital sentence abolished," he said, "but I do hope and pray fervently I will not die without hearing the good news that never again will a woman suffer the fate of the women victims, I sometimes see in my waking dreams."

But there were others whose demise revisited the executioner. Those who fainted, fought every step of the way to the scaffold, pleading for mercy that was futile but still years later rang in Berry's ear.

There was Alfred Sowley at Preston who shot to death his girlfriend and turned the gun on himself – unsuccessfully. He cried hysterically in the cell before being removed by five warders by force and dragged screaming to the scaffold, fighting with a manic force every inch of the way. In his dreams, Berry heard the condemned man's screams echoing off the prison walls.

The executioner should have been well used to the smell of fear and the tortured anticipation of the prisoner facing the final moment on earth – as he was at the time, when held his composure and his feelings in check. That was his job. But the memory of it many years later seeping into his fitful sleep began to unhinge him.

On more than one occasion he had gone through what he described as "a nervous breakdown" after an execution from which it took him two to three weeks to recover. A reaction that he managed to conceal from both his family and employers for most of his career.

In his book *English Local Prisons 1860–1900*, Professor Seán McConville gives another view of Berry, which is not at all inconsistent with accounts of the hangman's behaviour but is suggestive of another side to his character:

"The hangman whose misbehaviour is best documented was James Berry . . . within a few years he had fallen victim to the attractions of drink and the adulatory crowd. The arrival of a hangman in any country town was a matter of intense curiosity to the populace. A combination of freak show and festival of death. Decorum demanded an unobtrusive arrival and stay and a speedy departure; Berry frequently made a show of himself, inflaming his feelings and feeding his vanity."

This was possibly a harsh view of the man who was having a personal crisis of conscience but no doubt had taken to the pub to allay the desperation that was beginning to afflict him. If he seemed outwardly boastful, he might have been trying to bolster his shattered confidence, a sham by any manner or means. But the commentator was probably correct to be critical of his behaviour which was certainly reprehensible.

One of the men who would most often appear in the cast of his execution nightmares was Philip Henry Eustace Cross, whom Berry was assigned to hang on 10th January 1888.

Chapter 11

The Execution

During the period that had elapsed since his conviction, Cross had maintained his innocence and therefore had not made any confession even during the frequent visits of his spiritual comforters. He told the prison warders that he was not afraid to face death as he had done so very often in battle. He bore up well to the ordeal of three weeks of uncertainty in his cell until on the Saturday he received news of the Lord Lieutenant's decision not to intervene, but allow the law take its course.

And whatever courage had taken him up to the point of his execution it did not desert him then. The day before, he read the Bible and warders also read it aloud to him. Rev Mr Connolly reported that the prisoner was "constantly praying". Cross was bothered by the length of his fingernails and asked for a cutting implement which was naturally refused. On the Monday night he retired to bed at 10 o'clock and apparently after a fairly good night's rest rose at six o'clock on Tuesday, the fateful morning on which he was to pay the price for the awful murder of his wife.

After dressing and a light breakfast, he was visited in his cell by Rev Mr Connolly and at about seven o'clock by the Rev Mr Day.

Prayers went on, with Cross making the responses in a firm tone.

At eight it was time for the procession to assemble for the journey of forty yards to the scaffold. The governor of the prison did not attend the execution, because of his feelings about Cross and sent a deputy to represent him. The Deputy Governor led, followed by the two clergymen with the prisoner between, then four warders, the sub Sheriff and the medical officer Dr Moriarty.

Dr Cross walked firmly and never faltered, and his expression displayed no fear or trepidation. He was wearing grey tweed trousers and a knitted woollen vest; he had left his coat in the cell, either forgetting it or because he was advised to.

Halfway, Berry appeared and pinioned the prisoner's arms, at which Cross betrayed a perceptible shudder. It was a ritual that Berry followed religiously. The pinioning arrangement, he claimed, like the other arrangements for execution, was simple. A broad leather body belt was strapped around the waist and to this arm-straps were fastened. Two straps, an inch and a half wide, with strong steel buckles clasped the elbows and were fastened to the body belt in front.

On the scaffold the legs were pinioned by means of a two-inch strap below the knees. The rest of the apparatus consisted of a white cap shaped like a bag which pulled down over the eyes of the criminal to prevent him seeing the final preparations.

Scaffolds in use in various gaols differed in the details of their construction. Just three years previously, a design was drawn up in the surveyors department of the British Home Office.

The design was submitted to Berry, who approved it and suggested a slope or a level gangway in place of steps which could be awkward if the condemned person was nervous. It was usually dismantled afterwards but in some prisons like Cork it was left standing. The scaffold consisted of a heavy crossbeam into which bolts terminating in hooks were fastened to hold the rope.

The trap door or drop was the most important component. This was made of two massive oak doors fixed on an oaken frame, worked by a lever on a level with the floor over a deep bricked pit. When the lever was pulled, it moved a draw bar in the opposite direction so that the ends of the long hinges dropped through the openings causing the two doors to fall – both necessary to fall at the same moment.

Their great weight caused them to drop very suddenly, even without the weight of the criminal's body and they were caught by spring catches to prevent any possibility of rebound. The rope was the last but not the least of the legal apparatus available to the executioner and one to which Berry gave special attention. A leather washer which fitted the rope tightly was used to slip behind a brass ring, in order to prevent the noose slipping or slackening after it had been adjusted. In using the rope he always adjusted it with the ring just behind the left ear of the prisoner. This, he said was best calculated to cause instant death.

It dislocated the vertebra which was the actual cause of death, as opposed to strangulation. It also had the tendency to rupture the jugular vein which was also sufficient to cause instant death.

It was five minutes past eight. Berry placed the condemned man in position under the rope. His legs were pinioned and the white cap placed over his head.

Cross was of a fine build, over six feet in height, and while he had maintained his composure right to the drop he had aged considerably while in prison, his hair and beard colour being transformed from iron grey to absolute white. The condemned man's friends, the clergymen, were present to give him emotional support. Cross, grateful for their attendance, wanted to stand at attention, with respect, facing them as he died. Berry traditionally faced the condemned towards the wall. Each time Berry faced him towards the wall, the doctor would turn around and face his friends again. When Berry protested, the condemned man ignored him. Finally a prison official reminded the executioner that Cross was a respected soldier and turning back and forth might cause a botched job, the last thing Berry needed. He agreed and Cross was hanged facing his supporters.

This account of Cross wanting to face his comforters, the opposite of the norm of facing the wall and Berry ordered to comply would have re-enforced that sense of uselessness. Berry considered himself the last stage of legal retribution, as justifying his position, but this man offered him no comfort on that account.

It may have been that no punishment was too great, in the hangman's mind, for the sadistic crime that Dr Cross had perpetrated, but his self-possession in the face of Berry's rope diminished the purpose and caused a continued haunting in the executioner's nightmares.

Berry used to say: "When you read of a man walking firmly to the scaffold, it is nonsense. Some walk, some are carried. Of all the men I hanged Dr Cross was the only one who walked firmly."

The doctor was also one of the few "gentlemen", perhaps the only one that Berry had executed. He had gone to his death completely unmoved. Dr Cross had faced death in the army and he did not fear it when it was certain and only minutes away. For all the notice that the man he was going to kill gave him, Berry might well have not been there.

He did not speak a word and perhaps for the first time, Berry felt the full force of contempt for the hangman. Why did Dr Cross, who gave such little trouble haunt Berry more than the scores of other condemned who in various stages of collapse, terror, exaltation and madness went to the gallows, affect him in this way?

Was it the prisoner's indifference to his fate or his cold-blooded lack of recognition of his crime? As if the hangman was cheated out of the meaning of his role as the state avenger of brutal crime. The humiliation was transferred. As Berry recognised, Dr Cross was a gentleman and his friends were from the aristocracy and the upper classes.

The press were shown the scene afterwards but after a delay which the reporters objected to, noting that the Deputy Governor had not just been discourteous but insolent to them.

From about half past seven until a quarter to eight a crowd of about a hundred had gathered outside the main gate of the gaol in front of which a dozen police were posted. After the black flag had been raised, the crowd dispersed.

The body was cut down at nine o'clock and afterwards an

inquest was opened by coroner MJ Horgan in the guardroom of the gaol. There were two members of the press sworn on the jury, John McKay of the *Cork Examiner* and James Murray of the *Freeman's Journal*.

The Deputy Governor, a Mr Oxford, stated that the hangman Berry had left the gaol before the commencement of the inquest and he had no idea where he had gone. The jury was unanimous in asking for Berry and condemned the fact that the hangman had been allowed to leave before the inquest had concluded. The coroner then adjourned until the next morning and said he would further adjourn it until Berry was produced.

Before the adjournment the Deputy Governor had been questioned by the coroner on the obvious details of the execution, confirming that Dr Cross had been hanged and for what reason. Previous to that the jury had been taken to see the body and the scaffold. When questioned by a member of the jury, Mr Oxford said that the governor was ill (he was back at his desk after the execution) and that Dr Cross had made no confession.

He was put under a good deal of pressure by the juror McKay because they and the press were under the impression that the governor had ordered as little information to be given out as possible.

Dr Moriarty gave evidence as to the cause of death, injury to the neck caused by hanging and that death was instantaneous. Dr Moriarty said that Dr Cross had walked to the scaffold with the greatest bravery.

"I hope," he said, "I shall never see the like again."

The jury reiterated the desire to have the hangman at the inquest and Mr Horgan said that he had been produced in England to give evidence and he must appear here.

The inquest was reconvened the following morning when it emerged that Berry, his wife (who used to travel to lend him support and ensure his nerve didn't fail him for the task) and two detectives there to protect him had left the prison a few minutes before the previous inquiry began and caught the half past ten train to Dublin.

The inquest was resumed in the warder's room of the gaol. The coroner called the Deputy Governor and asked him if he had the witness, Berry, which the jury required and he answered in the negative.

He had asked the sub-Sheriff about the matter who told him that he had no power over the executioner. Mr Horgan then told the jury that he would do his best to get the executioner and he would start by issuing a summons for his attendance and therefore would adjourn the inquest until the 20th. As if this turn of events did not contain enough elements of farce, one of the jurors brought up the fact that the hangman Binns had carried out an execution under the influence of alcohol and Mr Horgan reminded him that Binns had been fired for the offence.

The jurors conferred and informed the coroner that they had unanimously decided that the proceedings should be adjourned until the executioner could be produced. When one suggested that a date should be selected when Berry was not attending to duties, Horgan told him that he did not care about his duties and adjourned the inquiry until Friday the 20th.

Dr Moriarty then told the coroner that the body of Dr Cross would not be buried in the meantime and the coroner replied that he could not help that. In the interim the authorities would make representations to the Lord Lieutenant for permission to inter the body.

Finally Horgan issued a summons for the attendance of the hangman. Berry replied in a letter to the coroner which read:

England, 12th January 1888.

Mr MJ Horgan, Coroner

Sir
Re, Dr Philip Cross hanged for murder at HM Prison, Cork, Ireland. In reference to the above, I beg to explain the reason I left the prison is because I never attend inquests either in England or in Ireland. I have been in Ireland several times but never attends (sic) the inquest unless something goes

wrong, and in the case of Dr Cross I never carried out a better execution in my experience as an executioner. He walked with a firm step and stood erect when the drop fell. He never moved a muscle or a limb.

The reason the delay of letting reporters up was in consequence to the religious ceremony be read after death by the chaplain of the prison. Certainly it took up a little extra time, and I am sure Mr Coroner, you will agree with me that it is a spiritual right to be read over the dead. There is a great many prisons in England where reporters is not admitted, and in most cases only one.

Trusting this letter will gratify yr morbid curious jury. I am, sir, yours truly,
James Berry

P.S. I have executed 113 convicts and only attended one inquest, and that was at Norwich, County Norfolk, England where the convict's head was severed from its body and I had to explain how the unfortunate accident occurred. If I attend the inquest which is adjourned until the 20th inst I shall be paid all expenses and my time in coming to give evidence, as if anything had gone wrong I should have stayed until the inquest was over.

If you like to forward me £10, I will attend Cork male prison on 20th inst, to give evidence as you may require upon the questions before mentioned.

13th January 1888

Sir
In your letter from "England" of yesterday's date, with the Bradford postmark, I have to inform you that it in my opinion your conduct in immediately running away to avoid the possibility of your being examined at the inquest, was to say

*the least, improper. The jury is entitled to the best evidence
before them, and that is the evidence of the executioner, whose
duty it was to take the life of the deceased. In this matter I have
issued a summons for your attendance on the 20th inst, and in
case you do not attend I will issue a warrant for your arrest,
which I trust may not be necessary.*

Yours obediently,
MJ Horgan

On 14th January County Inspector Cary of the RIC wrote to the
coroner saying that the summons issued for Berry could not be served
until the address in the summons was filled in and expenses paid to
the executioner for his return trip. He added that he resided outside
the jurisdiction for summons by coroners. The coroner replied that
he did not have Berry's address and was sure the inspector did and
said he had got a letter from Berry the address of which said England
with a Bradford postmark. And he was limited by an Act of
Parliament to a limit of 2 shillings for witness expenses. He said that
his jurisdiction for summonses extended all over the Empire.

The inquest resumed on the 20th at 9.30 for the third time. The
coroner questioned Sergeant Hall about the absence of Berry and
the summons, and he said he had received no instructions in regard
to the matter. Mr Horgan said that he had done all he could about
the matter of the missing executioner, the authorities had not
responded so there was nothing more he could do, adding, "I am
done with the matter." A juror Mr Nolan said that the authorities
could not find Mr Berry's address but if there was another to hang
they would find him quickly enough.

The coroner said he received a telegram from Berry that morning
and did not know whether he was playing a practical joke. He read
it out:

*"Well, I am not in gaol yet. Received no subpoena or summons.
Will attend on Wednesday if expenses are guaranteed. Berry."*

This was received with laughter from those present.

341

He also read out an anonymous letter he had received on the 16th with a Bradford postmark claiming that all that Berry was interested in was money, drinking and gambling and was looked on in Bradford as a perfect fraud; money, drink and debauchery was what he was after and when he returned from an execution he gave a full description in the beer house.

Clearly this was a way for the coroner to get back at Berry as he knew it would be reported in the newspapers.

He then adjourned the inquest *sine die* and if the authorities wanted to produce Berry, they could reconvene. It never happened.

There is an ironic endnote to the history of the scene of Berry's endeavours: Cork County Gaol where Cross endured his personal Calvary, and where his bones were interred, exists no more. Designed by the renowned Pain Brothers in the early 19th century, only the massive south entrance wall with its severe four-columned Doric portico survives. "A superb use of the classical idiom, creating boldness and severity," the portico, now dulled by time, was copied supposedly (and surely inappropriately) from the Temple of Bacchus at Athens. The rest of the extensive gaol, considered progressive in planning and concept in its time, has been obliterated by the march of education, having being bought and built over by University College Cork.

But this tension between incarceration and education existed from the start, as expressed in the following, written by Charles Bernard Gibson in the mid-19th century: "There is a common approach from the Western Road to the Queen's College and the County Gaol. This is not just the thing; nor is it in good taste." The students protested against having to share "the approach" with common criminals and eventually the present main college gates were constructed closer to the city. A smaller entrance to UCC still remains off "Gaol Cross" and to the students trudging by daily the façade and portico stand there disregarded and virtually invisible.

Chapter 12

The Last Word

The unlikely hero of the Coachford Poisoning Case was Dr Charles Yelverton Pearson, who like the great Alfred Swaine Taylor before him was a man of singular character, integrity and devoted to his calling and in every aspect of his long life maintained the devotion, care and attention to his profession that marked him out among his peers. He was the very antithesis to Dr Philip Henry Eustace whose merciless killing of his wife marked him as worthy of the company of Wainewright, Palmer and in particular Pritchard – men who disgraced their profession and used their skills in the pursuit of evil rather than good.

In the name of good and justice both Pearson and Taylor were subjected to criticism and indeed vilification at the hands of counsel in court cases and of others both in the lay and scientific spheres. But as men made of such strong mettle they took the brickbats and when unjustified treated them with the contempt they deserved. But neither man was disposed to be silent in the long run, in the face of those slings and arrows.

They would have appreciated the irony pointed out by Dickens, that everyone wanted to shake the hand of the murderer but not the hangman and the medical experts, without whose analysis and testimony the murders would have remained free from retribution and left to continue to practise their nefarious arts. There is little doubt that in the case of Palmer that despite the fact that he was serial poisoner that his conviction for the murder of John Parsons Cook was at the very least doubtful.

In Pritchard's case there was no contest and however self-serving and inadequate his confessions, he acknowledged his part in the awful crimes. The same, as we know, cannot be said of Dr Cross. There was no confession, no acknowledgement of the crime and therefore no expression of remorse for the pitiful end to which his wife was consigned.

Yet after his conviction there were also doubts raised on the matter of his guilt, which persist to this day.

The very fact that those doubts are entertained, whether capable of proof or not is of itself interesting and arise, in my view, from the relatively weak performance of the defence compared to the prosecution of the case. And certain sections of the judge's charge to the jury, which of course would not be tolerated now, but were then, but nonetheless could not be construed as anything but leading the jury in one direction and prejudicial to the prisoner.

It is also almost impossible not to feel sorry for anyone who has to suffer execution by hanging, as more than adequately displayed by the public at the last of the public executions, by such a great observer as Dickens and lastly but not least the hangman who despatched Dr Cross, James Berry. The fact that the man faced his fate with such steadfastness, enforces rather than diminishes that feeling. Like the hangman, one is subject to a form of sneaking admiration for his unflinching attitude to his fate.

But as unflinching, one has to remind oneself, as his attitude while subjecting his victim to death throes that lasted, not seconds but weeks. As many chroniclers of murder are wont to remark, not least Kate Summerscale towards the end of the great account of the Road House murder, *The Suspicions of Mr Whicher*, the victim is often too easily forgotten or passed over in the debates and controversies that inevitably surround such murders. Even murder in the majority of instances involves some human emotion; execution is by definition the very absence of it. That is not in any measure to alleviate the evil of murder but hanging provokes the very opposite reaction to the perpetrator than any proper retribution should. One could debate the pros and cons of this particular view of the case in that old lost phrase, *saecula saeculorum*. The best and worst fate that Dr Cross could have suffered was to end his life in prison.

Someone, on the other hand, had to speak for the victim, or rather allow the victim's voice to be heard, as it was from the grave, and that person was not among the counsel for the prosecution, or the witnesses, or the judge or the jury. It was Dr Pearson. He interpreted and translated the voice that came from the inert organs of Mary Laura Cross, almost perfectly preserved by the very instrument that caused her torturous illness and abominable death.

It was a voice that the murderer could justifiably have imagined was silent forever. It was not; through the medium of science, rather, it spoke volumes. In that context and the larger one of the infamous Coachford Poisoning Case it is entirely appropriate that Dr Charles Pearson – now long an occupier of his own grave, as are the prosecution and defence counsel, the witnesses, the jury, the spectators, reporters, commentators and the entire communities of Coachford and Dripsey – should have the last word.

On Friday, 3rd February 1888 he read his paper "The Medico-Legal Aspects of The Coachford Poisoning Case" before an audience of the Section of State of The Royal Academy of Medicine in Ireland. It was only three weeks after the execution, so there was huge interest in the reading and the doctor would not disappoint by being less than forthcoming, which was his style. This is an edited version of the speech with a minimum of commentary.

He started by saying:

"Owing to the very deep interest which has been recently aroused in this country and elsewhere, both in the minds of the public, in general and of the medical profession in particular, by an important criminal trial for wife murder in which I happened to be engaged as the principal medical witness, I think it desirable to bring under the notice of the profession, the chief scientific facts, together with such other points in the evidence that seems to me to be relevant to a consideration of the medico-legal aspects of the case.

"I also trust that the paper I now bring before you may serve the purpose of a permanent record, and consequently, in order that it might become intelligible to those of my future readers, who can have no other means of becoming acquainted with the case in all its bearings, I have felt compelled to introduce many matters of evidence of a non-medical nature."

After covering the background to the case, the post mortem and chemical analysis and evidence of symptoms in the victim and other medical matters Dr Pearson dealt with very revealing aspects of the case which were lost in the usual adversarial tendency to bury or hide truths in court for tactical reasons or simply because the counsel could not grasp the complexities of the evidence.

While the modus operandi of Dr Cross was fairly evident from the trial proceedings, the very detail and subtleties that typified the act of the secret poisoner were largely absent. It was left for this paper and speech to draw back a veil on the methods employed by the killer that would have quashed much of the speculation that arose immediately in the wake of the case and proved that Cross, far from being a blunderer, or the victim of miscarriage of justice, had made a close study of the instrument he chose as a weapon. There were a number of strands that Dr Pearson wove together to effect that unmasking.

In the area of the post mortem there was the liver which his slip at the magisterial inquiry led to such grief and which he dealt with in the opening of the paper. The liver of Mrs Cross had contained a considerable amount of the poison, so what did that indicate, apart from the confirmation of its ingestion?

"In the work of Wormley, in speaking of the quantity of arsenic present in the liver, the following passage occurs: 'According to the observations of Dr Geoghegan, this organ usually receives its greatest quantity in about fifteen hours after the poison has been taken, when it may contain as much as two grains.' I regret that I have been unable to discover any record of the observations on which this statement is based; accepting it, however, as being correct, while I readily admit that there is no record of such a quantity as three grains having been found in the liver, I still feel bound to maintain that no one can deny the possibility of such an occurrence in exceptional circumstances.

The statement of Dr Geoghegan goes to show that from the large quantity of arsenic present in the liver of Mrs Cross, we may arrive at the opinion that the last dose of poison must have been administered or taken at a comparatively short period before death – probably within twenty-four hours.

The presence of arsenious acid in the alimentary canal, in solid form, was a proof that some, if not the entire amount of this poison had been taken, or administered in an undissolved state. The white particles described as being present in the stomach and elsewhere, in addition to arsenic contained organic matter by the tests and beyond all possibility of error."

While the symptoms displayed by Mrs Cross during her illness were the subject of much evidence at the trial, there was a steering away from pinning down the precise cause of those symptoms. Dr Pearson replayed the main points of the evidence and concluded that Mrs Cross not only died from but presented during her last weeks of life well-marked and unmistakeable symptoms of slow arsenical poisoning; that from the distinct intervals of remission which occurred, followed by a return of the symptoms with increased severity, it appears that the illness was due to several successive and increasing doses of the poison and that it was impossible to conceive that any medical man could be under the impression that this was a case of typhoid fever.

There was also the matter of the missing arsenic, never brought up at the trial, in fact the defence emphasised the fact that Cross had had a week to get rid of whatever he wanted from the house but did not, evidence not contested by the prosecution. The good Doctor Pearson thought otherwise.

"Now it appears to me that there were various important points in the case which counsel for the Crown failed to bring forward; some of which I shall now briefly mention:

1. No attempt was made to show that all the facts, as detailed in evidence were consistent with the administration of strychnine at the close of the tragedy; that such might have been done I shall presently endeavour to prove.

2. No comment was made, which to me seems most remarkable, of the absence of arsenic with the exception of a small quantity of Fowler's Solution, from the collection taken from Mr Cross's surgery.

3. Although I stated in my examination that the administration of a narcotic would have the effect of diminishing or preventing the painful symptoms which arsenic might cause, and there was distinct recurrence of drowsiness and the administration of chlorodyne, counsel failed to catch the idea that the latter was evidently administered with this express object. Some additional points will be referred to when dealing with the subject of the defence.

"The defence was of a singularly weak nature, and might be said to consist altogether of two very eloquent speeches by counsel, which contained a good deal of matter foreign to the evidence, a large number of misrepresentations, many of them, no doubt, unintentional, and, as might be naturally be expected, in the absence of anything of a really tangible nature, a good deal of abuse of the Crown witnesses, myself, of course, included.

"One of the prisoner's counsel in his reply to the jury endeavoured to make them believe that the quantity of strychnine said to have been discovered (one hundredth part of a grain) was so minute that it was beyond human comprehension that anyone could discover it, because it was only one 43,750th part of an ounce. This gentleman also likened the liver to a sponge, which was only capable of sucking up a certain amount of any substance, and therefore, it could not possibly contain such an amount as three grains of arsenic; and strange to say, the learned judge, in his charge, seized upon this as being an excellent illustration.

"This shows the utter absurdity of anyone trying to deal with scientific matters on which they are totally ignorant. Scarcely anything could be more farfetched than the idea here conveyed; and even if the liver did act in the manner ascribed to it, it is a strange sponge, which itself weighing 21,875 grains could only absorb three grains – one 7,292th part of its own weight.

"The only (defence) witness produced, sister to the accused, who swore that she always considered the late Mrs Cross a delicate woman, with delicate stomach, subject to attacks of the heart; that she, the witness, frequently attended Mrs Cross during her late illness; and often brought her drinks and other nourishment; that on the night of Mrs Cross's death she went to bed about half past ten; that during the night she was roused by a little scream from Mrs Cross's room; this was followed by two or three little screams, after which she heard her brother go downstairs.

"During his absence she heard another scream or cry; she heard him come up again and re-enter the room; almost immediately after he came to her own room; she rose at once and went to the other room; she went to the side of the bed, and saw Mrs Cross lying quite still; her head to one side, and her hand as if it had been on her heart; she thought her dead, but brought the hot water tin from her own bed, put it on her hands, with the hope that it would restore her, but without effect; after that she went and lay on her bed, and rose in the morning about seven; the dead body of Mrs Cross was not rigid.

"The defence counsel also endeavoured to show that strychnine could not have been employed, as the evidence went to prove that the body of Mrs Cross was not of bent and rigid condition at the time of death or some five or six hours after.

"It might have been shown by the Crown that the conditions present immediately after death were not inconsistent with the termination of life by strychnine poisoning. I shall now proceed to prove that such was the case. It is well known that when death takes place from strychnine, as a rule, the body becomes quickly rigid, the rigidity usually persisting for some considerable time. When the person dies during a convulsion, and rigidity immediately supervenes, the distorted condition of the body and limbs may persist after death.

"This, however, is an exception and not the invariable rule, as counsel ingeniously, represented. In Taylor's *Medical Jurisprudence*, Third Edition, the following quotation occurs: 'The body of a person poisoned by strychnine, may, therefore, be found in a non-rigid state within the ordinary period after death.' And again: 'In other instances of strychnine poisoning, no particular degree of rigidity has been found at any period after death.'

"It is also a well known medical fact that in the bodies of those who died in an exhausted condition, either from disease, or otherwise, rigor mortis supervenes very rapidly, and is of transient duration. Now, I think it will be readily conceded that the later Mrs Cross, at the time of her death, owing to repeated vomiting and diarrhoea, must have had her nervo-muscular system reduced to a degree of very great exhaustion.

"We may therefore conclude, that whether a dose of strychnine, had or had not been employed to terminate her existence, in either case, post mortem rigidity would have quickly set in, and disappeared in an evanescent manner; so that it is almost certain that no trace of rigidity would have remained after the period which had elapsed between the occurrence of her death and the time she was first seen either by Miss Jefferson or the servants the following morning.

"When under examination, I was asked if I could account for the screams which were heard by Miss Cross and the servants; this I declined to do, as more than one cause suggested itself to my mind. The popular opinion which I have heard expressed is that they were due to the employment of violence. With this I do not agree; as I believe that if violence had been employed precautions would have been taken to prevent their occurrence.

"No explanation would account for them more satisfactorily than the supposition that they were produced by painful convulsions due to strychnine poisoning. I must, however, here point out that convulsions of a painful character are very frequently present towards the close of cases of slow arsenical poisoning. If, however, we adopt the latter suggestion, we must account for the presence of strychnine in the body of the deceased.

"This, I think may be readily done, as it is perfectly evident from the loose manner in which packets of this substance were left knocking about Mr Cross's surgery, it is not difficult to conceive that a small quantity might have been accidentally mixed with a packet of arsenic. I do not, however, believe that this was the way in which it came to be present.

"I shall now, briefly consider, from a medical point of view, the possible lines of defence which may have been adopted in this case: 1. That Mrs Cross did not die of poisoning at all but succumbed to some heart affection or natural cause. 2. That she did die of arsenical poisoning, and this might have occurred through self-administration, either by accident or design. 3. That she might have been poisoned by accident or design by others besides the prisoner.

"Now it is difficult to conceive how any sensible person, in face of the evidence which I have detailed – namely the presence of well-marked symptoms of arsenical poisoning during life, the distinct post-mortem appearances corresponding thereto, and finally the presence of arsenic in poisonous quantity in the body – could adopt the first of these defences; yet this has been the theory adopted by some of those who sought to prove the innocence of Mr Cross since his conviction.

"The possibility of accidental poisoning is clearly disproved by the history of symptoms detailed by Miss Jefferson. It may no doubt be said that a single poisonous dose of arsenic has been known to give rise to a prolonged and fatal illness, with distinct intervals of remission with the symptoms. If this view had been put forward it might readily be met by the assertion that if only one dose had been swallowed at the commencement of the illness not a trace of the poison would have been present in the system at the time of death.

"If it was suggested that others beside the prisoner administered the poison with criminal intent, in the absence of motive, it would have to be admitted that such must have occurred only at his instigation, in which case he would have been equally guilty.

"It seems to me that the only line of defence which might have met with a reasonable prospect of success would have to boldly admit the fact that the poisoning actually took place through self-administration, and that the prisoner was really under the impression that his wife was suffering from typhoid fever or some other gastro-intestinal affection, and that the chlorodyne was administered with the best intentions to allay the symptoms; and even it could be shown that small doses of strychnine might naturally be employed for a similar purpose.

"It might (if advisable) have been shown that arsenic is sometimes administered in typhoid fever to restrain diarrhoea, and is also frequently given to prevent the paroxysm of angina pectoris; and that strychnine is sometimes given for the latter affection as well to check vomiting. I need scarcely point out that no such case as I have here made out was produced for the defence; had such been done, I do not think it would have proved successful.

"If it was put forward that Mrs Cross deliberately took poisonous doses of arsenic on repeated occasions, with the object of committing suicide, we should have to believe that she subjected herself to a slow and painful form of lingering torture such as cannot be found recorded in toxicological literature. On the other hand it has been suggested that this lady was in the habit of taking arsenic as a cosmetic, or that she was an arsenic eater, such as may be found among the inhabitants of Styria.

"If she employed it at all for the former purpose it is nearly certain that it would have been in the form of solution and not in a solid state; this would have been the form of administration most likely to be chosen for medicinal purposes. If the latter theory be chosen, it will have to be admitted that arsenic-eating, after the manner of Styrians, is quite unknown in this country; yet even if such a practice had been acquired, can anyone believe that a person eating arsenic to benefit their health would continue to employ it in poisonous doses if it produced such symptoms? We are therefore, forced to the conclusion that the poison must have been administered by some other hand.

"Now, much fault has been found with the judge who tried this case for directing the jury that if they were satisfied that the deceased died from poisoning, they were bound to find the prisoner guilty. While I think he might readily have allowed the jury a little more latitude for the exercise of their own judgement, I utterly fail to see how he or they with the evidence before them could arrive at any other conclusion. It will be observed that, as far as my evidence is concerned, it merely went to prove the cause of death. And, in no way, implicated the prisoner.

"A critical examination of the speech delivered by the prisoner, previous to the passing of sentence, shows it to be wholly inconsistent. If some of the statements made by him were true, they could have been proved in evidence. It is interesting to note that his account of the destruction of the bottles does not correspond with that of his sister, nor hers with that of the police sergeant who overheard the conversation and wrote it down; and, strangest of all, he admits what Miss Cross did not, that there was patent medicine in the wardrobe that contained strychnine.

"It has been remarked that the prisoner, considering that he was a medical man, committed this crime in a very clumsy manner. I do not altogether agree with this. He selected a poison which was without *odour, taste or colour.* Therefore most easy of administration; he exhibited it in repeated doses, so as to produce a prolonged illness, and gave chlorodyne to mask the painful symptoms; he prepared her friends and relatives for her approaching death, gave a false account of her symptoms, and once she was buried, who would have heard of the Cross Poisoning Case, if the hasty marriage had not occurred, or had remained a secret for months?

"On calmly reviewing the entire features of the case in the most unprejudiced and dispassionate manner, which I have done on repeated occasions, I cannot for one moment conceive how any sane person can bring themselves to believe, even if they say so to others, that Philip Henry Eustace Cross was innocent of the crime, for which he was deservedly executed.

"After the conviction of Mr Cross, a powerful effort was made by a considerable number of individuals to obtain for him either a reprieve or an alteration of sentence. Of those who took part in this matter, there were some who were naturally actuated by interested motives; there were some who were influenced by purely benevolent feelings and deserve the highest commendation; many did so owing to their entire disapproval of capital punishment in general; some few existed who either asserted their belief in the prisoner's innocence or thought there was some slight doubt about his guilt; while I believe the greater number attached their signatures to a memorial simply because they were asked to do so.

"Numerous letters were written to the local press, a few of which contained some shallow arguments in favour of the prisoner's innocence. Notwithstanding that some of these letters contained gross misrepresentations (many of them no doubt unintentional) and numerous statements of a nature calculated to reflect on my professional reputation, up to the present I have treated them (as, I trust, I could afford to do so) with silent contempt, as I felt that any refutation of them by me, at a time when the memorial on behalf of the convict was under consideration, would be certainly calculated to diminish its prospect of success, and would, in addition, have the effect of making me appear to act the part of Crown advocate – a position throughout the entire case I most carefully refrained from assuming."

Dr Pearson then went on finally to deal with some of the correspondents who questioned his competence and findings and the victim's state of health prior to her death.

"One correspondent (although a medical man) having pointed out that arsenic was an occasional impurity of chloroform, and that the latter entered into the composition of chlorodyne, asked the (apparently to him somewhat profound) question: 'Did the analyst test the chlorodyne for arsenic?' It will probably gratify this gentleman to know that the analyst did so, with a negative result, not however with the object he supposes of detecting this substance as an impurity, but of ascertaining whether the chlorodyne had been employed as a medium of administering the poison. I scarcely think it possible that it would have occurred to any medical man, save the writer of the letter referred to, that the presence of *dissolved arsenic in minute quantity* in the chlorodyne administered to Mrs Cross would have accounted for the presence of arsenious acid in *solid form and poisonous quantity* in her stomach and intestines.

Another writer (a clerical gentleman) makes the audacious statement: 'I am in a position to know that this lady (meaning Mrs Cross) has been for the past six years or seven years or more continually suffering from affections of the heart, the lungs and the stomach.' The question will be naturally asked: How was he in a position to know? Listen to his own answer. He says: 'I can swear that I have heard this said of her over and over again by one who knew her intimately.' Evidently we may conclude that the intimate acquaintance was not a medical man. Could anything be more utterly absurd?

Further on the writer says: 'There was sworn evidence that three grains of arsenic were found in the liver – three times as much as any liver could absorb or as the whole faculty had ever discovered in a human body since the world began!' The untruth of the first portion of this statement has already been shown; as regards the latter portion of it; the writer of the letter referred to will probably blush when he hears that as much as two ounces, or over 870 grains, have been found in the body of a person who died from arsenical poisoning. Again he says: 'The analyst did not know the fact that the human liver could not possibly absorb more than one grain of arsenic.'

Unfortunately the analyst still remains ignorant of this 'fact'. He also mentions the fact that the analyst said that strychnine was taken or administered to hasten death. This statement is a pure invention of a fertile imagination. I disregard any further remarks of this gentleman as being unworthy of serious attention, nor shall I allude to some of the language employed by him; but I trust when he is afforded the opportunity of reading these few lines it will have the effect of deterring him from rushing into print on a subject on which, from his own showing, not to speak of other considerations, he must be profoundly ignorant."

Thus did Dr Charles Yelverton Pearson deal with the case with which he had been intimately involved and, in relation to his detractors, game set and match might just adequately describe the result.

Chapter 13

Aftermath

There was nothing but melancholy in the dark skies over Shandy Hall. The black night had enveloped the countryside, everything cold and motionless. The sombre trees around the house had the aspect of gigantic hearse plumes, black and awful – a fitting backdrop for the young mistress in her widow's weeds. The dark winter lay in a state of seemingly permanent suspension, frozen by the claw of the awful recent past. The house and its inhabitants paralysed by the dreadful secrets, cast to the winds but giving no relief. The pall of death hanging over every corridor, lurking in every corner.

The crushed inhabitants must have had great difficulty in dealing with the fresh and painful memories of the trial and execution, living as they were in a strange world which had been manufactured by the whole process surrounding the foul deed. The consequences must have been both profound and depressing. All, both directly and peripherally played roles in the tragedy that had been played out on a public stage and were now like abandoned playbills scattered across the footpath outside the imposing silhouette of the dark theatre.

There is little doubt that the now-reluctant young mistress of the household must have ordered the bedroom of her predecessor to stay permanently locked.

The silence from that room, nonetheless, must have resounded in Shandy Hall like the screams in the early hour of the fateful June morning, clinging on and torturing the imagination of all who had been safe in their beds when the mistress and poor mother suffered the agony of her last hours on this earth.

Mary Laura might not have survived the ravages of the effects of the primary poison and succumbed to the secondary cause of heart failure brought on by exhaustion. It seemed that her physical humiliation could go no further. So weak and permeated by pain, she could not bear her bed to be changed daily, preferring to lie in the discomfort of her own waste.

This did not seem to bother her medical attendant. The constant, yet distant and perhaps mocking presence, who could not rouse himself from his bed to deal with her discomfort long after the servants had retired for the night. His ears plugged, his face to the wall. Some time after 11 o'clock on the night of the 1st of June, her infernal sentinel gave his grevously ill patient a medicine with the usual explanation that it would ease her symptoms.

Within twenty minutes she began to feel uneasy sensations, stiffness at the back of the neck and twitching in her muscles. Then a feeling like someone was pressing the front of her neck. She tried to lie still but could not stop moving her neck from side to side to escape the sense of suffocation.

Sometime later a wave of ice cold swept over her from her toes to her head and back again and later a burning as if a fire had replaced the ice. Suddenly her calves cramped and then like a bolt of electricity spread through all her other muscles. Her backbone was starting to arch and her toes curl under her feet. Her jaw locked and her mouth opened in a fixed grin.

She began to groan but it did not attract the attention of the doctor who had retreated to his bed on the other side of the room as he did every night. She realised with a rising panic that there was nothing going to be done for her. Throughout her illness she had never experienced anything like this. She was terrified and again gripped by suffocation.

Her fingers gripped the sodden and soiled sheet. There was no sense of the time or the time that had passed. There was no remission. As before, she was seized again by a series of spasms, now spreading everywhere, and her bowels involuntarily emptied. The pain was intolerable and then another convulsion gripped her and another.

Her breathing became more and more rapid. She moved her head slightly. He was standing in the corner. Just standing, doing nothing, saying nothing. Watching. Her head seemed to be fixed and paralysed, incapable of movement, she could feel the fearful thumping of her ribs, her breath rattling from her mouth.

She began to choke and let out a scream and another and another and more rattling like a decreasing drum rhythm. She screamed but nothing came out, her thundering heart lurched, her skeletal hands gripped the sheets. A long sigh issued from her gaping mouth. The dark curtain fell. It was all over, at last.

The effects of a murder, in any family, at any time casts a shadow of gloom and darkness that lasts for all of the generations that follow. The legacy never goes away. Family, friends and the community are dragged into its vortex. There is a stain that is not easily wiped out. The passage of the years may diminish the impact but it never goes away. Memory of it is as merciless as the event, continually debated over the hearthstone of the dismembered family and the torn community.

It is like one of those ruined castles that dot the landscape of County Cork, constantly eaten away by the tentacles of time and the erosive punishment of each successive passing season. Decrepit in the warm light of a summer's day but eerie and haunting in autumn twilight and almost alive under the shadow of a winter moon, still there full of memories.

There is a realisation of the emptiness of this life, the

nothingness of its ephemeral achievements and ambitions. Murder strikes the very vitals of society, confounds its very existence. The victims outside the event are myriad. And doubt, irrespective of the outcome, is never far away.

The doubt and unfathomable aspect of a case as this when the perpetrator goes to the grave without leaving the extended families of all involved an explanation or confession which might enable them to somewhat grasp the nettle of their fate and in later years achieve a state of understanding or at the best acceptance. It was not an honourable concession that Philip Henry Eustace Cross was going to grant. He deluded himself to the last, despite his bravery when faced with the scaffold, that he was an innocent man but if not may have felt that by leaving that impression he would in some way, with a legacy of doubt, spare his family from the real and awful truth. The opposite would be the actual effect, as they were left to wonder and fret and forever be denied a proper and ultimately comforting resolution.

While Dr Cross was incarcerated in prison, and now facing the ultimate conclusion to his life on earth, his wife Evelyn gave birth to his son, named John, on the 23rd of December – a week after the trial began – confirming that his mistress was pregnant long before his wife's death. The child's birth was recorded in the Macroom Registrar's District by his nurse Mary Martin who had been present at his birth. Normally this record would have been made by the father, but in this instance, that was not possible.

It may well have been the pregnancy that drove Cross across the line that every killer must go to make the appalling decision to deprive another human being of the greatest of gifts: life. He had pursued the affair and gratified his passion for quite a while with no seeming conflict in his mind about his established status as a husband. Ultimately that would have become a problem as it always does. But a sudden urgency entered the adulterous equation sometime about the start of May.

If indeed Effie had conceived in the bedroom of the North Wall Hotel on the 29th of March, it must have been about the time of the murder that the fact of her pregnancy would have been confirmed. And the comfort and convenience of the affair would have been removed, most particularly for the young governess. The stigma of her condition in Victorian times is almost impossible to imagine. Not only her family's reputation and her own, but also her livelihood was on the line to be obliterated. She was lost, she was doomed and what was she to do? She had nowhere to go, once it was no longer possible to conceal it. Even her family might reject her and in any case she could not bring such utter disgrace on the respected Skinner name and her proud family line.

So the only person she could appeal to was the father of her child. But what could he do as he was already married, albeit to a woman he had come to hate and had quite a while ago treated abominably in a verbal tirade? From as far back as January in his exchange with Mrs Madras, he had talked of the possibility of his wife's impending death. Proof that it was in his mind, then perhaps more in hope than expectation. A seed had been sown and when another one had, this could have pushed him into action.

The only way to allay Effie Skinner's fears was a promise to marry her, no doubt as soon as his ailing spouse had passed away. When might that be? Sooner rather than later; he was a medical man after all. They were together again at the end of April and not long after Mrs Cross experienced the first symptoms of her fatal illness.

If the date had not been arranged, the rough time of the marriage must have, because at some stage in June, the pregnancy would become obvious. And some urgency, some deadline must provide the only explanation why Cross abandoned his apparent practice of administering the poison in soluble form, after weeks of doing so and gave the arsenic in solid form just a day or two before he added strychnine on the night of 1st June.

Perhaps, however, the strychnine and a sudden end were always part of his planned modus operandi. If so, his plan was devilishly conceived and calculated. He waited until the 29th of May to write to Humphrey Marriott in England of his sister's serious illness.

Then, when Humphrey had scarcely received the letter, Cross used the strychnine, thereby ensuring that he had no time to travel to Ireland, no time to intervene. On the morning of Mary Laura's death he wired Humphrey and then wrote again, not just to impart the news but to say the burial would be quick – thereby blocking any notion of Humphrey's to attend the funeral of his sister.

He added that he would be going to England to tell his children, a cover of course for his rendezvous with and marriage to Effie. And coincidentally, at this time, he had received a letter from his lover.

There were two letters to Humphrey Marriott not read at the trial which revealed a great deal about his callousness, his psychology and his intent.

His letter, dated Saturday 4th of June, was admitted into the Magisterial Inquiry in August but for obvious reasons not allowed admission in the trial of December. That being so, because the first inquiry was held in front of a magistrate who was only deciding on the matter going forward to trial, but if presented to a jury the letter could be prejudicial to the accused. Hugely so, given the contents.

Letter of 4th June

My dear Marriott,
The last rites were duly carried out this morning in Magourney Church graveyard, the family burial place having been discarded for this reason: the vault was full and only by poking around could room have been found for her alone. So, as she had no regard for that ground, we decided that, as I had been born at, christened in and attached to Magourney Church all my life with poor dear Laura that there we should like to be laid side by side, as there was plenty of room left in the graveyard.

I had her quietly buried, half-privately – with a carriage and pair to her last (I feel sure) heavenly home. I had dear Emma and other friends' wreaths buried with her; those of our acquaintances we laid on her grave, which received her not a moment too soon, as the weather was very close. I got your letter on my return, and of course was not surprised at your not coming to her funeral, and in fact I thought it would be useless to ask you as the poor soul could offer you no welcome such as she'd gladly have done many a time those last eleven years.

When weak she said "Remember me to Humphrey, the children and all, as I fear I might not see them again." I think she loved you better than anyone else. In her eyes, HM could do no wrong. Poor thing, she will be missed by Bessie and Etta, neither of whom seem to care much about her loss, not having shed a tear yet, nor are they likely to. "It is a pity about poor Mother" is the only expression of regret I have from either of them yet.

It is truly sad the state of these children, but I suppose they cannot help it, not being answerable to a certain extent for their action, and they both can still read well, and Bessie in her own way is inclined to do something, in short all she can. Poor Etta, I grieve to say, is hopeless. Most likely I'll go over next week, to break the event to the dear ones in England, who so far have only been informed of their mother's dangerous illness; that, in a way, may well prepare them for the sad event. If I go, I'll go down and see you for an hour or so, as my time will be very short.

I hope none of you have given the children news about their mother. Please leave that to me.

P.H.E.X.

Given the circumstances then, not to mind later events, this was a communication which not only beggared belief but was of a singularly evil character. The vault, he said was full and by only poking about could room be found. What an image to present to a loving brother, quite apart from the lie he gave it by saying that his wife had no regard for it. And so he would be laid with her side by side – a statement sufficient to raise the hairs on the back of anyone's neck.

And, of course, "*[the grave] received her not a moment too soon, as the weather was very close*" – another gruesome image of appalling insensitivity when addressed to a grieving relative. If anything could have indicated his intent, that was it – to inter his poisoned wife as quickly as possible and thus not allow the man he was writing to an opportunity of coming to the funeral.

And then his clumsy switch of attention to the lack of grieving on the part of his two slightly disabled daughters, complaining about their lack of expression of regret. But where was his? Nowhere to be seen. But he tries to engage his brother-in-law by a disgusting diversionary tactic using his children. Their mother is dead, but look what I have to deal with!

What does that suggest but a reason, down the road, to explain why he married the object of his passion, as he so gratuitously explained in his address to the court? "She was wanted in the house to look after those poor children."

Of course, he never went to see Humphrey, as he had promised.

He had one thing in his mind, and one thing only: marriage to Effie Skinner.

In the next letter, dated 5th June, he mentioned again that the burial was not a moment too soon in consequence of the heat of the weather. He says that Humphrey Marriott would have been too late for the funeral which took place at 6 a.m. on the 4th June. "*You should have had a long journey for an unpleasant purpose into the bargain.*" Again, an almost pathological lack of sympathy: burying one's sister is not normally referred to as "an unpleasant purpose" as if it were an unwelcome everyday chore best avoided if possible.

He went on to chronicle Mary Laura's attacks of the heart and how she used to be so ill with these.

And then comes a peculiar reference which apparently had to do with Humphrey's sending of cheques to his sister. "*I enclose a cheque, defaced, and had some difficulty in finding it, as I never examine anything about those, when they come, or rarely so.*" Presumably he wanted to ingratiate himself with Humphrey by returning the most recent of Mary Laura's cheques, at the same time claiming clumsily in passing that he had no interest in their periodic arrival at Shandy Hall with the implication that they were in his wife's sole possession. And no doubt he was hoping that Humphrey would send a replacement cheque and even continue to pay Mary Laura's allowance for the sake of the children. Again, one notes the crassness – indeed the insult – of implying that Humphrey would be concerned about the fate of his last cheque at such a juncture.

There is then mention that the news of their mother's burial has been given to his children by their schoolmaster and mistress. "*Still, the intention was good, if a little injudicious,*" he told Humphrey.

One can only imagine what the Attorney General would have done with the evidence of those two letters. He was not given the opportunity, which as it transpired he did not need.

The real reason for Cross's haste to marry could not have been brought into the trial but nothing else could adequately explain it. Whatever actually transpired, both parties would take it to their respective graves.

As for his poor Evelyn, the object of the murderer's passion and seeming motive for the killing, she, given the publicity and destruction of her character, must have wanted to get away from Shandy Hall and forever distance herself from every aspect of the circumstances that crushed her. She, the vicar's daughter, must have been devastated with guilt and remorse. If there was any possibility of redemption, she would seek it in obscurity, and she did. She eventually left the scene of her passion and torture, certainly within two years and no doubt returned to her family in Scotland. She was still a young and beautiful woman and must have had some prospects of a new life. And possibly another relationship. It took time but so it was and she went on to marry again, this time a man of more modest means but, she might have remarked to herself, so much the better.

On the 27th of October 1898, she married Patrick James

Robertson, a commission agent for gelatine, at the Registry Office, St Giles, London. Her husband was the son of a farmer in Fife; in a peculiar but appropriate way Effie was returning to her roots. Obscurity was what, no doubt, she craved, and that it what she got. Not that, for one moment, would the past ever leave her mind, but at the very least she could now get on with her life.

She did and the couple had a child, a daughter Mary, who was born in 1902. In the 1911 census, Evelyn Forbes Robertson was living in Paignton, Devon, with her mother, Anne Henrietta Skinner, now widowed, and her daughter Mary, then aged 9 years. The census detail revealed that she was married and working in a nursing home. He husband was not recorded, but he no doubt was away on work, in his capacity of a salesman.

It might have been a far cry from the position of the mistress of Shandy Hall, the wife of gentry, but no doubt the young woman had left those ambitions far behind, and hopefully had some peace, some consolation and some love, to somehow dull the pain of the past. She at least experienced some normality and was a proud mother who was present at her daughter's wedding to Robert May in Kent in 1925. Her daughter was 23, Effie was 60.

She had but twelve years to live. Evelyn Forbes Skinner Cross Robertson died on the 30th of July 1937 at Pennshyn Lodge, Margate, Kent as a result of exhaustion, brought on by cancer of the kidney, which had spread to her back and was confirmed by an X-ray. The death certificate recorded her as a nursing home proprietress and her husband Patrick James Roberston as occupation unknown. Her daughter Mary May signed the certificate, giving the distinct impression this time that Effie's husband was not around, possibly had not been for a long time. She was seventy-two years of age, nine years older than her first husband when he was consigned to eternity.

It seems that Effie's son John Cross went on to marry Pricilla Morgan Lewis on the 24th of December, 1909 in St Andrew's Church in Fulham, just a day after his twenty-second birthday. His wife was aged thirty, the daughter of David Morgan Lewis, a solicitor.

The marriage record confirms that John, who was then using the name John Eustace Cross, was a medical student. It is thought that he changed his name and emigrated to Australia at some stage and died there in the 1950s. Certainly, in 1911, Priscilla Morgan Cross was recorded as living on her own in Fulham, with some Tasmanian medical students as lodgers, suggesting that John may have left at that stage – perhaps to send for her when he was established.

There have been no records unearthed for the three eldest children following the murder of their mother and execution of their father. It is said that Humphrey Marriott was very kind to his nephews and nieces and indeed in one instance appeared as a witness to a wedding. However the census returns for Abbots Hall in 1881 and every subsequent decade up to 1911 could not confirm if any of the Cross orphans went to live with their uncle.

Sophia became a governess, an irony in itself, and was found working with the Churchill family in London in the 1901 census. On the 14th of July 1903 she married William Ranson Cooper, a consulting engineer and son of William Cooper, an accountant. Her uncle Humphrey George Marriott and brother Henry Eustace Cross witnessed the marriage. Sophia and William had one son, Maurice Ranson Cooper, born in 1905.

The eldest son Richard (Bob) qualified as a doctor, emigrated to New Zealand, married and had eleven children. He had inherited Shandy Hall but, in Guy's Almanac Postal Directory, Henrietta Cross is householder in 1891 and a Mr Patrick Murphy in 1907, indicating that the house was sold.

The second son Henry became a vet. In the 1891 census of England, he was attending the Queens's College in Taunton, Devon, Somerset. Ten years later he was studying in Edinburgh, living as boarder with the Kerr family. He was in the British Army in Egypt and wrote a book: *Diseases Of The Camel,* which apparently is the definitive writing on the subject.

Twenty years after the murder and hanging, barrister Timothy Healy records that a youth made his way to Cork from abroad to ask a solicitor about the mystery of the deaths of his father and mother as he had been brought up in ignorance of the family tragedy. Which of Cross's sons this was, is not recorded. It seems unlikely to have been a son of Mary Laura as they would have had Humphrey Marriott to recount the details of the tragic tale. Effie's son John seems to be the most likely candidate and Healy's reference to the death of his mother possibly an error. Healy claims that the solicitor sent him away no more informed than when he came, but why this should be is an equal mystery as such a murder not only would have dwelt long in the public memory but also in newspaper reports. There would have been little justification in the solicitor sparing an energetic young man of even the barest facts. If the young man was indeed John, one way or another his trip to Cork may have uncovered facts which led to his change of name and country.

The Caulfields moved to England, first to Midsomer Norton near Bath, circa 1890, and the 1891 census found the family living at 10 Nightingale Road, Portsmouth.

The census recorded:

John Caulfeild (sic), aged 52, retired Army Captain, born: Ireland.

Theresa, wife, 42, housewife, born: East Indies.

Gwendoline 17, daughter, born: Southampton.

Walter 16, son, born: Ireland.

Edith 11, daughter, born: Ireland.

Geraldine 8, daughter, born: Ireland.

Gordon 6, son, born: Ireland.

John Caulfield died on 12th December 1892, in Yalta, Silchester Rd, Kingstown, Co Dublin. He was 53. The death certificate, registered by his son Walter S, then 18, gave the cause of death as cerebral softening which could have been caused by a stroke, brain haemorrhage or degenerative changes, and bronchopneumonia.

This is a bacterial infection of the lungs, characterised by chills, fever, high pulse and respiratory rates, cough with purulent, bloody sputum, severe chest pain and abdominal distension and can lead to respiratory failure and congestive heart failure. Presumably this was secondary to the main cause.

Theresa later married Thomas Hennessey on 29th March 1897, at Colchester Registry Office, Essex. She died on 3rd May 1911, at 1 Kingway Mansions, Hove, Sussex and was buried on 6th May at Hove cemetery.

The youngest son, Second Lieutenant Gordon Caulfield died aged 32 on 30th November 1917, in the Battle of Cambrai. The Clifton Rugby Club History website says: "It has not been possible to positively identify L Caulfield, who joined Clifton in 1913–14, as there is no Caulfield with the initial 'L' listed as having died in World War I by the Commonwealth and War Graves Commission. It is thought, at the moment, that his initial on the War Memorial and in the book *50 Years with Clifton Rugby Football Club* is incorrect. The Club Annual Dinner that took place on Saturday 5th April 1913 at Fortt's Restaurant included a G Caulfield. The best guess is that this is 2nd Lieutenant Gordon Caulfield, who died on the 30th November 1917 at the Battle of Cambrai. The name Caulfield is also listed as Caulfeild."

There are reportedly descendants of the Cross family now in New South Wales in Australia.

Local Coachford historian Anthony Greene met Cross's grandson who seemed to know little about the case. It struck him that it was not a tradition in the family to keep it alive – not surprising, given the nature of the crime and the outcome.

Charles Yelverton Pearson, Emeritus Professor of Surgery of University College Cork, died on 13th May 1947, aged 89. He had been on the staff of the college for fifty years when he retired in 1928.

By the time he was forty, he had become Professor of Surgery at Queen's College, a position he continued to hold until 1928, when the university conferred on him the title of Emeritus Professor. He was a member of the council of the university and the senate of The National University of Ireland. In 1916, he succeeded the late Sir Charles Ball as honorary surgeon to the King in Ireland.

One of his daughters by his second marriage was a doctor. His two sons were Dr Charles B Pearson of Cork, and Mr William Pearson, Professor of Surgery, Dublin University.

Henry Tyacke was subsequently moved around the country and achieved some notoriety with involvement in policing protests in the increasing political agitation over the land question and consequent evictions and arrests. His greatest policing moment it seemed was behind him and, at one incident in Waterford, he and his force were the subject of the jeers and taunts of a crowd after an eviction.

He also was in 1901 the subject of criticism by a nationalist MP in Parliament in relation to an incident after the trial of two county councillors at Loughlynn, Co Roscommon, under the Coercion Act [an emergency act to establish law and order, many of which were passed between 1801 and 1922]. A crowd had gathered outside the courthouse and a police force under DI Tyacke threw a cordon and ordered them to retire. The Member for East Galway apparently tried to remonstrate with the inspector and was told to mind his own business. Another incident was mentioned and the complainant was demanding that the Attorney General should say under what law these proceedings were carried out. Ironically, the Attorney General was none other than Baron Atkinson who had defended Dr Cross but now was on the same side of the fence as the inspector.

The 1911 census found him now a County Inspector in Dunmoe, Co Meath, at fifty-two years of age living with his wife Ann Mary thirty-five, who he had married in 1896 with one child and four servants. He died in 1948 at eighty-nine years of age.

New York Times, December 3, 1911

EX-HANGMAN ARRIVES HERE

James Berry, Now an Evangelist,
Comes in on The *Cedric*.

Among passengers arriving yesterday from England on the White Star *Cedric* was James Berry who was official hangman in Great Britain for several years and gave it up 18 years ago to become an evangelist. He gave an eye to the reporters suggestive of the length of drop he would like to give them. In his career as a public executioner, Berry said he had hanged 193 persons and assisted in the hanging of 500 others while he was the hangman's apprentice. He said that the post was not an enviable one.

One reason Berry gave for retiring from his position of hangman was the discovery he hanged two innocent persons. They were proved innocent years afterward by the confession of the real murderers. He has written two books, 'From Scaffold to Pulpit' and 'My Experience as an Executioner'.

He said that one of the best-known men he had hanged was Lieut Colonel Cross of Shandy Hall, County Cork, who murdered his wife and married the governess.

Four years after that execution in 1892, the medical officer in Kirkdale Prison interfered with the hangman's drop calculation resulting in the near decapitation of the prisoner. In March of that year Berry wrote his resignation, not knowing that when his tenure was shortly up it was not going to be renewed by the Home Office. After eight years his career was over.

Berry had been suffering from depression for some time but now he became suicidal and decided to end his life by jumping from a train. He was in the station having bought the ticket, when his dejected appearance was noted by a young man who had entertained similar thoughts and was making it his business to save others. He brought Berry to a mission where he talked to an evangelist and said that he felt that he had been possessed by the evil demons from the men he had executed. After two and a half hours of unburdening his soul, the hangman was "saved" and began his own evangelical career, preaching against the evils of capital punishment.

When Berry had accepted his first appointment as executioner, his family raised strong objections and his neighbours shunned him. He had ignored the entreaties of those closest to him and took on a role that was also totally unsuited to his basically gentle and caring nature. He always claimed it was to feed his family but he could not have chosen a worse way to do it.

He fooled himself by thinking that he had invented a more humane method of dispatching his clients but he could not escape the naked truth of the fact that he was, in essence, a State-approved murderer. This realisation took a terrible toll on him, mentally and physically. His cherubic early looks were wiped away and replaced by a ravaged countenance which chronicled every line of his torment.

James Berry died in 1913 at sixty-one years of age.

John George Gibson MP, resigned his position as Attorney General the year following the Cross trial and was appointed a High Court Judge. He had married his cousin Anna Hare of Deerpark, Co Tipperary, some years before and they resided in 38, Fitzwilliam Place, in Dublin. He died in June 1923 at the age of seventy-seven.

His adversary at the trial, John Atkinson, went on to have a highly distinguished career. Three years later he was appointed Attorney General, a post he stayed in for only a year. He was elected a Conservative MP for North Londonderry in 1895. He was again appointed Attorney General and this time lasted ten years in the position. He then became a judge and Law Lord. He retired in 1928 and five years later died in London aged eighty-eight.

Timothy Healy MP recorded in his memoirs that a leading member of the judiciary was dining with Lord Justice Murphy in early January 1888. Later in the evening as he was preparing to leave the judge asked him if he might consider stopping the night. Replying to his host that he was unable to comply with his request, regretfully, he enquired why the judge felt the need for his company overnight.

"Well," he replied, "Dr Cross is being executed in the morning."

Clearly, the fact was weighing heavily on his mind and he felt the need of company. The judge, we know, had broken down, overcome by emotion during his charge to the jury. A charge that had been roundly criticised afterwards, as Dr Pearson soberly remarked, for not leaving the jury enough latitude to make up their own minds. The judge's conscience was obviously bothering him.

We had the reluctant hangman Berry torn by the implications of exercising his awful duty. Then the considerable support for mercy being exercised on behalf of the condemned man and the Governor of the gaol absenting himself from the execution. Quite apart from the crime, the punishment excited highly ambivalent feelings.

One must remark that it would be a person with a heart of stone who would not have felt some sorrow for the fate of Dr Cross as he faced his last moments. On the other hand, one would also have to take into account the awful suffering inflicted on the victim Mary Laura Cross at the hands of her executioner. And the necessary indignity of the treatment of her mortal remains in the pursuit of justice on her and society's behalf.

Her wracked body interred and exhumed, not once but twice. Organs removed and subsequently destroyed. In her last weeks and moments of life her body and mind subjected to the most foul humiliation and indignity. And then scientifically torn apart in a manner in which compassion plays no part. Inevitably forensic investigation must have its way and is impervious under such circumstances of criticism. This is the price of bringing the murderer to task.

In the dramatic maelstrom that surrounds the act the victim is lost and becomes almost a cipher. Although that should not be, that is the way of it, then and now.

There is a haunting image after the first post-mortem in Coachford at the end of July 1887. The coffin of the victim, born into great privilege in the historic Abbots Hall and with some expectation of happiness in life, being drawn on a handcart back to the grave where she had been so hastily interred. To rest but a short while and again with the absence of any decent care.

The victim of any murder should not be forgotten in the storm of activity that succeeds its consequence.

Mary Laura Cross in your silent tomb in Magourney Graveyard in County Cork, our fervent hope is that you will not be forgotten.

Selected Bibliography

BOOKS AND ARTICLES

Altick, Richard D, *Victorian Studies in Scarlet: Murders And Manners in the Age of Victoria*
(WW NORTON AND CO, NEW YORK, 1970)

Atholl, Justin, *The Reluctant Hangman: The Story Of James Berry; Executioner 1884–1892*
(THE ANCHOR PRESS LTD, 1956)

Ball, Elrington F, *The Judges in Ireland 1221–1921,* Vol 2,
(DUTTON AND CO, NEW YORK, 1927)

Berry, James, *My Experiences as an Executioner,*
edit H Snowden Ward
(LUND & CO, 1892)

Burney, Ian A, *Poison, Detection, and the Victorian Imagination*
(MANCHESTER UNIVERSITY PRESS, 2006)

Collins, Wilkie, *The Woman In White*
(LONDON, 1860)

Cooper, Anthony, "50 Years of Anglican Ministry in Cologne, 1850–2000"

Dickens, Charles, *Hunted Down*
(LONDON, 1859)

Doyle, Arthur Conan, *A Study In Scarlet 1887;*
"The Adventure of the Speckled Band" from
The Adventures of Sherlock Holmes
(LONDON, 1892)

Duke, Winifred, *Six Trials*
(GOLLANCZ, LONDON, 1934)

Gillman, HW, "History of a Townland in Muskerry, Cronodymore" (*Journal of the Cork Historical and Archaeological Society*, Ser. 2, Vol 1, 1895)

Healy, Timothy, "Legal Memories" from *Letters and Leaders of My Day, Vol 1*
(THORNTON BUTTERWORTH, LONDON, 1928)

Healy, Maurice, *The Old Munster Circuit,*
(MICHAEL JOSEPH, LONDON, 1939))

Hodge, William, Publisher: *Notable English Trials*
(series published from 1911, Edinburgh, 1921)

Hufton, Olwen, *The Prospect Before Her; a History of Women in Western Europe 1500–1800, Vol I*
(HARPERCOLLINS, LONDON 1995)

Hughes Kathryn, *The Victorian Governess*
(HAMBLEDON, LONDON, 2001)

James, Henry, *The Turn Of The Screw*
(LONDON, 1898)

Jarvinen, Taviki, "The Victorian Governess: The Romantic Heroine in Victoria Holt's production v Social Necessity in Victorian England"
(MA Thesis. University of Tampere, Finland, 1998)

Johnston, Colonel William: *Role of Commissioned Officers in the Medical Service of The British Army.* Edited by A.L. Hodge.
(ABERDEEN UNIVERSITY PRESS 1917)

Langbein, John H, *The Origins of Adversary Criminal Trial*
(OXFORD UNIVERSITY PRESS, USA, 2003)

Le Fanu, Sheridan J, *Wylder's Hand*
(NEW YORK, CARLETON, 1864)

Lewis, Samuel, *A Topographical Dictionary of Ireland*
(LEWIS & CO, LONDON, 1837)

Macinnis, Peter, *Poisons from Hemlock to Botox and The Killer Bean of Calabar*
(ARCADE PUBLISHING, NEW YORK, 2004)

McConville, Seán, *English Local Prisons 1860-1900: Next only to Death*
(ROUTLEDGE, LONDON, 1995)

Maurice, Mary Atkinson, *Governess Life: Its Trials, Duties and Encouragements*
(JOHN W PARKER, LONDON, 1849)

Parry, Dr Leonard, *Some Famous Medical Trials*
(SCRIBNER & SONS, LONDON, 1928;
REPRINTED BY BEARD BOOKS, WASHINGTON, 2000)

Pearson, C Yelverton MD QUI FRCS Eng, "The Medico-Legal Aspects of the Coachford Poisoning Case" *Dublin Journal of Medical Science 1872–1920*, Vol 85, January–June 1888 (Springer, London)

Prior, Pauline M, *Madness and Murder: Gender, Crime and Mental Disorder in Nineteenth-Century Ireland* (Irish Academic Press, 2008)

RIC Outrage Papers, Index (National Archives Ireland)

Roughead, William, *The Murderer's Companion* (Kingsport Press, 1941)

"The Trial Of Dr Pritchard" *Notable Scottish Trials*, (William Hodge, Glasgow, 1906.)

Summerscale, Kate, *The Suspicions of Mr Whicher, or The Murder at Road Hill House* (London, Bloomsbury, 2009)

Taylor, Dr Alfred Swaine, *On Poisons In Relation to Medical Jurisprudence and Medicine* (Churchill, London, 1848)

The Principles and Practice of Medical Jurisprudence, (London, 1865)

Thestail, John H, *Criminal Poisoning: An Investigational Guide for Law Enforcement, Toxicologists, Forensic Scientists and Attorneys* (Humana Press, USA, 2000)

Vaughan, W, *Landlords and Tenants in Mid-Victorian Ireland* (Oxford University Press, 1994)

Vincent, Adrian, *A Gallery of Poisoners*
(TIME WARNER, LONDON, 1993)

Walker, William, *The Life and Times of the Rev. John Skinner,
M.A., of Linshart, Longside, Dean of Aberdeen*
(SKEFFINGTON, LONDON, 1883)

Watson Katherine D, *Poisoned Lives: English Poisoners
and Their Victims*
(HAMBLEDON, LONDON AND NEW YORK, 2004)

White's *Directory of Essex* 1848

NEWSPAPERS

Auckland Star, New Zealand

Cork Examiner

Constitution or Cork Morning Post

Cork Herald (*Cork Daily Herald* from 1860)

Evening Post

Hibernian Chronicle (later *Cork Mercantile Chronicle*)

Irish Times

Munster Advertiser

New York Times

People's Press and Cork Weekly Register

Skibbereen and West Carbery Eagle

Southern Reporter (*Irish Daily and Southern Reporter* 1871)

Te Aroha News , New Zealand

MICROFILM SOURCES

Cork Examiner

Cork Evening Post

Cork Weekly News

Cork Constitution

Cork Daily Herald and Advertising Gazette

Weekly Herald, Cork

Irish Times

GENEALOGICAL SOURCES

Baptismal Records, Scotland and England

Burial records Inniscarra 1896–2002

Calendar of Grants of Probate and Letters of Administration, Ireland 1888

Census for County Cork, 1901 and 1911 (only existing census)

Civil Registration Records, Scotland

Cork Central Library, Grand Parade Cork

Cork City and County Archives

English Census 1841–1911

Family Heritage Centre, Wilton, Cork

General Register Office, England: Marriage and Death Records

General Register Office, Ireland: Birth Records

Griffiths Valuation or the Householder's Index taken 1851–3 in County Cork Irish National Library

Mallow Heritage Centre

National Archives of Ireland

Radleys of Cork, Genealogy Website

Scottish Census 1841-1911, various locations

Testamentary records in National Archives.

"Tracing Your Ancestors in County Cork" by Nora M Hickey.

University College Cork Library Archives

WEB SOURCES

Ancestery.co.uk

1911 census.co.uk

Familysearch.org

gro.gov.uk

irishroots.ie

Questia.com

scotlandspeople.gov.uk

Wikipedia

OTHER SOURCES

Court Records: Prior to 1924 serious criminal cases were dealt with at an Assizes in each county, the records of which were maintained by the Clerk of Crown and Peace. Lowest courts prior to 1924 were Petty Sessions. National Archives hold most of those court books for the period 1858–77. Surviving court records are still stored in Four Courts.

Records, HM Prison at Cork for Males, Prisoners awaiting trial on custody 22nd October 1887.

Genealogy of
Evelyn Forbes Skinner

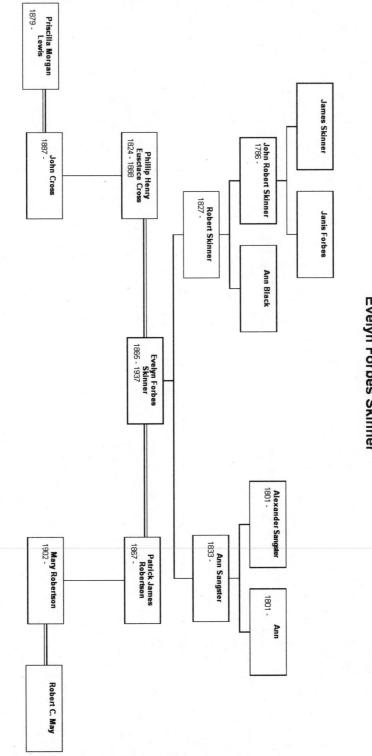

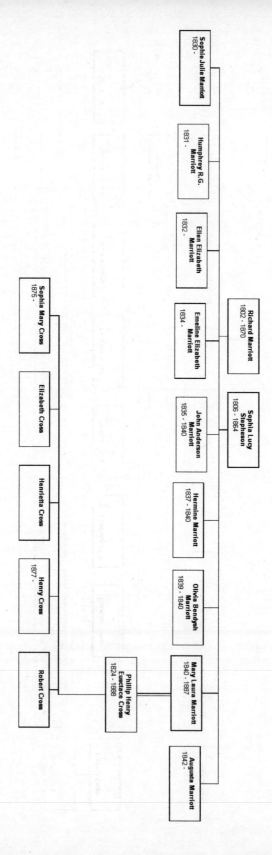

Genealogy of
Mary Laura Marriott

Sophie Julie Marriott
1830 -

Humphrey R.G.
Marriott
1831 -

Ellen Elizabeth
Marriott
1832 -

Emeline Elizabeth
Marriott
1834 -

Richard Marriott
1802 - 1870

Sophia Lucy
Stephenson
1806 - 1864

John Anderson
Marriott
1835 - 1840

Hermine Marriott
1837 - 1840

Olivia Bendysh
Marriott
1839 - 1840

Mary Laura Marriott
1840 - 1887

Augusta Marriott
1842 -

Phillip Henry
Eustace Cross
1824 - 1888

Sophia Mary Cross
1875 -

Elizabeth Cross

Henrietta Cross

Henry Cross
1877 -

Robert Cross

Genealogy of Phillip Henry Eustace Cross

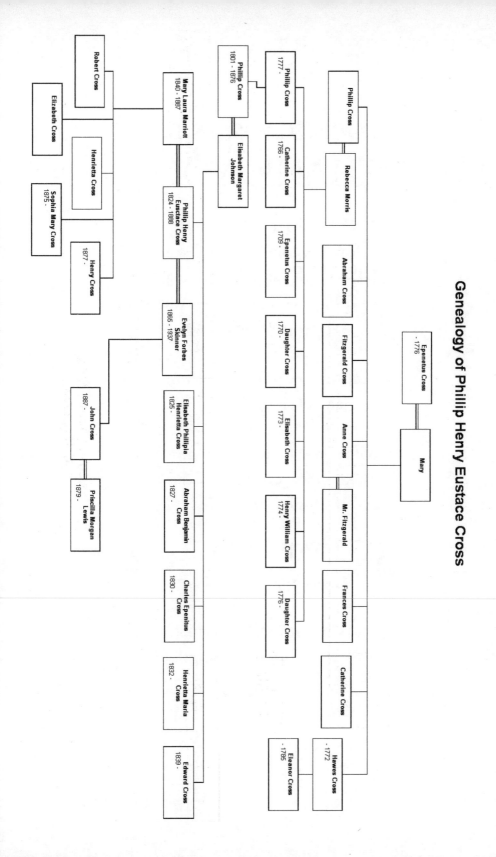